By MARGUERITE LABBE

All Bets Are Off
Ghosts in the Wind
Make Me Whole

The Triquetra Trilogy
My Heart Is Within You
Haunted by Your Soul
Our Sacred Balance

with Fae Sutherland
Bee Among the Clover
Lotus in the Wild

Published by DREAMSPINNER PRESS
http://www.dreamspinnerpress.com

MAKE ME ME
WHOLE
MARGUERITE LABBE

Dreamspinner Press

Published by
Dreamspinner Press
5032 Capital Circle SW
Ste 2, PMB# 279
Tallahassee, FL 32305-7886
USA
http://www.dreamspinnerpress.com/

Make Me Whole

Cover Art by Melissa Gay
http://www.melissagay.com

Cover content is being used for illustrative purposes only
and any person depicted on the cover is a model.

ISBN: 978-1-62798-055-5
Digital ISBN: 978-1-62798-056-2

Printed in the United States of America
First Edition
August 2013

Ayla and Adara, thank you for the inspiration, this one has been a wild ride from the beginning.

Chris, my love, you are always there whenever I need you, whether it's to brainstorm, critique, or to offer sympathy when I feel like I'm losing my mind. This story couldn't have been done without you. Thank you for everything you've done.

THE VOW

THE sounds of the encampment surrounded Dexios and Lykon—the snap and crackle of the fires, the soft moans of men pleasuring themselves mixing with the snores of those who grabbed what rest they could. Dexios and Lykon had made their own little sanctuary behind the brush, closer to the shore, wrapped up in their blankets, cloaks, and each other.

Their urgent coupling had erased the fears of the day, yet Dexios was unable to put those fears completely behind him. It intruded upon his thoughts, pushing him to consider the days that would follow. He slid his hand down to Lykon's muscled stomach and splayed his fingers. In the calm following the day's battle he found that being near did not seem to be enough. He wanted to be nearer still.

Lykon chuckled, laid his hand over Dexios's, and twined their fingers together. "You're restless tonight. Share your mind with me, or is it my touch you seek again?" His voice dropped low with seductive intent as he stretched before settling in Dexios's arms again, fitting against him as if he belonged there. Dexios held him closer, luxuriating in the warmth of Lykon's back and the way his buttocks pressed against his groin.

Dexios wanted to ensure Lykon would always be there, and once again his thoughts jerked back to the day's harrowing battle. Lykon was safe. He was here. Dexios's arms tightened around him. "Reinforcements will arrive on the morrow," Dexios said and kissed the side of Lykon's neck, breathing him in. The blood and sweat had been washed away earlier, replaced with the clean brine of the ocean and Lykon's own scent. "The fighting will be fierce once the enemy realizes they are cornered. They will not give way without a struggle."

Lykon twisted to look back at him. "Whether they lay down their arms or continue to fight is of no matter. The outcome will be the same." He smiled, a slow, sensual upturn of his lips that heated Dexios's blood. "My sole concern is how many days I have left with you before we are sent home. I want to make the most of every moment." He kissed Dexios, sliding a hand into his hair. "Come, I do not wish to speak more of battles, not when there are pleasures to explore."

Dexios shifted and turned Lykon onto his back. The moon shone down on his face, illuminating the strong lines of his jaw and nose. The camp quieted for the night, allowing Dexios to hear the sound of the waves washing against the shore in the distance. Fitting, all things considered, and Dexios prayed that Cythera would hear his words to Lykon and bless them.

"The end of the war does not mean we have to part." He stared down at Lykon, hovering over him. "I would rather stay by your side."

Lykon frowned, slid his arm around Dexios's waist, and pulled his weight down on him. "You do not speak sense. They will expect us back at home. We have duties awaiting us that have been long ignored."

"Duties that others have taken up while we fought to keep them safe." Dexios could not deny the want inside of him anymore. Not after the fierce fighting earlier today. Not after seeing Lykon fall and thinking the worst. The vivid memory still chilled him, the image etched behind his eyes of the enemy standing over his lover, spear poised to take his life. Somehow Dexios had found the divine strength to get to him, to stop the blow.

He slid his arms under Lykon, held him close, and reassured himself with the heat of his body. Why was Lykon not bothered by the same memories? Mere moments after his own close encounter with death, Lykon had saved him in return by shoving him out of the way and blocking a lethal strike to Dexios's unguarded back.

They had both almost died this day. For what? So they could part after their friendship had changed into a relationship far more profound? Dexios loved him. He had not believed himself capable of such deep emotion until he had found Lykon. The fate he wanted for them did not include living apart and never seeing one another.

"What is it you are trying to say?" Lykon pushed him aside and sat up, bracing his hands behind him as he looked at Dexios with his eyebrows drawn together and a slight grimace twisting his lips. "Speak your thoughts plainly. Do you wish for us to join a mercenary unit to find another battle? I have no desire for more bloodshed. We have been fighting for years now. We've done what we set out to do. Our families and lands are safe."

"No more fighting." Dexios was done with seeing Lykon in danger, of tending to his wounds, and having his own wounds stitched by Lykon. "If we both go home we will not see each other again. At least not often enough for what I want."

Dexios knelt in front of Lykon. His heart pounded, his chest tightened. "You know what is in my heart, Lykon, how I feel about you. You have said that you feel the same. Is it true?"

Lykon stretched out his hand and cupped Dexios's jaw. "I do. Don't doubt that. I do not wish to think of what may happen on the morrow or the day after. You worry too much about the past and the future. Only the here and now matters. Love me here and let me love you in return."

Dexios closed his eyes and turned his head to kiss Lykon's calloused palm. He had tried to live in Lykon's moment, and he thought he had succeeded until today. He could not get the image of the spear out of his head. He had almost lost Lykon earlier. When the war ended he would lose him still. Lose him to his family and the other life that awaited him. It made him ache inside to think so. "I want more. I want a lifetime with you. Say you want the same."

"I do, but I do not see how we can have it." Lykon brushed his fingers along Dexios's jaw. "Our wants are passionate, not practical. We cannot let our hearts rule our minds."

"Why not?" Dexios set his jaw, opened his eyes, and caught Lykon's gaze. "We both have younger brothers who have taken up our duties at home, younger brothers who are about to take wives to breed more sons and daughters. Our families would demand too much if we returned home. We will have done our duty when this war ends. Let us find a place where we can be together. A place by the shore all our own."

"What of our lands, our inheritances? Do you not wish to return home to see your family at least, and let them know you survived?"

"We can let them know together. I will travel with you to your home, and then we can visit my family one last time. I do not care for either lands or inheritances if you are not with me. We will be rewarded with many riches when the enemy is routed. We can use that coin to start over."

"You ask much." Lykon angled his body away and the uncertainty on his face made Dexios's stomach clench. "I had not given thought to abandoning everything."

"Not everything." Dexios cupped Lykon's face in his hands and turned it toward him. Dexios had never seen him look afraid before, not even during the fiercest battle. "I will be with you."

Lykon remained quiet as he searched Dexios's face. He must have seen something there that reassured him because some of the tension left his body. "I admit, I am unsure about returning home again after these last few years. I am not the same person I was when I left. I have no desire to marry and tend to the land...."

He looked away, the silence falling rich with unspoken promise. Dexios held his breath, waiting to hear what Lykon would say next. Some answers could not be prodded and pushed for. Then Lykon slanted a glance at him and continued in a softer voice, "And I have no wish to be parted from you. You have caught me unawares. I did not realize you harbored such thoughts."

"I did not realize it either until today. I do not think I could have borne it if you had died."

Understanding flickered in Lykon's eyes. "You stopped the spear. I had no doubt that you would. We have guarded each other's backs well."

Dexios brushed his thumbs over Lykon's cheeks and the rough scrape of unshaven skin grounded him. Not knowing had become an agony that tore him open more than any gaping wound. "Say you will go with me. Please, I love you."

A smile flickered over Lykon's lips and he leaned closer to brush his mouth over Dexios's. "Yes," he whispered.

Dexios sat back on his heels as relief washed through him. He grinned and kissed Lykon hard on the mouth. "Say it again. Swear it. Swear it in her name."

Lykon laughed and tugged Dexios down on the makeshift bedding with him. "I swear it by Cythera, and the waves that gave birth to her shall hear my vow. I love you, Dexios. I will go where you go and I will stay by your side." He kissed Dexios before he could respond and said against his lips, "No more words. Show me that you want me."

CHAPTER ONE

GALEN KANELLIS stared at the four huge unmarked packing crates that filled the museum's small storage room to the point that he had just enough space between each crate to slip through to open them. He scratched his head, frowned, and tried to remember what he'd ordered that would take up so much room. They were good on supplies for the studio, and the gallery gift shop had more than enough stock. Besides, nothing he ordered would've come in crates about to fall apart.

He called out to his personal assistant, Suzane Eberly, as he grabbed a crowbar. "I thought we weren't going to have the pieces for the new exhibit shipped until Ella had a chance to do the mural. Are any of the boys still here? I'm going to need some help."

The crates looked as if they'd been waiting at the bottom of the abyss, with dried-up algae and barnacles clinging to the sides. The metal banding had rusted through in some parts, making it easy to pull off. The wooden slats were gray with age, the nails holding them down also rusted. Galen began prying off the lid to the nearest crate. He'd take a quick peek, no more, before help arrived, just long enough to assuage his burning curiosity. Nothing set his mind going with possibilities like an unopened box.

The slats cracked and splintered the moment he applied pressure, so Galen stopped to put on a pair of gloves before Suzane saw and threw a fit. He'd managed to get most of the lid removed in sections by the time he heard her heels coming toward the storeroom. "Where the hell did those come from?" Suzane demanded from the doorway.

Galen set aside the crowbar with a clatter and pulled off the top before he peered over his shoulder at her. She had her brunette wig on this morning, pulled back into an elegant twist, and was still on her power suit kick. Oh boy. That meant she was in her no-nonsense mood, and that wasn't nearly as interesting as her blonde hippie days.

"I have no idea," he admitted, yanking out handfuls of moldy straw. "Isn't it cool? And I don't care either, as long as it fits the new exhibit. It's missing something." He paused and gestured with his hands, trying to visualize it. "A center point to build the rest of the exhibit around. It's been driving me nuts. No matter how much I rework the layout on paper, I can't picture it as a whole."

Suzane examined each of the crates, then turned to Galen with a frown, her eyebrows drawn together and her gray eyes far away. She probably had a checklist in her mind to match the one in her ever-present folder. "Where's the shipping information?"

"Didn't see any." His fingers encountered layers of wool, and the thrill of discovery made his heart leap. Galen pulled out his pocketknife, then sliced with care through the padding. "Come on, baby," he crooned low under his breath, "show me what you've got."

"Four crates mysteriously appear in the middle of a locked storeroom, with no shipping information, and you're not in the least bit suspicious," Suzane said in exasperation and smacked him on the arm with her folder. "You are familiar with the story of the Trojan Horse, aren't you?"

Galen nodded, only half listening as the gleam of metal appeared under the wool. He put away his knife and peeled back each layer. "Yeah, Greek story, right? Big horse, bad things. It would be amazing if this fits the new exhibit theme. Do you think it's that old? The crate is falling apart."

"If they were that old somebody would be clamoring for their return. Ancient relics just don't pop up out of nowhere." Suzane took the shred of blanket he handed her and wrinkled her nose. "Personally, I think it's a prank. Who packs art in straw and old wool these days? It's a hoax."

The last layer of the blanket fell away to reveal a full-sized statue of a man in ancient armor; Galen's breath caught. "Oh my, my, my, he's beautiful. Help me get him out. I want to see him in the light." *Nick would love to see this.* Galen shook his head with a pang of regret. It seemed like everything these days reminded him of the lover he'd walked away from. It was true, though; Nick would have gone into spasms of joy over this beauty. He had a passion for ancient art and a love for wreck diving. How he ended up as an HR manager still confused Galen.

"Wait a minute." Suzane grabbed his arm when he reached to pull out the statue. "For the love of God, let me get you some help before you hurt it or yourself." The thought of damaging the statue made Galen pause. "And while we're waiting for the boys, we're going to have a nice discussion about where these came from and what you plan on doing with them."

Galen ran his hands over the statue, humming to himself as Suzane disappeared from the doorway. The statue was cast from some kind of metal, bronze most likely, with a nice verdigris, but it was hard to tell in the shadows. He hoped Suzane would be able to find some helpers. There were usually people hanging out in the attached studio every day either working on their own art, admiring others' projects, or just enjoying a safe place to hang out. And if Knox was in today, that would be even better, since he worked for an art moving company and would know what to do and have the equipment to do it.

To distract himself, Galen pulled out the layout sheet that he had stuck in the back pocket of his worn jeans. After a few moments of searching, he located the pen behind his ear and began rearranging and making notes, though he knew he wouldn't be satisfied with the flow of the exhibit until he saw what was in the other crates. If they were anything like the statue, he'd have to get them up, fiddle with the arrangement itself instead of looking at it on paper. It was only February. He still had several months to get it together. Ella's mural came first.

Suzane returned and launched into a lecture about proper documentation, verification, and dating. There were probably some other things mixed in there, but they slipped his mind almost as soon as he heard them. He nodded, made assuring sounds, and scribbled while she talked. Knox had to hurry up; if he didn't get all of those statues out of the boxes soon he was going to jump out of his skin. This was better than the Christmas when he was ten, when he was so sure that the giant box in the garage had held a new bike.

"What do you think?" Galen asked as he stepped back and gestured toward the layout with a flourish.

"Mr. K? You needed something?" Knox Marwick hovered in the doorway, his broad shoulders filling the space. He was a big kid, taller than Nick…. Galen broke off the thought with an inward groan. Five months, three weeks and six days, and still Galen thought about him more every day. He couldn't pinpoint when that had started happening.

"There you are! You have to come see this." Galen grinned at Knox and waved toward the crates. "Would you get the statue free and help me see what's in the other crates? Like right this minute? I get the impression that I'm going to be contracting you to move and set them up for me. But I need to see them to be sure."

"Not a problem. It shouldn't take me long to break them down. If you want, I can call my boss and see if they can send some extra men when you want to haul them to the exhibit room."

"That would be great." Galen grabbed his layout sheet and squeezed by him. "Suzane and I will get out of your way."

"What's the point in looking at your new layout when you're just going to change it again? You won't stop playing around with it until everything is in place." Suzane leaned over to study the doorknob and lock on the storeroom door. "It doesn't look like it's been tampered with."

"Why would anyone break in just to leave art behind instead of stealing it? I'm sure we'll find the paperwork once it's all cleared away." He handed Suzane his layout and she took it with a sigh. "You have to admit, it's missing something."

"Yes, only I doubt this trouble-waiting-to-happen is going to fill that void."

Galen's eyes fell on the uncovered first statue. A sense of reverent awe filled him and his jaw dropped. The man stood with his legs spread slightly apart, his arms outstretched and curled as if he had been in the midst of an embrace. Sunlight streamed through the window, giving the metal a burnished, glowing quality. The aged bronze with a nice warm patina made Galen's fingertips itch to caress it. "Oh wow, will you look at him? He's perfect."

"Yeah, he's pretty hot." Knox carried out the sections of crate and the shreds of wool. "I'll be right back to get the rest."

Galen moved closer and ran his hand over the man's muscled arm. The metal was smooth and strangely warm. His hair lay in a shaggy mess about his head, which was tilted to one side, his lips parted and pursed. He made Galen think of kissing. It had been too long since he'd been kissed just right. He only had himself to blame. He'd been the one to put a temporary moratorium on casual flings. That was after he'd broken things off with Nick only to wonder *what if* too many times when he was alone at night.

"I think you're crazy if you intend on actually making this a part of the exhibit." Suzane came up beside him and gave his shoulder a shake. "You don't even know if it's authentic or not, or how old it is, or why someone would just give it to you with no information or explanation. It's going to come back and bite you in the ass, I just know it."

"Bites on the ass can be fun."

Suzane smacked him with the folder. "You're incorrigible. I'm serious. You've sunk your entire inheritance into this museum. I'm not going to let you ruin all your hard work because someone dangled a statue of a half-naked muscled man in front of you."

"The authenticity can be researched." Galen flashed a smile at her. "That's what you're good at. I want you to find everything you can about him. As for who our mysterious donor is and why they were so generous, I don't care. If I ever meet them I'm going to kiss him or her."

"People don't give things for nothing."

"Where's your sense of adventure? Besides, the upcoming exhibit is new homoerotic interpretations on the ancient world, so even if it isn't old it'll still work."

Suzane groaned. "You don't even know if it's homoerotic or not. Remember the theme for your museum? Gay love, sex, and life? You can't have a centerpiece for a new exhibit that runs counter to what you've established. Not after all the work we've put into making a name for it."

Galen knelt down to examine all the glorious little details, the ridged lines on the man's legs indicating scars, the realism in his hands as they gripped someone who had disappeared long ago. "I'm not sure about erotic; maybe the second half is in another crate," he mused, though for the life of him he couldn't figure out how they'd fit together, much less how they'd come apart in the first place. "But there are definite gay overtones."

"And what makes you think that other than wishes and a dirty mind?"

Galen twisted and looked up at her as he pointed to the base of the statue. "There are two discarded helmets, which makes me think two men are involved."

"Damn, you're right." Suzane sighed and pulled out her phone. "Okay, I'll look into it. I have to admit, he looks Hellenic in style."

Knox returned and began working on the second crate. The nails screamed in protest when he pulled apart the top and it fell apart. Galen gave Suzane a grateful smile. "Did I tell you that I like your new brunette do?"

She rolled her eyes. "I'm immune to your sad attempt at flattery."

"Go do whatever you have to do to prove me right. Please, prove me right. Get whatever tests and research you need. These statues are to stay on site. Whatever funding or overtime you need, it's approved. You're the best; I've told you that, right? I'd be lost without you."

Suzane made an exasperated sound, though her eyes lit up with pleasure. "Yeah, I know. You need me. I'll work on getting this big boy dated." A wicked smile crossed her lips. "Hey, maybe you should call what's-his-name who you refuse to mention. That wreck diver. 'Cause these statues look like they came from one, and he might have some insights."

"You're an evil woman." Before Galen could say anything else, the second statue was revealed, the same man, now naked in every glorious detail and fully aroused. "Oh my God, just look at him. Can you freaking believe it, Knox? People are going to come here in droves just to see him."

"You have to put these statues in your exhibit." Knox came to stand beside him. "Don't let her talk you out of it. You're the owner, right?"

"Galen!"

"I'm the owner, she's the boss." Galen tore his eyes away and pulled out his cell phone. "Looks like I have some calls to make. Shout when the rest are uncovered."

"Will do, Mr. K."

Galen climbed to the top of the tower to his office. He loved this small square room, the highest point in the old firehouse that he'd bought and renovated. A huge half-circle window dominated two sides of the room and the other sides contained two more windows next to each other so he had an almost panoramic view of the Seattle neighborhood. He'd left the exposed brick walls alone, and, with the polished wood floors, they gave the room a homey feeling.

He propped his feet up on his desk as he stared at his cell phone. He should call his lawyer, have him look into any insurance claims, see what it would take to keep the statues in-house. He would keep them no matter what it took.

Nicholas Charisteas. Galen's thoughts drifted right back to the man who refused to get out of his head. He hadn't spoken to him in months. He doubted Nick would want to hear from him now, even if he had left him an open invitation to contact him when he got his head out of his ass.

Galen smiled and tapped his phone against his cheek. He'd deserved that. And a fired-up, passionate Nick took his breath away. He scrolled through his contacts until he came to Nick's name—the only one of his flings that he'd programmed in there.

This wasn't the first time he'd looked up his number, and once again he hesitated. There would be no way around things getting complicated. He didn't know if he was ready for complicated. And it wouldn't be fair to come bursting back into Nick's life if he wasn't. Of course, there was always the possibility he was being too arrogant. Nick might have zero interest in him after all this time.

Galen hit Send before he could change his mind and his stomach jumped when the phone rang. What was he thinking? To his consternation and relief, a young man answered, and it took Galen a moment to unscramble his brain long enough to realize that he'd accidentally called Nick's work instead of his cell.

"I'm sorry, Mr. Charisteas is in a meeting. May I ask who's calling?"

"Just tell him Galen Kanellis called." He paused and his stomach sank further. He was an idiot. This was stupid. And Nick was going to laugh his ass off if he knew how much he had tied himself into knots over a simple phone call that Galen would've shrugged off six months ago.

"Hey, Mr. K." Knox's excited voice came up through the hole in his office floor that still contained a fireman's pole and cut through Galen's circling thoughts. "You have got to come see these dudes."

NICK CHARISTEAS ducked into his office and dumped the stack of files on his desk. He was in hell. Absolute, literal hell that involved endless wait times on the phone and reams of papers that kept getting higher every day. Financial security was not worth this bullshit.

He flung himself in his chair and pinched the bridge of his nose to ward off the incipient headache. If he could just clear his mind of insurance forms for ten minutes, he'd be golden for the rest of the day. He took out his darts and swiveled his chair around to the small dartboard he'd stuck onto the bookcase.

The first dart landed next to the outer rim and Nick winced. He did not want to explain to management how another book got punctured. He took careful aim and the second hit dead center. By the time he ran out of darts, the tension in his shoulders had started to ease and the knots in his stomach had unraveled. Nick rose to grab the darts for another quick round when his eyes fell on the poster of Santorini he had tacked to the wall.

Six more months. Then he would have three blessed weeks on a charter boat in the Greek Islands, diving, getting back in touch with his roots, and hopefully this time, bringing back the prominence to his family's name. That's why he worked this job. It gave him the pay, the insurance, and the vacation time for these twice-yearly jaunts around the world. He came in sick, saved up every scrap of leave just for these little escapes. If he was the one to find the Dexios Collection, it would be his ticket back home. Finding the Collection would fix everything.

Nick's phone rang and he peered at the display with a grimace for the name there, Jessica Blandford, no doubt calling to bitch again about staffing. Nothing made her happy. Nick ignored the ringing and turned back toward the dartboard. He threw the dart harder than he intended and it sank all the way up to its shaft into the workplace safety sign he had hanging next to the bookcase. "Crap."

A brisk knock at the door made him jump and cast a quick glance at the offending dart. Before he could answer, the door opened and his assistant Sean walked in with several message slips in his hand and two paper cups of coffee.

"You have a meeting in ten minutes, and you might want to call Jessica back before it starts."

"I do?" Nick sat up at his desk and pulled up his calendar. "I thought I was free to catch up on paperwork for the rest of the afternoon."

"You were, but this came up regarding you-know-who, and they want it addressed immediately."

Nick scowled and shuffled through the files on his desk. "Got it, thanks. Any other messages I should know about beforehand?"

"No, I think they can wait. The barista you've been ogling wrote his number down for you." Sean handed him one of the coffees with a number emblazoned on the side without batting an eyelash.

Nick took it with a slight flush and a cough. "Thanks, sorry about that."

"Not a problem." Sean handed him the slips of paper. "Jessica called twice, Hodson's Funeral Home sent a fax about the insurance papers for McCleary, that teller in the Market Street branch, oh, and somebody named Galen called. I didn't quite catch his last name, sorry."

"Galen Kanellis?" Nick dropped the message slips on his desk unread as thoughts of work and considerations of a hot barista disappeared right out of his head, all because of the power of one name. He had made such a fool out of himself over Galen.

"Yeah, that's it. He didn't wait on the line long enough for me to get the spelling of his last name. He didn't leave a number either."

Nick's heart twisted, and he squashed the burgeoning hope inside of him before it could take root. He'd been down that road with Galen, and he'd crashed hard right into the wall of reality. "Okay, thanks." Nick waved him off and stared unseeing at his desk as he remembered the last time they'd been together.

Wow. Galen Kanellis. Nick had written him off as a lost cause. It seemed like the only things they had in common were an interest in art and some fabulous sex. He had been such a sucker for those dark eyes that had held secrets Nick had never been able to get him to reveal, secrets and pain. Galen had been running from something and running hard.

"Hey, Sean. If he calls back give him my cell number." The words were out of his mouth before he could stop them and reconsider. Oh, what the hell, what did it matter? It wasn't like Galen would call twice. Of course, Nick could do it first.

Nick snorted and picked up the fax from the funeral home. No, if Galen really wanted to hook back up with him he had to show Nick. He wouldn't accept dribbles anymore. Not after he'd already lost his heart once and had it handed back to him. Not after Galen had walked away without looking back.

He should have been used to it by now. His mom left. And she'd contacted him and his brothers later on too. Nick still didn't understand what her motivation had been, because it hadn't lasted a whole year before she was gone again.

He rubbed his temple when the headache threatened to return. At least Galen had given him the courtesy of honesty. He hadn't lied and pretended to love him, then walked away after he'd gotten what he wanted. Better to lock the door on his past. Nick didn't have the time or energy to waste on people who didn't stick around. He wasn't that little kid anymore to set himself up with false hope. His mom and Galen made their choices, and they had to live with them. Not him.

Nick glanced at his watch. He had enough time to call the funeral home back to give them what they needed so the family could scratch one worry off their list. That was something he could do, that and dream of Santorini with its sunsets, caldera, beaches, and wonderful food. He could almost taste the roasted leg of lamb and the pita bread slathered with taramasalata.

It was a long shot, but maybe the Dexios Collection had made its way back home somehow. All of his other leads had dried up. It wouldn't hurt to start at the beginning, and at least he'd be doing his diving in a picturesque location this time.

Galen would look scorching hot laid out on the charter boat's deck.

Nick growled to himself and picked up the phone. He was not going to think about him anymore.

CHAPTER TWO

"WAIT, a little more to the left. On the third one, the angle's off," Galen said as he studied the arrangement of the statues again.

Knox blew out his breath and straightened as he gestured to the other workmen. "You know, Mr. K, the first twenty times I looked at his ass I was all for this. Now, I'm too tired to admire it."

"We're almost done. This is the only one that's still bugging me." Galen watched with his arms crossed, worrying his lip as they adjusted the angle again. Knox knew what he was doing, but telling himself that didn't make the adjustment any less nerve-racking. Nothing could happen to these statues.

Four unfinished statues, all seeming to be caught in a miderotic moment, one man who waited for his other half to complete the embrace. The bronze gleamed with a life of its own over taut muscles that looked as if they were just waiting to move again. In his head, Galen had already given the statues names: The Kiss, Fellatio, Copulation, and Afterglow.

Galen stood back after the statue was shifted and looked over the arrangement again. "I think we've got it this time. That's perfect."

Knox began picking up his equipment with a look of relief on his face, and Galen walked the room from the beginning of the exhibit to the end. He'd set up cones to take the place of the pieces that hadn't arrived yet. Suzane would kill him when she discovered he'd gone ahead and set up the statues as the center point. She hadn't finished her research, and the dating on the statues would take some time, but he had to see what it would look like in the room.

And he was in love.

"What do you think?" he asked Knox as the young man coiled the straps that had steadied the statues when they'd been moved.

"Oh, you already know my opinion. I just wish they'd been finished. It seems a shame to go to all the trouble to make four halves of a statue instead of four whole ones."

"What about you, Ella?" Galen called to the only other occupant in the room, a young woman in the process of painting an Asian-themed Daughters of Sappho mural along three of the walls. Galen had been captivated by her initial designs that mixed traditional Asian style with a vibrant modern palette. To see her sketches penciled out on the walls brought a satisfied smile to his lips. He couldn't wait to see them completed with a roomful of people admiring her hard work. This exhibit would lead to good opportunities, and not just for the museum. He just knew it.

Ella Zhu came toward them, wiping her paint-spattered hands on a rag hanging from her belt loop. She stripped off the bright cotton kerchief that protected her long links of dark braids and stuffed it in her pocket. The unusual combination of a broad nose in a round face with dusky skin and long, narrow eyes gave her an exotic look. "I think I'd like it more if they were naked women instead." She examined the statues, walking around them with a thoughtful expression. "They'll be popular, though. I agree with Knox, they look a little odd as they are. What was going through the sculptor's head when he came up with these?"

"I believe they were made this way on purpose, to make people think." Galen looked over the progression of statues, all of the same man, and most of them in naked, erotic poses that left much to the imagination.

He paused before each statue, drawn to the solitary figure and unable to explain why he evoked such an emotional response from him, aching loneliness and yearning. At times it reminded him of what he'd gone through after Bryan had died. Other times it made him remember all the good things about being in a relationship, made him long for another one.

He couldn't seem to stop tending to the statues and fussing over them. He had to have them in his museum even if it turned out they weren't as old as he suspected or if they were created as somebody's idea of a joke. They were beautiful and just what this room needed. He could now picture the whole exhibit finished and ready for patrons with the smaller items ensconced behind their glassed enclosures, the statues on the low platforms, with Ella's brilliant murals finished.

Galen stepped up to the second statue. In it the naked man stood with his legs wider apart than in the first. The lines of his muscles spoke of tension, and the corded throat with his head thrown back, the parted lips, and half-lidded eyes conveyed pleasure. His hands were outstretched low in front of him and his cock jutted out from a nest of curls. Every time Galen laid his eyes on him in that stance it brought a visceral punch of desire to his gut.

Galen imagined the man's companion on his knees, leaning forward to take the offering. Maybe he could talk Knox into doing some of his charcoal renderings to complete the set on paper. If Galen had any of his inherited fortune left, he would give a good chunk of it to see them complete. He turned toward the third statue and heard the sound of Suzane's heels on the hardwood floors as she entered the room.

"I hate to admit it, but they look good," she said, her tone grudging. "I think they will really bring the display together. Now if we could just get the people at the British Museum to part with the Warren Cup for a year, I'd be the happiest woman alive."

"Does this mean we're not going to have an argument about them staying?" Galen crouched in front of the third statue. The man leaned on his hands and knees, back arched, buttocks clenched in midthrust. "Because I'm keeping them. Did you have any luck on the research?"

"I found some maddening, vague hints to an obscure myth about a pair of lovers who pissed off a goddess. One of them, Dexios, got turned into a statue. You know those crazy gods in mythology, always having to take matters to an extra level. Someone could've used the story as a basis for your hottie. If that's the case, the timing could be right. Just do me a favor and don't go announcing this until we know for sure."

Suzane laid her hand on his shoulder and waited until he looked up at her. "These statues belong to somebody, and they might want them back. We should look into what legal standing we have. And if they turn out to be a big, fat joke, I don't want to see your reputation screwed with because you let your passion overrule your judgment."

Galen turned back and traced the intent furrow across the man's brow. Something about Suzane's words struck a chord deep inside him. Dexios. Why did the name sound familiar? Maybe he had heard it from Nick. He had two loves: geek stuff and wreck diving to salvage lost art. He seemed to recall Nick mentioning statues a couple of times, though Galen was pretty sure that wasn't why it was familiar.

Nick. Thinking of him awoke the ache again. Galen would love to see Nick's excitement over this discovery, to hear his thoughts about where they might have originated. Hell, it would be just good to talk to him, period.

"And sometimes you lose too much when you let go of passion." He rose and shook his head. "Sorry, I don't know where that came from."

"Are you okay? You've been pretty distracted the last few days." Suzane's voice came from far away as Galen's fingers dropped down to the man's full lips and jaw. "I know this place is your life, but when was the last time you went out? Had a hot date?"

Galen shrugged and stuck his hands in his pockets. "Dating is overrated. I haven't been able to get into it." Meaningless sex, on the other hand... he'd gotten pretty used to those kinds of hookups. Until Nick. The man had brought feelings into the matter, and Galen had been unable to reciprocate at the time. Now that he'd regained his equilibrium again it seemed he would be paying for his sins by having Nick haunt his thoughts on a constant basis.

Suzane squeezed his arm. "It's been almost two years since Bryan's accident. I'm sorry I made the comment about dating. I know you can't put a time limit on mourning, but you can start living again. Find new things to enjoy outside of your work, a hobby maybe. Hell, get a cat."

"I've been giving it a lot more thought lately. I'll take it under advisement."

"You always say that. One day you might actually listen and I think I'll die of heart failure. In the meantime, why don't you try sleeping in your apartment more and your office less? I'll leave my research notes on your desk before I leave."

"Hey, Suzane?" Galen caught her hand and gave it a squeeze. She was dealing with her own crap and still had the energy and compassion to be a pillar for him when he needed it. He hoped he did the same for her. "Thank you."

"Anytime."

Galen watched her go, grateful for her unwavering support and friendship for the last five years and finally at a point where he could tell her. It was like he'd been stunted since the night of Bryan's accident, a part of him ripped away, and he hadn't been able to find a way to fix the empty hole inside of him.

Being at the museum and watching his dream come to life helped. He felt almost normal until he went home and the echoing loneliness hit him. Time had eased it even more. And Nick had borne the brunt of his inability to let anybody new close. If he had one regret in this last year, Nick was it.

He turned to the final statue, struck again by the way it stirred him up inside. The man lay on his side, his arm curled around as if clasping another body to him, his head bowed with a tender expression on his face. "You really loved him, didn't you?" Galen crouched down and slid his fingers down the length of the man's arm.

"Make me whole."

The low, deep voice with a strange accent sounded right next to his ear. Galen jumped and fell back on his ass at the murmur and glanced around the room only to find that Knox had left and Ella had gone back to her mural. "What the hell? Did you say something, Ella?" No, that had been a man's voice, no mistaking it.

Ella shook her head, her face inches from the wall while she worked on some small detail. "I didn't hear anything."

He got to his feet and dusted himself off while he stared at the statue. Man, he was losing his mind. Maybe Suzane was right—it was time to get out of the museum for a bit. He pulled his phone out of his pocket as he left the room. It had been a couple of days since he'd called Nick, and he'd been thinking of him even more. A little thrill of anticipation raced through him. It would be good to hear his voice again, and maybe hearing about the mysterious statues would pique his interest enough for a dinner date. Nick liked talking art. It wouldn't hurt to try, and if Nick didn't want to see him again, he only had himself to blame.

But maybe, just maybe, the heavens were smiling down on him and Nick was still interested.

NICK hung up his suit coat and opened the cockatiels' cage. Rory chirped and twittered before he climbed to the door and squawked. His mate, Amy, cocked her head, let out a trill of greeting, then went back to preening her feathers. "Let me change, and you can help me cook dinner." He brushed a finger down Rory's brilliant yellow crest, and the cockatiel rewarded him with a tender nip on his finger.

He yanked off his tie, tossed it over a chair, and was already shrugging out of his dress shirt by the time he reached the bedroom. This was the best part of the day—getting home and changing into something comfortable with birdsong in the background. Ten minutes later, dressed in track pants and a Team Zissou jaguar shark T-shirt, he returned to the kitchen and grabbed a can of soup to heat up on the stove.

Rory glided into the kitchen and landed on his shoulder. His talons dug through the thin T-shirt as he shifted and found his balance. Amy called out to him from the living room and Rory answered with a series of whistles before ending his conversation with a gentle nibble on Galen's ear.

"Oh, you have time for me now, is that it?"

Nick's cell phone sat on the kitchen counter and the lit-up message icon mocked him. When he saw Galen's name on the screen after all of these months, it had been a shock, and it brought back a whole flood of desires and feelings he'd thought he'd dealt with and shoved away. Apparently not. Even now, he was still wrestling with them. He wanted Galen, and not just in his bed. The memory of Galen's smile still captivated him and made him want to see it again. He'd never smiled enough.

So Galen had called back. Nick had honestly thought he wouldn't. The first twenty-four hours he'd debated whether or not he should pick up the phone first. The second, he'd congratulated himself on being right and not falling for Galen's tease. The third day he'd cursed himself for letting an opportunity pass him by. Now what the hell was he doing? He still stared at the icon and still resisted listening to the message after several hours. He had to be touched in the head.

He dumped the can of Italian Wedding Soup into his saucepan, added a little roasted garlic and some seasonings, then set it to simmer. Amy winged in, lit on her perch on the back of a chair, and bobbed her head along to the radio that Galen had going above the microwave. "What do you two think? Delete or listen?"

Rory launched himself from his shoulder and joined Amy. Rory had been incredibly pitiful until Nick had found a companion for him. It made Nick smile to see them, Rory a beautiful shade of gray that contrasted with Amy's pristine white. Both had the yellow crest, though Amy's was a paler shade, and both had the orange spots on their cheeks, which made them look like cheery troublemakers in Nick's opinion. "You two are no help."

Finally, he picked up his phone, set it to speaker, and hit the voice mail button. He'd regret it the moment he deleted it if he didn't listen first. Moments later, Galen's low, husky voice filled the kitchen and Nick's pulse leapt. He didn't understand how he could've let one man get under his skin so much.

"Hey, Nick. I know you probably never expected me to call." Nick stopped stirring the soup. Was that nerves in Galen's voice? No, that would require Galen to desire something past his own immediate gratification. That brought memories of a naked Galen back to his mind. If Galen knew anything, it was gratification, and Nick's body hadn't forgotten that either.

"I've been thinking about you a lot. I didn't think I had the right to call until I had my head on straight, and then it seemed like too much time had passed and you didn't need me stirring up things again."

Nick added some more pepper to the soup and took out a bowl. He should just delete the message and not respond; he didn't need the heartache. Galen would get the point, and after all this time he doubted the man would try another hookup again, but he continued to listen, curious despite himself.

Galen paused before continuing in an excited voice. "So I have these statues that showed up in my storeroom. They look Hellenic or maybe Roman in origin, and I wondered if you'd be interested in taking a look at them. I know you've done some wreck diving and you like art history. I thought you might have some insights into them."

The tiny hope inside him died and Nick ground his teeth because he shouldn't have allowed himself to feel it at all. Business. He should've known better to think that Galen would've wanted to speak to him for anything else. It was time to delete the voice mail and drop the past. Galen had made it very clear from the first night they met that he had no interest in pursuing a relationship. Nick should've known better than to think he could change his mind.

"The statues are strange, obviously old, and they seem only half-finished. It looks as if there should be a mate to them." Galen's voice trailed off and Nick froze, his skin tingling as adrenaline raced through him. *No fucking way.* "A missing lover…. I've never seen anything like it. I think you'd be fascinated. Please give me a call back. I should be at the museum for the rest of the day; maybe we could have dinner together. I'd really like to see you again."

Nick's hands trembled, and the wooden spoon he'd been stirring with clattered down on the stovetop. The Dexios Collection. It had to be. How the hell had Galen come across the statues? They'd been lost before over the many centuries, and they'd always somehow ended back in his family's hands, except this time.

He had to find a lawyer, get the paperwork proving ownership. Only that meant he'd have to talk to his dad. Nick winced at the thought of another painful, awkward conversation with him. His brothers were even worse. He'd have to deal with lectures along with the awkwardness. He did not want to put up with that right now.

Nick switched his thoughts back to the problem at hand. Galen would want to keep them. Nick couldn't blame him there, but they belonged to him. No, wait, he should see the statues first, make sure they were the Dexios Collection before he started jumping around all over the place and causing trouble.

There was a long pause, and then Galen continued in a softer voice that cut through Nick's thoughts. "I'm sorry for the way things ended between us. I was an ass, and it's past time I acknowledged it. I just thought you should know, I *am* sorry."

Nick stared at the phone, and his mouth dropped open. The tension that gripped him ever since Galen started to talk business melted away. Nobody could tie him up in knots and turn his emotions inside out like Galen. Damn the man. Nick couldn't help the small smile that crossed his lips. Wasn't that what had enthralled him in the first place?

Nick shoved away the thoughts of a nonexistent relationship and concentrated on the important issue. First things first. He had to establish whether or not the statues were the Dexios Collection. After that he could go from there.

Nick grabbed his phone, called Galen back, and cursed under his breath when it went to voice mail. "Galen, it's Nick. Call me back. Look, if those statues are what I think they are, it's huge. They've been lost for decades. Please call me back. I want to take a look at them. How the hell did you manage to get your hands on them? Call me, please, I don't care what time it is when you get in."

He tossed his phone on the counter, willed it to ring, and drummed his fingers while he stared. He glanced at his watch with a curse. The museum would've been closed for hours, which meant that Galen was probably off to one of his clubs, trolling for a hookup. Nick couldn't wait till morning. He had to see those statues. And if they were the Dexios Collection, they were his. Galen would have to come to Nick on his terms for once.

Last time they'd started with the sex and had somewhat become friends. At least that's what Nick had thought until they parted ways. But if Galen had felt anything other than lust for him, he surely wouldn't have waited this long. This time, Nick was determined to keep their relationship focused on purely business. He would not fall for Galen again.

"I hate to do this to you, guys, but it's back into the cage you go. I'll be back as soon as I can, I promise." He lifted Rory and Amy to his shoulder. Amy screeched when he transferred her to the cage and Rory followed, his crest flattening in distress. "I'm sorry, guys. I'll make it up to you; I'll bring out the bath tonight."

Nick headed for the door and turned back with another oath to shut off the stove. At this rate, he'd come back to a gutted apartment. *Good going, Nick, good going. Get a fucking grip.*

CHAPTER THREE

GALEN shut his laptop with a sigh and rolled his chair over to look out the arched window to the side of the desk. Night had fallen hours ago; the moon had risen above the window so the only light that spilled across the pervasive gloom came from the little lamp on his desk. The Space Needle stood out like a beacon against the bars, clubs, and theaters that sparkled like a field of fireflies across the cityscape. That nightlife had drawn him in once.

He walked over to the window, leaned his arm against the brick, and looked down. Nick hadn't called him back, so he'd sent queries out to some other scholars he knew at the university to see if they could track down more information on the myth Suzane had discovered. So far he hadn't been able to find out any more than she had.

Nick hadn't called him back. His thoughts flitted back to that very important fact. Well, if he wanted some kind of sign, that was the slap in the face he needed and no doubt deserved. He had no business being disappointed, yet that didn't stop the sinking in his gut and chest. Would it have been too hard to have taken a chance with Nick six months ago?

Galen stuffed his laptop in its carrying bag and grabbed his keys. His stomach rumbled with the demand for sustenance with more substance to it than coffee and pretzels. He checked to make sure the massive fire station doors along the workshop and the storefront were locked tight. When he reached the doorway to the museum proper, Galen paused and shut off the alarm. He wanted one more look at the statues in their proper setting before he went back to his empty apartment.

Shadows blanketed the hallway, but he had grown accustomed to making his way through the museum with just the security lights for illumination. The museum wasn't that big, and it didn't take him long to get to the new exhibit. Galen paused in the doorway, stunned by the sight before him. The security lights hadn't been set up here yet, but the row of skylights stretching across the roof faced the rising full moon, and the room was awash with a pale-blue glow. In the shadows and light, the statue facing him looked almost alive, ready to move at any moment and finish the action he'd started.

Galen walked over to him, his heart thudding, and laid his hand on the man's forearm. How surreal. For a moment it almost seemed like heated flesh beneath his fingers and not cooler bronze. "Who are you, Dexios? And why do you seem so familiar to me?"

Silence answered him, and Galen had the insane urge to slip under those embracing arms to press himself up against the man. He stepped back with a short, uneasy laugh and stuck his hand into his pocket. With his luck he'd get stuck. He didn't want to hear Suzane's laughter the next morning when she found him entangled with a statue. He'd never live it down.

This obsession, this inability to get these statues out of his mind, was unhealthy. He needed to go home and relax, as Suzane had suggested. Go home and find some way to get Nick out of his thoughts.

"Shouldn't you prefer flesh and bone to metal? You never were one to put your faith in the mystical."

Galen stiffened and spun around to face the man in the wide arched doorway. Adrenaline raced through him and his breath quickened. At first all he could see were shadows, and then the man stepped into the moonlight. He wore no undershirt beneath his breastplate and the studded leather fringe that hung from his waist did nothing to hide his muscular thighs. A teasing smile played on his lips and his eyes held mysteries in the shadows and light. Galen couldn't tell what color they were or what the man intended. "Would you kiss these lips now that I stand before you?"

Galen's breath caught on a wave of recognition. "Nick?" Wait, no. Not quite, but similar. This man's hair came to his shoulders in thick waves, unlike Nick's short, rumpled style groomed to look careless. Old scars ridged his arms and legs. And though Nick worked out, this man had hard muscles all over as if he drove himself all the time. In fact, now that he looked at him closer, Galen was uncomfortably reminded of his sexy statue. They even had scars in the same places.

The back of his neck prickled with uneasy awareness. If he turned around, would he still see it standing in its place behind him? He wavered between looking over his shoulder and keeping his eyes on the strange man before him. It was a ridiculous thought—statues didn't wake up and move around. He really needed to get away from this place and take a break if he was having thoughts like that.

"Nick? That is an interesting pet name, not one you have used before. What does it mean?"

Galen stumbled back, almost falling as the man moved closer. His hands caught a hold of metal and he clung to the reassurance that he hadn't lost his entire grip on reality. This man wasn't the statue come to life. "Who the hell are you?"

The coaxing smile died and his eyes widened. "You don't remember? A part of you always does. Could it have been so long this time?" He tapped Galen's chest just over his heart. The physical contact was another small comfort. The strange man wasn't a figment of his imagination, though Galen supposed an intruder wasn't a better option. "How can you not remember me, remember us?"

Galen looked over his shoulder at the control panel on the wall. He needed a better nighttime security system, maybe even a guard. "I don't know how you got in here or what possessed you to dress like that, but I suggest you leave before my security comes." The man did not react the way Galen expected him to with that desperate gamble. Instead, a puzzled look crossed his face as strong hands settled on Galen's hips.

"I do not understand the words you say. You look different, yet I know it is you born again to bring me to life." Those hands on his hips tugged, and Galen gasped as groin met groin with a hot tingle of awareness. Oh yes, hard all over. Damn, it had been so long since he had another man against him. And the resemblance to Nick made it even more disorienting. "Kiss me, Lykon. Make me whole again."

Lykon? Galen's brain whirled, and he latched onto the only thing that made sense to his muddling thoughts. "You're the one who spoke earlier today." Galen hadn't been losing his mind when he thought he heard the words earlier, even if he was losing his mind for real now.

"I will always find a way to reach out to you."

A hot man who just happened to look an awful lot like a cross between Galen's statue and an old lover, dressed up in ancient gear.... Oh, what the hell, Suzane said to live a little. Galen refused to believe he was having a mental breakdown. So that meant this had to be a dream brought on by equal parts of obsession over the statues and Nick. The situation was too weird otherwise.

Galen ran wondering hands over the man's shoulders instead of pulling away. It felt kind of nice to have him so close. In a strange way it felt familiar too. And the familiarity had nothing to do with his memories of Nick.

"And how am I supposed to bring you to life? I have to say that, for a pickup line, it's not one I've heard before," Galen murmured. The man smelled as if he'd just come off a battlefield with only enough time to dump some water over himself for a cursory wash. And for some reason the lingering scent of blood, sweat, and leather did not turn Galen off; instead it stirred a primal and ancient instinct in his gut. It made him dizzy, and the stirring inside him turned toward a tugging for release.

"Well, for you and me it starts with a kiss." The man slid his arms around him, and he pulled Galen closer. His pulse jumped at the sensation of leather, metal, and warm muscles pressed up against him. He found himself gripping the strange man's biceps, and his thoughts spun in a tighter circle. A kiss. There was no harm in one little kiss between strangers. He'd done that too many times to count. Yet this was different. It was so much more than a kiss, and Galen couldn't pinpoint why.

"Kind of like Sleeping Beauty," Galen murmured.

The man was shorter than Galen by a couple of inches, and he lifted his head to graze his lips along Galen's jaw. "So smooth.... I think I like you clean shaven. Tell me more of this Sleeping Beauty."

"Oh, you know, evil fairy godmother who curses a princess to sleep until a handsome prince wakes her with true love's kiss. My sister and I loved the Disney version when we were kids." Lips smiled against his jaw, and Galen shivered when the man turned his head so the rough rasp of whiskers scraped his skin.

"I think the tale may have some similarities to our own. We should share them another time. Right now it feels too good to have you in my arms again. It's been centuries since I last kissed you."

Before Galen could ask for the story now, the man's lips settled over his own, and his thoughts scattered. The museum fell away and the sense of rightness, of coming home, came over him when the man's mouth moved over his. His firm lips nudged Galen's apart, and his breath caught as his tongue swept in. Galen pressed himself closer with a groan. A strong hand gripped his ass, fingers flexing and kneading, and the hot rush of desire snapped Galen's immobility.

His arms came around the man's shoulders, and Galen held him tight as they kissed. His taste brought an ache to Galen's throat, a yearning for a man who seemed so familiar and yet so unattainable.

Lips were bruised and stung from the intensity of their kiss, and desperation filled him. More. Galen needed more. He needed skin on skin. He needed to feel alive again, to glory in surviving another battle, another day.

What the…. Galen jerked back, and his breath came in quick pants. He stared agape at the man standing before him, a man who had subtly altered in Galen's perception. "What's happening to me?" A presence inside of him had come to the surface; another man's thoughts crept into his head. And before Galen's stunned mind could force out the invasion, Dexios gathered him close again, and the intruder took control.

"Dexios," Lykon whispered. His hands fisted in Dexios's hair, and his throat tightened so much that no more words could force their way out.

"There you are, Lykon." Dexios tightened his arms, and a flicker of a smile touched his lips. "Kiss me again. I've missed you."

Lykon groaned and tugged his head back over. Desperation exploded as their mouths met again. The need to apologize, to beg for forgiveness, disappeared under the wave of need and heat. They'd almost lost each other, but they were together for the moment and it wasn't too late. His hand slid down to the ties holding Dexios's armor, and something wrenched deep inside him.

Galen came rushing back into himself as the other presence faded. He jerked away, bringing a hand to his temple to ward off the dizziness. His knees buckled, and he had the faint impression of strong arms catching him before darkness fell.

"GALEN, for the love of God, wake up."

Galen groaned as someone shook him. He turned to roll over, moving to pull the covers over his head and let out a squawk when he fell to the floor instead. He sat up, looking around at his office in confusion. Suzane crouched down next to him, her brow furrowing. "Are you okay? You landed hard."

He scrubbed a hand over his face and glanced at the couch with a frown. He didn't remember falling asleep there. "Yeah, sure. What time is it? Did you bring any coffee?" As he stood up, Suzane's nostrils flared and her mouth tightened. Uh-oh. "What's going on?"

She punched him on the arm. "You fell asleep without turning on the alarm. What has gotten into you lately? We could've been robbed. You could've been killed. And you have the nerve to ask me for coffee."

Galen caught her hand before she whacked him again. When Suzane got all worked up she sometimes forgot to hold back. The spiky red hair today was enough warning of her mood. "Of course I set the alarm. I always do as soon as you leave." Then the events of the night before flooded back and his cheeks heated. He had turned it off again before he got thoroughly kissed by a crazy man who broke in dressed up in ancient gear, and passed out in the process.

He was such an idiot. Not just an idiot either. His abstinent streak must have done him more harm than good if he swooned from one kiss. This couldn't be more embarrassing.

"You might as well go ahead and tell me," Suzane said in disgust. "I can see it all over your face. You forgot, didn't you?"

"No, I set it, but I wanted to do one last check before I left." Galen looked away and tugged on his ear. "I passed out in the new exhibit room." He refused to mention the strange man. Dexios. If Suzane knew that he'd let an intruder kiss him after everything else, she'd drive him to the nearest hospital herself.

The tightness faded from her eyes and lips, replaced with concern. Her hand went to his forehead. "How are you feeling now? How'd you get back here?"

Galen glanced at the couch again and ran a hand through his tangled hair. "I have no idea. I must've roused and stumbled back. I don't remember. And before you bring it up, no, I'm not going to the doctor. I feel fine. It's never happened before, and it's not likely to happen again."

In truth, he felt a little strange. Not sick, just… off… as though a door inside of him had been unlocked. He couldn't explain why the thought occurred to him, only that it seemed right.

Last night had just been a weirdass dream, and it might be time to see a psychiatrist if he couldn't tell reality from a dream. Intruders didn't kiss the people who caught them breaking and entering. If the victims were lucky, they just got knocked out while the intruders stole everything they could.

"I just need to eat breakfast and drink some coffee. It had gotten late, and I was getting ready to grab dinner. That's probably why I passed out."

Suzane shook her head and dropped her hand. "Well, you go do that, and I'll check the place to make sure nothing's been touched, though I doubt it. Not even you could sleep through being robbed."

Galen shouldn't be content for her to look in his place, but his head remained in a fog, so he nodded and gave her a distracted wave instead of going with her. Another flash of concern crossed Suzane's face. He ignored it and turned toward his bag on the floor next to the couch. Minutes later he sat at his desk with a hot cup of coffee and his laptop booted up. He had to find out more about those statues. Not knowing was driving him crazy, and the mysteries kept piling up.

His phone rang, and Galen's heart gave a strange little twist when he saw the name on the screen. Nick. Wow. Galen's one and only what-if had called back, and here he'd been thinking of cutting his losses and moving on. What little they'd had before had been good. He now suspected they'd just touched the surface of how good it could be.

"Hey, Nick." Galen shifted on his chair and leaned forward to set his elbows on the desk. "Thanks for calling me back."

"Finally. I didn't think you were ever going to answer. I've been calling since last night." Any awkwardness at hearing from him again after all this time faded at the excitement in Nick's voice. "Are you serious about the statues? How the hell did you find them?"

Galen frowned and his stomach tightened. There was no "hi, how you doing" from him. Despite Nick's excitement, the greeting seemed impersonal and not at all what he expected. Not at all like the Nick he'd known.

"Why don't we meet for breakfast, and I'll tell you what I know? If you're interested we can come back to the museum and you can take a look at the statues. Do you think you'd be able to give me some insights into them?"

"Actually, I'm on my way to the museum now. I'll stop and pick us up something." Before Galen could reply, Nick hung up.

Galen stared at the phone. Nick was fired up, and to his disappointment it wasn't over seeing him. He got up to see if he had any spare clothes in the closet off the small office bathroom in the base of the tower. He didn't want to know how he looked after he'd slept on the couch all night. It was stupid to worry about his appearance when Nick was coming by on business, but Galen found himself changing and washing up as best as he could. When he got back to his office, Suzane was waiting for him with her notebook in hand.

Her eyebrow rose as she took in his dress pants and matching vest. "You don't have a meeting on your schedule for this morning."

"It just came up." Galen buttoned the cuffs of his shirt and resisted the urge to take one last look in the mirror. "How's my museum? Everything secure?"

"Yep, you lucked out. I thought for a moment there was something weird with the statue of the two men kissing. It turned out to be my imagination."

Galen froze as he reached for his hairbrush in the desk drawer. "Wait a minute, what did you say? Two men kissing? Not just one?"

"Of course two, it wouldn't make much sense with one even if the others are unfinished." Suzane gave him a look that accused him of being simpleminded. "Are you sure you're not sick?"

Galen leapt for the fireman's pole and zipped down. His palms had broken out into a sweat and it made for a faster trip than he normally had. He landed hard, the shock jolting through his entire body.

"Galen! Are you trying to break your damn neck? Hold up, wait for me."

He bolted through the workshop and raced toward the new exhibit. It was early enough in the morning that nobody noticed his mad dash or heard Suzane yelling as she chased him. As Galen rounded the corner, he stopped and caught a hold of the wall. His heart lurched then sped up again, and the reaction had nothing to do with his sprint. The first statue stood there complete, the two men caught up in a passionate embrace.

"What the fuck is going on?" Galen walked out of the room, gesturing wildly. He was losing his goddamned mind. That was the only explanation. Or maybe he was still in the middle of a very vivid, very real dream. He counted to ten and turned back to steal another peek at the statue.

It stood there, solid and utterly changed. It was everything he had imagined it would be and so much more. A part of him wanted to freak out, but he pushed it back for the moment so he could fully appreciate the changes.

"Oh wow." Galen's breath came out in a rush, and he took a step closer as Suzane caught up to him. Whatever she said didn't register as he approached and ran reverent hands over Dexios and Lykon. They were gorgeous and looked as if they'd been cast at the same time as one piece instead of two that fit together. Lykon was pressed up against Dexios, hands buried in his hair, the passion between them almost palpable. "How?"

"How what?" Suzane asked in a disgruntled tone. "What has gotten into you? I swear you've been all moony over these statues from the moment they showed up. See, they're fine, just like how we left them."

Galen shot her a startled look, and the uneasiness returned twice as bad. She had to have seen the changes. He couldn't be the only one who remembered the statue being half-completed. He called over Ella when she walked into the room carrying her paint equipment. "Do you see anything different about this one?"

Ella tilted her head and pursed her lips while she studied it and shook her head. "I see two dudes doing the tongue tango, Mr. Kanellis."

"Yes, that's how it is now, but that's not how it looked yesterday." Galen flung his hands out gesturing toward the first statue, then around to encompass the other three, which had remained unchanged. Only the first had become whole. "Yesterday it was one man."

Ella's eyes widened and she exchanged a silent glance with Suzane who patted him on his arm. "No, it's been the two ever since you found them," Suzane said in a gentle voice.

Galen fisted a hand in his hair and groaned when another thought struck him. How would he explain this to Nick? He was on his way over here at this moment, expecting to see four unfinished statues. Galen would never be able to convince him it wasn't a hoax.

"We're so screwed."

"You're worrying me." Suzane caught his arm. "What's going on?"

He'd like to know that himself. He pulled Suzane out into the hallway so Ella couldn't overhear and sat down on the bench. He could still see the statue through the archway, and the sight mocked him. "I think I'm still dreaming. I must be dreaming. Pinch me."

Suzane pinched his arm hard enough to leave a bruise. "Ow!" Galen jerked away and glared at her. "Not so hard."

She shrugged, looking unapologetic. "Gentle wouldn't have gotten the point across. You're not asleep and neither am I. And apparently you see something different with this first statue than the rest of us."

"So I'm crazy."

"I wouldn't say that. You've been… preoccupied lately, in your own world, and I'll admit it bothers me, only because I don't want you to lose sight of the rest of the world." She took his hand and laced their fingers together. "There has to be an explanation for everything. We might not see it now, but we'll find it."

Galen stared at his hands. She seemed to be taking this awfully calmly. Maybe she was just humoring him. "Do you believe in ghosts?"

"Of course."

Galen stared at her, a little thrown off by her immediate agreement. "No, I mean real ghosts, like haunting-an-object ghosts."

Suzane rolled her eyes and shot him a look of fond exasperation. "I didn't think you meant Casper. There has to be something else going on, because none of us are crazy, and there's been something strange about them since the first day. For God's sake, Galen, they appeared in the storeroom out of nowhere. We both know that someone couldn't have gotten in all those crates without one of us knowing about it. And we've found no documentation on them at all."

Galen didn't respond as he stared at the statue. It was enough to make him wonder if last night hadn't been a dream. "Nick's on his way over. He seems to know something about them. At least he sounded pretty excited, though I'm not sure if he's going to freak out over the difference or accept it like you did. I don't know what to do."

"Well, you ignored me before, when all you could see was how perfect they were. And I'm not sure if you're prepared to listen to me now."

"I'll listen. I may not agree, but I'll listen." Galen tore his gaze away from the exhibit room. "And they still are perfect. They're just a bit weird too. I don't know what to think anymore."

Suzane looked thoughtful and patted his arm. "Here's my advice, because I know you're not going to give them up now." She paused, eyeing him, and Galen grinned with a shrug. She knew him too well. "Unless you start thinking they're dangerous, run with it and enjoy the ride."

"Aren't I normally the one taking risks and you're the one telling me to step back and think things through?"

"It's a little late for that. You've already opened the door, and even though it's more than a little unsettling, I think realistically it's too late to back off now. Which you won't, so the point is moot." Suzane frowned at him, and Galen knew he'd better divert her now before she started thinking about how he hadn't listened to her warnings at all.

"In the meantime," Galen said, "we have to step up our research. Something freaky is going on, and I want it solved before we open this exhibit. It's your mission to track down the previous owners of these guys. Drop everything else and concentrate on that. Someone has to know something."

"I will," Suzane agreed, "but you'd better swear to me that you won't hide anything weird from me. If something else happens that doesn't seem normal, I want to know. And if I ever find you passed out in your office again with the alarms off I… I don't know what I'll do, but you won't like it." The fierce light in her eyes blazed again, and Galen got up before she decided to get even more outraged on his behalf.

"There's no need to glare at me like that. I promise." Galen paused and considered telling her about the intruder from the night before, but a glance at his watch told him how late it was getting. He'd talk to her later. "I need to get ready for my meeting. I'll come find you when it's over."

"You'd better."

Galen turned and walked out, trying to think of what he was going to tell Nick. From the excitement in his voice he had to know something about the statues, a lot more than Galen did. Would he also not see the difference like Ella and Suzane, or would he think Galen was screwing with him?

CHAPTER FOUR

NICK suppressed a little flutter of nerves as he climbed the stairs into Galen's office. The only reason he came was to see the Collection. However, the sight of Galen, looking so smooth and sexy as he stared out of the window lost in thought, brought a hard punch of old longing to his gut. His dark-blond hair fell in an arc around his face and emphasized his high cheekbones and full mouth.

He looked away when he found himself concentrating on those lips. Instead he swept his eyes over Galen's body. The man wore a suit like he was born in it. It accentuated the lean lines of his body. The silvery gray looked good on him, so did the bold-blue dress shirt. It wasn't fair that Galen could affect him on such a visceral level when he remained pretty oblivious to Nick in return.

And Nick did not want to be caught ogling. "I brought coffee and muffins," he said, breaking Galen's reverie as he set them down on the desk.

Galen swiveled his chair around and rose, welcome lighting up his warm brown eyes. "It's good to see you again."

Galen stepped forward and hesitated, his hand outstretched in a way that made Nick think Galen couldn't decide between a hug or a handshake. Nick solved the dilemma by taking his hand briefly before letting it go. Business, that's it. A dozen little social niceties leapt to his tongue and none of them emerged.

Of all the people to find the Dexios Collection, why did it have to be too-sexy Galen Kanellis who fucked like an Olympic gold champion? It was a cruel twist of karma that Nick's body and heart had such vivid memories of him.

Galen's eyes swept over Nick once before he gestured to the chair. "Please, sit. Thank you for coming."

"Thanks for seeing me. I know I pretty much barged in here without thinking about your schedule." *Finally.* Words passed Nick's lips, ones that didn't make him sound like a bumbling idiot.

"You're the one with all the meetings and deadlines. I get to make my own rules when Suzane lets me. I'm glad you came."

Nick had the craziest thought that Galen was nervous. He kept rubbing the back of his neck and rearranging folders on his neat desk. It had to be Nick's own nerves talking. He wasn't sure what to do or say after all this time. He had been so angry when they last saw each other, and it had taken a long time to let go of that anger.

Nick covered up his unease by handing Galen one of the bags and paper cups of coffee. "Peace offering?"

"I like the idea of a fresh start." Galen glanced into the bag and threw Nick the easy smile that had snared him from the first moment their eyes had met at the bar. "Blueberry. You remembered my favorite."

There were too many things about Galen that were seared into his memory. Nick sat back and took a sip of his coffee. Best to get down to business and get out of there before his mind started up on everything he should've said or done that might have convinced Galen to give their relationship a fighting chance. "You never said how you got your hands on these statues, and my curiosity is killing me."

"This can't go past this office or my assistant will kill me," Galen said in a low voice and waited for Nick's nod while he buttered his muffin. "They showed up in my storage room about a week ago. They were wrapped in wool and stuffed in old crates with rusted nails, craziest thing. They didn't have any paperwork with them at all. Suzane thinks somebody is messing around with us." A troubled expression crossed Galen's face and his gaze went far away again.

Nick sat forward; his heart beat faster, chasing away the flutters in his stomach from seeing Galen again. It was possible that it could be a hoax, but as often as those statues disappeared, they always showed back up again. And this wouldn't be the first time they appeared with no explanation.

"That's interesting. The Dexios Collection was lost at sea during World War II. Many different salvage companies tried to locate them without any success. I've been searching myself for years. Was there any water damage?"

"No, they look perfect to me. They're gorgeous." Galen glanced away as if he didn't want to meet Nick's eyes and shuffled some papers on his desk. "Maybe they're not the Dexios Collection. It would take magic or a miracle for there not to be some damage, and I don't believe in miracles."

What about magic? Nick's tongue begged to ask. What did Galen believe in? He was acting so oddly. On the phone he'd sounded as excited about the statues as Nick; now he seemed almost hesitant.

Nick's hand trembled, and he set down his coffee cup hard, almost spilling the contents. This had to be the Collection. He had waited his entire life to get a real glimpse of them in person instead of scrutinizing photographs and drawings. If they were here, he'd have a chance to study them in intimate detail like his Uncle Stavros had. He'd be able to face his dad with pride and get an acknowledgement out of him. Sometimes dreaming wasn't a waste of time.

"Can I see them?" The look of unease returned to Galen's face, and a hot, hard knot blossomed in Nick's chest. He wouldn't let Galen keep him from what belonged to him. "What is it?"

"The Dexios Collection is four statues that appear to be missing their other half, right?" Galen studied Nick with an intent look.

"Yes. That's the way it's always been." Nick glanced at the door. He couldn't get over the impression that Galen was stalling. He needed to see those statues now. To his surprise, Galen's expression fell even more. "What's going on?"

"You'll have to see it to believe it." Galen rose and set his coffee down. "Come on, I'll show you. There's no way I can explain it. Something's changed with one of them."

Nick followed him down the spiral staircase and held back all the accusations he wanted to say. If his Collection had gotten damaged under Galen's watch.... He didn't know what he would do. He'd searched too long to find them. And the sideways glances Galen kept shooting him didn't help his frame of mind at all.

When they entered the gallery, Nick's jaw dropped, and he stared at the whole statue, unable to process at first what he saw. "What the hell? Is this some kind of joke?"

A young, light-skinned black woman turned toward them and rolled her eyes. "Okay, I don't get it, Mr. Kanellis. You've been pinballing in and out of here for the last hour. What has got you so worked up?"

"Nothing. Nick here has some information about this Collection. I'm hoping he can solve some of our mysteries. Would you give us a bit, Ella? I'll let you know when the room is available again."

"I'm at a good spot for a break." Ella wiped her hands on a rag and made quick work of taking care of her equipment while shooting them curious glances. "I'll be in the studio."

Nick paid little attention to either of them as he moved to study the statues, starting with the last three. They took his breath away. The pictures he had didn't do them justice at all, and he had no doubt in his mind they were a part of the missing Collection. He felt lightheaded; his heart froze and then pounded. Oh, wait till his dad and brothers saw this.

Nick ran his hand down the statue's back, and his eyes stung. He'd found them. They were real and right here. He didn't have to dig into his savings to haul them from a wreck site to the U.S. He didn't have to search for a museum that would display them while letting the Charisteas family retain control.

By the time he turned back toward the first statue, Ella had left and Galen stood transfixed, staring at the two men embracing. Nick's chest tightened. Near the end of their relationship before Galen had left, he had looked at Nick with that same soft, glowing expression. The expression had given him hope and had him saying words that he'd known were better left unsaid.

"You see it too, don't you?" Galen asked and touched the shoulder of the new man. "The statue has changed. Everybody else seems to think this is the way it's always been, except for me." He met Nick's gaze, his eyes troubled. "And now you. I was afraid you'd think I was trying to trick you."

"I still might." Nick couldn't believe it. He'd heard tales of the statues changing, and he'd always chalked them up as fairy tales.

Nick walked around the statue and examined it closer, but he had to admit it didn't look like an addition had been tacked on after the fact. The embracing men seemed to be one solid piece, though a test for age would reveal that for sure. "So, are you going to explain what happened?"

Galen spread his hands and opened his mouth with a shake of his head. "I don't know if I can. I doubt you'd believe me. I'm not sure I believe it myself."

"Try me, you'll find I'm amazingly open-minded about some things." A niggling suspicion had Nick taking another look at the statue. Most of his family had been skeptical about the legend surrounding it, but his uncle had been convinced the tale had merit. Nick had spent hours poring over his journals when he'd been a teenager, and the dreamer inside him had been captivated by Dexios's story.

Both men looked familiar... however, with the lip-lock they had going, he couldn't be sure. Nick cast a sharper look at Galen, who shrugged as faint spots of color appeared on his cheeks.

"This was still a single man when I went to check on them last night before leaving." Galen hesitated and shook his head. "Oh, never mind. I'm sorry, it sounds too crazy even to my own ears."

Last night Nick had dreamt of Galen kissing a strange man in his museum. He'd woken up to one hell of a boner and stirrings of an old jealousy. Until now, he'd passed the dream off as a natural reaction after hearing from Galen, given their unique history. His suspicions returned even stronger, and Nick shoved them away. Galen was right. It was too crazy to contemplate. This was real life, not a fairy tale.

"Let's go back to your office and finish our breakfast. I'll tell you what I can about the statues." Then he had to decide whether or not he would let Galen keep them at his museum. He wanted them to be seen. They deserved to be on display, especially after so many years of being lost. To give Galen the opportunity meant he'd have to work with him, see him day after day and know that Galen was unreachable. He could touch, Galen wouldn't mind that, but he wouldn't be allowed to keep, and that's what Nick really wanted.

"Okay." Galen brushed his fingers across the statue's jaw. "It's beautiful as one piece, isn't it?"

Nick had to admit it was. As stunning as he'd always found the pictures of the original, this one called to him on a much deeper level. What would they be like if somehow all of them came to be completed? His gaze drifted to Galen, and he snorted to himself. Not if fulfilling the legend relied on Mr. Noncommittal over there. Galen wouldn't understand commitment if it slapped him in the face. Besides, it was just a story, a wildly romantic, heartbreaking story.

"Yeah, they're amazing." Nick resisted the urge to touch Galen's shoulder, to cup his face. He couldn't be so close to him like this and not have such thoughts. He spun on his heel to head back to the office, and Galen fell into step beside him.

"The quick version of the myth is that Dexios, the solo man in the statues, was in love with a fellow soldier, Lykon. They pledged their fidelity to each other, but when the campaign ended, Lykon broke his promise so he could return to his old life and left Dexios behind. Heartbroken, Dexios went to the island they had planned to make their home and gave in to despair. The goddess of love heard him and, out of pity, changed him into a statue to wait for his fickle lover."

"The goddess of love, hmmm? You mean Aphrodite? I'd hoped this tale would be grounded in a little more truth," Galen said as they climbed the spiral staircase up through the tower.

"You wanted to hear the story. You didn't say anything about truth." Nick sat down and picked up his coffee again. He grimaced as he took a taste. It had gone lukewarm. "Unless something happened last night to make you think there was more to the statues than pieces of art. Belief is power, and the names of gods and goddesses change with the people who follow them. It doesn't mean that the spirit doesn't exist."

"Let's not argue philosophy. What happened next?"

"At some point, Lykon returned looking for Dexios and instead found the four statues of him. The goddess appeared and cursed him to be reborn over and over, searching for his lost love and unable to have him."

Nick leaned back and folded his hands on his stomach as Galen shifted with a frown. "You mean there isn't anything in there about the statues becoming whole?" he asked.

Nick waged a fierce inner debate over whether to tell him more and decided that if Galen were going to continue to hold out about what happened the night before, Nick wouldn't spill all of his secrets either. He had a lot he wanted to consider before he let Galen in more.

"There's a whole body of research on them that I haven't delved into for a while. The answers should be there. You see, the statues are more than an area of study for me—it's family history. The Dexios Collection belongs to the Charisteas family, and I have the paperwork to prove it."

He waited for that to sink in, for Galen to realize he could snatch possession of them right from him. Galen's eyes widened, and when he opened his mouth, Nick held up a hand to stop him. "I have a number of journals from past family members that pertain to the Collection. Most are in Greek, but my uncle's mentions, on occasion, some of the statues changing like yours did. It never went beyond three, and they always reverted back to only Dexios."

Nick considered telling Galen that the other journals backed that up, but decided not to. He didn't want to reveal how much information he had just yet. Not until he knew what Galen was going to do. He didn't want to get any more invested in opening doors with Galen than he already was.

"The belief is that when all of the statues are made whole, the lost lovers will be reunited. I'll admit the family has always been rather split on whether or not the statues really changed. Most seemed to think the men who came up with the tale enjoyed a little too much opium, or whatever their personal recreational drug choice was at that time."

Galen turned his head and stared out the window. Nick studied his profile in the silence. He used to kiss the long bridge of Galen's nose when they lay spent in each other's arms. He wondered if Galen remembered the little things like that.

Galen turned back toward him and leaned forward. "Which are you, Nick? Are you a believer?"

"Let's just say, I've always wanted to believe." Nick paused and leaned forward too. "I had a dream about you last night, of you kissing a man in Greek armor who you called Dexios. If you want to keep these statues as part of the exhibit, you will have to tell me what happened between the time you left me a voice mail and this morning."

Galen's eyes widened, and he frowned as he pulled back. "I seem to remember telling you once I didn't like ultimatums. You're basing your distrust on a dream."

"No, I'm basing it on our history."

"Trust goes both ways. Did you ever think to ask yourself why I kept my distance, or did you assume the worst about me? I was honest with you from the very beginning about what I wanted. I never lied to you. You changed the rules on me and got upset when I pulled back."

Nick rose and took two steps toward the staircase before he turned to face Galen again. He had asked that question many times. He still wondered what lay behind the easygoing demeanor that Galen had projected that invited closeness but wouldn't accept any ties. And to make it worse, Galen had to remind Nick that he'd walked right into a broken heart with wide-open eyes.

"I didn't come here to bring up our sordid past. I came to see if the statues were really the Dexios Collection."

"And to lay claim to them?" Galen rubbed the arms of his chair, his gaze fixed on Nick. "That's what you're good at, isn't it? Staking a claim on the things you want."

Nick flushed and looked away. "I didn't come here to fight, Galen," he said, his chest tightening even more. "Why're we arguing?"

Galen sighed and his voice softened. "You know why. I don't like a threat hanging over my head. I don't know if you're trying to goad me or if I'm trying to goad you, but I think we should take a step back and think things through, then try to talk again."

"You'd like that, wouldn't you? Step back, retreat behind that no-man's-land you put yourself on." Nick came around the desk toward Galen. He'd thought that time apart would've eased his knee-jerk reaction to Galen pulling back, but apparently not. He should back up himself and not engage Galen. Not after all this time. He couldn't open that door again and risk Galen hurting him just like last time. What kind of a man did something like that? A masochist, in Nick's opinion.

"I think we should get back to the topic at hand. I'm sure you want those statues to be seen just as much as I do. What better place than here? Let me show you the plans I have for the whole exhibit. The opening is going to be huge, and your Collection will be right at the heart of it. After all this time, don't you think Dexios deserves that?"

"I meant what I said." Nick ignored Galen's impassioned plea and leaned over the desk until their faces were inches apart. "If you can't be honest with me about what's happening with those statues, my statues, then I'm not going to let you keep them. They're important to my family, and I'm not willing to leave them in the hands of somebody I can't trust. Something happened last night, something that changed one of them in a significant way. I want to know what you did and if you think you could do it again."

Galen's gaze darted away and came right back. He dragged a hand through his hair with a sigh. "I need some time to consider it. I'm still not sure it wasn't a dream myself. I haven't had a chance to think it all the way through."

Nothing had changed; disappointment cut sharp and deep, and it infuriated Nick that he'd let himself think something might've changed. When Galen had apologized in his message with that warmth in his voice, Nick had let himself soften.

"You have twenty-four hours. I'll have found another place for them by then. Do your thinking, and do it quick."

"Come on, be reasonable," Galen said, and though his voice remained calm, his hands kept moving, betraying his agitation. "You don't need to resort to threats."

"You'll tell me what I want to know?" Nick held his breath. *Come on, Galen, let me in a bit. Give me some reason to hope that maybe, just maybe we can make a relationship work out.*

Galen glanced away.

"I thought not." Nick straightened and grabbed the remainder of his coffee. He had to get out before he lost his temper. He never should've even tried. He could've sent a notice through his lawyer and never had to deal with Galen at all. "You know how to reach me if you change your mind."

"Wait."

Screw that, Nick thought. He was done with waiting.

"Come on, talk to me," Galen said in a softer voice.

"That's the fucking point. You aren't talking." Nick paused and stabbed his finger toward Galen. "How am I supposed to trust you? Tell me that. This is important to me, and if you're going to dick around, we can do it through lawyers."

Galen jumped up as well, all trace of entreaty vanishing as his eyes flashed hot. "You can't just walk in here and take them. We're the ones who found them."

"And I'm the one that owns them."

They stared each other down, the tension crackling in the air. Nick had never seen Galen pissed off before, and if there hadn't been so much riding on the line, he might find it kind of hot. There had to be some legal way of getting the Collection back without screwing with the museum and its reputation. He didn't want that, no matter how much this whole situation tied him in knots.

"Look," Nick said, striving for a calm that seemed to stay just out of reach. "Let's just both separate and cool down before we say anything else we regret."

Galen motioned toward the stairwell with a jerky nod, his jaw clenched, and his hand shoved into his pocket. "I'll give you a call."

Nick bit back a hot retort and headed down. Yeah, right, he wasn't going to hold his breath on that one.

CHAPTER FIVE

"WHY won't you talk to me?" Galen stood in front of the unmoving statue and strained to listen for any whisper of sound. The heating system sighed as it cut back on, but no other noise broke the silence. The museum had been locked down for the night, and it hadn't seemed to make a damn bit of difference. His mystery man hadn't shown himself.

"Dexios, please, talk to me. Tell me what's going on." Galen went from statue to statue, and they all remained silent. Whatever he had unlocked the night before, both with the statues and within himself, seemed to have retreated, leaving him with too many questions and no way of getting the answers. At least he wasn't delusional. Nick had seen the change too, and Galen clung to that knowledge.

Everybody else looked at Galen like he was crazy if he mentioned that something had changed about the statues, everybody but Nick. Well, Suzane believed him, but she had no memory of how it looked originally. And he had asked Nick point-blank if the Collection consisted of four unfinished statues, and Nick had confirmed it. So, why were they the only ones who remembered something different? It made no sense.

Galen had to remind himself that just because Nick saw it and had a dream that mirrored last night's events didn't mean he would believe Galen. How could he when Galen, who had lived it, didn't even believe it himself? He couldn't even tell Suzane, though he'd tried, because he couldn't think of how to say it without sounding delusional.

Pacing, he tried to decide if Nick was bluffing about having papers that proved his ownership. His thoughts jumped around as he tried to remember all the legalities of the situation and whether or not he could claim salvage rights. He could give in and tell Nick what he wanted, but he didn't want the threat of having the statues removed hanging over his head on one of Nick's whims.

Galen couldn't say why he was reluctant to share what had happened. It embarrassed him, yes; still, that wasn't the real reason. It was intensely personal, in a way that Galen couldn't explain. And if he couldn't tell Suzane, who had become his friend and whom he trusted and loved, then he couldn't tell Nick, who threw his weight around with threats and seemed like he harbored his hurt.

He turned back to Dexios and Lykon, and somehow, the statue of them kissing mocked him. What would it be like to be locked in an eternal embrace with someone he loved? It had to be better than this hollow emptiness.

He touched Dexios's jaw and slid his finger over their joined lips. The metal held a chill that hadn't been there before and was nothing like the heat of Dexios's kiss. Last night had awakened feelings he'd buried months ago. He'd almost forgotten how much he loved kissing, loved having strong arms around him and the hot rush of desire they brought, the comfort.

Getting the chance to see Nick again this morning had reminded him of so many other things. When Nick's color rose and his eyes heated, Galen remembered all the little warning signs. Galen lost count of how many times they'd ended up naked when Nick got his temper going.

He'd missed Nick's intensity, the way he had of waking him up inside, making him feel more alive than dead, and that scared him too. If he woke up, he'd be vulnerable, and Galen had never wanted to go back to being vulnerable. When they had been together all those months ago, Nick made him realize he missed being held. He missed having someone to turn to in the middle of the night. And the urge to confide in him, to let him come closer, to surrender, had grown stronger with every encounter.

And that made him run. He hadn't recognized it then, but he did now. He'd run from everything Nick represented. Galen sighed and turned away, trying to think about what he might've done last night that had triggered Dexios to emerge and come talk to him. Unless he'd hallucinated the whole encounter.

Galen had been looking at the first statue when Dexios had spoken behind him. No. That wasn't right. He'd stepped back away from it when he'd been struck with the insane urge to kiss it. Dexios had even commented on it, something about preferring flesh and bone. Who knew how long he'd been watching?

He glanced at the second statue and his cheeks heated even though nobody was around to see him. He checked over his shoulder to be sure. He could experiment and see what would happen if he knelt in front of Dexios, leaned toward the jutting, hard cock. He glanced at the security camera and his flush deepened. *Idiot. Don't even consider it.*

Galen returned to his office and tried to shrug away his embarrassment. Meeting Dexios had to have been a dream somehow shared between Nick and himself. Maybe if he explained that he'd passed out, it would placate Nick enough so he could keep the statues in his museum, though Nick would probably demand to know how Lykon had gotten to be part of the statue, and Galen had no answers for him.

He still couldn't believe that Nick had dreamed about last night's encounter. How the hell was it possible? Galen had been spun into a world where normal rules didn't seem to apply, and it was weirding him out. He would've thought it was a trick on Nick's part, but there had been no way he could have known what had happened between him and Dexios.

Galen leaned back in his chair and stretched out his legs on top of the desk. He knew he had fucked up what rapport they'd once had, but he'd never expected Nick to use such tactics. The little hope he'd harbored, that maybe they could give things another try, had faded. Maybe it was for the best. Galen wasn't sure if he really wanted to open himself up to another person the way he had with Bryan, even if Nick tempted him. Nick had gotten underneath Galen's skin and made a home. Seeing him today had reminded him of that fact.

Galen had gone from being in a long-term relationship to being alone, and after a time the loneliness had driven him out to the clubs and bars. Hookups, threesomes, and random encounters had kept him going for a while, until Nick had made him realize how empty and self-destructive they were. And once he'd quit sleeping around, where had that left him? Alone again.

He flipped on the monitor at his desk and accessed the camera in the new exhibit room. The statues hadn't moved and remained solitary except for the first. He could solve last night's dilemma by looking at the camera recording, but God help him, he was afraid. He didn't know what he would see. He didn't even know what he wanted to see.

The same argument played over and over in his mind. If he had imagined it, how had Lykon appeared? And how come only he and Nick noticed the changes?

Galen stared at the statues until his temples began to ache, and he still didn't have any answers. Maybe he could seduce Nick into letting him keep them. His conscience flinched at the thought. No, he couldn't toy with Nick's emotions again. It wasn't fair.

Enough. He had to look at the recording and then decide what to do. Galen accessed yesterday's footage, and his pulse leapt as he hit play. The image flicked on, bright from the morning sun that streamed through the windows. Ella stood back, studied the mural, and as the camera panned the room Galen leaned in to hit Fast-Forward.

The sun glinted off the statues, including the first one of Dexios and Lykon. Galen froze, and his head spun as he tried to process it. What the fuck. He checked the time and date stamp then stared in disbelief at the whole statue. The sour taste of disappointment filled his mouth. He was crazy; there was no other way to put it. Delusional. Hallucinating.

He clicked on another file from a few days before with the same results. All the way back to the first day when Knox carted the statues in, and sure enough, it depicted the two men bound in an embrace. Somehow when the change had occurred, it had rippled back in time. Not only had it affected the memories of the people around them, it had also affected the cameras and who knew what else.

Galen sat back and drummed his fingers on his desk. There had to be a rational explanation for everything, from the statues' strange arrival to the change last night. He'd been too besotted and excited over the exhibit to question it then, and now all of Suzane's questions haunted him. And Nick was involved. Seriously, what were the chances that the guy he'd been obsessing over owned the Collection?

He switched back to yesterday's footage and fast-forwarded it until he saw himself enter the room. At least if he made a fool of himself, nobody else had to see. Galen leaned forward to study the black-and-white image as he watched himself walk toward the Collection. He stared at the statue until his eyes burned and didn't notice anything change, even when he got to the part where he'd been tempted to kiss it.

A flicker onscreen stopped him, and he held his breath as his image whirled around to confront someone. He needed sound. Why hadn't he invested in sound?

The man came further into the room, and Galen's heart quickened. Dexios. He wasn't insane. It wasn't a dream. Oh damn, Nick had to see this. Somehow, between the two of them, they'd figure out what happened. Maybe this would be enough for Nick, and he'd let the museum keep the statues.

Maybe this would be enough for the two of them to start over. He wanted to stay mad over Nick's ultimatums, but he always had a hard time doing that once the heat of the moment was gone. Now that he had calmed down too, he could see where Nick was coming from. He had no reason to want to work with Galen, and the Collection seemed important to him. They'd just have to find a way to work it out as adults.

Galen flicked off the program and saved the file to a hard drive. He headed out to the bus stop and tried to call Nick, but the call went to his voice mail. He hoped it didn't mean that Nick was out and unavailable. If they were going to work together for a while, Galen wanted to find some way to heal this breach between them.

"Nick, in case you decide to listen to your messages, I'm on my way over. I have something you'll want to see."

NICK stared at the journal in his hands without seeing it as he weighed the pros and cons of calling his dad. Most likely he'd want to call a family meeting. Nick couldn't find a museum for the Dexios Collection without telling them, and they could help. And if Galen tried to wrest the statues from him, he knew without a doubt they'd band together to stop him.

He'd convinced himself that finding the Collection would solve all his problems. Now he felt like he'd been tied to a snowball that dangled on the edge of a steep incline. There would be no controlling it once it went over. His feelings for Galen and his family only added to the mix. Ever since Nick had left San Francisco, he'd talked to his father and brothers on rare occasions. When he had, the conversations were strained and awkward. He'd much rather have a tooth extracted without painkillers than go through another silent meal with any of them.

As always, thoughts of his dad and brothers made him want to squirm inside. They had reached out to him a few times, making a token effort at reconciliation. The knock on Nick's door jerked him out of his reverie, and he set aside the journal.

"Maybe whoever it is will go away," he said to Rory, who bobbed his head and chirped at the sound of Nick's voice.

He could sidestep the whole problem of his family for a short while if he figured out a way to work with Galen and keep the Collection with him. Nick had to admit that he'd acted like a heavy-handed jackass earlier. Yes, Galen was hiding something that had to do with the statues changing, but maybe it was something that couldn't be explained easily.

The knock came again, more forceful this time, and Nick rose with a sigh. It was almost nine o'clock, and he wasn't in the mood to be sociable, so whoever was at the door had better have a good reason to be there. The surly greeting died on his lips when he opened the door and saw Galen on his doorstep with entreaty in his eyes. His heart jumped. He'd waited a long time to see his expression so open, without that cool reserve, and knowing it irked him even more.

It didn't help that Galen still wore the suit from this morning. Earlier Nick had been able to resist thoughts of stripping Galen of his vest and shirt just to see if his chest was as smooth as before, his nipples still as sensitive. Here at his apartment was a whole different tale. Galen hadn't even come through the doorway, and already Nick was consumed by thoughts of him, compounded by very erotic memories.

"What do you want? I'm not looking for another fight tonight."

Galen winced and gave him an apologetic smile. "I'm not here to argue with you." He held up a flash drive. "You want to know what happened last night? Here it is."

Nick could only stare. Out of all the scenarios he'd imagined, Galen backing down wasn't one of them. "What's on the flash drive?"

"Last night's security tape from the exhibit room. I watched the first part to make sure I didn't imagine it all, but I haven't seen the whole thing." Galen seemed to steel himself and met Nick's gaze square on. "I'm sorry for my knee-jerk reaction earlier. You were right. The statues are yours, so I need to be more open with you about what's going on with them."

Well, dammit, he really hadn't expected that at all. Nick glanced at the flash drive, then met Galen's eyes. "I'm sorry too. I came in there ready to fight, and I didn't give you a chance. I shouldn't have given you ultimatums."

Nick held out his hand, and Galen gave him the flash drive. "I'll take a look at it and give you a call in the morning."

"Wait." Galen stuck his foot in the door before Nick could shut it on him. "Come on, let me watch it with you. It's only video, there's no sound. I can tell you what was said, and we can figure out where to go from there. I have questions, and I'm sure you will too. It'll go faster if we look at it together."

Nick studied Galen, at war with himself. The last time he'd let Galen into his apartment, it had gotten ugly. And they were already on edge with each other. To have Galen so close would bring all those temptations right back to the surface again. He'd like to believe that he was over Galen, but his reactions proved otherwise.

He couldn't deny that Galen was right, though. He'd have questions, and he'd want answers. Curiosity outweighed his misgivings. "Fine, come in." He opened the door and stepped back. "What made you change your mind? Is it just because of the statues?"

Galen shook his head. "I'll admit I hate the idea of losing them, though that isn't why. The reason I didn't say anything earlier was because I didn't think you'd believe me about what happened. I didn't believe it myself. It's insane. But somehow you're involved too, and I need to talk to somebody who sees the things I'm seeing. And I'm really hoping you can help me make sense of it."

Nick took a closer look at him. Galen had changed since he last saw him. He hadn't noticed it earlier, but the infuriating wall he always kept up seemed to be gone tonight. The tightness had disappeared from around his mouth, the unhappiness he tried to hide in his eyes. Before there had been an air of desperation about him, as if he'd been running from something or trying to fill a hole. Nick could never figure out which. Even that had faded.

Maybe they had… no, better to squash that line of thought before it started.

"I have to agree with you on one thing. I think you're the only person I know who might give credence to the family legend." Nick gave him a small smile. And that alone was worth the ache of being in close proximity with Galen and not being allowed to touch. It didn't stop Nick's fingers from itching to do so. Would he find other changes if he kissed Galen?

The cockatiels sang out a greeting as they entered the living room and Galen grinned. "I see you found a friend for Rory. What's its name?"

Galen remembered his pet's name. That both touched and flustered him. Not two minutes into his apartment and Galen already had him off balance. They hadn't exactly just hung out at his place, and Galen had always refused any invites to linger the whole night. Still, he remembered. "That's Amy."

Galen shot him an amused glance. "You're such a geek."

"You're not one to talk if you picked up on my homage to *Doctor Who*."

He led Galen over to the couch and opened his laptop on the coffee table. Galen sat on the edge of the couch, his hands clasped together as he leaned forward. Whatever was on the clip really had him going, and that only made Nick more curious. When the clip started, Galen pointed toward the whole statue on the screen. "This is what's really screwing with me. Last night, when I came in, Dexios was still by himself. How come that's not showing here?"

"It's the same with the old pictures I have of the Collection. In all of them the first statue is whole. I checked them when I got back from the museum." Nick grabbed the journal from the table and flipped through it until he found a photograph to show Galen. "I think the same thing happened in the past. And if the legend doesn't get fulfilled, I bet the security tape and the pictures will revert back to the way they're supposed to look."

"I'd love to know why we're not affected when everyone else is."

Nick had his theories, and he didn't like them one bit. His feelings for Galen were his own. He didn't want them bound up with the legend. Besides, it couldn't be possible. Their relationship had ended with no hope in sight. So the statues had to be reacting to another couple. Maybe Nick had a long-lost cousin he didn't know about who worked at the museum.

Another man stepped into view on the screen, and Galen's breath caught. Nick sensed his heightened awareness, and when he stole a glance at Galen he couldn't miss the rapt expression on his face. Whoever this man was, he had certainly made an impression on Galen. *Fucker.* Nick clenched his jaw and suppressed the white-hot surge of jealousy. He didn't give a rat's ass who Galen ogled.

Then Nick got a closer look at the strange man on the screen. His skin prickled and broke out in a wave of goose bumps. He knew that man. He'd dreamt of him last night with Galen. He'd read about him in the journals. He was a myth come to life. Dexios. Holy fuck.

"What are you two talking about?"

Galen shrugged and two spots of color appeared on his cheeks. "Nothing much. He seemed to mistake me for Lykon. And he asked me to make him whole." Galen shot a sideways glance at Nick. "I thought I heard the same phrase when we first brought the statues out to the exhibit room, but Ella was in there too, and she didn't hear anything."

He gestured toward the screen, drawing Nick's attention back to it. "Actually, I mistook him for you at first. There was something about his eyes and the shape of his face that reminded me of you."

Nick started to respond, then the action on the screen changed as Galen and the strange man kissed. Nick's gut clenched. He had seen Galen kiss many men, but not like this; even through the screen, the energy between them sparked. Nick tore his eyes away before he got himself worked up. He had no claim on Galen. He never had, and he needed to keep reminding himself of that before he lost his self-respect.

The moonlight seemed to shimmer around the statue of the men embracing, and Nick thought he saw them shift to embrace each other tighter. "Did you see that?" He pointed toward the screen as the moonlight brightened even more.

"Weird, I didn't notice that last night. I was—What the hell?" Galen jerked back away from the computer, his face pale, then leaned forward again to hit Pause.

"What is it?" Nick leaned forward too, and studied the statues, searching for whatever had startled Galen.

"Hold on, let me play this back in slow motion. This is about the time I started to feel real strange. Like there was another presence in me fighting to come out, and suddenly I recognized Dexios. No, more than recognized, I knew him as well as I had known…." Galen trailed off and started the clip again. "Now look at my face when we break apart."

Nick frowned and peered at the couple. He didn't see anything out of the ordinary, definitely not anything he hadn't seen before. Then just as Galen began to pull back with a shocked expression, his face changed, his features shifting until the man who looked back at Dexios had only a passing resemblance to Galen. The features were similar, but the other man's hair was curly, his cheeks unshaven, and his shoulders broader.

They kissed, a torrid, desperate kiss, and clung to each other as if they were afraid they were about to be torn apart. This was different from when Nick had watched Galen kiss the other man. That had him wanting to stake a claim on Galen, but this made his heart twist in empathy. Their desperation was almost palpable, even through the camera.

The man in Dexios's arms stiffened and went limp. As Dexios caught him midfall his features returned to those of Galen's, and another indistinct figure rose from his body. It became solid, turning into another man dressed in Greek armor. The man who had possessed Galen. Dexios said something, and the other man gave him a sad smile, touched Dexios's jaw, and turned, disappearing into the statue.

CHAPTER SIX

"I KEEP telling myself it couldn't have happened, yet it did," Galen said softly. The situation was strange enough without adding in the thought that he'd been possessed last night by some ancient spirit and somehow it had entered the statue. The only thing that kept him from freaking out entirely was having Nick next to him and knowing that other than passing out, no harm had come to him at all.

Galen and Nick watched Dexios lift Galen and carry him out of range of the camera. Nick sat back, his expression troubled as he continued to stare at the quiet exhibit room. "I woke up this morning in my office." Galen turned toward him on the couch and indulged in the chance to watch him. "I'd hoped that I dreamt the whole scenario, because my other thought was that I had a mental breakdown. Either I'd been hallucinating, or I'd let an intruder get away with breaking into my museum. Neither was a happy thought. Now that I know I wasn't crazy, it's even scarier knowing that something had changed me."

Nick remained silent, and he worried the corner of his lip, his brow furrowed in thought. Galen studied Nick's profile: the long nose, the heavy brows, and strong chin. His gaze returned to Nick's lips, firm, sexy. He remembered how Nick got the hint of dimples when he smiled. He loved Nick's mouth, and thoughts of leaning over to kiss him crowded his mind.

"What did you dream last night, Nick?"

Nick finally looked at him, his brows still drawn together, and Galen wasn't sure if there was awe or fear in his eyes. "Almost everything that happened on the tape. Then it became me kissing you, and not Dexios, and when the dream changed again, we were making love in some camp near the sea, only it wasn't really us. I can't explain it."

Galen had dreamt, too, though he didn't remember the details. Nick's words tugged at him, conjuring up wisps of half-formed musings that had filled his night. The idea that they had shared the same dream was ludicrous. However, there were a good many incidents that had happened ever since those statues showed up that could be called the same. He didn't know what to think anymore.

Nick rose, slamming the laptop lid down and startling Galen out of his thoughts. "Dammit, you couldn't have called before? Six months without a word, not even an e-mail or text to let me know you were doing okay."

They were going to have it out. Somehow Galen wasn't surprised. Deep down he knew he wouldn't have been able to come over tonight without discussing their aborted relationship. And this was a normal conversation, though uncomfortable, a step back from the weird. He craved that sense of normalcy. Once they talked, they'd both know where they stood with each other. He needed to know if Nick was involved with someone else because Galen did not poach on anyone's territory. Despite how heated the vibes were that had been passing between them since he arrived, there were some lines he wouldn't cross.

And the pain in Nick's voice that he tried to disguise with anger made Galen more than a little ashamed of himself. Now all of his excuses for not calling seemed to be just that—empty, cowardly excuses.

"I thought about it more than once, even went so far as to pick up the phone a couple of times," Galen said, his elbows on his knees as he stared down at his hands. "The longer time went on, the more I thought about it, not less like I'd assumed I would. I didn't realize how much you'd already become a part of me."

"Why the hell didn't you call?" Galen looked up only to be pinned by Nick's reproachful gaze. Before he could find the words to reply, Nick continued. "I left it as your decision. I didn't push you or come begging for you to give us a chance. I expected you to back off, not disappear entirely."

"Remember what I said when we first hooked up?"

Nick threw up his hands and disappeared into the kitchen as one of the birds called after him. Galen rose with a frown and took two uncertain steps in that direction when he heard the fridge door open and the clink of glass against glass. Moments later Nick returned with two beers and he handed Galen one. "Look, I know I broke the rules when I—"

Galen held up his hand and shook his head, interrupting him. "I didn't mean it as an accusation. I'm sorry for how I reacted when you first told me how you felt. I wasn't ready for any of it. Not for how you felt about me and sure as hell not for how you made me feel again. I wanted to be dead inside and I couldn't, not with you. So I ran."

Shock crossed Nick's face, and he sat down across from Galen, then took a long drink from his bottle. "I always thought you were running from something. I thought maybe a bad ex. I never thought I might've been the cause."

"No, you were right. I was running, and not from an abusive relationship. And you didn't do anything wrong. You were yourself, and it drew me in and scared me at the same time." Galen took a seat on the other couch and set the bottle down untasted.

"I cared, more than I wanted to, about your feelings. I didn't want to string you along, give you false hope, and wind up hurting you even more. When I called you, I wanted to be sure it was because I was ready and not out of a selfish need to see you when I couldn't promise to be what you needed. It was different when I'd believed we were using each other. I couldn't continue when it changed."

"Why didn't you tell me all this then?" Nick looked so bewildered that Galen wished he could find some magic way to make things better. Rory lit onto Nick's shoulder and he stroked his feathers with a finger. Galen remembered the strength and gentleness of those hands, and he wanted them again. "I would've backed off, given you the space you needed."

"You? Come on, I'm telling the truth. You need to give me the same courtesy. At least be honest with yourself. Having something you want out of your reach drives you batshit. You would've tried at first. I know you would've, but...."

"I'm possessive?" Nick broke in, and a rueful smile touched the corner of his lips when Galen shrugged. "Yeah, I suppose I am."

"It's one of the things that drew me to you, and at the time I couldn't open myself up to someone else." Galen's mind flashed back to that horrifying night. The pouring rain. The terrible sounds of glass shattering, metal crumpling, and Bryan's scream. He banished the dark memories with a firm shove. He couldn't go back, only forward. He'd spent too much time as it was wallowing in the past, blaming himself for things that couldn't ever be fixed.

"You're right." Nick leaned forward, his gaze intent on Galen's face in a way that made his heart skip a beat. "It would've made me nuts. I was already making myself crazy. I knew we could be so good together if you'd take the chance. And seeing you flirting with all those other men, knowing that some were taking you home and that I had no real claim on you, yeah, it did raise every possessive instinct I had."

Galen glanced down and took a sip of his beer. That's how they'd met, hooking up for a semianonymous threesome. They'd returned more than once to the same dynamic. Galen had gotten off on Nick's hot, possessive eyes on him when someone else touched him, fucked him. And Nick had gotten off too. He couldn't deny that. That's why they both had kept going back for more. Nick had been the closest that Galen had come to seeing someone regularly in a long time.

Then something had changed for them both. Galen had no idea when the line had been crossed. He found himself losing interest in having a third person with them, and Nick had gotten pretty vocal against it as well. More and more often it had become the two of them alone. It had changed from just sex to hanging out at the clubs beforehand, sometimes even meeting for a quick dinner.

And it had all come to an abrupt halt when Nick admitted he loved Galen.

"That being said, I couldn't have told you what was going on in my head anyway. I needed to face it first and understand what drove me. I needed to know what I wanted out of life." Galen lifted his head and met Nick's gaze. "I'm sorry I ran. I'm sorry it hurt you."

"So am I."

They stared at each other, neither of them quite ready to break the silence, to take the next step. At least that's what Galen hoped Nick's silence meant. Maybe he'd already moved on. If that were the case, well, Galen would have to learn to live with it. He couldn't lay a claim when he'd given up that right six months ago. He had to know before it ate him up inside.

"When I called you the first time, it wasn't about the statues. I remembered how much you liked art history, and I hoped they were enough to pique your interest and get you out to dinner." Fuck. He was going about this backward, and Nick's expression remained unreadable, which did not help the nerves plucking at him. "I guess what I'm trying to say is… are you seeing anybody else right now?"

Nick rubbed his palms on his jeans, then leaned forward to grab his beer. Rory launched from his shoulder with a raucous cry and glided over to his cage where he continued his barrage of irritated calls. "No, I'm not seeing anyone." He took a long swallow of his beer, his gaze everywhere but on Galen. "Are you still partying every night?"

He didn't say what Galen knew had to be uppermost in his thoughts. Was he still sleeping around? Fair enough. He could understand why it would be a deal breaker for Nick at this point.

"There hasn't been anybody since you."

Nick's eyes jerked toward him, widening. "For real?"

"You showed me how empty it was. Besides, it would've defeated the purpose of getting my head clear. I don't want random strangers anymore."

Nick looked as if he wanted to say something. Instead, he rose and walked over to the bird cage and fussed with it. Galen watched him and gave Nick a chance to gather his thoughts. The tension over the statues had broken, and the big question that had loomed over him ever since he'd decided to call Nick had been answered. They'd both had a chance to bring up the past and now Galen didn't know where to go from here.

Their future remained uncertain, a dark labyrinth rising up before him. If he opened up the door and Nick stepped through, he'd be vulnerable again. Six months ago the thought would've had him both angry and scared and not even willing to consider it. Now, after seeing Nick again, remembering all those things he'd missed about him, had him thinking that no matter what the future held, not trying would be the worst thing he could do.

"What do you want?" Nick asked with his back still to Galen.

Galen hesitated at the question. What right did he have to ask Nick for another chance? Nick turned toward him and cocked his head to the side. "Come on, when you called, what were you looking for? A hookup for old time's sake? A few drinks at a bar before we went cruising?"

Galen stood up and walked over to Nick. He'd wondered for so long if he'd imagined the hum of energy between them. If anything he'd downplayed it. The currents were still there and they still tugged at him. He was aware of Nick all along his skin, and they hadn't even touched yet. When he neared, Nick shifted as if he was about to step back, but he didn't.

"I wanted to ask you out on a date."

Nick wet his lips and stuck his thumbs through his belt loops. Galen resisted the instinctive urge to lean in closer and kiss him. He wanted to know if Nick still wore the same aftershave. If Galen pressed against him would Nick have the faint spicy scent that had haunted Galen for weeks after he'd left?

"A date?"

"I know it wasn't our MO back then. I want something different this time. I want us to really get to know each other in a way I wouldn't have let happen when we were together before. I wouldn't have called you if I wasn't serious. I'm not trying to play games with you."

Nick's green eyes darkened, and he shoved a hand through his hair, making the tumbled spikes stand out even more in random tufts. "Let me think about it."

"Fair enough." Galen resisted the urge to touch him, because if he did, he knew he'd kiss him. If nothing had changed, that would lead to the both of them naked in Nick's bed, and Galen wanted to show him things *had* changed. Nick was already wary enough of him; no need to add fuel, to make Nick think he was after sex before leaving again.

Besides, he hadn't come here for seduction tonight. He wanted to figure out what was happening with the statues and whether or not he'd be able to keep them for his exhibit. Okay, that was a lie. He'd also wanted to know if Nick was still single and interested. Now that Galen knew where he stood, time to back off.

"It's getting late. I'd better go." Galen turned away and retrieved his flash drive. "Do you think we could get together sometime tomorrow? I'd like to talk about the statues again. Between us we might figure out what'll happen next."

Nick seemed to be relieved about the change in topic, and it gave Galen a little pang of regret to see it. "Yeah, why don't I come by after closing hours? I'll bring us some dinner, we can talk about it and check out the exhibit again. Maybe we can trigger another visit from Dexios."

"Sounds like a good plan. Bring the journals too. I wouldn't mind taking a closer look at them." Galen frowned as he thought about what he'd seen on the tape. He did not want to be possessed again, to have someone else control him. "You said you'd read about the statues changing. Was there anything about possession or anybody getting hurt?"

Nick's brow furrowed, and he shook his head slowly. "I don't remember anything in them that applies to what happened to you, but it's been a while. And I'm sure there's nothing violent in them. I would've remembered that. So, I think you're pretty safe."

"Okay, that makes me feel a little better." If Galen looked at the situation with a clear mind, the worst that had happened to him was the embarrassing fainting spell. Dexios had taken care of him instead of leaving him crumpled on the floor and that had to stand for something.

Nick walked him to the door and dropped his gaze to Galen's mouth. Galen's heart pounded. The tension spiked and then faded under a wave of uncertainty. Nick stepped back, his eyes showing the same emotions Galen felt. It was like neither one of them had a clue where they should go from here. "Good night, Galen."

"Night."

Galen walked away, sensing Nick's stare hot on the back of his neck all the way to the outside stairwell. And when he got home, he relived every moment of the whole day. While the statues were one mystery, Nick's heart was a whole other one.

A VOW BROKEN

"*I* CANNOT *stay, Dexios.*" *Lykon glanced toward his love and continued to roll his few belongings up in his cloak. He hated that look in Dexios's eyes, that confused, hurt, desperate gaze. In the years that he'd known Dexios, he'd never seen an expression like that before on his face.*

"*We made a promise to each other. Do you remember? We vowed that when the campaign ended we would stay together. You cannot mean to foreswear that oath.*"

The quiet desolation in Dexios's voice made Lykon question his resolve. He never wanted to hurt Dexios.

"*I remember.*" *That night had been special, blessed by the gods, but they could not stay in their little nest, wrapped up in each other to the exclusion of nothing else.* "*I am sorry, I need to see to this by myself.*"

"*What is so urgent that you have to return home now and so secretive that I cannot go with you?*" *Dexios caught his arm as Lykon started to tie up the bundle.* "*Look at me, curse you. Look at me and tell me why.*"

Lykon pulled back, and his heart ached. He couldn't think when Dexios touched him. All he could think of was sinking into Dexios's embrace and agreeing to all the plans his lover had for them without giving them full consideration. He needed to get away, get some perspective before he made such decisions.

He considered and discarded several excuses before he decided that he owned Dexios the truth.

"*This passion between us, it....*" *He paused and tried to find the right word. It unsettled him.* "*It is too strong. There is no reason with it. I agreed to abandon my family for you without thought of consequence. I did not think the vow through, and it is not like me."*

"Your family does not need you anymore than my family needs me. They are cared for and their needs seen to. We shed blood for their safety for these last few years. Why should we sacrifice more? It is not as if we are leaving them destitute." Dexios grabbed Lykon's shoulder, and Lykon wondered if it would be the last time he felt the grip of those strong fingers. Would Dexios wait for him, or would he find another to fill his life? "They do not need you, I do."

Lykon could not harden his heart against that naked plea. Dexios was not a man who normally let himself be so vulnerable, and the thought frightened him even more. How could he live up to such expectations that Dexios had for them? Lykon had seen passion flare and die once too often. Better to hurt Dexios now, before they got in too deep, than hurt him more later on.

And if Lykon harbored doubts now, what did that mean? Time and distance would clear his thoughts, and then he could make a decision about his future. Not here and now, clouded by the way Dexios made him feel.

"I am sorry, Dexios. I need to think this through on my own." His lover's hand fell away from Lykon's shoulder, and the ache in his heart intensified in response. He wanted to say he would return, but he didn't know that for certain. He'd already broken one promise. He didn't want to give Dexios false hope and break another.

"Will you return to me?"

Lykon flinched at the quiet question. Even now, Dexios seemed able to read his thoughts. His lover knew him like no other. "I will make no more vows to you until I am sure I can keep them. I do not know if I will return. I want to, yet I do not know what the morrow will bring. Give me this time I need, Dexios. Please."

"You ask much of me."

Lykon turned to face Dexios, and when he reached out to touch his face, Dexios stepped back out of reach. "You asked much of me too."

"You could have asked for time before you made your promise. I would not have denied you." The vehemence in Dexios's voice took

Lykon aback. He did not want to part with Dexios harboring such anger toward him. Even if it had merit.

"I should have. I did not think, not when you were looking at me the way you were. When you do that I find it impossible to refuse you anything." Lykon sighed and finished tying his bundle together. He could not give in this time, or he would always have doubts that he made the right decision. "That is what you do, you catch me up in your net, and I abandon all thought. Perhaps I should have done it before. It seemed senseless to think ahead when we did not know if we would survive each day."

"If you find it impossible to refuse me, then do not do it now." Lykon closed his eyes as Dexios stepped toward him and cupped his face. He savored the sensation of those calloused palms against his cheek. The heaviness in his chest grew until it became a weighted rock that threatened to crush him. It would be too easy to lean in and kiss him, give in and let Dexios carry him away with his plans for their life.

He wished he had Dexios's strength of purpose, to have the certainty without doubt or fear. He'd lived the last few years with that uncertainty every day, not knowing what the day would bring, what horrors he'd see. And he'd dealt with it by living in the moment, ignoring the morrow and laughing the fear away. Now that it had all changed again he was as lost as a boat on the sea in a fierce storm. If he didn't ground himself, he'd be swept away.

"You do not understand. You are so sure of our future, of us. Do you not want me to have the same surety?" Lykon whispered and felt Dexios stiffen, the tenderness fleeing from his cupped hands.

"You are right. I do not understand how you can have doubts about us." Dexios's hands fell away, and it seemed as though an abyss had dropped the ground away between them. Lykon opened his eyes and flinched from the mute betrayal in Dexios's gaze. Dexios's reaction was far worse than Lykon had feared it would be.

"Have I ever betrayed a confidence or treated you in a manner not to your liking, Lykon? Have I ever given you reason to doubt my commitment to you? I thought we belonged together. Perhaps I was mistaken."

"I only ask for time."

"No, you ask for time with no assurances given. You expect me to let you walk away while you leave me with nothing save for the hope that you may return. How long am I supposed to wait for you to think, for you to discover what it is you want? How am I supposed to know it will not happen again if you do come back?"

Lykon wanted to ask for his trust, yet how could he when it seemed as if he had no trust in Dexios by taking this time for himself? A visit home would clear his mind, give Dexios a chance to do the same.

"I will not leave you in darkness, wondering and waiting." He flung his bundle over his back. He should start out. He had a long trek back to his home and an even longer journey awaited Dexios. "I will get word to you. This does not have to be good-bye."

Dexios took a step back, his expression cold and hurt. "Why should I believe you when you will not even try now?" With that he turned and walked away, and Lykon sensed a gaping emptiness inside of him as he watched him go until he disappeared over the hill. More than once he almost called out to him, and each time the words died on his tongue.

I love you. Please wait.

Lykon had no right to ask that. He'd find a way to make this up to Dexios, once he was able to get some perspective. He did not want any regrets later because he rushed into decisions now. Better this small regret now than a bigger one later. Only, as he trudged in the opposite direction, the regret seemed almost overwhelming.

Some time. Please, Cythera, just grant me some time and clarity of purpose. Then I will know how to proceed.

CHAPTER SEVEN

"YOU'RE eyeing the phone like it's a spider about to pounce."

Nick jerked his head up to see Sean standing in his open doorway, his expression so smooth that Nick knew he had to be holding back a laugh.

"There isn't a spider in the world that would dare come onto my desk. It would be seen as an act of war, and I would be forced to answer with a full-on frontal assault."

"I remember that fierce battle in the supply closet. I think the whole office heard your shouts of 'die, die, die.' But I digress." Sean held up a file. "Your two o'clock has been cancelled. Did you still want me to make the copies?"

"Yeah, I'll want to reschedule. Do me a favor and hold my calls for the next fifteen minutes. I need to take care of something."

"Will do."

The door shut, leaving Nick alone with the phone and an all-too-familiar squirming inside of him. He should call his dad at night; the butcher shop would be busy at this time of day, but he didn't know how long his meeting would go with Galen tonight, and he couldn't hold off telling his dad about the statues any longer. Before he decided to once again not call, he grabbed the phone and dialed.

"Charisteas Quality Meats. How can I help you?"

Some of his tension unknotted at the sound of the woman's voice. At least it was Sophia, his brother's wife, and not Jason himself, though Nick had to admit that his relationship with his oldest brother had improved since Nick had gone to their wedding. "Hey, Sophia, it's Nick. Is Dad around?"

"Nick! I'm glad you called. We were meaning to call you to tell you the news." The sound of her voice faded, and Nick heard her shouting for his brother. He groaned and dropped his head into his palm, then dragged his hand through his hair. This would not be the quick check-in that he'd been going for. "Hold on, Jason's picking up in the office."

Before Nick could get a word in, the phone clicked over, and Jason came on the line. "You must've been reading my mind. How've you been?"

The casual tone seemed… forced, and Nick bit back a sigh. Yep, Nick thought, it was going to be one of those conversations. He should've asked Sean to interrupt him after ten minutes. "Been getting by. How about you? Sophia said you had some news."

"Lots of stuff happening, man, you're missing out." Nick bristled at the implication that he should call more. It was one of Jason's favorite points to harp on. It went both ways. His dad knew how to dial a phone, so did Jason and his other brothers, Stefan and Damian. He held his tongue as Jason continued. He didn't want to argue today. "Stefan got accepted into a graduate program, so he's heading back to school in the fall; and Damian finally popped the question, so you can plan on traveling sometime next May."

Damian had been dating someone seriously? Mr. Casanova? Nick's stomach sank as the distance between himself and his family seemed to grow by another couple hundred miles. He'd thought they'd made some progress with everyone when he'd returned to San Francisco for Jason's wedding; now it seemed like he'd been cut out all over again.

"Sounds like you all have been busy. Tell them congrats for me." Jason remained quiet, and Nick sensed the weight of his disapproval through the phone. He shifted in his chair, searching for something to say so the silence wouldn't become strained or before Jason could start in on a lecture. "What else is going on? Sophia implied you two had something to share too."

"You're going to be an uncle." Nick grinned at the pride in Jason's voice, and all the little nagging frustrations and resentments eased. Oh wow, another generation of little Charisteas kids. His dad must be strutting around excited as he could be, telling all the regular customers when they came in. Nick could picture it as clear as if he stood in the shop himself. "The baby will be here sometime around New Year's."

"That's awesome. Wow, I'm really happy for you two." Nick wanted what Jason had: to be in a relationship stable enough that they could consider adopting. Not that he was looking for that right now. Hell no, he wasn't ready to be a dad, but he wanted the promise of that someday. He wanted his dad to acknowledge his partner when he found one. He wanted too much. Or as his dad would say, he was a dreamer with his head off somewhere when he needed to be grounded.

"Sophia and I talked about it, and we want you to be the baby's godfather," Jason said.

Nick sat back in his chair as his breath came out in a rush. He dragged a hand through his hair and looked at the poster of Santorini on his wall. Godfather? "I… I don't know what to say. Won't that piss off Damian? You two are really close." As soon as the words were out of his mouth he wished he'd kept it shut. This was a chance at a new connection with his family, and he needed that.

"Sophia and I agree that we want you. Damian was my best man. He'll get over it. So what do you say?"

It occurred to Nick that Jason picked him for the same reasons he wanted to say yes. He didn't want to lose all of his ties with his family, and it seemed that at least one of them didn't want Nick to disappear altogether either. If Jason was willing to live with the fallout since he lived in San Francisco with everybody else, Nick couldn't do anything less.

"I'd love to, I…." Nick paused, his chest tight as he searched for the words. "It means a lot. Tell me when, and I'll be there. I swear."

"Sweet. I knew I could count on you."

Nick shifted in his chair again as the never-ending guilt panged. He had to stop letting everything they said get under his skin. "I hate to rush, but work calls, and I know it's busy at the shop. Is Dad there? I wanted to talk with him too."

"Sorry man, Dad's dealing with a truck," Jason said with a note of apology in his voice. "I'll tell him you called, though. He'll be happy to hear it."

Nick swallowed back his disappointment and the resentful thoughts that sprang into his mind. His dad had no way of knowing he was going to call. Get over it. "Okay, tell him I'll call him back when I get a chance. Take care."

"Hey, wait." Nick tensed and steeled himself for familiar words. "About Damian and Stefan, call them and tell them you're happy for them yourself. Trust me on this. It's got to start somewhere."

Whatever, they could've called him and given him the news themselves instead of using Jason as their spokesperson. "I'll think about it. I promise. Gotta go, bro. I'll talk to you later."

Nick stared at the phone for a long time afterward, debating whether or not to call Stefan and Damian before dropping the idea. One call a day was stressful enough. He'd think about calling them tomorrow.

GALEN looked at himself in the mirror one last time and smoothed a hand over his hair as he tried to quell the nerves that plagued him. This was not a date. Nick was coming over to discuss the Dexios Collection, and he'd already made it clear that he was less than enthusiastic about the thought of dating. Galen tried telling himself that the nerves were just because he wasn't sure what Nick had decided to do about the statues, but he knew it wasn't the truth, at least not entirely.

He looked forward to seeing more of Nick, to having the chance to talk about things other than business. Galen turned away from the mirror with a sigh. He didn't even know what Nick was looking for or what he wanted. And he didn't want to ask and bring up old wounds in the process. They'd already hashed it out enough.

A day at a time. Wasn't that what his mom always said? *Just take things a day at a time, and they will work themselves out.* He wished he had her patience and serenity.

At least they'd started out on a different footing this time. They hadn't jumped into bed at first sight, so that had to be progress there.

Suzane's head popped up through the stairwell, and she knocked on the landing. "Looking good there." Her eyes held questions that she didn't ask, for which Galen was grateful. He didn't want to discuss Nick, at least not until there was something to discuss.

"What are you still doing here? You should be home resting and gathering your strength for tomorrow." He frowned at her as she climbed the rest of the way into his office. "I thought you went home a couple hours ago."

"I wanted my desk clear before I left." She shot a pointed glance at the clutter on his desk. "I did a final sweep of the place. Everything is locked down tight."

"Thanks, I have a business meeting with Nick Charisteas here tonight. He's agreed to help us authenticate the statues." Suzane's eyes lit up with what seemed like curiosity, and Galen decided to give her something else to occupy her attention. "Actually, I have a confession. There's a bit more to the story than that. The Collection belongs to his family, and he's trying to decide on whether or not he's going to let us keep them."

Her gaze sharpened, and her voluminous pants swished like a long skirt as she began pacing up and down. Galen wasn't sure how to describe her new look, maybe Victorian Goth. Her long, black hair was done in tight ringlets with a vivid purple streak over one ear. It was an improvement over the power suits. It fit her whimsical nature far more than the serious look had.

"You don't think he'll try to remove them, do you? It would be a disaster."

Galen thought back to their conversation last night and shook his head. "No, I think he's happy to know that they'll be shown. We just have some details to work out."

"Do you think he knows anything about why there are so many mysteries about the statues? Like where they came from or why the one changed?" Suzane paused with her hand on her hip before she resumed her pacing.

"He said they had a tendency of disappearing and reappearing. Apparently, there are family journals that might shed some light on it all. I'm hoping he brings them tonight." Galen got in her path, forcing her to a stop. "It'll be fine, I'm sure of it."

Suzane gave him a worried look. "Are you really sure? Maybe I can come in after my appointment tomorrow. We can work on a strategy to change his mind if he decides to move the statues. Or I could stay late, and we can wear him down together and get as much information out of him as we can."

Galen caught her by her shoulders and gave her a reassuring smile. "The last thing I want you worrying about tomorrow is me or this place, okay? You're going to have enough on your mind. And I want you taking all the time you need to keep your strength up. You don't have to be fussing over me so much every day. Give yourself a couple days before jumping back in here."

Apprehension chased across her face, followed by a wry expression. "Fussing over you occupies my thoughts. It gives me something to think about after the chemo, other than puking my guts out."

Galen gave her shoulders a gentle squeeze and searched her face. The chemo took more of a toll as the months wore on. "Is there anything else I can do to help? Your son is taking you tomorrow, right? You don't need a car? I can arrange for one." It wasn't enough; he should offer to take her himself, only the thought of going to a hospital and sitting in a waiting room was something he could not stomach, even if it made him feel like a coward to admit it.

"I am fine, I promise." Suzane cupped his face in her hands and smiled at him. "Clint will be there, same as every other time. I know you don't like to talk about me being sick. I know it scares you, and I appreciate the offer. A few more rounds of chemo, and then hopefully, none of us will have to think about it at all. It'll be done and over with."

Galen admired Suzane's guts. She almost never complained, and even on the days when she was worn out, with dark rings under her eyes, her complexion pale, she still faced the day with a kind of verve that amazed Galen. "I love your optimism." He leaned down and kissed her forehead. "We'll have to do something to mark the occasion."

She patted his cheek and pulled away. "Enough sentimentality. You're as bad as my son." Suzane stepped back and looked him over once more. "Now go charm the pants off Nick Charisteas, and make sure those statues stay with us."

"Yes, ma'am." Galen tried not to think of her suggestion literally. Getting Nick's pants off had been a main theme in his dreams all last night. He did not want to complicate this meeting with unrequited lust.

The issues between them were tricky enough, and Nick could be prickly when he wanted. "I promise to be on my best behavior and to not antagonize him."

Suzane paused and looked over her shoulder. "I know that innocent tone. You already antagonized him, didn't you? Oh God, do I want to know what happened? Am I going to have to spin this?"

"No, you don't want to hear the tale. It'll just make you think violent thoughts toward me." If Suzane had known that Nick had issued an ultimatum to him yesterday and he hadn't tried to ease the situation right away, she would've dragged him to Nick's apartment by his ear. "All you need to know is that I apologized and gave him what he wanted, so everything is good now. I have faith that Nick and I can work out the complications."

Suzane laughed and shook her head. "I sense there's a deeper story that I'll expect to hear at another time. Good night, Galen. Try not to leave the alarm off and to antagonize Mr. Charisteas while I'm gone. I'd like to come back to see the museum in one piece."

Galen spread his hands. "Hey, it's me."

"That's the part that makes me worry."

NICK smiled at the slight woman emerging from one of the small off-to-the-side entrances of the museum. There was something familiar about her. She paused when she saw him approach and smiled. "You must be Mr. Charisteas." He recognized her then—Galen's private assistant who he saw in passing yesterday morning. She looked completely different. "I'm so glad to meet our expert. I'm Suzane Eberly."

Nick shifted the takeout bags and shook her hand. "Pleased to meet you, just call me Nick. Is Galen inside? I meant to get here before you shut down for the night."

"He's in his office waiting for you." She tilted her head to one side and studied him in a way that made Nick wonder what Galen had told her about them. "Are you going to let the statues stay?"

Relief and disappointment swept through Nick. Galen hadn't shared with her their past or how well they knew each other, which was good. He didn't really want people thinking they were together, even if

Galen had made hints that they could pick up where they left off. He still wasn't sure what he thought about that. A wise man wouldn't want what Galen offered.

"I'd like to get another look at his plans for the whole exhibit. I'll admit I wasn't paying attention because I was too excited to see the Dexios Collection." Nick smiled at her to ease the worry on her face. "But they're staying, and I'm going to make sure that a real buzz is created around the opening of the exhibit. It's been too long since the last time those statues were seen."

Her expression lightened, and she beamed at him. "Perfect. I'll leave you two to discuss the terms." Her eyes slid down to the takeout bags. "Mmm, Pauli's, good choice." She unlocked the door and waved him on through. "Do you know where his office is?"

"Yep, I was here yesterday morning."

"Oh yes, I forgot, sorry. Once the day is over, my brain shuts off. Since you already know your way, I'll be off." She headed down the street toward the streetcar stop with a backward wave.

Nick was struck by the quiet stillness of the museum after the heavy door shut and the lock engaged. It was even quieter than his office at the bank headquarters. Sometimes Nick had to turn his radio on to fill the silence when he worked late. Galen didn't seem to have the same need, though he'd think that a place like this would almost have to hold ghosts.

He climbed the spiral staircase up into Galen's office and found him moving a small table to sit in front of one of the large arched windows. There was something romantic about it with the view and the setting in the old fire station tower. The sun was lowering in a series of brilliant reds and purples, and the light streamed through the window, bringing out the warmth in the brick walls and the honeyed wood of the table. Maybe it would be better if they ate at the desk.

"How's it going?"

Galen jumped and spun to stare at him with wide eyes until he seemed to register Nick's presence. Then he straightened with a smile and scooped up a stack of papers. He wore another dress pants and vest combo, this one a charcoal with a deep red shirt. Nick preferred the suits to the clothes Galen used to go barhopping in. It was still sexy yet not so blatant. "I was expecting you to call when you got here. For a moment there, I thought you were Dexios."

"I met Suzane coming out, and she let me in." Nick came into his office and set the bags down on the table. "Do I look that much like him?"

Galen cocked his head to the side and studied him. "Not so much. It's more in the stance, I think. There are similarities, and in the shadows he reminded me of you."

Somehow the statement reassured Nick, though he couldn't say why. He opened the bags and began pulling out containers of soup and salad, leaving the pasta alone to stay warm. "I wouldn't have recognized her if she hadn't said something. She looks the complete opposite today."

"She likes to play around with styles, that's for sure. It's helpful, though. I can gauge her mood depending on her hair and dress." There was more to it, Nick was sure, but he didn't press Galen for details when he didn't offer. If there had been one thing he learned about Galen it was that if he didn't want to discuss something, he didn't. There was no sense in them starting off the evening butting heads.

"Do you have any idea what you could've done to have caused Dexios to appear when he did? Has anybody else here had any similar experiences?" Nick asked instead as he arranged the table with the napkins and plasticware.

"I haven't asked anybody else if they heard the statues talking like I did the first day. And no one's mentioned anything strange other than the fact that they appear to be unfinished." Galen dropped the papers on his desk, opened a small fridge nearby, and pulled out two bottles of water before he kicked it shut again. "I did skim through the security recordings since the statues appeared in the storeroom and didn't see anything else strange. So I have no idea what could've motivated Dexios to appear when he did."

"I have pasta fagioli soup and Italian sausage with white bean, which do you prefer?" Nick held up the cartons of soup as Galen set the drinks on the table.

"Doesn't matter, I like them both. You pick because I'm laying claim to the chicken cannelloni I spied in the bag. It smells like heaven."

Nick grinned and handed him one of the soups. "That's okay, I got two." They sat down and spread out the feast, the scent of garlic and rosemary rising in the steam as they took the lids off the soups. Nick dunked a slice of bread in his pasta fagioli as he considered the problem. "So did you try again? To replicate what you did before?"

"Yeah, last night before I decided to check the security footage. I begged Dexios to come out and talk to me. I didn't even hear a whisper in return." Galen nudged Nick's ankle, and the brief touch made Nick want more. Why not agree to a date, a dinner somewhere quiet where they could talk about nothing and everything? "Maybe it's too soon to bring it up, but I'm dying to know if you've decided what you're going to do about the Dexios Collection."

"I'm not taking them anywhere. They belong with your exhibit." The smile that crossed Galen's face brought a pang to his heart. It was a genuine smile, not one of practiced seduction. He liked this smile more. "Maybe the both of us will be able to find the trigger tonight."

"Or it's just as possible that Dexios got what he was after and now wants nothing else to do with me." Galen crumpled a napkin in his hand and let his spoon drop back into the container of soup. "You saw it. It was like I was possessed with the part of me that recognized Dexios and disappeared into the statue. Maybe that's why he didn't appear again. Whatever was inside of me is now back with him."

"No, that would imply it's over, and somehow I doubt that. We're just getting started. After all, there are three other statues to complete." Galen stared down at his soup, stirring it, his expression troubled, and Nick touched the back of his hand. Maybe other things had changed; maybe he could get Galen to open up some and let him know what was bothering him. "What is it?"

"I'm not sure what made Dexios come to me, but what if kissing him is what completed the first statue? If what you're saying is true, maybe whatever was inside of me isn't entirely gone, and it's not going to stop with the kissing." Galen pushed aside his soup and leaned forward, crossing his arms on the table, his expression serious. "Can I tell you something without you taking it the wrong way?"

Nick's gut clenched. He thought he might have an idea where Galen was going with this, and he already didn't like it. Dammit, he didn't have the right to not like it. Galen was a free man. He could do whatever the hell he wanted. Even if it meant carrying on with Dexios. "Don't worry; I'll keep my baser instincts under control."

Galen searched Nick's face for a minute before nodding as if he'd made a decision. "The night Dexios appeared I had an urge—no, it was stronger than that, almost a compulsion—to kiss the statue. I even got close to slipping under his arms. Last night I had the same compulsion to interact with the second statue, and I resisted. Maybe that's why he didn't appear."

"And you think if he does you're going to have to suck his cock if we want the next statue to be completed?" That came out harsher than Nick meant. He could tell by the way that Galen flushed and looked away that it bothered him. It unsettled Nick even more because it wouldn't have bothered Galen in the past.

"It's just a theory. I can't think of anything else I did that was different."

Nick had to admit, Galen's theory made sense, though he couldn't see how it was as simple as that. If completing the statues just involved sex, he was pretty sure Dexios would've been able to seduce somebody into it a long time ago. Besides, the family journals indicated that a relationship was needed and that the statues only served as a kind of barometer for that relationship. He'd have to read and refresh his memory, but Nick was pretty sure that the relationship had to be between one of Dexios's and Lykon's descendants. And he couldn't see how that had anything to do with Galen. Until yesterday morning, Nick hadn't spoken to him in months.

"I'm sorry, that came out wrong, and I did promise to keep it together." Nick pushed the rest of his food aside, his appetite gone. "What do you think about going forward with your idea? Are you going to try it?"

Galen shrugged and finally met his gaze. "I'm not sure at this point."

CHAPTER EIGHT

GALEN watched the conflicting emotions on Nick's face and understood the struggle. He had the same obsession to see those statues completed. Galen had envisioned them whole even before he'd known it was possible. Now that they had a direction they could go in, a theory they could try, Galen couldn't help but feel ambivalent.

He wouldn't have a problem experimenting if it only involved himself. Dexios was gorgeous, and he could kiss like the devil. If having a fling with a spirit from the past would make those statues whole, he'd do it. At least it wouldn't be another meaningless encounter forgotten almost as soon as it happened.

Only it wasn't just Galen involved. Now Nick was too. As he looked at Nick, Galen realized his feelings for the other man ran much deeper than he'd allowed himself to recognize before. He didn't want to hurt Nick again, even if it meant that the rest of the statues would remain unfinished.

An ancient voice inside of him screamed at the thought, probably that same someone who had emerged the first night to return Dexios's kiss. Lykon. Galen rubbed his chest. It was weird to think that somebody could have been inside of him all this time. Had Lykon been aware during Galen's entire life, or had he woken up when Galen kissed Dexios?

"We have to do something," Nick insisted and began packing away the remainder of their unfinished soup. "If it's my feelings you're worried about, don't be. I've seen you with other men before. Hell, I've participated. So I'm good. If all it takes is the willing sacrifice of your ass, I say go for it. You looked like you were enjoying that kiss enough."

Galen winced. That stung, deserved or not.

Galen studied Nick's face. He couldn't tell if he was being sarcastic or defensive. An even scarier notion was not knowing if the compulsion to see those statues whole had grabbed a hold of Nick harder than they had Galen. Or maybe he was wrong, and Nick just didn't give a damn anymore. His heart sank, and he stood up to help, trying to hide how much that last thought bothered him.

"It wouldn't hurt to at least try to draw Dexios out," Galen said. "He might have all the answers we need. I suggest we try talking to him first before we make any other decisions. Agreed?"

"Sounds like a good idea." Nick slipped the last carton in the bag, opened his mouth as if he wanted to say something, and paused. The lines of defensive wariness around Nick's mouth had Galen wanting to make him smile and see the flash of dimples instead.

"What's up?" Galen prodded and took a step closer to him. As much as Nick accused him of holding back, of hiding, he wondered if Nick reacted that way because of what he saw in himself. There were wounds in him, old ones that he hadn't noticed before because he'd been too wrapped up in his own hurts. "Talk to me."

"I want to see this through to the end because I need to have those statues completed. I've made this Collection the focus of my entire life. It's why I wanted to study art history. It's why I let my brother take over the family business even though my dad had pushed me to do it. Ever since Dad told me about my uncle and the legend, it's fired my imagination."

Galen frowned and tried to read between Nick's words. There was more to this that he wasn't saying. He had the impression the statues were vitally important to Nick for reasons he kept to himself. He waited until he realized Nick wasn't going to add anything more.

"I know a little bit of how you're feeling if not the extent. I didn't even know that the statues existed until they showed up in my storeroom."

Galen turned away, assailed by a riot of conflicting emotion. The last person who had been able to get to him like this on such an instinctive level was Bryan. He didn't know if he was ready for this. He'd thought he was when he'd called Nick. It had been two years. What if he wasn't ready for the give and take, the compromise, and the work it took to be in a relationship again?

"So what you're trying to say is you want me to fuck him." Galen looked over his shoulder at Nick. "Any means necessary, right?"

Nick winced and ran a hand through his hair, leaving it in a mess of tufts. It gave Galen the urge to touch it as well, to calm them down. "Yesterday, I would've said yes."

Galen's heart skipped a beat, and he turned around again to face him. Did he still care? Any urge to run and put distance between himself and this aching vulnerability disappeared under the need to know. "What about tonight?"

Nick looked at him, a helpless expression in his gaze. "Tonight, I say you do what you need to do. Yesterday, I would've pushed for it. I would've made cruel comments about your past. I would've said things I didn't mean, that I would've hated myself for, and I still would've sacrificed you if it solved the puzzle." Nick shrugged with a rueful twist to his lips. "Then you showed up last night and opened yourself up to me in a way I had always wished for. And you dropped the crazy notion of a date on me—"

"Dates," Galen cut in and took Nick's hand in his. "I'm telling you right now, if you agree, I'm not going to be content with one date."

"Okay, dates." He took a step closer, and Galen's heart jumped again. He'd taken the time to change into more casual clothes before coming over tonight. Galen liked the way the worn denim clung to his thighs and how the black T-shirt stretched across his shoulders. The casual look suited him; Galen found it more exciting than the suits Nick tried to wear. "I need to know one more thing before I go against common sense and agree to that."

"Common sense is boring. Let a little more of Nick the traveler and wreck diver out, and tell the good angel on your shoulder to go screw himself."

Nick chuckled and untangled their fingers to cup Galen's jaw. "Screw the risks; is that your new philosophy? I bet you've taken that fire pole down a few times, haven't you?"

"More than a few, much to some people's horror." Galen couldn't concentrate on risks though, not when Nick's mouth was so close and anticipation made him long for even more contact than just his hand. He closed the distance between them, pressed his body against Nick's, and slid his arms around him. "So, what was it you needed to know?"

Nick's gaze dropped down to Galen's lips, and the tension between them stretched even more taut than before. Why had he ever thought that burying himself away was better than this feeling right now, the expectation, the warmth, and the emergence of emotions so acute they were almost painful?

"I need to know if we've still got it. I stayed awake half the night wondering." And before Galen could respond, Nick's lips met his own, gentle and coaxing. The ache inside of him swelled, expanding almost to the point of pain. Galen clutched the back of Nick's soft T-shirt and held him close as he kissed back.

This was much sweeter than their past kisses. This was the way Nick had tried to kiss him a few times in the middle of the night when they had lain naked in each other's arms. And this had always been when Galen had realized it was time to go home. Nick's mouth moved over his with a tender pressure, making Galen crave more contact just like this.

Nick's lips urged Galen's apart, and his tongue swept in, bringing a hot rush of desire with it. Galen groaned and unclenched his hands to hold him closer. How could he have forgotten how much Nick could turn him on? It had never taken much—a touch, a glint in his eye, a brush of his lips, and Galen was filled with thoughts of finding the nearest bed so he could strip them both bare and let him fulfill all those promises.

Galen's breath quickened as the kiss deepened. The coaxing sweetness disappeared when their tongues tangled and the heat rose. The couch, it couldn't be too far away. As the thought flitted through his mind, the kiss ended, leaving Galen's head spinning and his body wanting more. That had been better than he remembered.

"Well that answers that question," Nick murmured, still holding him close.

Galen grinned and pressed another kiss to Nick's lips. Nick was willing to give him another chance. He hadn't been certain even though Nick had agreed to a date. The kiss eased his mind because there was no way Nick would've kissed him like that unless he had made up his mind to try again.

"Did you have any doubts? Wanting you was never the problem."

Nick shook his head and stepped back. "Come on, let's go see Dexios."

Galen gestured toward the rest of the food they hadn't touched. The sun had set completely, and Seattle had come alive with lights. Whether it was a clear night, like tonight, or a rainy night that made the lights seem wreathed in a watery nimbus, the view was always spectacular up here. He couldn't think of a better place and time to show Nick that he meant what he said.

"Why don't we have that first date now? Dexios has waited a long time. He can wait a little longer."

"Are you sure this is what you want? You know how I felt about you."

How he felt. Galen considered that along with his next words. He wanted to reassure Nick, to give him those little white lies that lovers said to each other to keep that air of romance. He sensed that Nick would recognize and reject anything that wasn't as completely honest as he had been before.

"A hundred percent? No. Life is unsure. I like the way you make me feel, Nick. That's what I know. And I know that right now I'm in a place where I want more than a warm body next to me. I want you, and I'm willing to work for a chance with you again."

At first Nick didn't say anything, and then he gestured toward the table. "Fair enough. Let's finish dinner, but this is not our first date. This is business. If you want a date, take me out on a real one. Not a meal in your office that I brought, where we're going to be talking about the Collection."

"Understood." Galen pulled out Nick's chair. "How about Saturday?" Neither of them had to work on Sunday, so they could be out as late as they wanted. Galen figured he'd need a full-on campaign to win Nick back; might as well start off strong. He'd never had to woo anybody before, and he found himself looking forward to romancing Nick.

"Saturday?" Wary suspicion flickered in Nick's eyes, and then he spread his hands and the expression vanished. "Why not? I'm all yours."

Not yet, and that was his own fault. However, Galen's thoughts already churned with plans to change that.

GALEN led Nick through to the museum proper, turning on lights as he went. "You have a lot of space," Nick said, glancing up at the tall ceilings with their exposed beams and skylights. He peeked into the wide room that contained the combined gallery for local gay artists and the gift shop. Galen wanted more artists to showcase than the ones they already had, yet he knew that it was a slow, patient progress. They were still continuing to grow. "How much work did you have to put into remodeling?"

"More than I want to remember. This place was a mess when I bought it."

"I like how you left it so open." Nick pointed to where the wall ended halfway up between the workshop and gallery so that the rooms were open to the roof.

"Yeah, with all the skylights I didn't want walls going all the way up. I left it the same way on the museum side too." Galen paused as they headed out of the gallery and pointed out Knox's charcoal rendering of a man sitting cross-legged by a pond. "That's one of the kids who uses the workshop. I gutted the inside and divided it in half. The front half is the workshop and gallery, the back half we split into three rooms for the museum. When we opened, we only had one exhibit."

"Nice. It really works that way. Are you using all the space now?" Nick asked as they moved down the corridor to the back half of the building.

"Nope, we still have an untouched room for a third exhibit." Galen flipped on the lights to the first exhibit room. Framed and matted photographs lined the walls and spiraled inward on tall stands that led to a central area with comfortable chairs to encourage conversation. "This exhibit is all about expressions of love, and it was our first."

Nick walked down alongside the wall, his arms crossed as he studied the photographs. "I should've come to check this out before. I'd heard of it around town and from you. I didn't really picture it, though. This is amazing."

He paused in front of a picture of an older gay couple. Their linked hands were liver spotted, their hair wispy, and yet their eyes were still bright as they looked at each other. There was an unspoken lifetime in that glance.

Galen loved that picture too. He wanted that for himself one day. To find the person that he could grow old with and still be in love with forty years later.

"Thanks. The new exhibit with the Dexios Collection is much more erotic. I'm impatient to get all the pieces into place so I can see it instead of staring at the layout on paper and imagining it."

Nick continued on through, his thumbs hooked through his jean belt loops. "Do you know what you're going to do with the third room yet?" Nick looked over his shoulder to where Galen lounged against the opening to the exhibit.

"Not yet. We're taking it one exhibit at a time. To be honest, I was worried at the beginning that we would tank. I wasn't sure we'd be able to fill the place up with enough art, much less get people to pay to see and to buy from the gallery. I should've had more faith."

He watched Nick with his closed stance and the way he kept steering the conversation into safe territory ever since they sat down to finish dinner and realized he was making small talk, backpedaling from the emotions and realizations unleashed with that one kiss. And Galen was letting him. He needed to figure out what he wanted out of this relationship and fast before it led to the sex they both knew was coming. It was time to regroup, think things over before they had their date. Because no matter what happened, there were going to be consequences.

Nick turned back toward him and gestured toward the hallway. "Well, let's see if we can lure Dexios out."

They paused in the doorway to the new exhibit. Galen reached over to flip the light switch and hesitated. The lights seemed too harsh and glaring with all the moonlight flooding through the skylights and high windows. It was still almost full, just starting to wane, so there was more than enough light to see by.

Nick stepped over to the first statue, touching his shoulder in a gesture curiously reminiscent of the one Galen used that strange night. "It seems almost magical, there's a feeling in the air," Nick murmured.

"Yeah. It caught me up in its spell even before I got the crates open and saw them." Galen moved over to the second statue to see if the compulsion would come again with Nick there to witness it. His eyes slid over Dexios's naked body, the muscles tense with desire, and it struck him in the gut hard and fast. A presence came awake in his mind, made his heart flip, and Galen shoved it away.

He touched Dexios's chest, and his hand slid down to the statue's taut stomach. He couldn't help picturing Nick there instead, cock straining, waiting for Galen to take him into his mouth. He shuddered with a soft groan, and then Nick was there, taking him by the elbow and turning him away from the statue, muting the spell it wove.

"Are you okay?"

Galen met Nick's worried eyes and nodded, torn now between turning around and kneeling in front of Dexios, and wrapping his arms around Nick and kissing him until he forgot all about the statues and lost his wariness toward Galen.

"Yeah, I'm fine. Remember the compulsion I told you about?" Galen clutched Nick's biceps, trying to drown out the siren song of the statue behind him and struggling to hold down that part of him that wanted to wake up and answer the call. Nick nodded, searching his face. "It's still there. Stronger, actually. You don't get the same impression?"

"I'm afraid that's all you." Nick looked around the room, and Galen remembered Dexios and did the same. "I wonder why it's only you."

"Because you carry my Lykon. He has been reborn within you and you have to be the one to free him," Dexios said. They both looked to see the first statue move, Dexios's head turning to regard them. His half of the statue shimmered, and he stepped free of it.

Well, that answered that question. He must be descended from Lykon, weird. A flash of protectiveness crossed Nick's face, and he stepped forward to place himself in front of Galen. "What if he doesn't want any part of this curse of yours?"

"Nick, it's okay." Galen laid a hand on his shoulder and stepped up beside him. The last thing he wanted was Nick barging in and making his decisions, and he didn't want Nick hurt, so he'd have to proceed very carefully. "What do I need to do? The other night we kissed, and someone seemed to wake up inside of me. You saw him, and then the statue became complete." Galen gestured toward the second statue. "Do we have to act out every statue for Lykon to be free and the curse ended?"

Dexios came toward them, and Galen sensed Nick tense. He reached over without thinking and took Nick's hand in his. Dexios stopped in front of them with an ancient sadness in his eyes. "Forgive me. I get confused when too much time has passed between one rebirth and another. I've waited so long. I thought at first you were Lykon, and I forgot myself. I should not have kissed you."

"So, you're not going to try to seduce him anymore?" Nick asked, drawing Dexios's attention to him as Galen tightened his fingers around Nick's. "How else is he supposed to let Lykon free?"

"By letting go, embracing life instead of holding onto the past, though that advice would serve the both of you well." Dexios looked at Galen and smiled, somehow Galen got the impression that he was looking through him to the person inside of him. He sensed a tugging in return. He took a step closer, lifting his free hand to touch Dexios's cheek.

"It won't be enough, will it? Just letting him out. We're missing something," he said as Dexios closed his eyes and turned his face into Galen's touch.

"You are. It's up to the both of you to fulfill the conditions of the curse. But I am not permitted to tell you how." Dexios opened his eyes, turned his head and kissed Galen's palm. The sensation inside of him tugged harder, and Galen gasped, going weak when a sense of vertigo hit him. Nick steadied him as he slumped, and his warm voice murmured in Galen's ear, only Galen couldn't make out what he said.

Instead he sank inward, struggling to reach that place inside of him, fighting to let it go, yet afraid, so afraid it would swallow him whole.

CHAPTER NINE

"WHAT'S wrong with him?" Nick asked, his voice harsh with anxiety as he eased Galen to the floor. Nick sat beside him and gathered him close again, his stomach clenching, his thoughts jumping. "Is he going to get hurt? I don't remember reading about this in the journals."

"I do not know why he reacts in this manner. None of the other vessels have." Dexios stared down at them with a worried frown nested between his eyebrows as Nick glared back at him. "Perhaps he holds on too hard. It does not seem as if it causes him any injury."

"He passed the fuck out again! Obviously something is wrong."

Dexios knelt on the other side of Galen, leather creaking and metal clinking against the cold floor. "I can see Lykon in him, sense him. They are bound together very tight."

"Maybe being with you is what he needs," Nick said with a sigh. It was hard to admit. The kiss earlier and Galen's reaction to it had given him some hope that maybe they could start over again. First, he needed to decide if he really even wanted to. It would be too easy to give in to temptation. He didn't want another six months like the last, and Galen wasn't giving him any guarantees that he wouldn't walk again. "If it'll wake up Lykon and reunite the two of you, I don't think Galen would find it a hardship at all."

Dexios's head jerked up, and he stared at Nick with incredulity. "You would allow him to lie with me?"

Nick's lips twisted in the approximation of a smile. "I have no claim on him. Galen does what he wants, when he wants, and with whom he wants. We aren't together in the way you seem to think we are."

Dexios looked alarmed for a moment, then desperation etched lines around his eyes and mouth. Galen stirred and reached for Nick with a sigh of his name, his eyelids fluttering as he struggled to waken.

"I think your claim on him is stronger than you believe," Dexios replied. "I know the torment you go through. Be patient. I was not, and I regretted it for a long time."

"What do you mean?" Nick grabbed Dexios's arm, and Galen sat up with a soft gasp.

"What...? Where...?" Nick started to reach for him until he realized with a chill that it wasn't Galen, not anymore. His cheeks had several days' worth of thick stubble, his body seemed bulkier, and his features had shifted in a subtle way and become a little more roughhewn.

"Lykon!" Before Nick could react, Dexios had swept the man into his arms, and they were kissing as if they expected to be torn apart again at any moment.

Nick shifted away and averted his eyes. *Whoa...* way to be the sudden unnecessary cog in this wheel, intruding on a private moment. To his surprise he wasn't jealous in the least because he knew that wasn't Galen. It was more than unsettling. What if Galen couldn't come back? What if he was trapped in his own body while Lykon dominated it?

He glanced toward the second statue, hoping to see the moonlight gathering around it as it had the night the first statue changed, but nothing seemed out of the ordinary. The kiss between the parted lovers didn't seem to have any effect on it at all.

Lykon moaned, and Nick's gaze jerked back toward them. *Christ.* He even sounded different from Galen. Nick's heart twisted, and his fears sharpened, souring his stomach. Lykon had waited thousands of years to be with Dexios again. He'd come close and lost him again so many times. Dexios said that Lykon and Galen were bound tight. The thought of losing Galen again when they were on the cusp of having a new chance jolted Nick into action.

Without thought, Nick lunged toward the intertwined couple and sank his hand into Galen's hair the way that he liked, fisting it. "Come back to me, Galen," he urged and pressed closer. "Remember who you are."

Nick found the sweet spot on the nape of Galen's neck and gave it a rough nip. In the past when they'd engaged in threesomes it didn't matter how hot the third person was or how much Galen was into the moment, whenever Nick did that he never failed to capture Galen's attention. It would be no different now.

Galen broke the kiss with a rough groan and twisted toward Nick as his features shifted back to normalcy. Nick couldn't resist those proffered lips even as Dexios released Galen. The same instinct from their past seized him. He had to mark and claim Galen so that if he left again, he'd always come back for more.

"Nick," Galen murmured just before their lips met. His arms wrapped around Nick, pulling him close and holding on. The heat of their kiss stole Nick's breath as Galen kissed him back with a hunger that made his body ache. All the pent-up heat and frustration fed that kiss as lips bruised and tongues demanded more.

Galen lay back on the floor, stretching out underneath Nick, tugging him down. Nick felt the pressure of Galen's cock against his thigh, the unmistakable throb of his arousal. "Kiss me again," Galen rasped and lifted his head, taking the kiss before Nick had a chance to respond.

Nick heard Dexios get up, and a part of him wanted to stop him, to get answers, but he couldn't seem to control or stop himself. He slid his hand up Galen's thigh and squeezed the lean muscle. Galen groaned against his lips and rocked up against him. Nick shifted and settled between Galen's thighs, and a hot electric current zinged between them as their groins met. Even through his jeans and Galen's pants the contact of his cock against Galen's flooded Nick's mind with potent memories.

Nick's fingers fumbled with the buttons on Galen's vest before he stripped it from him. Urgency gripped even harder when Nick pulled Galen's shirt free from his dress pants. Buttons pinged off the polished hardwood floor as he tore open Galen's shirt, anxious to touch his warm skin again, to smell him. The warning voice inside of him shouted even louder. Nick ignored it with a growl and bent his head toward Galen's throat.

Galen shoved him away and sat up, breathing hard. In a flash Dexios knelt next to him again and reached for him. "Lykon?"

Galen batted his hands away and scooted back. "I'm not your and Nick's ping-pong, dammit." He lifted his head, his eyes wild, and Nick was both relieved to see that he was still Galen and ashamed of how rattled he looked. It cut right through the lust that still gripped him.

"I'm sorry. Are you okay?" Nick asked, sitting up himself as he eyed Galen and the strange man who hovered next to him. He couldn't tell if Galen was a little paler than normal, or if it was the moonlight that leeched the color from him.

"What is this ping-pong?" Dexios asked with a perplexed expression.

"A ball, never mind." Galen pulled himself to his feet and waved them both off when he swayed. "Leave me alone, just give me a second. I'll be okay." He moved to the wall and leaned against it, taking several deep breaths. He stiffened, and then, as before, a figure seemed to rise from his body and become solid next to him. Nick gasped, and Dexios let out a low moan that went beyond mere longing. The sound was enough to make Nick's eyes sting.

"Lykon, you cannot keep doing this," Dexios said in an unsteady voice. "It is not our time yet."

"I will make the time when I can. She never proscribed this."

Nick watched Lykon move over to Dexios, and the two embraced. He found himself stepping backward toward Galen until he reached the wall, and Galen caught his hand, linking their fingers. Oblivious, the two lovers continued to hold onto each other, Dexios's face pressed against Lykon's neck, and a moment later they vanished.

Nick let out an explosive breath. "I'm not sure I know what happened or if we accomplished anything."

"You and me both. I think the only thing that I got out of this is a new fetish for the scent of leather and aching balls." Galen gave his hand a quick squeeze before letting go. Already Nick could sense him putting distance between them even though he hadn't actually moved one inch. He looked away; his hair fell across his face, obscuring his expression.

"How are you feeling? You scared me when you collapsed like that. You scared the both of us. And then you changed, and I didn't know if you'd come back." Even now that it was over, that unease lingered.

"Much steadier now that Lykon isn't fighting for control." Galen turned toward Nick, leaning his shoulder against the wall and shoving his hand in his pocket. "I think we should both call it a night and talk again tomorrow."

"I'm not sure if I'm comfortable with you being alone right now. You were laid out on the floor not too long ago. Let me at least see you home." He was tempted to ask if he could stay, but he didn't want to obliterate the line that he'd drawn. He'd already stomped on it a few times this night. Once Galen was away from the statues, he should be safe.

"No, I'm good. Lykon's doing whatever he's doing." Galen turned away and fisted his hand in his hair at the nape of his neck. "God, this is weird. I need some time to process this. You don't know what it's like, having someone else in you, trying to push you aside. A part of me really wants to freak out, but I think it's a little late for that. Besides, what I sense from Lykon has absolutely no malice in it, and that makes me feel a lot better."

Nick couldn't imagine not being in control like that, and the thought made him want to bolt. It had to be an even stronger instinct for Galen, who'd left the last time things got complicated. Nick felt like he was doomed to care for people who left. Not this time; this time he wouldn't allow it to happen with meek acceptance.

He turned to face Galen and laid his hands on either side of the wall next to him. Galen's breath caught as he leaned in toward him. "You're not thinking of running on me again, are you?"

Galen shook his head, and some of the tension eased from his body as he slid an arm around Nick's waist. "I'm not going anywhere. I have to see this through, with the Collection, with you. I'm sorry if I gave you the wrong impression when I slammed the brakes earlier. When we do hop into bed again, I want it to be because I'm thinking clearly and not because I'm clouded with hormones not entirely my own. I want it to be just you and me. Nobody else, especially not some legend come alive."

Those words were sweeter than Nick could have imagined. He could handle an unsatisfied ache if it meant that Galen was all his when the time came. "I like the idea of you being all mine."

Galen grinned and hooked his finger through Nick's belt loop, tugging him closer. "I thought you might."

Nick succumbed to temptation and closed the space between them, trapping Galen against the wall. The kiss started out gentle, and Nick pulled back with a smile when it heated again. "Come on, let's get out of here."

They gathered their belongings from Galen's office and walked to Nick's car. His worries about Galen being alone tonight eased once they left the museum and it was apparent that Galen wasn't lightheaded in the least. Nick resisted the urge to pull him close for another kiss good-night. He had the impression that Galen wanted some space tonight, without any demands from him, and he was used to that. Despite the fact that he agreed to a date, he wasn't going to let himself get drawn into Galen's appeal again. "Be careful getting home."

"Hey, wait a sec."

Nick paused in the act of sitting in the front seat and glanced over at Galen, who stood on the sidewalk, his hands deep in his pockets. "Yeah?"

Galen walked over and crossed his arms over the car's doorframe. "I'm glad I finally worked up the nerve to call you, and that has nothing to do with the statues." The unexpected statement darted under his defenses and touched him right in the spot that Nick had been striving the hardest to protect. Galen dropped a kiss on his lips and walked away, leaving Nick staring after him.

"Galen!"

He turned around and Nick grinned. "I'm glad I called you back too."

GALEN returned to the museum just as dawn broke over the city. Something had happened last night, not only with the statues, but with Nick too. Maybe enough happened that the second statue would be whole now, and he couldn't wait to see it. He'd tossed and turned all night, first agonizing over what they could do to break the curse, then caught up all over again with thoughts of Nick, memories of before, and half-formed dreams of what might be. Dreams that he knew he wanted with more certainty now. No more second-guessing himself. He wanted the way Nick made him feel.

He'd fought those emotions for so long, thought he'd gotten a handle on them, and this time around Nick had snuck up on him even faster than before. All of his fight had gone. He did want to be in an exclusive relationship again, and not just with anybody either. Now he'd have to convince Nick he meant it.

The taxi pulled up in front of the museum, and Galen paid the driver. This was getting to be too much of a habit. He used to be good about taking public transportation until the Dexios Collection showed up in his storeroom, and the habit had started to slide. He was too impatient to wait on the slower commute. He really needed to suck it up and get back to his old routine, maybe start biking too, when summer came. No, what he really needed to do was grow some balls and start driving again.

Galen's stomach twisted, and he shoved his hands in his pockets as he crossed the street. *No, no, not yet.* He didn't need another round of nightmares, haunted by the sound of exploding glass, of Bryan's scream. That's what happened the last time he'd tried to get behind a wheel. What if he lost Nick too? It was bad enough worrying over Suzane. He couldn't handle losing one loved one after another.

The brightening sunrise deepened the rainbow colors that arched across the giant bay doors of the old firehouse, and the sight never failed to make him smile. The hanging baskets of greenery spilled more color across the brick façade. When it warmed up a bit he would add flowers to those baskets. This was his place, built from the inside out, and he wasn't going to spend the day thinking dark thoughts. Besides, he had too much to do, starting with making sure he erased the security footage of Nick and him rolling around on the ground tearing at each other's clothes.

Galen's cheeks heated as he recalled that. The buttons! He had to find them before Ella came in to work on the mural. He hurried down the hall toward the exhibits, and when he walked into the new room his stomach plummeted. The second statue still stood there incomplete, and the searing loneliness of it made Galen ache in return.

It was too early to call Nick, so he sent him a text and a picture of the statue before getting on his hands and knees to search for the scattered buttons. "I don't understand why it didn't work," he muttered under his breath toward the statue. Telling himself that he was talking to Dexios and not the air didn't ease his self-consciousness one bit. "We kissed, Lykon appeared, and the two of you went off together, so what the hell are we missing?"

He sat back on his heels and glared at the statue, which seemed oblivious to his irritation. Dexios implied that it wasn't about the sex or Galen being with him, but dammit, what else could it be? There had to be something in the myth that would give them a clue. He'd grill Nick about it when he got the chance or else the frustration would drive him crazy. He also needed to find a copy of the myth himself. Maybe he could find one at the library or online. He'd ask Suzane where she found her reference.

Galen rose, stuffing the handful of buttons in his pocket. He went to the second statue and stared at Dexios's face. The half-lidded eyes seemed to hold more pain than pleasure right now, though he was sure that only he and Nick would be able to see it. Everybody else would see the heat, the sexual tension. "I saw you two together. Why didn't it work?"

"Please, help us." The bare whisper seemed to shiver in the morning air.

"Tell me what I have to do." Galen growled in frustration as he grasped Dexios's shoulders. The metal was cool under his grip, lacking the odd warmth it sometimes had. The statue remained silent, and Galen almost shook him before he recovered his composure. It wouldn't solve anything, and how would he explain it to Nick if the statue got knocked over and damaged?

As he headed up to his office, his cell phone rang, and he smiled when he saw Nick's name. "What are you doing up at this time?"

"Cursing the lack of coffee and you for sounding so damned awake. What's your excuse for this god-awful hour?"

"I got here early to check it out and to remove last night's evidence. We left buttons scattered everywhere." Galen's voice echoed as he headed up the stairs in the tower.

"Oops." Nick didn't sound at all repentant. "How are you feeling? No more dizziness or fighting off Greek warriors last night?"

"Nope, made it home without a problem." And crashed hard.

"I got your picture. So last night was a bust, and nothing's changed."

"You said it." Galen stuck the buttons in his desk drawer and tossed his keys on the desk. "I'm not sure what else we can do. I did hear the statue whisper again, asking for help, but there were no new miraculous appearances."

"That's odd," Nick said, his voice thoughtful. "I don't remember any mention of whispers in my uncle's journal. I'll look again. Maybe it didn't register when I read them."

"Or maybe he didn't write it down because he didn't want his family thinking he'd lost his mind," Galen said.

"There is that. Look, we need to talk about last night," Nick replied, and Galen's heart sank. Nick didn't say it, he didn't need to. Galen was pretty sure that what he wanted to talk about had less to do with the statues and more to do with them. "And not at the museum either."

"How about lunch?" Galen checked his calendar. With Suzane gone and Heather off for the afternoon, he needed to be there most of the day. Maybe Knox would be interested in manning the front for an hour or two if he was free.

"No, I don't want either of us having to rush off to be someplace else. Are you free tonight?"

Galen held his breath as anticipation grabbed him. This was an opportunity, to get Nick alone without the statues getting in the way of the two of them. "We could have dinner at my place. I'm not a bad cook." There, it was out. He'd never invited Nick over to his apartment before, even though the other man had hinted about it on more than one occasion. He waited, stomach clenching for Nick's reply.

"I'd like that," Nick said in a softer voice. "Does six work for you? Can I bring anything?"

Galen sat back, the knots in his stomach easing. Nick hadn't dismissed the idea even though they hadn't had their date yet. If he ran to the market at lunch and stashed the groceries in the fridge here, he would have enough time to get dinner started before Nick arrived. "That works for me, and if you want to, you can grab a bottle of wine. You know what I like."

The long pause on the other end heightened his nerves, and when Nick spoke again there was a slight strain in his voice. "I know I keep asking this, and this is the last time. Are you sure? I'm not trying to be difficult, but I can't start something that isn't going to go anywhere. Not again. I want you to be as honest with me now as you were then."

The panicked clenching returned tenfold, and Galen shut his eyes, which turned out to be a mistake because the moment he did, he saw the tilting whirl of lights as the car spun out of control again and the flashing strobe of emergency lights cutting through the rain-streaked, spider-webbed glass. This was it; either he drowned or headed toward the shore, time to put the past behind him.

"I promise to be completely honest with you." Galen hesitated, trying to get his thoughts together. "You make me want to try, and I haven't wanted to do that with anybody in a long time. I don't know if I'm going to panic and try to pull away again. I do know that I… I care about you, a lot. And if you're willing to see where this goes, then I am too."

"Fair enough. I'll see you tonight."

Galen's heart flipped as Nick hung up on the other end. He wasn't sure what Nick meant about that; still, the other man hadn't cancelled their date for the weekend. It wasn't what Galen had planned for their first date, and maybe Nick wouldn't call it that even if Galen did. A date. How long had it been since he had a date and not a hookup? He didn't know, but it felt nice to anticipate this one.

CHAPTER TEN

GALEN spread the savory mix of spinach, feta, onion, and dill on top of the layers of phyllo dough and then laid another buttered layer of dough over the small casserole dish. Spanakopita was one of his favorite meals, and the recipe had been handed down for generations in his family. He liked it because it had much less dough than in other versions he'd ordered in some of the local restaurants. In his opinion the filling was the best part.

He slid it in the oven and turned to clean up before Nick arrived. If he didn't keep busy, nerves would take over. He'd never invited another man to his apartment, the place he'd shared with Bryan. In the last two years, it had ceased to be a home and merely became the place where he slept and ate when he could be pulled away from the museum. Starting renovations hadn't helped make the apartment feel like he was embarking on a new beginning. Maybe inviting people here would.

Galen loaded the dishes in the sink and wiped down the cool slate counter. Out of all the rooms, the kitchen was his favorite, with its muted red walls and pale honey cabinets. This was the first room he'd made his own, and it was the room he spent the most time in when he bothered to come back at a decent hour.

He started in on the dishes and was almost done when the doorbell rang. He paused, his stomach jumping as he eyed the clock—right on time. Was he ready for this relationship talk? Even if it was a casual relationship for the moment, what if Nick decided he couldn't risk it?

The doorbell rang again, and Galen took a deep breath. If Nick was willing to swan dive into another try, considering he'd been the one to be hurt last time, the only thing Galen could do was give it a go as well. If he lived in fear of falling in love and losing that person again, he would never move beyond this little, lonely box he'd put himself in. And if Nick decided to run, Galen wasn't above pursuing him.

Nick's eyes lit up as Galen opened the door. And the smile that crossed his face made Galen question all his worries over what Nick wanted to talk about. Because if he was nervous, it didn't show. Nick had taken the time to change out of his suit into jeans and what looked like a brand new polo shirt. "I was beginning to think you'd gotten trapped in your exhibit room and I'd have to go rescue you."

"Nope, you caught me with my hands in the sink and soap suds up to my elbows." Galen stepped back to let Nick in and gestured toward the kitchen. "I wanted to get dinner in the oven before you got here." That was a bad idea, since working on dinner during their conversation would've given him something to concentrate on. Thinking about it made his tongue clumsy and his stomach knotted.

Nick held up two brown bags, the neck of a wine bottle sticking up from each. Another bag hung from his wrist. "I wasn't sure what we were having, so I bought a Chardonnay and a Pinot Noir."

"Good choices." Galen took the bags and waved his hand toward the couch. "Take a seat and let me put these away."

"I have a hard time picturing you being domestic," Nick said in a teasing voice from the living room. "I keep remembering you flirting at the clubs and bars, or smooth and sexy in your suits at the museum, not running around your apartment in bare feet."

Galen's heart sank to his stomach, and doubt crept in. Nick didn't know him at all. He knew the façade that Galen had put up after Bryan died. He'd never seen him in a worn T-shirt in the workshop with the kids, trying to help them pull a project together, or his wild excitement whenever he discovered a new artist or found a new piece for the museum. Suzane and Heather saw that, Knox and Ella, and a few of the other kids who'd managed to get close before Galen could shut them out. All Nick knew of him was some sex-crazed, barhopping, empty man.

Galen set the bottles down on the counter and pulled out two wide-mouthed wine glasses. When he entered the living room with the wine, Nick was standing by the fireplace, looking over the array of photographs that marched along the mantel. Most were of his family, a couple of Galen and Bryan. He didn't think it was right to bury them in a drawer and hide them away, but now he wondered if he should have.

"I don't usually wear suits at work. Not unless I'm meeting somebody important." Or trying to impress an ex-lover with something he wasn't. Idiot move there.

Nick turned around and must've seen the unease on Galen's face because he came closer and took a wine glass with a reassuring smile. "Hey, I like this side of you, it's much more approachable."

"You don't know me." Galen sat down on the couch and set his wine on the glass-topped table. "That guy you had feelings for? That wasn't really me. I hope you're not disappointed in the real version 'cause I'm done with the way I was before."

"The guy I knew then was maddening and frustrating because I knew there was a lot more to him. I could see glimpses of the real him, and that's the part I wanted to see more of." Nick sat down next to him, his expression serious. "And I've gotten to know him more these last couple of days."

"I think you're certifiable for risking getting hurt again," Galen said under his breath and Nick must've heard him because he laughed. "But I'm glad you are."

"I play it safe more times than I care to think about. I hope it's worth it. We'll see." He looked away, his expression thoughtful, and took a sip of his wine before he met Galen's gaze again. "Promise me one thing tonight?"

"What is it you want?"

"Tonight should be about us, trying to figure out where we're going from here and enjoying each other's company. I don't want to talk about the statues or the curse. I don't want those distractions. I just want to relax with you. Though, for the record, it doesn't count as the first date. I want to see what you've got planned for Saturday because the gleam in your eye when you mentioned it has got my curiosity up. Is that okay?"

"You must have read my mind." Whatever Nick wanted to discuss, it wasn't to suggest leaving this as a business relationship. Galen bit his lip. "Can I ask one thing first, and then we won't mention Dexios or Lykon again tonight? I swear."

"Shoot."

"Last night, when Lykon took control and Dexios kissed him, you interrupted." A shuttered expression dropped over Nick's eyes, and Galen just knew he had been right to be worried. Nick had been jealous. Not that he didn't have cause, but their past was one thing, and Galen didn't want it clouding their entire future. "Why? 'Cause I'm telling you, it wasn't me kissing him. I had no control."

"I wasn't jealous, if that's what you're thinking." Nick shook his head, and the closed-off expression disappeared. "Hard to believe, I know, but you're right, it wasn't you. Lykon looks different; hell, he smells different. I jumped in because I was afraid Lykon would take you over completely in order to be with Dexios any way he could. I was afraid you'd be lost and trapped. It was pure instinct that had me reacting the way I did."

A slow smile spread across Galen's face as relief poured through him, drowning all those stupid little anxieties he'd let plague him all day. "Good to know. You can bite my neck any damn time you think you need to. Let me tell you, it worked better than an electric shock." He reached for his glass and took a sip of wine. "Want to help me make the salad for dinner?"

"Not yet." Nick set his glass aside and reached for him. "I've been thinking about this most of the day."

Anticipation leapt up as Nick leaned in and kissed him. Galen's lips parted under the warm assault, and his heart quickened. He hadn't let himself think past the lust that he'd always had for Nick to the emotions underneath. Now he didn't try to hold them back. Warmth and tenderness mixed with his desire in a heady rush of pleasure that beat all the hot, quick, backroom encounters between them before.

Galen pulled Nick closer still, sinking into his arms, savoring the slow thrust of Nick's tongue. He tasted like the wine he'd been drinking… and Nick. Galen had missed the taste of him. The kiss broke with one last little nibble on Galen's lower lip that sent a ripple down his spine and a fantasy of laying Nick naked on his bed to explore his body with similar nips and tastes.

"Feel free to accost me with your lips anytime the urge hits you." Galen stole another quick kiss and pulled back with a smile.

NICK loved the warm, open expression in Galen's eyes. It revitalized his entire face. He didn't know how he'd missed it before. He'd mistaken Galen's reserve and sensual escapades as someone who had no need for anybody else and who lived for the pleasure of the moment. Maybe at the time Nick had been right about the second part; now he was beginning to think he'd been dead wrong about the first. He hoped so.

"Come on, let's get the salad together," Nick said, and Galen rose, holding out his hand to help Nick up. "What's for dinner? It smells amazing."

"Spanakopita. With a name like Charisteas you'd better like cooking from the old country." Galen peeked into the oven and steam came out redolent with the scent of spinach and cheese. "My mom wasn't too happy at first when I told her I was gay. Since then she's come to terms with it, and she got along with the boyfriends I brought home. I don't know if she'd be happier to hear that I'm dating again or that you come from a family with Greek roots too."

Nick winced. Galen's words brought back very uncomfortable memories of when he'd come out to his dad and brothers. He probably should've tackled his family members one by one instead of trying to get it over with all at once. Then again, he knew he couldn't have handled rejection after rejection. Whatever had happened between Galen and his mom then didn't seem to be weighing on Galen's mind now. And it wasn't a topic Nick was eager to explore tonight.

"I happen to love spanakopita."

Nick glanced around the kitchen as Galen shut the oven door and adjusted the temperature. This room seemed much homier than the cream, glass, and austere metal of the living room. He preferred the kitchen.

"I hope the rest of your place is more like your kitchen and less like your living room," Nick said. "I didn't want to step on the carpet at first."

Galen handed him his wine glass with a laugh. "I know. I was afraid to eat and drink in there for a long time. It's not really my style at all." He took a sip of his wine. "I've been trying to redecorate but been so busy with the museum that I've only gotten around to a few rooms. I need to do it, though. This place looks like I have multiple personalities."

Nick had the impression that there was more to the story. He cocked his head, but Galen didn't seem inclined to add to what he'd said. Nick watched him as he went to the fridge and rummaged around. Did it have anything to do with those pictures of Galen with another man, pictures where he'd seemed happy?

"Can I ask you a question?" Nick took the bowl and a bag of romaine lettuce that Galen gave him.

Galen hesitated and then shrugged. "Ask away."

Nick dumped the bag in the bowl as Galen retrieved feta cheese, kalamata olives, a tomato, and a red onion. At this rate he was going to have to beg for leftovers at the end of the night. If Galen's spanakopita was half as good as Nick's aunt's he'd be a happy man. "Back when we used to hook up, you seemed hell-bent on seducing every man who crossed your path."

Two hot spots of color bloomed on Galen's cheeks, and Nick paused in surprise. The Galen from six months ago wouldn't have cared less what anyone thought of his behavior. If he'd been called out on it, and he had been a couple of times, he'd lifted one eyebrow with an expression of amused disdain and told them that if they didn't like it they could go find someone else to play with.

"I was in a very bad place then, and after you, empty sex seemed pointless," Galen said as he washed the vegetables, the set of his shoulders tense. "But that wasn't the question you wanted to ask. So what is it?"

Nick remembered that Galen said he hadn't been with anybody else since they'd parted. He had a hard time remembering the question, with his cock concentrating on the fact that Galen hadn't been touched in six months. For a man as naturally sensual as he was…. Damn, Nick wanted a long, hot taste of all his pent-up passion.

"Nick?" Nick looked up from the package of feta he was clutching to find Galen watching him, his brown eyes warm with a teasing look. "I think it wouldn't take much imagination to know where your thoughts went."

Nick gave him an unabashed grin. "Very naked thoughts. You drove me crazy enough when you were a glutton. I'm not sure I could handle you after a dry spell, but I'd be more than willing to try."

Galen laughed and turned away from the sink to lay a quick, hard kiss on his lips. "You'll get your chance. Now what was it you wanted to ask me?"

"This is what I wanted to talk to you about tonight. I'm trying to get a handle on your mindset." Galen said he wanted to date, and other times he still seemed distant. If he knew what was going on in Galen's head, he could prepare better. He hoped Galen wouldn't take this the wrong way; still, he had to know before he let himself fall any further. "Why is it you seem so reluctant to be in a committed relationship? Is it just not your thing? Or were you burned at some point?"

The amusement fled from Galen's face, and his gaze reflected an old pain. Why hadn't Nick realized that maybe Galen's heart had been crushed? He was such an ass for not considering that. He would bet his trip to Santorini that the man in the photos was behind Galen's hurt.

Galen brought the tomato and onion to the cutting board and began dicing the tomato. "I wasn't always like that. Actually, I preferred being in a relationship over casual dating."

Nick walked over to him and laid his hand on Galen's shoulder. Galen tensed, then relaxed, reaching up to touch his hand. "What changed? Talk to me."

Galen looked at him, and he seemed so lost that Nick leaned in and brushed his lips across Galen's. He cupped Galen's face, coaxing and tender, and Galen sighed against his lips, taking the offering. This new vulnerable side to Galen had Nick aching to discover more about him, to peel back all the layers until he discovered all those parts that Galen hid away.

"I was with someone for quite a few years, and he died," Galen said. "There was an accident with a drunk driver, and he was gone so damned fast." He pulled back and returned to his dicing. "So yeah, after that I didn't feel much like risking my heart."

"I'm so sorry." Nick couldn't imagine a loss like that or trying to fight to find some sense of normalcy afterward. Now the whole way Galen acted before, the distance he put up, it made sense. He ached for the pain that Galen must've gone through. "I wish I'd known."

"I wasn't ready for you to know." Galen shrugged and swept the diced tomato into the bowl. "The hurt of it is gone, but I'll admit, the fear that it'll happen again, that's still there."

"That's understandable." Nick sensed that there was quite a bit more that Galen wasn't saying. There was still an open wound in him, maybe half-scabbed over, but it still seeped blood. "There's more isn't there, about the accident?"

Galen pressed his lips together and nodded. "Yeah, but can we not talk about it tonight? I'd rather relax and enjoy the evening with you than discuss something so damned depressing."

Nick hesitated and wondered just what Galen was holding back—not that it mattered from Nick's standpoint. Walking away now wasn't an option, not when he was starting to get to know the real Galen. And Galen wasn't saying he'd never tell him, just not now. He could respect that.

Nick turned back to his part of the salad and said the only thing he could think of. "It's okay. The invitation is open for whenever you're ready."

Galen gave him a grateful smile. "I don't know why you keep coming back for more when it seems like I keep slamming the door shut. I have to know why you came tonight when I didn't give you the reassurances you were looking for."

Nick sprinkled the feta over the salad greens and began tossing it with the olives. "I appreciate honesty. You played straight with me last time. You didn't string me along, and you put an end to it when I told you how I felt. Another man might've played it out until he was bored, but you cared enough about my feelings to step back. I was pissed at first. Now I'm glad you did. And you were honest with me last night too. Just keep doing that."

"I don't want to give you false hope." Galen checked Nick's progress and started to slice thin slivers of onion. "I don't want to hurt you again."

"We'll take it a day at a time. We don't have to rush into anything. I'm not going to push you into giving me more than you can." Nick added the dressing and red onion that Galen brought over. "The things you've said, the way you've acted these last couple days, has shown me that you're at least willing to try, and if there's a chance you'll come to feel for me what I feel for you, I have to give it a try as well."

Galen looked as if he were going to say something and instead reached down into the oven to pull out dinner. The top crust had turned a flaky golden brown, and Nick's stomach rumbled at the scent, which reminded him of happier family gatherings when he was a boy. "Now that we've had our profound discussion, what do you say about risking my carpets, taking dinner into the living room, and finding a movie?"

Nick jumped on the chance to retreat onto less treacherous ground. No more talk about statues or relationships. He wanted to relax and have a little fun.

"I brought something that might grab your interest." Nick pulled a couple of DVDs out and grinned at Galen. "How about a little of the Seventh Doctor? I have my two favorites, *The Silver Nemesis* and *The Curse of Fenric*."

Galen snatched one of the DVDs out of his hand with a chuckle and shot Nick an amused glance. "You're such a geek."

"And yet, I don't hear you saying no." Nick waved the other DVD enticingly. "What do you say? Good food, a geek fest, and some snogging on that pristine couch of yours?"

Galen tossed the DVD back at him with a laugh. "I say yes to all three. And it just so happens you've picked my favorite Doctor. He was my first."

"Mine's Peter Davison. I love how he was always trying to take care of everyone and getting frustrated when they got into escapades anyway."

Galen bit the corner of his lip as he transferred a steaming helping of spanakopita onto each plate. It was a little charming, the way he concentrated so hard on some tasks, and when he blew a lock of hair out of his eyes, Nick chuckled. This new side of Galen had him entranced. Galen glanced at him and grinned in return. "So it had nothing to do with him being young and blond?"

"That certainly didn't hurt." Nick scooped the salad into smaller bowls, and they made their way into the pristine living room, juggling food, wine, and DVDs. Galen set his load down and tugged the glass coffee table closer to the couch.

Five minutes later they were sitting back, shoulder to shoulder, with loaded plates on their laps and wine close at hand as the DVD started. Nick studied Galen's profile as a little hope blossomed in his chest. He'd wished for nights like this: simple, homey nights where they shared their interests and enjoyed each other's company. The reality was so much better.

"LOOK at you, making such a mess." Nick laughed at Rory's antics as he rolled around in the water, splashing it all over the table. That was his favorite thing to do. Amy preferred it when Nick ran the water in the small fountain so she could duck her head under the spray. "Silly bird, you really love your baths, trying to get all pretty for your lady friend, huh?"

Amy stopped preening her damp feathers long enough to chirp an answer to that, and Nick grinned. "Yeah, you know what I'm talking about."

His cell phone rang, the screen showing Galen's name, and a flush of warmth struck him. Last night had been everything that Nick had dreamt of the first time he'd hooked up with Galen. They'd had fun, curled up on the couch together, watching the old *Doctor Who* episodes and stealing kisses.

"Hey there," Nick answered as he got up to get some paper towels to sop up the mess. "How are things going at the museum today?"

"Let's say… interesting. Do you have a minute? I don't want to bother you if you're busy."

The hesitance in Galen's voice sparked Nick's curiosity. "I'm totally free. I have an appointment later, so I took off from work for a mental health day. Spring assessments are coming, and I'm not going to get another chance for a while. What's up? Is it something with the statues?"

"I think so, but I don't know if it's a product of wishful thinking or not enough sleep. Nobody else can see it. Hold on, I'm e-mailing you a clip from the security footage. You take a look at it and tell me what you think."

"Sure." Nick dried his hands and flipped open his laptop in the living room. "I take it that means Lykon isn't a part of the second statue yet."

"I'm not saying a word until you see the clip. I've asked Suzane, Ella, and Heather to take a look at it, and they don't see anything. If Knox shows up, I'll have him take a look too, but I'm not holding my breath. These statues have been a mystery since they showed up, and there are some days when I worry I've lost my ever-loving mind."

Nick opened his e-mail and clicked on the message from Galen. "Okay, hold on, I'm watching now." The clip opened up, showing the exhibit room, the light dimmer from the rain that came down steadily outside. Ella was lying down on a scaffold, painting with an intent look on her face. The camera panned, revealing the statues, and Nick frowned. They looked exactly the same.

"I don't see anything."

"Dammit. I *am* losing it," Galen said with a real note of worry in his voice.

The camera shifted, and a light shimmered out of the corner of Nick's eye. "Wait." He hit the rewind and watched again. Just as the camera moved out of view he saw it, a strange coalescing light around the second statue where Lykon should be. He hit pause and leaned closer. He could almost make out the image of Lykon, but as Galen said, he didn't know if it was just because he wanted to see it. "Is that Lykon in the second statue?"

Galen let out an explosive breath of air. "Thank God, I'm not crazy. I don't see it all the time, just sometimes. So something is going on with them. Maybe we triggered a change, but damned if I know what we did."

Nick sat back, frowning as he watched the clip again. He was half tempted to stop by the museum to take a look at it for himself, but what he really should do was find those old journals that he'd packed away and see if there were any clues in them that he wasn't remembering. Until now, those journals had been nothing more than a cool story and a link to the Dexios Collection. Now they might be just what they needed.

"We'll figure it out," Nick assured him. "Until then, you're not crazy. I see it too."

"At least I'm not alone in this insanity." Galen laughed. "I'd better get back to work. It's almost time for Heather's lunch, and I'm covering the front for her. I'll talk to you tonight."

"See you." Nick hung up the phone and watched the clip again. So weird. The sounds of splashing had stopped coming from the kitchen. "Are you two hooligans done?"

Rory had finished his bath and had settled on the terrycloth towel that Nick had laid out for him. He sometimes got soaked, though it didn't seem to be too bad today. The towel let him get off the excess before he got a chill. Nick whistled at him as he cleaned up the mess and flipped on the radio for them.

The journals had to be in the apartment somewhere. Nick remembered packing them as he prepared to leave San Francisco. He also remembered his dad bitching about his dreaming ways and that it was time to put childish things in the past. He'd change his tune when Nick told him about the statues... he hoped.

Nick dug through the hallway closet, pulling out old scuba equipment, extra flippers; he really needed to pick up some new stuff before his trip to Santorini. Most of this could be tossed. He dragged out the box tucked in the back corner and stole a peek. The scent of old leather and the dry mustiness of yellowing paper hit him. A hot leap of excitement struck him and awakened a sense of anticipation.

He picked up the box and carried it into the living room. He had loved the story of his dad's uncle and the mysterious lover he'd met during the war and moments of magic. He used to read it before bed, especially after he started to realize that he was different from his brothers, and that he might have more in common with his great-uncle than just a name. Uncle Stavros had been in love with another man.

Nick settled back on the couch with his uncle's journal in his hands and a glass of iced tea on the table. There had to be a clue in one of these that would help him. Uncle Stavros had been in Greece during the Italian invasion, and the statues had been in a private museum run by his father. He'd met the other man when the British came to Greece's aid.

Nick lost himself in the tale and suffered the same pang of empathy that he had as a teenager when Uncle Stavros's heart had been broken. There didn't seem to be many clues to the statues in that journal. Uncle Stavros had been more concerned with the war, and his lover, than what had been going on with Dexios and Lykon.

"You should not be looking in those old books for answers."

Nick dropped the journal and scrambled to his feet with a startled yelp at the sound of the voice in his living room. Rory and Amy went silent as Dexios came forward, his helmet tucked under his arm.

"What the hell are you doing here? I thought you couldn't move that far away from your statue," Nick said. Dexios, with his armor and sword, seemed to take up all the space in the small living room, and having him there was more than a little unnerving.

"I am tied to you as much as I am tied to the statue."

Nick had started to suspect that he was Dexios's reincarnation, as Galen was Lykon's, and this pretty much confirmed his suspicions. "Why won't it help? Didn't the people who wrote them have similar experiences? We're just trying to figure it out to help and to make sense of it all."

Dexios's stern expression softened. "I know, but this journey is a leap of faith, a dream to dare. Reading the accounts of the men who failed will only cloud your vision."

Nick glanced at the box, full to the brim with records, photographs, and artistic renderings of the statues. There was so much in there to discover. One of the birds trilled, breaking the silence, and Nick looked up to find that Dexios had disappeared again.

CHAPTER ELEVEN

IT HAD taken quite a bit of pleading on Galen's part, but he'd managed to convince Heather to stay all day long to run the front of the museum on a Saturday. Normally, he did that stint. It was one of his favorite days of the week because they were busier than others, and he got to dump the paperwork for a day in favor of interacting with patrons.

If he'd had any other first date in mind for Nick, he wouldn't have begged her; however, when he'd seen the ad for the Emerald City Comicon, he'd known it was perfect. And Saturday would be the best day of the con. The way he looked at it, both he and Nick were holding back. He figured that the only way they'd relax and be themselves without any pretense would be by immersing themselves in a day both fun and interesting. And if there was any way into a bona fide geek's heart, it was a comic book convention.

Galen bounded up the outside stairwell and knocked on Nick's apartment door. If they hurried, they'd have a chance to grab a bite of breakfast before they had to queue up. He wasn't sure how long the line would be, but the website warned him, and he wasn't about to ruin his surprise by taking it lightly.

He checked his watch and knocked again. The morning air was cool and damp on his skin. It was not the kind of Saturday to encourage waking up and getting out of a warm, comfortable bed. Nick answered with his toothbrush in hand, his hair in disarray, and his pajama bottoms riding low on his hips.

Well, hello.

Galen's eyes slid over Nick's bare chest. He had the lean, sleek, muscled build of a swimmer. Fine, dark-blond hair sparsely covered his torso and thickened to a trail down his stomach. Galen had to admit to being a fool for not allowing himself the chance to wake up to that before.

Desire stirred, and Galen had to remind himself that he'd promised Nick dates, not casual fucks. They should have at least one date before Galen lured him back to his bedroom and talked Nick into having his way with him. Besides, they would be late, and Galen didn't want to miss one minute of Nick's reaction when he realized where they were headed. He'd had a hard enough time keeping silent all week.

"You're fifteen minutes early and you're cheerful." The accusation in Nick's voice had Galen's eyes jerking back up from Nick's naked skin to his face.

Galen grinned. "And you are rabidly antimorning and underdressed."

"Aren't most sane people at this time?" Nick stepped back to let him in and dragged a hand through his already rumpled hair. His living room was dark with the shades still drawn, and one of Nick's birds trilled a greeting filled with curiosity as Galen came in. "Just give me the fifteen minutes. I need to jump in the shower and down some coffee if you want replies that aren't belligerent."

"Wear something comfortable. We're going to be doing a lot of walking."

Nick paused in the doorway to his bathroom and shot a narrow-eyed look at Galen, taking in his jeans and sneakers. "That's all the hint I get? Be comfortable, and you're expecting me to exercise?"

"Yep." Galen grinned at him, perversely entertained by Nick's morning surliness. It was kind of sexy, though that might also have something to do with Nick's half nakedness and Galen's reawakening libido. He flipped his hands at him. "Hurry up. Trust me; you're not going to want to drag your feet on this."

The bathroom door shut on Nick's mutters, and Galen chuckled. The soft whoosh and flap of wings went by him; then Rory landed by the window and pecked at the wooden slats covering it. He fixed one eye on Galen and called out a very clear demand. "I agree, Rory. It's darker than a dungeon in here."

Galen turned the blinds to let the gray morning light filter into the room. The clouds couldn't seem to decide if they wanted to drizzle or break apart to let the sun through. He was hoping for sun, at least until they got out of line. Then the weather could do whatever it wanted.

Nick's living room invited people in; no wonder he'd felt out of place in Galen's. The furniture was mismatched with a long, leather sofa and a deep, comfortable-looking green recliner. He kept the hardwood floors bare except for an area rug under the coffee table. It had a lived-in appeal Galen's place was missing. Galen's favorite part was Nick's mural of photographs taken from his travels: wooly sheep dotting a field in Ireland, the steep, rocky walls of a fjord in Norway. There were a few of Nick alone, none with friends or family.

Another picture caught his eye, this one older, yellowed on the edges, not as crisp and clear as pictures nowadays. A man who looked a lot like Nick around the eyes stood next to the first Dexios statue, leaning against it. The smile he had for the camera seemed intimate, warm, and Galen wondered who had taken the photograph.

The sound of the shower stopped, and moments later the door opened. Galen couldn't have stopped himself from stealing a quick peek if his life had depended on it. A short towel swathed Nick's hips and water beaded on his skin. The urge to lick it from Nick's body welled up within Galen. Nick paused, looked back at him, and a smile broke out on his lips.

"Like what you see, sweetheart?"

"You know I do." Galen smiled back at him and made a little motion with his hand. "Go, change, before I say screw our schedule and pounce you. You just might end up kicking yourself for it later."

"You're forcing me to choose between my sex drive and curiosity. Not cool, not cool at all," Nick called back as he went down the hallway to his bedroom. "For the record, Saturdays and schedules should not exist. It's amoral."

A few minutes later Nick emerged in jeans, sneakers, and a gray T-shirt that said "Men of Scarves" with Sherlock, the Fourth Doctor, and Harry Potter underneath. "Does this meet with your approval, O Ringmaster?"

"It's perfect." Galen tossed Nick his jacket. "Ready?"

"Yeah, let me get the kids in their cage first." Nick caught Rory in gentle hands and transferred him to the cage as he let out a screech of protest. Amy was harder to track down. He finally got her down from the cabinets in the kitchen and let the two of them complain about their incarceration.

"So any more unannounced visits from Dexios?" Galen asked as Nick grabbed his keys and stuffed them in his jacket.

"Nope, once was enough. How about you? You're the real magnet. You've had Dexios visiting, Lykon poking, and we still don't know how those statues showed up in the first place."

"Things have been quiet, for the most part. I'm sure it won't last, but for now I'll take it." Galen grinned and caught Nick's hand. The statues were the last things he wanted to think about today. He was too excited to see Nick's face. "Come on."

"Please tell me that coffee is on your agenda."

"Yep. I figured we'd need some food to fortify us for the day ahead." Galen shrugged back into his own jacket as he stepped outside. The morning air still held a cold nip, but he thought the threatening rain might hold off. "First stop, the Metro, then breakfast and caffeine, then my surprise."

Nick groaned and locked the door with a shake of his head. "You're an evil man, Galen Kanellis. Evil."

"One does try one's best."

Galen had a hard time resisting Nick's attempts to get the surprise out of him during their Metro ride. It was the anticipation of seeing his expression when they reached the convention center that stopped him from spilling his guts. Thirty minutes later, hot coffees in hand, and the remains of their breakfast sandwiches in their stomachs, Nick paused on the sidewalk outside of the café and turned to Galen.

"Now that I feel semihuman and it's at least almost an acceptable hour to be awake on a Saturday, where to next?"

Galen grinned and pointed across the street. While they'd been inside the line had gotten longer and now wound around the side of the convention center that they faced. "There."

Nick glanced over with an expression of bewilderment, and his eyes widened. "The Emerald City Comicon? For real? That's awesome." He caught Galen's face between his hands and dropped a kiss that tingled Galen's lips.

Galen laughed and tugged his hand to get him moving. They glanced both ways, then ran across the street, dodging traffic. "I can't believe you agreed to go out with me today. I would've thought you had already made plans to go."

"I did with some friends, but I cancelled to go out with you instead." They got into the end of the line, standing next to a family of four dressed up like the Avengers. A grin broke out over Nick's face. "Now this has to be the most kick-ass first date I've had in a long time."

Pleased with himself, Galen took a sip of his coffee. "I'm glad you decided to cancel, though I have to admit, given your love of cons, I'm surprised you did."

Nick gave him an odd look, then tangled their fingers together long enough to give a quick squeeze. "I guess I wanted to see what you had in store for me more than I wanted to go to the convention."

Warmth spread through Galen's chest, and satisfaction filled him. It had been a gamble, and it wasn't what he would've normally chosen for a first date, but he'd made the right choice. Now he just had to convince Nick that he'd also made the right decision in giving him a second chance.

NICK had promised himself he wasn't going to fall for Galen. Not again. He'd bide his time and enjoy himself until Galen flitted off somewhere else. Now look at him. All those damned emotions were waking up inside of him again, urgent and aching, and he wanted to scramble back and call the whole thing off.

He couldn't think of any other guy he'd dated in the past who'd be willing to spend an entire day at a convention, not even the ones who'd had their own latent geek tendencies, like Galen. It was probably a good sign he'd been dating the wrong men.

He set down the painted Harley Quinn glass and glanced over at Galen, who was taking more photographs. He'd been stopping everybody who had a cool costume and getting them to pose. It seemed like he was having fun too. Nick had worried for the first hour or so until he realized that Galen's enthusiasm wasn't going to wane.

Galen was the perfect guy, and that's where the trap lay. It was too late to backtrack and call it off. It was like coming to the realization that he was screwed halfway up the long first climb of a rollercoaster. He couldn't demand to get off when he was already strapped in and on his way.

Nick turned toward the vintage toys all still packed away in their pristine original boxes. He'd never had the patience to put them away and not play with them. He didn't know how people had that kind of fortitude and foresight. The minute he got them, they were out of the box. Right now his old Millennium Falcon was stored away under his bed at his dad's house.

A wave of longing hit him. There were times when he wanted to wind back the clock and do things in a different way. An arm slipped around his shoulders and squeezed. "Hey, what'cha thinking?" Galen asked, leaning his head toward Nick's. "Must be serious."

"Nothing much." Nick set the toy down. "About my dad and all the junk I still have at his house. It must make him nuts to have it around."

"Yeah, my mom is forever calling me about getting the last of my stuff out of the garage." Galen's arm fell from his shoulder, and Nick found himself missing the casual touch. He had never considered himself much of a touchy-feely kind of guy, and he'd forgotten how much Galen was forever touching, a hand to the cheek, a quick hug, a clasp of fingers. He even found himself doing the same. "Sometimes I think it's laziness on my part, other times I think I don't want to cut that last tie to home. It's ludicrous, it's not like she's going anywhere…." Galen trailed off, then gestured with his hand. "Oooh, will you look at that? Scarves, just like the ones on your T-shirt."

Nick stared after Galen as he crossed over to another vendor on the other side of the aisle. His dad had never complained once about Nick's remaining belongings, and it made him wonder if Galen's second theory was more insightful than he thought. Life used to be uncomplicated when he was a kid, and now it was one big snarl of conflicting, confusing threads.

Galen wrapped a slim, black scarf around his throat, tossed one end over his shoulder, and turned toward Nick. "What do you think?"

Nick chuckled and shook his head. "Very dashing. I don't know how you manage to pull it off. I'd look ridiculous."

"It's a skill." Galen reached into his back pocket for his wallet, and Nick shook his head as he went over to him.

"Let me." Galen had been spoiling him rotten all day; the heavy bag stuffed with comics that Nick carried was a testament to that. All in all, Galen seemed to be enjoying taking in the sights and sounds more than showing any interest in serious collecting himself. And Galen looked pretty sexy with that scarf.

"Thanks." Galen dropped a light kiss to Nick's lips that brought a longing for emotional intimacy that Nick had missed before. It was there, just waiting to be grabbed this time, and it was terrifying.

They soon reached the end of the show floor, and Galen dug out the map of the convention. "Where to next? We have about an hour before the panel you wanted to see starts."

Nick contemplated heading over to the Artist Alley to get some of the comic books signed, but the thought of a few moments of quiet time with Galen and the chance to sit changed his mind. "Let's see if the line's already formed for the panel or if we can grab seats early."

"Good plan."

Galen caught his hand as they snaked their way through the crowd, and a flush of warmth went through him. Galen was going to make him crazy. He made it easy to forget the past and contemplate a future. After a few moments, Nick pulled his hand back and shifted his bags to both hands.

Nick had been a complete idiot and taken a look through the rest of those journals despite Dexios's warning. Story after story had been the same: betrayals, heartbreak; the only things that had been different were the details. There had to be a way to make the statues whole, fulfill all the conditions of the curse, and keep his heart intact at the same time. He was not going to end up like his uncle or all the other men in his family before him. They'd allowed themselves to be completely taken in, to fall hard. If he kept his feelings out of this, then they could all come out winners.

Maybe he should tell Galen the whole story about the statues. He cast Galen a sideways glance and decided against it. No, it would complicate the situation and quite probably make Galen bolt early. He couldn't let that happen until the Dexios Collection was completed.

He knew far too well that it was easier said than done. He couldn't make someone stay who was hell-bent on leaving. His mother had taught him that lesson. He'd begged while she'd packed. He'd cried as she walked out the door. He'd believed every word of her promises when she'd come back, even though his brothers had been more pragmatic. No matter what he'd done, he hadn't been good enough, and she'd left again.

"Why do you look so sad and angry?" Galen asked as they reached the line. There were a few people ahead of them, so they would manage to get good seats up front. "You not having fun anymore?"

Nick squashed down the old anger and resentment and forced a smile. "Sorry, I am, really. Hell, I should be asking you that question. Are you enjoying yourself?"

"To be honest, I thought today would just be okay other than being with you. I was looking forward more to your reaction than to the con itself." Galen looked around at the crowded convention hall, and he gave Nick a grin. "But it's a lot more fun than I expected."

"It takes a certain open mindset." Nick leaned against the wall and set his bags on the floor. He felt Galen's eyes on him, and it jumbled him up inside even more. He liked this new side to Galen, yet it unnerved him at the same time. Galen's self-preoccupation in the months before had allowed Nick to mask some of his own emotions. He didn't think he'd be able to get away with that much now. Galen was more perceptive than Nick had given him credit for.

"So what's bothering you?" Galen asked in a low voice, and when Nick glanced at him he couldn't miss the concern in his expression.

"I have a lot on my mind. Family stuff."

Galen grimaced in sympathy. "That can be the worst. I kinda wish my mom would worry about all of us a little less. She checks in on us often."

Nick turned to face him as he remembered something Galen had said before. "So your mom was upset when you told her you were gay, huh? How long did it take her to come around?"

"She was mostly just disappointed. She'd always dreamed of seeing me, my brother, and sister married off, with lots of grandkids for her to take care of. It took her a couple of months, though she tried not to let me see it because she didn't want me to think she was rejecting me. She came to see that I can still give her all that one day, just differently." Galen worried his lower lip, his gaze thoughtful. "When we finally talked about it, really talked about it, she let it go."

"What about your dad?" Nick had never heard Galen mention him, not even once, now that he thought about it.

Galen shrugged and stuck his hand in his pocket. "He died when I was real little. I barely remember him. I'd like to think he'd be okay with it." He turned his head and gave Nick a nudge. "How about you?"

It was on the tip of Nick's tongue to give his usual spiel about his dad and brothers, and then he hesitated. "To be honest, sometimes I wonder if I gave them a chance. Other times I'm pretty sure I made the right decision to move out of state after I told them."

"Sometimes distance brings perspective," Galen said in a low voice as other people joined them in the line.

"And sometimes it's just running. I'm not sure which side I fall on," Nick admitted, and it was more than he'd ever allowed himself to give. He was a little surprised at himself, but Galen could be so easy to talk to.

"Maybe it's both."

Galen had a point. It didn't have to be either, and he didn't really want to think about it anymore. This was his first real date with Galen, and he'd been brooding silently through too much of it. There had to be some kind of dire punishment for going to the Emerald City Comicon and letting his fears screw with him.

Nick took Galen's hand and thrust his chin out toward a man dressed as Khal Drogo. "Do you think I could pull that look off at a con?"

Galen shook his head. "You've got the body, but you're too light. He's dark and menacing."

"I can be menacing," Nick said in mock outrage and scowled at Galen who seemed not at all intimidated.

"When you show me menacing I'll say okay, until then I suggest Legolas."

"You have a thing for elves?"

The corner of Galen's mouth lifted, and there was a look of mischief in his gaze. "I have a thing for you."

The last six months may have been hell on Nick, but he couldn't get over the changes they had brought about. Just with that look he fell a little harder, and no warnings in any journal seemed to make any difference. "You're dangerous."

Galen burst out laughing, and Nick found himself laughing with him. "You've named me evil and dangerous in one day. Maybe I should be the one dressing up as the barbarian warrior."

The image of Galen dressed like that, with his chest bare, rose in Nick's mind, and he sucked in a breath. "I could see that. However, he's not evil, and you just proved you are."

CHAPTER TWELVE

"WHEN Order 66 came through, I quit my job and opened a comic book store in—"

"Stop it." Nick gasped, laughing so hard that his stomach ached and he had to stop to clutch the railing outside of his building. He didn't know how Galen was able to recreate some of the more colorful personalities they'd met that day with such devastating accuracy. "Not the guy who swore he was a modern-day Jedi."

Galen turned oh-so-innocent eyes on him, an image that shattered with his sudden grin. "Sorry, I couldn't help myself. I don't know how that dealer said it with such a straight face."

Nick shook his head and dug out his keys as they climbed the steps to his apartment. "I don't know how you can repeat it with a straight face."

Galen slipped his arms around him as Nick stopped in front of the door to unlock it. "I like hearing you laugh," he said in a husky voice. "And seeing you smile like this."

Nick's fingers suddenly trembled, and he fumbled at the lock before he managed to get the key in.

"I had a good time today." Nick's feet were sore; he was tired from the endless walking and noise since they'd stayed from opening to close. Over the course of the day he'd somehow managed to forget all of his worries and fears. They were back now, hovering in the back of his mind, and he knew they wouldn't be enough to keep him from inviting Galen in. He just hoped he wouldn't regret it in the morning.

"I'm glad." Galen pressed a kiss behind his ear, and it made Nick a little light-headed. The tiredness vanished underneath his craving to get Galen naked in his bed.

Nick turned around to face him. "Do you want to come in for a bit?"

Galen searched his face, as if sensing the meaning behind his words, and then he gave Nick a smile of regret. "I would love to, but I won't. Not on our first date."

Equal parts disappointment and relief swept through him. "Well, I guess we're going to have to have a second date."

Galen laughed and slipped his arms around Nick again, pressing him back against the door. "We do, and a third, and a fourth." He tilted his head up as Nick closed the space between them and kissed him. Desire overrode common sense at the feel of Galen's body up against his and the eager way he kissed Nick back. He didn't think it would take much to get Galen to yield and change his mind. And he couldn't help wondering if Galen would stick to his new principles.

Nick groped for the doorknob behind him and stumbled back into the apartment, pulling Galen with him. He kicked the door shut, dropped his bags on the floor, and kissed Galen again. Hands slid under the back of his T-shirt, cool from the night air against his overheated skin. Nick twined his hands around the ends of Galen's new scarf and imagined it wrapped around Galen's wrists and tied to the headboard. He wanted to push his boundaries, taste Galen's surrender. He groaned and heard Galen's breath catch in response as he pushed him back against the door.

This time Galen was the one trapped, and Nick tasted his eagerness in the play of his tongue and the way he gripped him, his body taut with hot energy. Nick pressed his thigh between Galen's legs and felt the hard length of his cock through his jeans. Nick's heart raced as he slid his hands down to grip Galen's ass and pull him closer. Galen rubbed himself against Nick's thigh with a throaty groan, and his breath escaped with a little sigh of loss as the kiss broke.

"One more," Galen murmured and lifted his head to kiss Nick again.

Nick leaned back out of reach and pinned Galen's wrists to the door. Galen's eyes widened, and a tremble rippled through his body. Nick's heart pounded harder. They'd flirted with these games before, though they'd always pulled back. Nick hadn't dared to press, and

Galen hadn't invited more. He seemed to be inviting it tonight with the sudden suppleness of his body and the unmistakable throb of his dick.

Galen wet his lips, his eyes hazy with need. "Please. One more kiss."

Nick's cock ached, and that simple little "please" was enough to make him breathless. He kept Galen's hands pinned as he leaned closer, staring right into his eyes until their lips were so close he could feel Galen's breath against them. He'd expected Galen to pull back, not beg for more, and he didn't know whether to feel triumphant or disappointed over how easy it was to seduce him.

He brushed his lips over Galen's, felt him press closer, and then Nick shifted and sought the warm curve of Galen's neck instead. Another harder shiver went through Galen as he turned his head to give Nick better access. "That's wrong, going right for my weakness."

Nick grinned against his throat, lips nibbling, tongue tracing the rapid beat of Galen's pulse. He let his mouth wander until he found the right spot, and Galen squirmed against him. "Don't," he said with a strangled whimper even as he arched his neck a little more and pressed closer, as though he couldn't make up his mind to struggle or stay put. "Please, dammit, you tease."

Nick chuckled and nipped him below his ear, then again at the sweet spot where his neck curved to meet his shoulder. Galen melted against him with a wanton sound caught in his throat. "Oh yeah, right there."

"Are you sure you won't stay?" Nick asked and circled the spot with his tongue before moving back up toward his nape. "I haven't even gotten started teasing you."

Galen jerked his hands free and fisted them in Nick's hair. He tugged him down and kissed him hard on the lips. "God, you make me crazy, you bastard."

"It's entirely mutual." Nobody could make him feel as reckless and out of control as Galen did.

Galen kissed him again and let go of him with a shake of his head. "I can't, Nick. I'm not giving you any more reason to doubt me."

Nick stepped back, stunned by Galen's insight. Was he that transparent? As much as he wanted Galen, he needed to know that

Galen really planned to stick around this time. It seemed that no matter what Galen did, he managed to get Nick all muddled up inside. He took a deep breath, willing his libido to calm down. He was going to need a cold shower; at least he wouldn't be the only one. "Okay, then."

Galen caught his hand and kissed his knuckles. "Another time."

"I'll hold you to that." Nick touched the curve of Galen's jaw and smiled at him. "I get to pick where we go on our second date."

"It's a deal. Make it soon."

Nick leaned his forehead against the door after Galen left. Right now his heart was grateful for Galen's refusal, but his cock was pissed off. Galen seemed sincere. But past experience and the depth of his want to trust made him wary. He wanted to believe that Galen would be different from his mom and the rest of his family. He wanted to believe that this situation wouldn't play out in the same way that every other Dexios and Lykon reincarnation seemed to have ended.

He locked the door and picked up his packages, determined not to brood about it. They had a good day; he wasn't going to ruin it. He laid the bags on the couch and opened the cage for his birds. Rory popped his head out first and fixed Nick a look with one bright, beady eye. "How's it going, buddy?"

Rory twittered and glided out of the cage to take up a perch on the back of the couch, moments later followed by Amy. Nick grabbed himself a beer and took a long swallow. It was quiet in his apartment. Too quiet. He was restless, all that excess energy built up with nowhere to go. He flipped on the radio and took another sip of his beer as he returned to the living room. Maybe if he read some of his new comics he'd settle down.

Nick stretched out on the couch and tried to get his mind off Galen despite his body's insistence on remembering how it had felt to hold him and kiss him again. His gaze fell on his great-uncle's journal, and he reached over to grab it from the coffee table. The leather was old, the binding cracked in a few spots, and the yellowed pages held the musty smell that books got.

He read through some of the journal entries and soon found himself engrossed in Stavros's slow fall with the soldier from Britain. He read a passage where Stavros struggled to sum up the other man and was struck by one line. *He has a love of the moment and a fear of the future.* Boy did that sound familiar. The description could easily fit Galen. To be honest, it could fit Nick too.

He paused at a photograph of Stavros Charisteas and looked into familiar eyes. His dad had always said that Nick reminded him of his uncle. He'd been named for him after Stavros had passed only a few months before Nick's mom had gotten pregnant with him. Nicholas Stavros Charisteas. It sent a chill through him. How could he be the same man as Stavros, the same man as Dexios?

It was strange to think he was the reincarnation of a man born hundreds of generations before, even stranger to think he was the reincarnation of his dad's favorite uncle. Nick frowned and pulled out his phone and brought up his missed calls. His dad had tried to reach him earlier. Nick hadn't talked to him in ages. He missed him.

Nick sighed and set the phone aside along with the journal. Not tonight. He didn't have the energy to deal with the struggle of who he was or his dad's recriminations, whether or not he deserved them.

GALEN stared up at the dark ceiling and took several deep breaths, trying to still the panic that clawed at him. He hadn't had that nightmare in several months, and there had been something different about it this time. He replayed it in his mind, knowing that trying to ignore it would only lead to more disturbed dreams. The recent nightmare mixed with memory made the images even more potent. He could feel the rain on his skin through the shattered windows. He could feel the hot, slick blood on his hands.

He shuddered and sat up, pushing the sheets away from his overheated body. He didn't want to remember. Not tonight. The day had been so much fun. Those were the memories he wanted on his mind tonight, seeing Nick's face light up as he got his comics signed, feeling the strength of his arms when he pinned him and kissed the breath right out of him before they said good-bye.

Galen scraped a hand through his hair and went to the bathroom to splash some water on his face. A presence fluttered in his chest, and he touched a hand to the spot. That had been happening more often now; Lykon stretching, awakening, and trying to impinge his awareness on Galen's. Galen still didn't understand how the four of them were tied together. And he didn't want any more blackouts.

The cold water banished the last emotional vestiges of the dream, and Galen was able to think back on it without his heart constricting. It had been the same old nightmare, complete with horror and heartbreak. Nothing had been different until….

He frowned, remembering the sound of the sirens and looking up through the windshield for the source with a last desperate, fading hope. Only this time, among the gathering onlookers and witnesses trying to help, another man stood out. Dexios.

In tonight's dream, Dexios had stood in the rain, watching him with sorrow on his handsome face. Galen's hands tightened on the chill, metal water basin. Had Dexios actually been there that night? An icy sensation rolled over him at the thought, followed by a rage that left him shaking with its intensity. Was that what had distracted him and caused the accident?

Lykon stirred again, coming fully awake, and Galen batted him back down, using his anger to give him strength. Had Bryan died because some ancient jackasses had found him too inconvenient to their story? He shook his head violently to dispel the thought. *No, no, no.* They wouldn't. That was taking speculation too far. He'd never to able to look at Nick without wondering if he didn't let it go now.

Galen glanced up at the mirror and found Lykon staring back at him through his own eyes. He snarled, lashing out at the image. His fist connected with the mirror and the sound of shattering glass, the sudden appearance of the spider-webbed crack across the glass, knocked the anger right out of him.

Galen stared at the distorted image of himself and breathed a sigh of relief when he saw his own eyes. His knuckles throbbed and stung. He glanced down and shuddered at the blood welling from his knuckles to slip down his fingers. Blood on his hands. He wasn't sure if he was still dreaming or not.

Shaking, Galen turned the water back on and slid his hand underneath until the blood washed away. Dexios couldn't have been there that night. Galen would've remembered something as blatant as a man standing by the side of the highway in full, ancient battle gear. His nightmares were getting all mixed up with his obsession over the statues. He was awake and overreacting to a dream that he had thought he'd already put behind him.

His knuckles ached as he examined them, but the damage wasn't too bad, none of the cuts deep enough to require real attention. He winced as he looked at the mirror and the smear of blood across the center of the cracks. He didn't need to see that every time he came into the bathroom, so he tossed a towel over it to hide the damage until he could get it fixed.

Galen tended to the worst of the cuts and then tugged on a pair of jeans and a hoodie. It was one in the morning, too early to head to the museum, and it would be a while before he could get back to sleep. He wondered if Nick had the same trouble sleeping. He doubted it. He probably was dreaming of geek stuff, reliving the day. Maybe thinking of him. Galen didn't dare to hope. At least he didn't have someone fighting to take him over so he could go make nookie with the ghost of his lover.

He took down a shot glass and a half-full bottle of tequila. The smoky, smooth flavor exploded in his mouth and left a sweet burn on the way down. He poured another shot, then set the bottle and glass aside. Lykon pulled at his consciousness, taking advantage of Galen's distraction to make his presence known once again.

Galen rubbed his palm against his chest. "Leave me alone, will you? There's nothing I can do about the statues tonight, I'm sorry."

It should've felt like he was losing his mind, talking out loud to himself in the empty apartment. Instead, he didn't feel alone at all; it felt like Lykon was listening to him. The urge to get out, to take a walk in the cold night air came over him, and Galen found himself putting on his sneakers and shrugging into his leather jacket.

The air nipped at cheeks still warm from the shots of tequila, and the dual sensations invigorated him. He wasn't sure how long he wandered; the longer he stayed outside, the more bemused he seemed to get. A part of him questioned the wisdom of this jaunt, but the more aware side was confident he could handle any trouble that came his way.

Galen finally managed to flag down a cab, intending on heading back to his place and the warmth of his bed, and instead he found himself giving the driver Nick's address. He sat in the back seat, tapping his chest and worrying his lip as he tried to fight the urge that drove him forward.

It wasn't that Nick wouldn't invite him in if he showed up on his doorstep. It wasn't that the sex wouldn't be scorching hot. He knew deep down it would be a mistake. Nick already thought he was some kind of sex-starved nympho who had no real interest in any kind of a commitment, not even a casual one. This would just confirm it in Nick's mind.

Galen had been at a point not too long ago when he'd been ready to bolt at the slightest provocation, so he recognized the signs in Nick. In fact, he wasn't too sure of Nick's motivations. He could be giving this relationship a chance because of whatever he knew about those statues and what it took to end the curse. It hadn't taken as much work as Galen had thought it would to woo him back into being with him again.

If he wanted Nick to stay when the Collection was complete, he'd have to give Nick every reason to do so. He had to win his trust again. Galen stared out the window and brooded as the cab pulled up in front of Nick's apartment. The windows were dark, but that didn't stop the sharp jump inside of him, the pull to get out and climb the stairs to Nick's door.

"Stop it," Galen muttered under his breath, pressing the heel of his hand against his skin as though it would somehow contain Lykon.

"Hey, mister, you okay?" The cab driver turned in his seat, his eyes narrowing on Galen.

Galen nodded, not trusting himself to speak. He dug his wallet out and shoved some money at the cab driver and gasped out his own address. Lykon fought him, and Galen's vision went gray as he tried to hold on. He couldn't pass out now, and he wasn't going to be Lykon's fucking marionette either.

He unzipped his hoodie partway, dug his fingers into his skin, and the pain of bruises forming shocked him into some semblance of control. Galen shook his head, pushing Lykon down until the sense of his presence faded, though it didn't disappear entirely. His relationship with Nick was nobody else's business.

"Do you hear me, Lykon?" Galen said under his breath. "We're doing it my way or not at all. Stop trying to manipulate me."

The cab driver shot him another nervous glance through the rearview mirror. "Look, do you need me to take you to a hospital?"

A surge of panic welled up, breaking the last bit of Lykon's control, and the man disappeared. "God, no. Just take me home." He laid his head back and tapped his bruised and cut knuckles against the window, counting on the renewed ache to keep him in control until he managed to get back home. No one manipulated him.

A PROMISE OF PATIENCE

DEXIOS knelt on the shore, the sand digging into his knees until his skin was numb. He was frozen, unable to make any decision about a future that now seemed without purpose or joy. His plans were shattered, and no wound he had taken on the battlefield hurt as much as he hurt now. Lykon had deserted him and the betrayal had taken him by surprise.

Lykon had broken his promise the very same day they were given their freedom to leave and pursue their own lives again. He did not even try to find another way. And no argument or plea from Dexios had been able to sway him. Lykon didn't even offer hope for a future.

Dexios knew what would happen when his lover returned home. His family would ply him with problems that needed fixing, questions that needed answering, and Lykon would bury himself in the day-to-day. By the time his thoughts turned back toward Dexios the memories and emotions would have turned distant and cold. There would be no desire or reason to return to him.

Lykon could be single-minded when it came to a problem. It was one of the characteristics about him that drew Dexios in the first place. It had also been the cause of much vexation. He chose practicality over giving vent to his feelings. It had taken much effort for Dexios to get Lykon to open up. Now that Lykon had locked himself away again out of fear, he wouldn't readily open that door again. How had he missed the signs and not noticed that he had overwhelmed his lover with his plans?

"Why do you kneel on the shore all alone? Why does your soul weep?"

Dexios leapt to his feet, drawing his sword as he spun to face the voice that surrounded him. At first he didn't see anyone, and then he noticed a form in the waves that followed the curves of a woman's body. As the realization struck him, the figure rose, riding with divine grace as the surging wave transformed into a woman of unearthly beauty, clad in nothing but the damp tendrils of her hair.

Dexios gasped and averted his gaze as he fell back to the sand. "Cythera."

Words froze on his tongue, and he found himself unable to speak, unable to react as the sheer force of her presence touched him. Bare feet stopped in front of his eyes, sand clinging to delicate toes and the arch of her feet.

"I sensed your pain. Where is your other half?"

Dexios closed his eyes as another wave of grief washed over him. It seemed as if the pain had grown a hundredfold in Cythera's presence, and if Dexios had not already been on the ground he would've been bowed down by it.

"He has returned home to see to his family." Dexios struggled to lift his head and felt a slender hand tangling in his hair. "He takes his duties with utmost seriousness. He always has. For him, duty takes precedence." Perhaps Dexios should have shown Lykon that he had a duty to them as well.

"But what of love?" The hand tightened in his hair, and Dexios looked up at the goddess. She was beautiful, but there was an implacable resolve in her eyes that was terrifying to see, a will that went beyond human comprehension. "Duty is pale in comparison, boring and without life."

"Love does not come first with him." Dexios hadn't been able to get Lykon's last expression out of his mind, the baffled fear that he tried to hide by busying himself. It wasn't that Lykon didn't feel; perhaps he felt too deeply and did not know how to handle such strong emotion. Dexios wished now that he had taken time to understand why Lykon needed some distance.

"He made an oath to you in my name. Does that not mean anything to him? Does he dismiss me so lightly?" Cythera asked with an edge in her voice.

Dexios shook his head and tried to speak past the knots on his tongue. Fear broke through his sorrow, fear for himself, fear for Lykon.

The gods and goddesses were not known to be forgiving. "No, this is an exception. He needs time to think. He will return when the time is right. I know it."

He hoped it. One day soon, Lykon would come back to him of his own free will. He would not return unless he knew that staying was what he wanted. It would not be an ill-thought-out promise spoken in the heat of passion and the desire to make Dexios smile. So when Lykon did return, Dexios had no reason to fear that he would leave again. If he did. Please let him return.

"Time? Lykon spoke of time as well." A smile touched the corners of Cythera's lips. "I will make sure you have all the time that the two of you need. Would you like that, my brave warrior? Would you have the patience to wait for your wayward lover if given the chance?"

Dexios hesitated. He could say yes, but what if Lykon never changed his mind? He'd be stuck waiting for something that may never happen, prolonging the ache in his heart. He could choose to move on, let the ache heal and find someone new. His heart rebelled against the thought.

Then Dexios remembered the look in Lykon's eyes when he made the promise. Lykon did love him, of that he had no doubt. He would come back someday, and when he did, Dexios would be ready for him. He just had to be patient, not one of his stronger virtues, but if it was for Lykon....

Dexios smiled up at the goddess as certain of this vow as he had been of his vow to leave and make a new life with Lykon. "Yes, Cythera, for him I could have endless patience."

"Then I will give you this time." She paused and searched his face. "Perhaps this will give you some measure of comfort. Your other half does love you and already regrets his hasty retreat. In time he will come searching for you."

Dexios closed his eyes as some of the ache in his heart was replaced with hope. Perhaps they both needed to listen more and demand less. When they did see each other again, Dexios would tell him so. In the meanwhile, Dexios clung to the knowledge that Lykon would come. "Thank you, Cythera."

"Still, you both broke your vow said in my name." Dexios's eyes flew open, and he stared at Cythera in horror, shaking his head and unable to give voice to the protest locked in his throat.

"You said that he returns, so the vow stands unbroken, merely postponed." Dire fates rose in his mind, tales of all the punishments inflicted upon those who had offended the gods. *"Please, do not bring harm on him for leaving."*

"What of you for letting him leave?" Dexios had no reply as she paused, studying him with a small smile on her lips. *"You fought the enemy harder than you fought for him. I think you were susceptible to your own fears. You did not wish to push him too far, not knowing what you would find. It was easier to let him go."*

Again Dexios wanted to protest, but instead he searched his heart and was ashamed to realize the truth to her words. He had left Lykon in anger and haste, too hurt to listen to words, unable to give him then the patience he promised now.

He lifted his face and met Cythera's gaze stare for stare. *"I freely admit my own guilt. We both were at fault."*

"Done." The goddess's capricious smile widened, and Dexios felt his limbs become heavy as the world shifted. He tried to look down and found himself unable to move. Cythera touched his jaw. *"You make a very handsome statue, and you will be as eternal as the tides until your fickle lover fulfills his promise four times over and you accept him. Be well, Dexios, and remember your promise to be patient. I will be watching."*

Dexios tried to cry out as the goddess vanished, but no sound emerged from his frozen lips. He stood staring out at the sea, his arms reaching for something that wasn't there.

CHAPTER THIRTEEN

GALEN shut the journal with a snap and sank back into Nick's couch with a sigh. He wasn't going to get any answers from the mismatched lot of books. Most of Nick's journals were written in Greek and, despite his heritage and his great-grandmother's harping when he was younger, he'd only picked up a few phrases, most of them curse words. The one journal written in English, Nick's great-uncle's, seemed to have chunks missing, and what was there focused more on Dexios, which didn't help him at all with his Lykon problem.

Nick shot him a sympathetic glance and set another journal aside. "Getting frustrated with dusty old books and bad handwriting?"

"I reached my limit an hour ago." Galen stretched, and his back popped in several places. "I don't think I'm going to find any answers in those. I wonder if I could jiggle the museum's accounting books enough to scrape together some funds for a translation. How about you, have you discovered anything significant?"

Nick grimaced and pulled out a folder. "I've been looking at a couple different versions of the myth to see if I can find any answers there. I know it's a long shot, but what the hell. They're almost as confusing as the journals. They mention a test, but I think most mythic tales have a test. And they talk about Dexios's reincarnation making an offer to Lykon's, and that offer has to be accepted. But that could mean anything. I don't see how it applies to us or how that first statue changed. I could offer you anything, but I'm pretty sure it's supposed to be certain things."

Galen raised an eyebrow as he took the folder Nick handed out to him. "That is pretty broad. Well, at least we know it isn't sex based. Dexios said it had nothing to do with him kissing me, and the first one was made whole before we saw each other again, much less kissed."

He glanced through the contents of the folder and tossed it down on the cluttered table with a sigh. The myth wasn't going to help him either. The tale seemed to end after Lykon was charged with caring for the statues.

"Why don't you tell me what you're looking for? I know those journals pretty well, and something's been bugging you for a couple of weeks now." Nick came to sit next to him and urged Galen to turn so his back was to Nick. Galen sighed as strong hands started to knead the muscles of his back. "You're tense all over."

Galen closed his eyes and sank into the comfort of Nick's ministrations. It wasn't how he wanted Nick's hands on him. He'd much rather have naked-skin-to-naked-skin contact. Sometimes he thought his vow of celibacy got to him more than it did Nick. "I'm tired of Lykon trying to take over. He wants to push everything as fast as it'll go, and I think it's a mistake, but he won't stop fighting me. Is there a timetable I don't know of to break the curse?"

Nick's thumbs worked down Galen's spine, and despite his irritation, tension started to ease from his body. "I doubt it. Some of those journals go on for years about the statues. Lykon's probably reacting out of sexual frustration. I can sympathize," Nick said in a teasing voice. Well, that answered the question; Galen wasn't the only one thinking of taking their relationship to another level.

Nick kissed the side of Galen's neck, and a shiver of yearning went through him. Two weeks of dating and some really hot make-out sessions were putting a dent in his resolve. To be honest, just looking at Nick and remembering some of those long, sensual nights almost broke that resolve in half.

"Though in all seriousness, I think it's more likely that Lykon misses Dexios and is impatient to be reunited and have the nightmare over," Nick continued. "I can't begin to imagine loving and waiting for someone that long."

Galen could imagine it. He didn't remember too much about his dad; still, he knew his parents had been happy, enough that his mom had shown no interest in remarrying. She'd always said that if she found someone who gave her what his dad did she'd consider it, but she didn't want to search only for the sake of not being alone. Her life was full enough. His aunts and uncles were still married after decades of being together, and that was the kind of relationship he wanted. And the more time he spent with Nick, the more he thought about that kind of a lifelong commitment.

"Did you ever wonder what would happen if you stopped fighting Lykon?" Nick asked, his hands stilling on Galen's waist.

A chill went through Galen, and he looked back over his shoulder at Nick. "Too many times. The way I figure it, I'd either find myself naked with Dexios or you, and in both cases it would be my body, but not me, and I refuse to be used that way." Galen twisted around and cupped the back of Nick's neck. "When you and I get naked, I want to remember every detail."

Nick skated his hands up Galen's back as they kissed and his tongue thrust into Galen's mouth. He loved the way Nick kissed him, as if he wanted to stake a claim on him, bind Galen to him. It made him go all soft inside even as it excited him.

"I have a suggestion," Nick said against his mouth. "How do you feel about skinny-dipping?"

Galen pulled back to see if he was serious, and the wicked glint in Nick's eyes answered him. "I don't think the weather has warmed up enough for that. It's not even April yet, unless you're talking about dancing naked in the rain."

"No, however, that gives me other ideas. I have access to an indoor pool, and I guarantee that nobody will be there at this time of night." Nick grinned and gave Galen a nudge. "So what do you say, you up for it?"

A hot sizzle of naughty anticipation hit Galen. It had been years since he'd last gone skinny-dipping. "And how do you know nobody will be there this time of night?" Galen nudged Nick back. "Is this something you do often?"

"Swimming, yes; I do laps about four or five times a week. I like going at this time because I'm usually wide awake and I have the pool to myself." He stood up and stretched, then scooped up his keys. "Besides, we've been bent over these books for hours. We need a break."

Why the hell not? Galen was game. If he looked any longer at these books he'd go cross-eyed. Seeing Nick naked for the next hour would no doubt haunt his dreams that night. Still, doing it would be well worth the torture.

Nick tossed Galen his jacket and drew a light sheet over the cockatiels' cage. Amy and Rory seemed to be fast asleep, their heads tucked over their shoulders and their eyes closed. "It's not far. We can walk there from my apartment."

The air was cool and damp and the neighborhood quiet, with most of the windows dark for the night. Galen took Nick's hand as they walked, something he hadn't done with anyone in a long time. With Nick it felt right. "So how many laps do you normally swim?" He considered himself a fair swimmer, though he'd rather lie on a beach than fight the waves. He knew Nick did some wreck diving, but he wasn't sure how serious he was about the hobby.

"About sixty to eighty. It depends on my mood and how much frustrated energy I need to work out."

"You're kidding me, right?"

Nick grinned and shook his head. "Nope. I hate the gym, the thought of getting up early in the morning to go jogging makes me gag, but swimming, I could do that forever."

"I'd be lucky if I got five laps in before quitting."

"You'd be surprised, you build up stamina quick." Nick tugged his hand free and stuck it in his pocket. "So how's Suzane doing?"

Galen missed the warmth of Nick's touch. He hadn't missed the little ways that Nick would pull away sometimes, and he never could pinpoint what triggered the reaction. He seized on the change of topic, eager to share his worries with someone who wasn't emotionally invested in the situation. "To be honest, I'm a bit worried about her. These last couple rounds of chemo are kicking her ass."

"She's got a lot of fight in her. I'm sure it's wearying, though. Didn't you say she's almost done with that part?" Nick touched a hand to the small of his back, and the touch comforted Galen.

"Yeah, thank God." At least he'd managed to convince her to take some time off. She hadn't fought him that hard, which indicated how worn out she was. "One more after this last one. Her sister took her to a family retreat for a week. Just the two of them near the water."

Nick turned toward a low, darkened building and took out his keys. "I predict she'll return with as much fire as she's always shown, and she'll give you hell if you hover over her."

"I believe it too, I really do. It's just sometimes hard to watch." As Nick opened the door, Galen felt the humid heat, and the scent of chlorine washed over him. "My dad wasted away. I don't remember a lot, but I remember enough." The endless waits at the hospital, the scents, the heavy pall of sorrow and worry. He also remembered his dad's eyes, though. He had kind, smiling eyes.

"Sounds like you need to get your mind off your worries." Nick led him to the long square room that held a good-sized pool. The ropes for making lanes were coiled off to the side, and the building held a hushed, still quality. Most of the lights were doused, the corners of the room draped in shadows.

"How'd you get a key?" Galen asked in a hushed voice.

"I know the guy who runs the place. We've gone diving together a couple of times."

Galen glanced at Nick. He didn't seem at all concerned about being there after hours. "Don't they frown on people swimming by themselves like this?"

"It's swim at your own risk. They only have staff on-site at peak hours." Nick shrugged out of his jacket and tossed it down on the bench. He winked at Galen with a grin and his shirt followed. "If they caught us here naked I'd probably get kicked out, but it's a risk I'm willing to take."

He kicked out of his shoes, and he put his hand to his belt. Galen shivered and turned aside as his cheeks heated. Nick made him think the craziest thoughts sometimes, thoughts he'd believed he'd buried. He began to get undressed, folding his clothes on the bench as he went, and watching Nick out of the corner of his eye. The other man was soon naked, and Galen turned to watch him dive cleanly into the water. He swam with powerful, sure strokes, and now Galen could believe that Nick swam as many laps a day as he claimed. It explained those broad, muscled shoulders and the lean, taut waist.

Nick reached the other end, smoothly flipped under water, and headed back toward him. His head popped up near the edge, and he folded his arms on the tiles as he looked at Galen. "Why aren't you naked?"

"Sorry, I was too busy watching you." Galen shrugged out of the rest of his clothes and folded them on the bench to give himself a moment to recover from the sudden spate of nerves. He had no reason to be shy. After all, Nick had seen him naked on more than one occasion. This time was different, and he couldn't figure out why.

He heard Nick get out of the water, and his pulse jumped. An arm slipped around him and pulled Galen back against a very warm, very wet body. "You're stalling. Did you change your mind?"

Galen shook his head, unable to speak. He repressed a shudder of longing as he clutched at Nick's arm, and he wondered what the other man would say if he knew what he was thinking. It had been a very long time since someone had awakened those deeply buried fantasies of being bound or spanked. It wasn't a desire that Bryan had understood. Hints from his past with Nick made him think he might be more open to the idea.

As if he read his mind, Nick's hand slid down to squeeze his flank. Galen's mind spun dizzily, and his breath came faster. He had the urge to lean over and lay his hands on the bench and spread his legs apart. He wanted to hear the sound of a wet palm against skin echo throughout this otherwise still chamber.

The shyness returned tenfold, and he finally realized why. Nick mattered. He hadn't been with anyone who had mattered to him in such a long time. He wanted to win Nick back, but he also wanted Nick to fall for who Galen really was, the whole package. Not the mess that he had been before, but who he was now with all of his obsessions with his museum, his inability to be still for any length of time, and all those other bits and parts of him that he hadn't let show before.

"What do you want?" Nick asked close to his ear, hot breath sending a shiver through him. "Tell me."

Galen wanted Nick's hands on him rough and hard. He wanted Nick to make him expose himself so that he felt vulnerable and safe at the same time. He wanted Nick to take him back to his place and have crazy sex until they were both exhausted, and then he wanted to wake up next to Nick in the morning.

The words remained locked in his head, unable to make their way to his tongue. As much as he tried, he couldn't seem to get past the last hurdle and open himself up to Nick more. And right now, feeling the hard press of Nick's cock against him made it very hard to think, period. The man got to him on such a visceral level.

"Not ready yet?" Nick asked, and his lips curved against Galen's ear. "No worries. I'll keep waiting for you, but for now, it's playtime."

Before Galen could react to that statement and the shock of lust it sent through him, he found himself hauled back toward the pool. *Oh crap.* His surprised cry of protest echoed shockingly loud off the walls. Too late he tried to twist away, only to find himself falling toward the still surface of the pool with Nick's arms locked securely around him. The smooth, silky water engulfed him, the sensation very sensual against his bare skin.

Galen emerged and shoved his wet hair out of his eyes to the sound of Nick chuckling. He turned to see Nick swimming backward away with a shit-eating grin on his face. "The look on your face, sweetheart. Come on, swim with me."

"Okay, it's on, Nicholas. Just wait till I catch you."

Nick laughed again and stopped a few lengths out of reach. "You're sexy when you're wet. Bring it."

The smile on Nick's face and his playfulness eased Galen's worry that he was shoving the other man away. Maybe Nick could see that he was working on it. Maybe he could open up to him, let him know about what happened with his last relationship without Nick freaking out and putting distance between them because he didn't want to be the rebound guy. Those were thoughts for another night though, because tonight, Nick needed a kiss and a dunking.

"FIFTEEN more minutes, and then I swear I'm outta here," a testy voice cut through the air as Nick walked through the museum's front entrance the following Saturday.

"I can get it done in twenty if you'd frickin' stay still."

The sound of a heated discussion came from the workshop, and Galen kept peering toward it with his eyebrows drawn together in mild concern as he rang up customers in the gallery. Several others browsed the shop, and a couple was disappearing down the hallway toward the exhibit. It didn't look as though he would get a break anytime soon to eat the lunch Nick had brought for him.

Nick caught his attention, pointing toward the workshop, and relief crossed Galen's face. "Could you rein it in for me? Thanks."

"No problem." Nick poked his head into the workroom. There was only a handful of kids in there and one rather bored-looking model who kept getting distracted by the people walking by outside. He guessed that being the object of an artist's muse wasn't everything it was cracked up to be. The source of the argument seemed to be between him and the young, pimply faced man painting him.

"Almost there, just move your hand back and stop twisting around, please," the artist said, sounding like he was striving for patience.

Several pairs of eyes turned toward Nick, some curious, others disinterested as they went back to what they were doing. "Hey, are you Mr. K's boyfriend?" the model asked, sitting up as the artist hissed in annoyance and then turned a glare on Nick.

"That's me. I'm Nick Charisteas." This time all activity stopped as the rest of the room focused their attention on him. "I take it the rumor mill has been going strong."

"Knox told us he was seeing someone." Nick's lips twitched in a smile as the model sized him up. Looked like someone had a case of wishful thinking where Galen was concerned.

A long table was set up on one end of the room where most of the artists were gathered working on various projects. The model lounged on a dais, and the painter sat at his easel. There was plenty of room for more people to set up their own projects, and with the bay doors, Nick imagined lighting was rarely a problem.

"Galen wants you two to take it down a notch," Nick said with a pointed look at the both of them. "If people can hear you in the gallery and shop, it's an issue."

"Sorry." The model grimaced with a shrug. "We're almost done here anyway... right?"

"I'm done now," the artist replied, tossing his paintbrush into a cup of water. "This is a damn mess. Next time, I'm taking a picture and painting from that. You're the worst model ever."

The model opened his mouth to protest, his eyes flashing hotly, and Nick interrupted him before he could start. "Don't. Galen's made a real nice place for you here. He's alone today and frazzled, so don't abuse his trust in you. Got it, guys?"

"Got it." The artist started cleaning up his brushes with a quick, disgusted glance at his model. "I promise, no more yelling."

"Thanks." Nick wanted to linger and take a look around to see what everybody else was working on, but he sensed that he was an unwelcome distraction, so he backed out instead and left them to get back to their projects.

It had started to rain, the drops making a soothing background murmur against the skylights and huge, glassed-in bay doors. Galen was wrapped up with the final customer, so Nick found an out-of-the-way spot to watch and wait. He liked how animated Galen got when he spoke, always gesturing to emphasize points. Galen didn't just speak with his hands; his whole body gave away his feelings on a subject.

Watching Galen was how Nick knew he was holding back on several levels. Galen hadn't mentioned the accident that had killed the last man he'd loved since he last brought it up. Sometimes Nick was okay with that, and sometimes he couldn't help wondering when Galen was going to backtrack because he didn't know if Galen had completely dealt with that loss. There was something left unspoken, something that still bugged Galen. Nick had tried getting him to talk a couple of times, and somehow the subject always ended up changed. And until Nick knew what other hurt Galen held onto, he couldn't be certain of where he stood with him.

A part of him said that he should cut his losses before he got in too deep; his cynical side said it was too late, and that tiny, nagging voice of hope kept urging him to give it more time. After all, they'd only been dating a few weeks, which was a vast improvement over the casual, sexual fling they'd had before.

And memories of Galen wrapped around him at the pool, kissing the breath out of him, made it hard to remember that they had decided to take their relationship much slower this time. Why the hell had they decided that? Nick wasn't sure anymore. However, he was glad Galen hadn't given in and told him what he wanted that night. He didn't want their first time, after all these months, to be rushed with the threat of being caught hanging over them.

Nick wanted to explore the new side he'd sensed in Galen that night. He hadn't missed the suppleness in Galen's body as he'd leaned back against him, or the new shyness, with those sideways, longing glances as if there was something he really wanted but was hesitant to say what it was. Nick had wondered then if he had ordered Galen to tell him what he wanted, whether the other man would've obeyed.

Another night he just might test that theory.

Galen glanced over and smiled as the customer walked away with a frame wrapped up in several layers of protective insulation. "Is that lunch? You're a lifesaver."

"Yep, lamb gyro, with extra tzatziki sauce and feta." Galen's eyes lit up, and he reached for the bag. "Where did everybody go? I know Suzane's out, but don't you normally have someone else helping you on Saturdays?"

"Heather had a family thing today. She felt bad about leaving me all alone, but I told her no worries, she'd helped me out Comicon day, and I figured Knox would be in at some point. It turns out he's doing a big move, and it's going to take most of the day. Ella's girlfriend dragged her out for a break earlier, and I hate asking her to keep an eye out on things for me because it makes her a nervous wreck."

"Well, for the rest of the day, I'm all yours." Nick handed Galen a soda and the bag with the gyro and chips. "What do you need me to do?"

"You don't have to if—"

"I do want to." Nick looked around at the gallery filled with pieces created by local gay artists, the door that led to the workshop where young artists could gather in a safe place to express themselves. This place was a haven. This was the kind of job he'd dreamed of having in college, and somewhere, it got muddled, or he got lost. "I really like what you've built here. It sure as hell beats doing a nine-to-five, shoving paperwork around."

"Thanks, Nick." There was that adorably flustered look in Galen's eyes that seemed to pop up more often as they continued to see each other. It made him want to kiss the expression right off his face. "What was going on in the workshop? I couldn't make out what they were arguing about. Vincent delivered the supplies this morning, and sometimes they take that as an excuse to open everything new instead of using up the old or to fight over the new pickings."

The name sounded familiar to Nick in a way that sent an unpleasant prickle through him, but he couldn't place it. He only knew a handful of the people who helped Galen with the museum, so he must've heard him mention the guy before. There were more than enough things going on lately to make him question everything.

"It was more of a staffing problem. The model was bored and wanted to be anywhere else but on the stand." Nick glanced back at the workshop that was now quiet. "I think they've resolved it. The artist is moving on to other things."

Galen grimaced and unwrapped the gyro. "I know who you're talking about, and that relationship is going downhill very fast." He gestured toward the hallway that led to the exhibits and shot Nick a pleading glance. "Would you mind checking in on the rest of the place? I haven't had a chance to go back there since Ella left, and she normally keeps an eye and ear out for me when we're understaffed."

"No problem." Nick left him to his lunch and checked the open exhibit room. There were a few patrons looking about, and no one had ventured past the roped-off area in the hallway that led to the new room. Nick stared at the statues for a few minutes. They unsettled him and excited him at the same time. He wanted to see the curse broken but had little faith that it would be, and the whole situation left him feeling stuck in limbo.

He returned to the photograph exhibit and chatted with a few patrons, answering what questions he could. When he came back to Galen, he was cleaning off the counter from his lunch. "All clear, Galen."

"Excellent."

Nick's phone rang, and his stomach dropped at the sound of the ringtone he'd set aside for his dad. The calls had been coming more frequently, and each time he let it go unanswered, the cold, lonely sensation inside him deepened even more. He missed his family.

Galen crossed his arms on the counter. "You're not going to answer?"

Nick grimaced and shrugged. "It can wait." Though hadn't it waited long enough? He was only making it worse, and he knew he was making it worse, yet he couldn't seem to stop the twisted carousel he was on. It had gotten to be such a mess, and he didn't know who to blame anymore or how to set it right.

Galen studied his face and leaned closer. "Who is it? You never seem to answer the call. At least not when I'm around. And you've got a look on your face like it's the IRS or an obnoxious telemarketer."

"Oh no, nothing like that. It's my dad." Nick looked away, pressing his lips together.

"What is it?"

Nick hesitated, torn between wanting to get Galen's opinion on the situation and... to be honest, a little ashamed to go into it. "Nothing so.... Is there anything else I can do around here?"

"Look, I know it's not really my business to say something—"

"Then don't." Nick turned away so he wouldn't have to see Galen's expression change. He didn't know why he did that, shoved people away when he knew logically they were just reaching out to him. Logic seemed to have no control over his emotions. He rubbed his thumb over the cell phone case. He had to put a stop to this circling madness, and for the first time he admitted to himself that he was scared it was too late.

"If you want to shut me out, fine, but whatever it is between you and your dad, you need to find a way to address it, whether it's by talking to someone else about it, talking to him, or finding some Zen, because what you're doing isn't working," Galen said, his tone more exasperated than angry.

Nick turned back toward him and squirmed inside at the steady way Galen regarded him. "I'm sorry, I shouldn't have snapped at you."

Galen shrugged, opened a fat file stuffed with documents, and spread the contents out on the counter. "Don't be sorry; just do something about whatever it is that's going on inside your head. I don't like seeing you flinch every time the phone rings."

"What do you have there?" Nick asked, thrusting his chin out toward the file.

"Everything that Suzane was working on for the opening of the exhibit." Galen began leafing through the contents. "Catering information, stuff for the silent auction, and on and on. I don't know what's actually been done and what hasn't. I'd like to tie up some loose ends for her before she comes back so she doesn't go into panic mode."

Galen shoved a hand through his hair with a grimace. "And don't even get me started on the accounting chores I've let slide."

"Let me take a look at it." Nick held out his hand for the file, grateful for something to do. "Paperwork is my specialty."

CHAPTER FOURTEEN

NICK moved through the museum, turning down the lights and checking to make sure doors were locked. Galen was up in his tower office, going over the account books for the day. He'd enjoyed helping Galen out with the museum while Suzane had been gone, even if there wasn't much left to do by the time he got off work in the evenings.

Galen really did need more permanent help. He rarely took a day off that Nick could tell, and often he was juggling both running the place as well as staffing it if Heather couldn't come in. It was like the museum had become his whole life. Nick knew he had family nearby, but he wasn't sure how often Galen saw them, and he wondered what Galen had done for fun and relaxation before they'd started dating.

Suzane was returning tomorrow, and Nick hoped that Galen wouldn't mind him continuing to insinuate himself into the day-to-day activities of the museum. The thought of coming here after work got him through the daily grind even more than dreaming of his vacations had. And damned if it didn't wake up other dreams that he'd thought had died and been buried.

The work he did was practical, stable, and not at all what he'd wanted when he started college. But it was either change his major from Art History to something more marketable or quit school to come back and work for his dad. Nick winced. He hated that there was a little part of himself that still resented the ultimatum. He understood why his dad had pushed for the change. College had cost a lot of money that they couldn't really afford, and Nick hadn't had a plan for his life after he graduated.

Nick walked into Dexios's exhibit and was struck by how uncluttered it seemed with all of Ella's equipment moved out. Her finished mural was draped in shadows now, but he'd had the pleasure of being present at her very nervous unveiling earlier. Soon Galen would start bringing in the final pieces, and Nick couldn't wait to see how it all looked together.

Nick wanted his dad to see it too. He closed his eyes, stuck his hand in his pocket, and traced the hard outline of his phone. It was a little crazy. Ever since he'd left home he'd been sure that this Collection was his ticket back into his family. His dad would see that there was some merit in having a dream, no matter how improbable it seemed.

He could just hear his dad now, telling him that he was wasting his time with the statues, that they couldn't afford the insurance on them, and a hundred other practical details his dad would latch onto instead of seeing the wonder of having found something that had been lost to their family for decades. His dad wouldn't see those things, and his brothers would take his side, because once again Nick was causing trouble. He just wished they could understand that he needed some space to be himself and that leaving San Francisco wasn't a personal betrayal.

Was this what it had been like for his mom after she'd left? Maybe she had wanted to make amends and be a part of their lives only to feel too guilty, too afraid, until it just became easier to move on.

Nick did not want to move on. He didn't want to destroy those last ties, yet he was letting it happen without even a token protest. What the hell was wrong with him? If he didn't try he could forget about being godfather to Jason and Sophia's baby. He could count on Stefan and Damian never talking to him again. And worst of all, knowing he hurt them, hurt his dad.

"Why do you look so mournful?"

Nick turned to look at Galen, only it wasn't his boyfriend who stood at the entrance. The accent was wrong, the set of his shoulders not quite right. Lykon, not Galen, and it was Galen who he longed to confide in. "You shouldn't take control without his permission. He doesn't like it. It isn't right."

"You are hurting." Lykon stepped closer and reached out as if to touch him, and Nick stepped away.

"Yeah, well, there's nothing you can do to help." Nick pulled out his phone. Galen had urged him to call his dad several times since they'd last talked about it. He had asked Nick what was the worst that could happen. And each time Nick had brushed him off. He didn't even want to voice the worst.

He looked at Lykon, and all the frustration and anger at himself leapt up and turned on him. "Leave Galen alone. He is not your toy. He is not yours to use to get what you want. And we'll both fight you on that. I swear to God, if you keep grabbing at him like you have been, I'll make sure the curse never gets broken."

Lykon's eyes widened, and he took a step back. "You would not do something so evil." His expression became bewildered, and he shook his head. "I cannot believe you would have changed so much, Dexios."

"Let's get this straight. I am not Dexios." Nick stabbed his finger toward the statue. "Dexios is trapped in there, just as you are trapped in Galen. We may be parts of you reborn, but we are our own persons, and we do not need you pushing and shoving us around. Have you ever thought that maybe that's why every generation fucks this up? Next time you want to talk to me, you'd better ask Galen for permission first."

He turned his back on Lykon, his heart aching even more. He'd always dreamed of finding the statues, and this wasn't at all what he'd expected. It was supposed to be a triumph, but now that he had dived so deep into the mysteries surrounding the statues, he didn't know where the surface was or how to get to it before he ran out of air.

Nick called his dad before he could change his mind, his stomach clenching into a knot almost as hard as his fist, which hung at his side. It couldn't be too late. He had to find a way to fix this, because if he couldn't fix his relationship with his family, how could he hope to build anything with Galen?

"Nick, you worry an old man when you shut me out." Nick closed his eyes again at the sound of his dad's voice. He did sound old. The realization struck him hard. Old and tired and sad. He loved his dad's voice, and the sound of it brought a thousand memories, most of them good. "Have I done something that offended you? Have I hurt you in some way?"

How like his dad. Damian and Stefan accused Nick of being selfish, of being like their mom. And his dad blamed himself for Nick's silence, just as he'd blamed himself for Nick's mom leaving. "It's not you, Dad, it's all me. I'm sorry."

The silence on the other end of the line weighed on his soul, had him scrambling for some excuse to hang up before he heard what he didn't want to hear. Nick sat down on the edge of the dais that lifted up the first statue. He could sense Dexios behind him, and he wondered if Lykon remained in the room, lurking. He didn't want to turn around and see him watching out of Galen's eyes. He had to find a way to put a stop to Lykon taking over Galen before it got ugly.

"Explain it to me, because I've been trying to understand." His dad broke the silence, and Nick's heart contracted. "I thought maybe you needed to go explore yourself, so I tried not to resist when you moved out of state. I thought giving you space to breathe would bring you back, so I tried not to pressure you, and now I keep thinking that you're slipping away even more."

Nick traced his finger over Lykon's sandaled foot, the metal in the statue cool and textured against his skin. "I don't feel a part of the family anymore," he finally said, the words forcing their way out of his throat. "I've felt like I've been on the outside looking in for a very long time now."

The scuff of a foot against the floor alerted him, and he looked up to see Galen, his face lost in shadow. At first he wasn't sure it really was Galen at all until he came closer and Nick saw the concern in his eyes, a familiar expression, not one slightly foreign.

There was a question on his face, and Nick answered it by scooting over and patting the bare spot next to him. Nick didn't want him to leave. Galen sat down and offered Nick his hand, and after a long moment he took it with a grateful squeeze.

"Whose fault is that? You don't answer when I call. You don't return calls except for on a rare occasion, and when you do, you don't talk about what is going on with your life. You haven't been home for a holiday in years, and your brothers have little confidence that you'll be here this year. What else can I do to make you feel welcome?"

Nick looked down at his hand clasped with Galen's. It scared him. Close relationships had scared him for a long time. Only now he thought that maybe the longing to not be so lonely anymore, to not survive off superficial connections, outweighed the fear. And instead of pulling away and searching for privacy he clung to Galen's sure grip. Oddly enough, it seemed like he and Galen were battling the same issues, only he was sure Galen had a better grip on his than Nick did.

Nick wanted reassurance that his dad accepted him for who he was and not just Nick the dreamer. The subject of him being gay had not really been brought up since he came out to his family. It was like the huge elephant in the room that everybody danced around and nobody acknowledged. Not even Nick. He was afraid to bring it up again only to find more silence.

"Hey, Dad, remember those statues Uncle Stavros was so obsessed over?" Nick glanced behind him, and his breath caught as he found both Dexios and Lykon watching him from their embrace. Galen glanced up too, and shook his head with a wry expression on his lips.

"I don't understand. What do the statues have to do with anything? I'm talking about your family, and you're bringing up legends." His dad never raised his voice, but Nick could hear the palpable frustration in his voice. "Call me when you're ready to let me in. I don't want to talk about Uncle Stavros. I want to talk about you. I want to know about your job, whether you're seeing someone. I want to know if you're happy in Seattle."

"I am seeing someone," Nick blurted out, scrambling to find some way of keeping the connection before his dad hung up. And as soon as the words were out of his mouth he regretted them. What if his dad was still disappointed that he was gay, just as he'd been disappointed when Nick went off to college, or decided that he wanted to move, or a dozen other things that Nick could name?

"You are?" Cautious pleasure replaced frustration, and Nick braced himself for his dad's next words. "Who is it? Is he special? Do you care about him?"

He, not she. The tension that Nick had been carrying for years cracked at that one little word. He glanced at Galen, who watched him with the kind of support in his eyes that Nick had never imagined he could have from him. Galen made him feel like he was a whole person, not a shadow. And all those feelings he'd been fighting clicked inside of him. Nick loved him, maybe he'd never stopped. Only this time, there seemed to be a lot more of Galen to love.

"Yeah, I think he's pretty special." Galen smiled and squeezed his hand. "I'm at his museum right now, and we're in the middle of shutting it down for the night. Then we're grabbing something to eat."

"You do not know how happy that makes me." His dad hesitated. "I'll let you get back to him, but you'll call again right?" Doubt crept into his dad's voice. "I want to hear all about him and you. You'll call?"

Guilt made him want to squirm in shame. He really had let it get this bad. "Yeah, I'll call you this week. I promise."

Nick hung up the phone and stared at it for a long minute, trying to work through all the complex emotions and thoughts that crowded his brain. On the one hand, he wished his dad had let him tell him about the statues, but to know that he'd been so wrong about his dad's feelings over him being gay… that lifted the worst of the weight.

"Could have gone better?" Galen asked, leaning into him.

"Actually no, I think it could've gone a lot worse." Nick looked over at him as a hope that he hadn't dared to believe in surged to the surface. "I think maybe things might be okay."

Galen smiled and kissed him. "That's what I was wishing for, for you."

Nick twisted toward Galen and cupped the side of his neck. "You feel okay? Lykon didn't screw you up, make you dizzy?"

"I don't think we have to worry about him for a while. You scared him pretty good." Galen kissed him again and smiled against his lips. "Come on, I think we've both earned a drink."

"CLOSE your eyes," Galen insisted to Suzane as they stopped just before the new exhibit.

"Please tell me you didn't find some more mysterious statues while I was gone," Suzane said as she closed her eyes and extended her hand for Galen to guide her. "We're well into April, and the opening is only two months off. If you add anything new it's going to make the whole exhibit seem cluttered."

"Nope, nothing like that."

"And nothing else weird has happened? You can tell me. I prepared myself."

"I've gotten used to the weird," Galen said with a chuckle. "And nothing else has happened to freak me out. We're good, I swear."

Galen steadied her as he led her toward the first part of Ella's finished mural. It stretched from the entrance down the entire length of the next wall on either side, the colors vibrant, the scenes flowing from one to the next against a mountainous background. Ella had outdone herself. The robed women showed sisterhood and intimacy in the clasp of hands, a head bent toward another with smiles as secrets were shared. It wasn't as blatantly erotic as some of the other pieces in the room, but there was a cupped breast there, a flash of thigh in another place. It was simply beautiful.

"Okay, ready? You're going to swoon."

"Get on with it, you. I'm not getting any younger." The comment struck Galen with a bittersweet blow. The last chemo treatment had laid her low for days. And he'd missed her fiercely while she'd been gone with her sister. At least the time off had done her some good. Her color was back, and her attitude was all there.

"You're still my lady of the spring," Galen teased, moving to the side so he could see her face. "You can look now."

Suzane's eyes popped open and delight suffused her face. "Oh, it's perfect. So much more than I imagined." She moved closer, studying all the little details, and then slowly walked down the length of the wall and back. "You could stare at this for hours and keep finding something new to look at. Where's Ella? I have to congratulate her."

"She and her girlfriend took off for parts unknown for a bit. You know how Ella is. Besides, she put in weeks of work. She needs to recharge."

"She'll be back for the opening, won't she?" Suzane cast him a look of appeal. "You can't let her duck out. She deserves every bit of the praise she's going to get."

"Ella assured me that she and Nicole will be here," Galen replied with a smile. Ella had balked at the idea of attending the opening until Galen reminded her she was more than welcome to bring Nicole.

"I can't wait." Suzane turned around, taking in the room that was coming together piece by piece. By the look in her eye, Galen knew she was picturing how it would look the night of the reception, and he had to grin. If there was anyone more excited than he was about the opening, it was Suzane. "So who are you bringing?" Suzane said with a sly smile. "Don't count on me being your date. My son finagled that invite. And I swear if you say you're going alone, I'll kick you."

"As a matter of fact, I do have a date," Galen said, then lifted an eyebrow as Suzane's expression turned to surprise. "What? You didn't expect that, did you?"

"I knew it!" Suzane tapped him on the arm with her fist. "Knox told me that you actually left on time almost every night while I was gone and that a guy was hanging around, though he didn't say who. You haven't done that in months. I look forward to meeting whoever has dragged you out of your self-imposed isolation." She paused and narrowed her eyes at him. "It's Nick, isn't it?"

Galen grinned and polished his nails on his shirt, delighted by the way she started tapping her foot. He'd really missed her. "Maybe."

"Ugh, you're impossible." She threw up her hands and headed for the door. "I'm sparing you the indignity of me digging for details. I have a ton of e-mails and paperwork to catch up on."

"You do that, and I'll go see if Heather needs anything up front before I get started on my own work. It's about time we opened our doors for the day. Hey, Suzane," he called as she reached the entranceway, striding briskly in her impossible heels. "It's damn good to have you back."

Suzane laughed, the sound rich and warm despite the lingering circles under her eyes. "Darling, I'm too ornery to go anywhere."

Galen smiled and waited until the sound of her heels faded before he turned toward the second unfinished statue of Dexios. There were times, like now, when he could almost see a mirage of Lykon kneeling before him, still clad in his armor, leaning to take Dexios's cock in his mouth.

The echo of Lykon stirred inside of him, but at least this time he didn't struggle to come out. Not since Nick had made his threat. Almost a month had passed, and nothing had changed, except for those momentary glimpses of what the statue could be like if it was whole.

Well, nothing had changed with the statues anyway. He'd had weeks of nightly evenings with Nick, really getting to know him this time instead of being afraid to look past the surface, weekends filled with him. And if Galen was afraid he was falling when he left Nick all those months ago, that was nothing compared to how he felt now. Nick made him believe in second chances. He made Galen feel like he wasn't so broken anymore.

Nick had loved him once, maybe did again, and Galen still couldn't say what he felt for Nick in return. The words caught on his tongue, froze his throat. And maybe the remaining hesitance was why neither one of them had pushed that hard for sex. Galen wanted him without a doubt. There were nights when he left Nick's place, or when he walked Nick to the door of the apartment, where the sexual tension had him about to come out of his skin. He needed to get over this last hurdle, this fear of losing someone else he loved. It wasn't fair to Nick.

Galen needed to tell Nick about the night that Bryan died. He deserved to know why Galen had been in such a bad place for so long. Because apparently, the fear of loss still had a hard hold of him. He'd talk to him tonight. Galen smiled and touched Dexios's elbow. Maybe the conversation would help them both. He wanted to unburden himself to someone he trusted and to show Nick he could open up to him the way he wanted. The statue in front of him shimmered, and the image of Lykon became a little sharper, a little stronger.

"Galen! Galen!"

Galen was startled out of his reverie by Heather's frantic voice, and the mirage in front of him faded away. He bolted for the hallway and caught Heather's shoulders just before she barreled into him. "What's wrong?"

"It's Suzane. She collapsed." Heather's blue eyes were wide with panic, and all the color had left her face. "She's unconscious. What do we do?"

A chill seized Galen's heart. "She just left me and she was fine. What the hell happened? Where is she?" He took off down the hallway with Heather right behind him.

"I stopped by her office to welcome her back, and she was on the floor. There's blood. What do we do?"

"Is she breathing? Did you call 911?" Galen yanked out his phone as Heather stammered behind him, fumbling for an answer.

"I'm sorry; I didn't know what to do. I can't handle dead people. I go all to pieces when someone's hurt. And blood... I can't do it, I just can't."

Galen spun on her and stopped her babbling with a stern look as fury and terror seized hold of him. She'd left Suzane on the floor and didn't call an ambulance. She was just a scared part-time college student who'd gone for the first help she'd thought of. "Calm down, take a deep breath. Now, go around the back to meet the ambulance. You're going to have to direct them to her office."

He didn't wait for her answer and continued on. The 911 operator answered the phone as he reached her office. To his profound relief, Suzane was pushing herself up to a sitting position, her wig askew and dark curls straggling in her face. *Oh thank God.* He steadied himself with his hand on the rail before moving toward her.

Galen dropped to his knees to steady her and winced at the sight of a lump on her brow and the blood that oozed from the cut there. "Hey, take it easy. Don't try to get up. I think you whacked your hard head pretty good." He answered the 911 operator's questions and hung up after she said help was on the way.

"I don't need a damn ambulance," Suzane muttered, attempting to straighten her hair. "I'm fine, got a little dizzy. See, all better now."

"That's too bad," Galen replied, taking in her slightly unfocused look and the icy chill in her hands, "'cause they're already on their way. Looks like you might have a concussion."

Suzane groaned and pushed him, but it lacked her usual strength. "Call them back and cancel it."

"Nope. And you're going with them too, if they recommend it, or else I'll call your son," Galen said with false cheer, trying to hide how worried he was. Was it just a dizzy spell or was it something worse?

"You wouldn't." In the distance he heard the ambulance, and it brought back memories he'd rather forget, waiting for another ambulance, holding someone else he loved in his arms. This time it would end much differently.

"Try me, sunshine. Just try me."

CHAPTER FIFTEEN

GALEN sat in the waiting room, his elbows on his knees, his head down and hands clasped over the back of his neck. The doctors wouldn't tell him a damn thing, and they wouldn't let him back to see Suzane either. He would have to wait until Clint, Suzane's son, arrived before he would get an update. The only thing he did know was that she hadn't been admitted yet, and he could only hope that was a good sign.

He had come in with her, shouldn't that count? It didn't, he knew that, no more than it had counted when he'd wanted to sit with Bryan until his family got there. Galen squeezed his eyes tight against the memory. This wasn't the same. Suzane had knocked her head. The worst-case scenario would be that she had a concussion. They'd patch her up, maybe observe her overnight. They might have to keep an eye out for more dizzy spells. That was it. She *would* be going home.

There was no chance of her being dead in there while Galen waited out here on the vain hope of a miracle. Telling himself that didn't help any more than telling himself that the dizzy spell was a random incident and it had nothing to do with her cancer. What if... so many what-ifs crowded his mind, and his thoughts bounced from one to another. He couldn't do this again. He would go out of his skin if he waited here any longer.

He wanted to call Nick again. He knew that if he could get a hold of him, from whatever meeting Nick was in, he wouldn't be waiting alone. Nick would drop what he was doing and come right over. Galen straightened and picked up a magazine to leaf through. He stared at the pages with unseeing eyes, unable to stop thinking about how Nick would be there for him.

That was the problem. Galen wished he knew if he could give Nick the same commitment in return. He wanted to, but he didn't know if he could open himself up to being that vulnerable again. Not after being slapped in the face with another hospital scare. Fear had grabbed a hold of his guts and was hanging on tight. If something happened to Nick… he didn't know what he'd do.

That same sick fear also told him it was too late to save himself possible future heartache. Galen was too invested in Nick now. So, he'd better do something and do something quick to stop this freak-out he was having.

He tensed as he sensed Lykon stir, but for once there wasn't the least bit of a fight for possession. The last time Lykon had struck so fast he'd barely had time to register the attack before he took control. Galen supposed the man must've taken Nick's threat as a serious promise.

Good. Just because he sometimes liked to surrender control to someone he trusted didn't mean he wanted someone else to come along and yank it from him.

He jerked his head up as the door opened, then deflated when the doctor who came in moved toward a waiting couple. He tried Suzane's son's phone again and still no answer. Poor kid. He was going to freak when he got the message. He tried Nick again, both his work and his cell phone, only to have both go straight to voice mail. Galen hung up without leaving a message and shoved his hands in his pockets. He could sense Lykon even stronger now and knew even without the struggle that the man was dying to emerge, but he didn't.

This time when the door opened, Galen didn't move. He continued to stare at the magazine, his brain still caught in the same looping thoughts of wishing Nick were there, all mixed in with worry over Suzane and attempts to think more positively before he had a meltdown. Someone sat down next to him, and Galen was enveloped by the scent of a very familiar perfume.

Galen's eyes stung as he looked over at his mom. She'd always had a knack for showing up whenever one of her kids needed her the most. He didn't know what instinct led her, but it was dead on. And now she was here with her too curly, graying hair pulled back into a messy bun, with her faded T-shirt, worn sweatpants, and enormous purse stuffed to the point of not being able to snap shut. She must have come straight from the gym, determined to lose the last twenty pounds that she'd been trying to lose for as long as he could remember. He kind of hoped it never happened.

"I picked up Suzane's son from his class, and he's talking with the head nurse now," Anna Kanellis said without preamble and pulled out a tin of mints from her purse. She popped two in her mouth and offered him the tin.

"How'd you know I was here?" Galen asked and took a mint for himself.

"I called the museum looking for you, and Heather told me what happened. I got a hold of your sister, and she's going over to help." She fixed him with a stern look over the rim of her glasses. "You take on too much. You need to stop and ask for help sometimes. It really won't hurt your pride, I swear. Maybe sting it, but you're a big boy, you can take it."

Galen scrubbed a hand over his face. Oh God. Heather. He hadn't even thought about her running the place by herself, especially after the scare she had. He was an idiot. "Thanks, Mom." He'd have to call and give her an update as soon as he had one.

"You know I don't mind." She patted his hand. "How are you holding up?"

Galen shrugged and tried not to think about all the reasons for that question. He did not want to remember, even if they kept intruding anyway. "I'm here, aren't I?"

"That doesn't say much. You wouldn't not be here until you had answers, especially with Suzane being alone. You'd stay, no matter how much it hurt you. Now, tell me again, how are you?"

"Honestly? I'm a mess." He was sitting there contemplating running again from the best thing that had happened to him in a long time. He could lose Nick. The way he lost Bryan, the way he lost his dad... maybe even Suzane if the treatments stopped working. The thought made him want to shudder. Walking away meant losing him for sure. Nick wouldn't give him a third chance, and he couldn't blame him. Walking away meant that he would hurt Nick more than he already had. So, it wasn't an option.

His mom slid her arm through his. "And you're blaming yourself too, no doubt." Galen shifted in his chair. She knew him so well.

"You're nobody's keeper but your own. So stop assuming responsibility for others. They won't thank you for it."

Easier said than done, even if she was right. "So why'd you call the museum and not my cell?" Galen asked. She must've called the main line and not his office number if she got Heather. "What are you up to?"

"I am up to nothing. You're implying that what I'm doing is wrong."

Galen patted her hand on his arm. "Not wrong. Underhanded, maybe. Sneaky, definitely. But not wrong."

"You're letting your imagination run away with you." His mom scraped the escaped curls back from her face and retied her bun. "I wanted to invite you to Sunday dinner. You haven't been in a long time. And since I knew the excuse you were going to give me, I planned on nipping it in the bud before you tried."

"Meaning you were going to harass poor Heather or Knox or someone else into covering for me on one of our busier days."

"I'm not even asking for a whole day. I think you can get off early one Sunday every couple of months." It would be better if she at least looked exasperated about it; instead, the expression of insistent reason made him squirm now almost as much as it had when he was younger. Well, it was only a matter of time before she renewed her pledge to see that he was doing more than working all day, every day.

"Okay, you're right. I can do that." Agreeing cost him nothing except peace from her checking on him.

She paused, mouth parted, no doubt about to launch her next argument. Then she cocked her head and studied him. She didn't say anything when she sat back, her expression serene. He wished he knew what she was speculating. They sat in silence, waiting for Clint to come in with an update on Suzane. Maybe they already brought him back to see her. Galen's mom pulled out her latest crocheting project from her purse and got to work as if she was sitting in her living room and not keeping him from entirely losing his cool by her presence.

"Is it okay if I bring somebody to Sunday dinner?" *Shit*. As soon as the words were out of his mouth Galen scrambled for a way to take them back. It wasn't that he didn't want to tell her about Nick, because he'd love for them to meet each other. He just didn't want to talk about Nick while sitting in a hospital. "Not that I'm saying anything, just wondering."

"Any friend you bring is fine with me." She finished the row of stitches and pulled some more yarn out of the ball. "You know that."

Galen waited for her to ask who, but she didn't. She could be so unruffled at times; it was annoying and unnatural too. She knew she didn't have to ask because he'd eventually cave and talk to her.

She started another row and paused to look over her glasses at him again. "About what's eating at you right now, talk with someone. It doesn't have to be me. Or Suzane. Or your brother and sister. Maybe you could talk to that new friend of yours. You've been making steps toward moving on, and I'm happy to see it. Talking means it doesn't fester, okay? Take it from somebody who knows."

Galen slid his arm around her shoulder and kissed her temple. "I love you, Mom. Thank you."

She smiled and patted the side of his head. "Anytime, dear."

GALEN sat on the bench outside of Nick's apartment building, the late afternoon sun warm on his face. He was drained inside and out. Suzane's scare had woken up too many memories best left buried, and they'd all come roaring back today. At least it was just a scare. Repeating it did little to settle him, and every time he heard sirens in the distance, a quiet leap of fear grabbed a hold of his windpipe and strangled him.

"Galen? Why aren't you at the museum?" Nick's quiet voice broke through his thoughts, and Galen's eyes flew open. "Not that I'm not happy to see you early, but I thought we weren't meeting here till tonight. What's wrong?"

He held out his hand, and Nick took it with a warm clasp of his fingers. "I needed to see you."

"Okay, now you're worrying me." Nick tugged on his hand, pulling him up. "Let's go upstairs, and you can tell me what happened."

"Suzane fainted and gave herself a concussion falling in her office." A few inches in another direction and she could've died. He tried not to think like that. "I spent the morning with her in the ER before a room opened for her. They want to keep her overnight for observation." And how Suzane had protested. She'd ripped into him, her son, and anybody unwary enough to step into the room before she'd finally settled down.

Galen had taken it all and dismissed it because he knew deep down how afraid she was of hospitals, how she didn't want to end up dying in one. He'd lashed out more than once after Bryan had died, and she'd taken his tantrums in stride. He could do no less in return.

"Is she okay? Do they know what caused it?" Nick asked as he unlocked his door and ushered Galen inside.

"Her iron is very low. Her blood cells are taking longer to come back after chemo, and she's wearing out. Thankfully, it's almost over. I hate seeing her like this."

"I'm sorry, I didn't know or I would've been there." As soon as the door shut, Galen pulled Nick into his arms. He needed to know that he was real, to feel him, dammit, to feel period. Nick didn't resist, he held Galen back and kissed his temple. "You should've called me."

"I did, but you were in meetings, and I didn't want to scare you by leaving a message. I should've, but I was spending too much time talking myself into a very bad place." It felt so good to be held again, to be cared for. Maybe opening himself up to that vulnerability was worth it, just for the moments like this. "Then I realized I was an idiot and that I needed to be with you, so I came over."

"Come on, we'll order a pizza, I'll grab us some beers, and we can watch a movie, relax some," Nick suggested, starting to ease away. It was the same every night—they'd reach a certain point, and one or both of them would pull back. Not tonight. Tonight Galen needed to experience every bit of the heat between them.

"No." Galen kissed him, a tender brush of his lips that made him ache inside. He kissed Nick again, seeking more contact, and their lips parted in sweet, open-mouthed kisses that offered the slightest taste and left him needing more. "I don't want another quiet night. I want you."

Nick cocked his head and searched his face, a tiny line appearing between his eyebrows. "This isn't the bad place where your mind went, is it?"

Galen shook his head. He didn't dare tell Nick that he'd had the momentary thought of walking away, because he wasn't going to. Telling him would only hurt him for no reason and make him doubt. "No, I'm not reverting to old behavior. I'm not looking for a quick, meaningless fuck. I'm here because with you it does mean something, and I need that tonight. You fill up that empty place inside of me, and I don't want that to stop."

Nick smiled and dropped another kiss on Galen's lips. To Galen's relief, Nick didn't hesitate anymore. He didn't ask Galen if he was sure. He took Galen's hand and led him down the short hallway to his bedroom, tossing off his suit coat along the way. Sunlight spilled through the half-open slats of the blinds, making lines of light on the bed. Galen's heart pounded as Nick sat on the edge and kicked off his shoes before beckoning to him. "I have been imagining you naked nearly every waking hour these last couple of weeks. It's been making me crazy. And it's gotten worse since we went swimming."

"You and me both." Galen laughed under his breath and tugged his shirt off over his head as he slipped out of his own shoes.

"Wait a minute. How did I miss this before?" Nick's gaze locked on the tattoo low on Galen's left hip, and he snagged Galen's wrist to pull him closer. "When did you get a tattoo?"

Galen touched the top of it where it peeked out over the waist of his jeans. He tugged the material lower so Nick could see all of it. It wasn't big, about an inch or so high, very easy to miss, especially in the dim light of the pool. "About a month or so before I called you. I wanted a reminder. I seemed to need it."

Nick traced the outline of the stylized ankh with his fingertip. The light touch sent a wave of goose bumps over him. It had been too long since he'd let a touch matter to him. "What did you need to remember?"

"Lots of things, I guess. It changes from day to day. Sometimes it's that life goes on, and sometimes it's that life is meant to be lived, not merely put up with." Galen laid his hand over Nick's, taking in the press of his fingers. Their eyes met, and they reached for each other at the same time.

Nick bore him back down on the bed and kissed the center of his chest. "That's a sentiment I can agree with. Live with me."

Galen's heart leapt up, and before he could ask Nick what he meant by that statement, he was being kissed. He groaned, heat and desire sweeping everything else away. He pulled Nick's dress shirt free from his pants and began undoing each button slowly, in no rush despite the demands of his body.

Nick savored him, his tongue stroking Galen's in long, slow sweeps, his lips nibbling, making him dizzy. Galen parted Nick's shirt and slid his palms up Nick's chest. Why the hell had he waited this long? Why couldn't he have seen sooner that Nick was perfect for him?

"I want you, Nick. Just you, nobody else," Galen whispered against his mouth as the kiss eased.

"I'm going to hold you to that." Nick shrugged out of his shirt and kissed the design etched on Galen's skin. "Since we're being so honest with each other tonight.... Now that I've got you here and you're not hiding anymore, I'm telling you I'm not letting you go. So if you think you're going to change your mind, now's the time to tell me."

Galen stared up into the shadows of Nick's eyes and knew there was no going back. He was lost the minute he'd picked up the phone to call Nick about those statues. He'd known that then, even if he hadn't acknowledged it. "I'm not going to change my mind. Not about you. I'm in this to stay."

CHAPTER SIXTEEN

NICK stared into Galen's eyes, and there was none of the smooth bullshit he'd seen in the past. And he had no reason to not trust Galen's words, other than his heart feared to take the risk with him again. His heart was going to have to get over it because there was no way in hell that Nick was going to let this moment slip through his fingers.

He knelt up and got rid of the rest of their clothes, then stared down at Galen sprawled naked on his bed. He had him all to himself this time. And as head over heels crazy as he'd been for Galen last time, it was nothing compared to how he felt now. Then it had been like trying to worship a distant star or a quicksilver flame he couldn't touch without burning himself.

This Galen was so much more approachable and open. There was a kindness in him that Nick hadn't seen before. Now Nick was truly in love with Galen. Now he could see a future together with him. Whatever dark place Galen had gone to before hadn't stopped him from coming to Nick.

Galen sat up with a laugh and braced his hands on the bed. "You're looking at me like you don't know where to start because you want it all at once."

Nick laughed in return and rocked forward onto his hands and knees, feeling Galen's heat as he nuzzled his jaw. "You were right, we still had a lot to learn about each other, and so far I'm liking what I've discovered."

Galen tipped his head back, turning it to the side as he offered up his throat. A shudder rippled through him as Nick's lips drifted down. In that reaction he sensed Galen's anticipation. He'd wondered if Galen still preferred forceful over gentle, and his open invitation for rough nips and bites had Nick's cock surging.

"What do you want?"

"You know what I want," Galen replied in a voice thick with longing. He shifted his weight to one hand and sank his other hand into Nick's hair, pulling him closer. "Please."

Nick smiled against his skin, heat rippling through him as the edge of anticipation sharpened even more. He nuzzled and pressed kisses to his sensitive skin while Galen squirmed and panted, seeking more, a rougher touch, greater contact. Sensing the tension in his body, Nick slid his hand up Galen's ribcage. His thumb flicked the tightened nipples, making Galen groan.

"You're a damn tease."

Nick smiled again. "I've been waiting a long time for this, and I'm savoring every minute."

Galen's hand tightened in his hair, and before he could turn the tables on him, Nick bit him harder just the way he liked, enough to redden but not break the skin. Galen's breath came out on a husky groan, and his grip slackened as he trembled. "Oh God, do that again."

Nick loved the note of pleading in his voice, the way Galen's body became supple from desire and need. Galen's hand slid from Nick's hair to cup his cock and closed his fist around it, pumping. Nick kissed the spot where he'd bitten him, then shifted to another spot that made Galen shiver with a whimpering sound before Nick had even parted his lips.

"I think I could get you to do just about anything I wanted if I played with your neck long enough." Nick's teeth grazed it, and Galen squeezed his dick in answer.

"I think you're right. It makes me absolutely crazy." Galen turned his head and caught Nick's mouth, kissing him deeply. He lay back on the bed, pulling Nick down with him. Galen slid his hands all over him, exploring, teasing, wonderful hands, as his tongue played with Nick's. Now it was Nick's turn to shudder as the man underneath him reacquainted himself with Nick's body.

They broke apart, panting, and Galen stared up at him, his eyes dark with desire, sunlight slanting across his face. "I want to be helpless with you." A bit of uncertainty crept into his expression. "Unless that weirds you out."

Nick's breath came out in a rush. They'd hinted at that before, and Galen had always pulled back. He'd never been sure if it had been because Galen didn't want to trust that much or if he'd been afraid of his own desires, so he hadn't pushed for it.

"Not at all. Are you sure that's what you want?" Nick asked, even as his body screamed yes, to take Galen up on his offer, to hold him down and make him cry out and writhe underneath him. Galen must've seen the truth in his face because his uncertainty vanished and he gave Nick a wicked grin.

"Yes, I am, and so are you." He arched his hips and rubbed his cock against Nick's thigh. "All those times you held yourself back because we weren't alone or because you didn't think you had the right…. I sensed it, I wanted it then, but it wasn't the right time, and I kept second-guessing myself and the signals you were giving me. This time is right."

Nick thought his heart was about to beat right out of his chest as all sorts of dizzying possibilities swept through his mind. One thing at a time. He'd start out slow and simple and let Galen dictate how far he wanted to take this. This relationship was new enough that Nick didn't want to upset the delicate balance they'd found.

"God, I love you," Nick breathed and dropped a hard kiss on Galen's lips. He didn't give Galen a chance to respond to that sudden statement. He didn't want him to feel obligated to reply or awkward if he couldn't. The words had been clawing at him to come out for days now, and Nick was tired of fighting them. So he kissed Galen and fumbled for the bottle of lube and the box of condoms in his bedside drawer.

Galen ran his nails down Nick's back, making him arch with a hiss. Galen chuckled, his eyes wicked as he looked up at Nick. "If I'm going to be at your mercy, I want you to be at mine first."

"I always have been." Ever since the first moment he'd laid eyes on Galen, leaning against the bar, laughing at some joke from another patron. Their eyes had caught, the smile on Galen's face had changed from amusement to speculative, and Nick had to go over to introduce himself. All those endless nights of drinking and dancing followed by amazing sex had only increased Galen's hold on him.

Nick rolled the condom on and slicked both of them, and after he'd fingered Galen a little, stretching him, Galen shook his head and stopped Nick with a hand on his wrist. "No more, I'm ready for you now."

"You sure? You said it's been a while." Doubt niggled. Maybe Galen hadn't been entirely honest about how long it had been out of an effort to spare Nick's feelings. Even if he hadn't gone clubbing anymore, he was at the museum every day with gay men drifting in and out.

Galen kissed him hard enough to make his lips tingle, ending with a hard little nip that made them start throbbing. "More than sure. Rough and out of control, that's how I want it."

Nick flipped Galen over onto his stomach and stopped him from getting up on all fours with a hand between his shoulders. "This is where I want you." Galen sank right back down, a visible tremor running down his back. Nick pushed Galen's thighs apart and paused to admire the view, the tension in Galen's back and buttocks, the flush to his skin.

Galen wanted to be out of control and be at Nick's mercy? Then they were doing things his way. He got more lube and pushed two fingers into Galen, scissoring them. He was tight, the muscle resisting him and Nick's doubts disappeared. "Nick!" Galen reached back for him and Nick caught his hands, pinning them to the small of his back.

"Oh no, you wanted to be at my mercy, you've got to take what I'm giving you." He would give Galen rough, but he didn't want to hurt him. Galen squirmed, trying to get some leverage, and Nick used his knees to push Galen's thighs wider apart. "You should see the gorgeous sight you make right now."

"You're a bitch," Galen replied, but the laughter and hunger in his voice told Nick that he wasn't pushing it too far. "I can take it."

"I know you can. That's not the point." Nick continued to finger him while Galen clenched and rocked. His mouth was dry as he watched Galen struggle in the sunlight, thighs straining, ass taut until the resistance faded as desire took over, and Galen began trembling with little whimpered moans and sighs for more.

He released Galen's wrists, his heart pounding as he guided his cock toward Galen's entrance. "Please." Galen started to lift his hips up, and Nick gave one firm cheek a hard smack before palming it with a squeeze. Galen went still and looked over his shoulder at Nick with surprised eyes.

How far did Galen want to take this lack of control? "Hands on either side of your head." Slowly he obeyed, wetting his lips, his breath coming quicker as his gaze heated. "Don't move. Don't try to take me in deeper, or else you'll have to wait even longer while I play with you more. Okay?"

Galen shuddered and closed his eyes, and when he opened them again, they were so hot, burning right into Nick with his stare. "Okay."

The acceptance in Galen's gaze, the need, brought another punch to Nick's heart. He loved Galen, as maddening as he could be... or maybe because of it. He challenged Nick in so many ways and jerked him out of the rut that had become his life.

Nick smiled at him and gave Galen's other cheek a smack so he had matching red spots on each side of his ass. Galen squirmed with an "Ooohh," laying his head back down on the pillow. Another time he would have to see how Galen would react to a real spanking. This wasn't the only hint he'd had that led him to believe Galen might enjoy it too.

Nick began to push into him, fighting the urge to thrust into him with one stroke. He grabbed Galen's wrists, holding him down as he pushed deeper inside of him, his weight pinning Galen to the bed. Galen groaned, his body tensing at the invasion after so long. Nick nipped the back of Galen's neck, hard little bites followed by licks and kisses. With each scrape of his teeth Galen shuddered, and as Nick continued to play with his neck, Galen relaxed until Nick was fully inside of him.

Then it was Nick's turn to shudder. Galen's heat grasped him, the muscles tightening and relaxing around his cock. He began with long, deep thrusts instead of the hard and quick way he knew Galen liked. Galen cried out, writhing underneath him, trying to push back and unable to. He circled his hips, clenching around Nick, chanting his name.

Nick toyed with him. He whispered endearments as he brought Galen close to the edge, then pulled back to give them both a chance to calm down, only to start again until both of their bodies were damp with perspiration, and Galen was trembling and pleading, crying out into the pillow with each thrust.

"Please… so close… harder, dammit." Galen's voice was raw, aching, and it made Nick crazy inside. Galen was a madness that had sunk into his bones and blood, that elusive spark Nick had finally caught a hold of and wanted to keep by his side forever.

Nick let go of Galen's hands and slid out of him as he rose to his knees. Galen whimpered and stiffened, but didn't move other than to give Nick a pleading look over his shoulder. "Stop stopping."

"I love you." Nick hauled Galen up by his hips and thrust into him with one hard rock of his hips. Galen cried out, his hands fisting in the sheets.

"Yes. Nick, please."

Nick pounded into him, the room filling with the sounds of flesh slapping against flesh, Galen's sharp cries for more, and Nick's groans. Nick's fingers tightened on Galen's hips as he stared at the back of Galen's neck covered in dark red marks. He couldn't believe he'd done that, much less that Galen had let him. For all that Nick was ostensibly in control, it was really Galen who had the string around his heart.

It didn't last long enough. Both of them were too close. Galen shifted, stroking his cock with quick jerks until he came with a hoarse shout, his body tensing around Nick's cock as he tried to rock back on him. Nick's hands tightened hard enough to bruise as his hips snapped. Feeling Galen contract around him was too much, and the tension shattered. Galen lowered his shoulders, arching his ass up higher in offering as Nick buried himself inside of him, riding the hard, hot waves of his orgasm.

GALEN traced his fingers down Nick's arm, his body replete and more than content to lie wrapped up with him as his mind kept going. *I love you.* Every time he remembered Nick saying those words he trembled a little inside. It was humbling, the trust Nick showed him even though he'd been hurt in the past, and Galen hoped he was up to that faith. It made him want to show Nick a little of that trust in return.

"You still hungry?" Nick murmured. "There might still be some pizza left."

"No, I think we pretty much killed it." They'd spent the entire evening in bed, exploring, learning new things about each other and themselves. Even now the memory made his cock stir. They'd played until hunger drove them to order in, and then they'd taken the pizza to the bed, fed each other, and screwed around some more, letting out weeks of pent-up frustration.

"You seem restless." Nick rolled onto his stomach and gave Galen an assessing look by the light of the bedside lamp. His expression was neutral, which Galen had come to understand meant what Nick was feeling was far from neutral. "It's getting late. If you want to head home, I'll understand."

Galen shook his head and tangled his fingers with Nick's. "No, I don't want to go home. I'd like to stay." He didn't want to go back to his cold, empty bed when he could stay right here, warm, content, and aching with the weight of all he wanted to say.

A grin broke out over Nick's face, transforming the neutral mask, and it made Galen ache even more to see it. He wanted to see that smile for a long time to come. If he only dared to take the next step, to open himself up even more…. He'd made a promise to himself this morning, before everything had gone to hell, that he would tell Nick everything about the accident. "Good, now stop looking so sad, or else I'll start to think I've done something wrong."

"No, you've done everything right, and that's the problem." Galen had fallen in love with him, and it was too damn late to turn away and run. He'd tried that, and it hadn't been enough to get Nick out of his mind. All it had done was hurt him, even if Galen had needed that time.

"What's bothering you?" Worry crept into Nick's eyes. "I didn't take it too far, did I?"

Galen laughed and kissed the corner of Nick's mouth. "Oh hell no. In fact, I wouldn't mind if you took it a bit further next time. Though, if you tell anyone that you got me to beg like that, I will retaliate in kind."

Nick cupped his face, and his thumb brushed across Galen's lips, silencing him. "What is it? Something's bugging you. Is it Suzane?"

Galen stared at Nick and drank in his steadying presence. He could do this. He could put his trust in Nick, hoping he would understand why he brought this up tonight. "You asked me once why I avoided relationships, and I said that I wasn't ready to talk about it." Nick's admission of love had changed that. If Galen was going to go forward with their relationship, Nick deserved to know why Galen had closed himself off for so long.

"And you're ready now?"

"Yeah, but it feels a little weird bringing up Bryan when I'm naked with you. Actually it feels pretty rude and disrespectful. This is something that's not easy for me to talk about." Remembering that night, the cold rain lashing through the broken windows, the hot blood between his fingers, chilled him inside and out. Memories should fade after time, but those were still stark and raw. He couldn't pass an accident on the road without getting that hard, sickening jolt every time.

Nick's expression became thoughtful. "Are you bringing it up now because you feel safe talking about it now or for another reason?" His hands continued to cradle him, giving Galen the comfort and intimacy he craved.

"I'm saying it because you deserve to know and because I'm so tired of holding onto it. I need to let it go 'cause it ate me up inside for too long. It made me dead and afraid and…." Galen paused, the weight in his chest becoming heavier. It wasn't the mourning. He'd done that, let Bryan go. It was the fear that held him prisoner. Fear that it could happen all over again. Fear that he would lose someone else too soon.

Nick wrapped his arms around Galen and pulled him close. "Hey, I meant what I said earlier. This is me, not the sex talking. Whatever it is, you can tell me."

Galen laid his head on Nick's shoulder and smiled wistfully. How had he gotten to be so lucky not once, but twice? And this time the difference was Galen was certain what he had with Nick could last until they were old and gray if given the opportunity. "I was in a relationship for four years. I wanted it to be permanent, and Bryan wanted what he wanted, and at the time it was me."

"You didn't think he would stick around?" Nick asked, his fingertips skimming down Galen's back.

"Bryan… didn't take life seriously; everything was a lark or a game." Galen lifted his head and looked at Nick, finding comfort in the other man's steady gaze. "It was raining the night of the accident. I was driving, and we were arguing over his latest scheme. I was pissed because he wasn't being serious, and he thought I was being oversensitive and wouldn't listen to my concerns."

Galen closed his eyes, and every angry word came back to him. "A truck suddenly tried merging into our lane, and I swerved to avoid it and lost control."

Galen could still hear it, that angry high-pitched drag of the tires trying to find purchase on the road. He still felt the same hot spike of adrenaline as he fought to straighten the car. He remembered how the car skidded, heard Bryan's shout just before the terrible crash, the silvery cymbal clash of glass breaking and Bryan's scream.

Nick's hand touched his cheek, drawing his attention back. "Hey, you've gone cold. Come back to me. It's okay. You're not there. You're here."

Galen drew a shuddering breath. "It happened so fast. There was nothing I could've done." He kept telling himself that, but it didn't stop him from going over the details again and again. What if his attention hadn't been half on the argument? Would he have reacted sooner? Would he have seen the truck drifting back and forth in time to know it was a hazard to be avoided?

"It took the emergency workers far too long to get through the mess of backed-up cars on the highway, and by then it was too late. I'd tried to stop the bleeding, but there was so much. He bled out while I held him, and there was nothing I could do. Even knowing that if they'd come sooner it wouldn't have helped wasn't a comfort. Knowing that the guy in the truck had been drinking hadn't helped either. We were mad at each other. Our last words had been angry, and I can't forgive myself for that."

"I'm so sorry," Nick said, drawing him close again.

"I'd never told anyone before, that we were fighting." Galen laid his head down on Nick's shoulder and relaxed, feeling as if a huge, terrible weight had come off him.

"You need to forgive yourself, sweetheart. It was an accident. You had no way of knowing what was going to happen," Nick said in a soft voice.

"I know, at least in my head I know that. It doesn't seem to make much of a difference." Galen thought that he might've started himself on the road to self-forgiveness with his confession.

His arms tightened around Nick. "Thank you for listening."

Nick's rubbed his hands up and down Galen's back, offering more comfort. "So that's why I never see you drive."

"Oh God no, every time I get behind the wheel I freeze up. I can't breathe. I can't unlock my hands. I tried several times, and then I gave up."

"Well, I guess the next step in moving on would be getting you to drive again."

Galen stiffened, going cold all over again, and Nick tightened his arms around him. "Don't worry. We don't have to rush, and we can do it together, okay?"

Galen didn't answer at first, until bit by bit he began to relax in Nick's arms. He was right. That was the next step. He needed to do it for himself. "Okay."

Neither of them said anything else. Nick held him, and Galen held him back, vowing to himself that this time it would be different. He wasn't going to take one day with Nick for granted.

CHAPTER SEVENTEEN

GALEN stirred, and the unfamiliar weight of an arm across his stomach accompanied by the sound of a soft snore drew him out of a comfortable dream. He opened his eyes and turned his head to look at Nick. Sandy lashes fanned against his cheek and his fingers curled into a relaxed fist under his chin. The sexy dominating fire had fled, making him seem far more vulnerable in sleep. Galen was drawn to both the fire and the vulnerability. One made him ache with need, and the other had him all tied up in knots.

It had been a long time since he'd been tied up in knots like that. He rather liked it. A slow smile crossed Galen's lips as he tucked an arm under his cheek and turned so he could continue to watch Nick sleeping. The last time Nick did this to him all Galen could think of was running and putting some distance between them while he sorted it out.

Now, the last thing he wanted to do was run. His heart twisted with a little ache of recognition. He was in love with Nick. He had been for a long time, and he'd fought it and fled from it, and neither had done any damn good. And the funny thing was, after last night, he wasn't afraid anymore. There was always the possibility of losing someone. You couldn't hide out in a bubble forever. The scare with Suzane had reminded him of that. He'd thought he'd made himself safe by burying himself in the museum, and somehow he'd gotten attached to people anyway.

Nick's eyes fluttered open, and for a moment confusion shadowed his eyes before he gave Galen a sleepy grin. "You're still here. I thought you would've slipped off by now."

"Not going anywhere." Galen brushed his thumb over Nick's jaw, the morning stubble scraping his skin and reminding him fleetingly of Dexios. "I have absolutely zero interest in leaving."

"Words I love hearing first thing in the morning." Nick brushed his mouth over Galen's. "Thank you for staying."

"Thank you for listening to me last night." There hadn't been one nightmare to haunt his dreams. Galen thought that maybe, just maybe, by unburdening himself to Nick, opening himself up to what he offered, it might've let him finally start to put his memories in the past where they belonged.

"You know how long I've waited for you to trust me enough to let me in?" Nick kissed Galen again. "Thanks aren't necessary. I'll listen anytime you need me too. I love you."

Galen's heart did that hard little lurch of happiness again. He'd forgotten what it felt like. "I—"

"Don't." Nick brushed his thumb over Galen's lip, stopping his words. "You don't have to say anything, I'm not expecting it. And if it would make you more comfortable I won't say it anymore until you're ready to hear it. I wasn't planning on it. It just kind of blurted out of me."

Galen suppressed a chuckle and nipped Nick's thumb. "You can say it as much as you want. It doesn't make me think of bolting at all. I wasn't ready six months ago. I am ready now." He slid his hand down to Nick's, linking their fingers. "What I'm trying to say is that I lo—"

This time Nick stopped him with a kiss, taking possession of his mouth as Galen's thoughts spun. How was he going to tell Nick how he felt if the other man kept interrupting him? Not that he minded this kind of an interruption at all. His body ached, desire awakening him as memories of last night flooded through him.

"Don't say it." Nick pulled back, his eyes haunted as he touched his forehead to Galen's. "Don't say it until you mean it."

Galen started to say that he did mean it, but Nick kissed him again, a hard, desperate kiss that told Galen how raw Nick's emotions were when it came to him. It was crazy. For all of Nick's talk, now he was the one not ready to hear the words. It made Galen wonder if there had been somebody else in Nick's past who had walked out on him after claiming to love him. If that was the case, Galen was going to have to show Nick he loved him and keep showing him until Nick was ready to believe.

Galen tightened his arms around Nick, softened his mouth with a moan as Nick plundered his mouth, kissing him more deeply and taking claim. It had been such a turn-on when he offered to let Nick take control last night. He'd forgotten how exciting it could be, especially with someone he trusted. And maybe that total surrender would help Nick to see that Galen did love him. He'd never let Nick go that far before, let him get so close, and Galen craved more of that now.

Nick broke the kiss, a bit breathless as he looked down at Galen, who smiled back at him. He seemed to relax when Galen didn't try to admit his feelings again and nipped Galen's jaw. Galen shivered, arching up into him, turning his head so that Nick could get at his neck.

Instead, Nick touched Galen's throat with his fingertips. "I think I may have left a couple of marks."

Galen's cock throbbed as he pictured them against his skin, reminders of where Nick's mouth had been and how much it had driven him crazy. Galen's neck was his weakness, and once Nick started playing with it, he was a goner. "I'm sure you left more than a couple, and I don't mind at all."

"Well, you did ask for it, quite insistently and often." Nick grinned at him, his dimples coming out. "And then there was all the squirming and cursing."

"Remember last night when you smacked my ass?" Galen shuddered, going weak inside at the memory of those two hard stinging slaps. "I'd like for you to do it again because you want me squirming and cursing. You can pull me over your lap any time you want."

Nick's eyes heated, and before Galen could offer any more encouragement, Nick had them both sitting up. Galen gasped as he was pulled over Nick's lap, his hands pinned against his back. He could break the grip if he wanted, but he had no desire to. Nick's hand squeezed his ass, and Galen moaned in anticipation. This was further proof that Nick was the right man for him. Nick wasn't at all turned off by Galen's desire for a little kinky play. He understood it and wanted it too. It was like the missing puzzle pieces of his life were coming together bit by bit.

"Are you sure?" Nick asked roughly, and Galen nodded, rocking his hips to show Nick how hard he was.

"Oh yeah." Galen looked over his shoulder at Nick, love and trust tumbling inside of him. The words he yearned to say burned on his lips, but he didn't want to bring this morning's fun to a screeching halt. He'd have to show Nick how much he wanted him, how much he felt safe with him, how much he reveled in this new dynamic between them, how much he enjoyed Nick's company and friendship. "Believe me, if I didn't want it or if I decide to change my mind, I'll let you know."

Nick squeezed his ass again and kept his hand locked around Galen's wrists. He liked that illusion of helplessness, and he wondered how much it would take to get Nick to try a bit of bondage with him. Probably not much. Then his thoughts fled as Nick's open palm cracked across his cheek.

The sharp sting flooded Galen's body with heat, and before he could process that, another hard slap followed. His cock throbbed. He shouldn't like that so much. All those thoughts he'd had over the years that had kept him from pursuing this side of himself flooded his mind. He was a grown man, not a disobedient—his breath left him in a rush as Nick set a hard rhythm, and all Galen could do was writhe, lifting his ass in offering and anticipation of the next blow.

Nick surrounded him. Nick held him. Nick was laying his mark on him. Galen cried out, kissing Nick's knee, pleading for more as his throbbing cock ground against Nick's thigh between slaps. The heat rose and soon, even when Nick paused to squeeze, that stung too. Galen squirmed, fighting to keep his hands still, to keep from covering himself, and that excited him almost as much as his breath came in gasps and pants.

"Nick… oh God…."

And then it was over and Galen went limp, panting, face down, ass burning, cock aching. "Are you okay?" Nick passed a gentle hand over his ass, and Galen shifted with a moan.

"Yeah, just let me get my breath." Nick's cock pressed against his stomach, making his mouth water. As much as he longed for Nick to ride him hard now, he wanted even more to get his mouth on Nick and suck him dry. Galen tugged his hands, and Nick released him with a frown of concern furrowing between his eyebrows. Before he could speak, Galen shoved him back on the bed.

"Stop worrying. Let me show you how much I enjoyed you smacking my ass." Galen laid a kiss on Nick's mouth, then slid down his body and took Nick's cock in his mouth.

"Oh fuck, Galen." Nick threaded his fingers through Galen's hair. Nick's head fell back against the pillow as he groaned.

Galen rubbed his tongue along the shaft, cupped Nick's heavy balls, groaning as he sucked. He couldn't get enough of him. He deep-throated Nick, listening in pleasure to the sounds of his moans, reveling in making Nick pant this time. Soon Nick's fingers tightened in his hair, making Galen's heart race as Nick began to thrust into his mouth, moving slowly until Galen adjusted and moaned for more.

"How could I have forgotten how wicked your mouth is?" Nick groaned. "You looked so damn gorgeous across my lap. Fucking making me crazy."

Galen drew back and lapped his tongue across the head of Nick's cock, tasting the heady rush of musk and salt. "You can do that every morning if you like, and for the rest of the day, every time I sit down I'll think of you."

Nick's eyes went hot with a smoldering possessive look that had Galen wanting to crawl into his arms so he could tell him that he loved him back. Before he could say something, a discordant beeping cut through the moment, getting louder each second.

For a second Nick looked confused, and then realization made his eyes widen as he reached for his phone. "Son of a bitch!"

"What's wrong?"

"Fuck!" Nick dragged a hand through his hair and sat up, gently pushing Galen aside. "I'm sorry."

Galen sat back on his heels and took a deep breath, trying to still the throbbing in his cock. "Appointment?"

"Yeah, interview. Shit!" Nick scrambled into some clothes, muttering to himself and casting longing glances at Galen. "I'm sorry, if I could cancel it, I would. Stay as long as you want. There's a spare key by the door, lock up when you go." He dropped a hard kiss on

Galen's lips, making them tingle as he struggled to knot his tie at the same time. "See you tonight, and I'll make it up to you, I swear."

He looked so distressed that Galen didn't have the heart to be irritated. He had the luxury of being his own boss, Nick didn't. "It's okay." Galen palmed Nick's cock through his pants and gave it a rough squeeze, making Nick groan and his eyes flash. He grinned up at him, feeling downright wicked. "Just something to think about today."

"Evil imp. I adore you."

NICK paced the confines of his office, trying to get his thoughts together long enough to make it through the next meeting on staffing in an hour. The interview had been sheer torture, and if somebody quizzed Nick now about it, he wouldn't be able to recall one thing about the candidate. At least his notes appeared to be concise and complete. He hoped he didn't make an ass out of himself.

He sat down at his desk and poked at his notes, only to spin around in his chair to stare out the window again. He wanted to trust Galen, he really did. After all, Galen had opened up to him last night. Galen had allowed himself to be vulnerable in so many ways. He'd come to Nick when he needed comfort. None of that helped his mindset at the moment.

Nick wasn't being fair to Galen. He was demanding commitment from him when he still had hang-ups of his own, and he wasn't allowing Galen to give him that commitment. He wanted to believe Galen loved him in return, but life experience had taught him that love wasn't enough to make people stay.

It hadn't been enough to keep his mom with his family. It hadn't been enough to keep him in San Francisco. And it hadn't been enough to make the rest of his family allow him to be who he wanted to be. He was still Baby Nick, who needed to be watched over and guided. He didn't understand their need to second-guess everything he did, and they didn't understand his need to have the space to be himself. It was just one big clusterfuck.

Galen had already lost someone he'd been in love with, and he'd already proven that when emotions got too intense he ran from them. It was only a matter of time before he did it again, before he decided that the risk was too much. Nick wanted to believe that Galen was different now. God, he really wanted to believe. But Lykon ran, and Galen was Lykon reincarnated. And every other version of Lykon had done the same thing. Nick didn't know what he would do if Galen left again.

And to add to his unsettled irritation, his balls still ached, and no matter how much he tried to concentrate on the paperwork in front of him, his thoughts bounced between the memories of Galen with Nick's cock in his mouth, his ass in the air as he begged for more, and writhing across his lap as Nick spanked him.

Nick had tried for too many months to block such thoughts. It had gotten even harder since they started seeing each other again, but after last night Nick didn't think he'd ever be able to leash those memories again. It was going to be a freaking long-assed day.

How was it possible to both wish for the day to be done and fear its ending? Galen ran. That was his MO. The question that remained was how long it was going to take. Nick wasn't sure if he could handle waiting for the moment to come.

"You are so certain, without even talking with him, without trying to listen to what is in his heart."

Nick jumped and almost fell out of his chair as it rolled back. Dexios stood near the desk, his eyes flashing, hand on the hilt of his sword. "What the hell are you doing here? You have *got* to stop sneaking up on me like this."

"Just because you have studied the myth does not mean you know the whole tale. You assume much." Dexios slammed his helmet on Nick's desk. "There is a storm coming, a whirlwind of fear and doubt, and I do not think you have the fortitude to weather it. Who is really afraid? Galen or you?"

"You're damn right I'm afraid, and you should be too," Nick snapped as he rose to his feet. "I've been reading up since I last saw you, researching the family journals. I know that Lykon needs to make it right in another lifetime. I know that Galen is his descendent just as I'm yours, but if you're counting on Galen to be less fickle than Lykon was, I think you're placing your trust in the wrong person. And I'm the one who gets to have his heart broken again this time. I'm the one caught in the middle of all three of you."

"You do not know as much as you think you do," Dexios said in a furious, low voice. "Galen is not Lykon; they may have the same soul, but they are not the same man. Their experiences are different. You said as much to Lykon. And your experiences are different from mine, yet you seem determined to repeat my mistakes. I warned you not to read the journals."

"I love him." Nick turned away, thinking of Galen, of his smile, his animated way of talking when he was excited. "And I don't want to lose him, not like you lost Lykon, or how my uncle lost his lover."

How could he fix things if Dexios refused to tell him how to do it? He and Galen had to find the answers somewhere before it was too late. Now that he thought about it, he wasn't the only one who would get hurt from this; Galen would too, and that thought made him go cold inside. Look what happened to Galen last time his heart was broken. He had been carrying around a crushing guilt for years that had incapacitated him in some ways.

Galen had already lost his heart when he'd lost Bryan. Nick had heard it in his voice last night. Dexios shot him a disgusted look. "This is why we do not tell people how to break the curse. They think too much and forget to feel. You think you heard Galen's heartbreak last night. Did you hear what he was trying to tell you this morning?"

"What the hell?" Nick flushed a hot red. "Were you spying on us?"

The withering expression in Dexios's eyes cooled Nick's anger. "Not in the way you think. I am a part of you. I know what you know. And I know what Galen was trying to tell you, and you stopped him."

Nick looked away, his jaw clenching. "I should've kept my mouth shut and not told him that I loved him. It messed everything up last time. I don't want him to feel obligated to respond in kind. I don't want to hear him say it just to say it."

"Your reasoning is as faulty as your wits. Ask yourself, how did Galen react the last time you told him you loved him? Did he pretend to love you too, to spare your feelings?"

Sudden doubt filled Nick's thoughts. He wanted to believe so much, and Dexios was a persuasive bastard, but it was in his best interests to shove him and Galen together. Still, he was right. Galen had been honest with Nick in the past even though he knew Galen had not enjoyed hurting him and would have spared his feelings if he could have.

Maybe he did mean it now. The hope was almost too painful.

"I'll think about it," Nick finally said, and Dexios nodded, taking his hand off the sword hilt. Something about the action made Nick wonder if he'd have used it on him, curse or no curse, and a chill touched him.

"That is all I ask." Dexios looked off to the side, as if hearing some distant call, and he began to fade until Nick could see right through him. "I must go, but I have one last thing to tell you. When you study those journals written by men who have had their hearts broken, it would do you well to know that Lykon wasn't the only one who had broken faith."

"Wait a minute. What the hell do you mean by that? Lykon left you." Nick cursed under his breath as Dexios disappeared completely. "Come back and tell me what you mean."

The corner of his office remained empty, and Nick bit back another curse. He still had some time before the meeting. Maybe he could reread the multiple versions of the myth that he had. He'd have to glean some answers from them since Dexios didn't seem inclined to do anything other than lecture and give vague warnings.

As for Galen, all Nick could do was wait and see what happened. And in the meantime, Nick had his own trust issues to work through. Galen was dealing with his. He could do no less.

CHAPTER EIGHTEEN

GALEN breezed into work, riding on a complete high compared to how he'd left it the day before. Suzane had been released this morning and was going to be fine. He was going to be with Nick again tonight. He couldn't stop himself from grinning. He was like a bad chick flick movie star. He hadn't felt this good in a long time. He hadn't felt this… normal.

He did a quick walk-through of the public part of the museum, then unlocked the doors. The morning sun looked as though it was going to hold when he set out the Open sign on the cobbled walkway, so he brought out some of the hanging baskets of spring flowers as well. They didn't get much traffic on a midmorning weekday, though they could usually count on a few walk-throughs in an hour. Patronage had been building some as word got out about the new upcoming exhibit.

Galen took his spot behind the counter in the gallery and began checking his e-mail, though his concentration was shot. His thoughts kept returning to Nick. And it didn't help that every time he shifted in his chair, the slight twinge reminded him keenly of the fun the night before and this morning. He grinned again. Wow, it was incredible how free he felt after he'd stopped fighting and running away from Nick.

"Galen Kanellis, you are a hypocrite."

Galen stifled a grin at the familiar acerbic voice and looked at Suzane, who stood in the doorway, back in her pinstripes and bun. Oh boy. She was going to be on fire today. "Am I? I hope you haven't left a trail of bodies between here and the hospital. I'm not posting bail."

"When you fainted at work, you wouldn't even go see a doctor! I have one little incident, and the next thing I know you're packing me into an ambulance." The outrage in her voice made Galen's lips twitch, though he was careful not to smile.

"I knew what had caused my faint, and it hasn't happened since. Plus, I didn't knock my head going down. I didn't call the ambulance because you fainted; I called because of the blood and the lump on your head."

Though if Dexios hadn't caught him, Galen might've been knocked silly too. Strange, he hadn't given the statues one thought at all this morning. He'd been so wrapped up in Nick he'd forgotten about trying to break the curse. Galen looked at the bruise on Suzane's forehead and the small bandage that covered the cut. "I don't suppose I'd be able to talk you into taking the day off."

"Forget about it," Suzane said flatly. "I'm fine. They've given me something for the anemia, and once the chemo's done my iron count should go back to normal. And if you sic one of those kids on me to play nursemaid, the cops are going to be trawling the Puget Sound for your body."

"Yes, ma'am."

"Don't you 'yes ma....'" Suzane trailed off and looked at him again. "You're in a good mood. What's gotten into you? No nagging, no fussing, not off in la-la land over that new exhibit."

This time Galen wasn't able to suppress the smile. "Nothing, just glad to see you back." He rose and startled a squawk out of her by giving her a hug. He didn't like the idea of her being at work today, but at least here he could keep an eye on her. "I'll take care of any tours today if you'll take care of the paperwork on your desk."

Suzane shot him a suspicious look, shook her head, and relaxed. "Well, if you're not going to be a butthead about this, I won't bitch if you hover a bit. Just don't take it to extremes. It makes me feel like an invalid."

"I promise. Note of warning: when Heather comes in, I'm sure she'll be by to check on you. She went to pieces yesterday, so go easy on her. I bet Knox will be by too, after he gets off work."

Suzane snorted. "And I'll send her right down here to run the shop. That should get her off my back. As for Knox, have you thought about hiring him part time? He's here, whenever he's off anyway, and does the work. It wouldn't hurt to have one or two of the kids on the payroll part time. Heather's going to be leaving us in the fall, and when it gets busier, it can't be just the two of us up front. We should have some back up."

"I've been giving it some thought. I'll ask him when he gets here." Galen glanced back as the door chimed and a patron he recognized came in. She'd been eyeballing this sculpture for weeks and was weakening. By the time she left with the wrapped package secure in her bag and an invitation for the opening of the exhibition, Suzane had returned with a bulging folder stuffed under her arm and her slim laptop.

"The guys are here to finish installing the security lights in the new room. I don't know why you waited this long. It should've been done weeks ago." She settled herself behind the counter. "I can work on the catering here while you deal with them."

Galen knew he should've had that set up a while ago, but he loved seeing the statues at night without the harshness of artificial lighting to ruin their magic. Suzane would thwap him if he said it out loud, though. "They assured me it wouldn't be invasive and shouldn't take long. We have the alarms around the windows, so I think I'm only going to have them put in two lights since we already have some spilling in from the hallway."

"Whatever you think," Suzane said, already deep into her notes with a flush of pleasure on her cheeks. She really loved doing this part. The organizing, the media kits—she would be in heaven come opening night.

Galen made small talk with the contractor as they headed toward the new exhibit room. He slipped his phone out, intending on sending Nick a text when he saw the second statue whole. Whole. He gasped and the phone dropped from his fingers. Oh God, it was gorgeous. It was better than he'd expected.

He ran forward to look closer as the contractor said something that Galen didn't register. Lykon knelt before Dexios, an expression of pleasured anticipation on his face as he leaned toward Dexios's cock, his lips parting to take it in.

Nick had to see this. Galen reached for his phone, looking around when he didn't see it. The contractor handed it to him, looking bemused. "You dropped it and broke it all to hell. Is everything okay?"

"Oh yeah, everything's perfect. It's better than perfect," Galen breathed, pocketing the shattered shell of his cell phone. "We've marked the spots for the lighting with tape." He vaguely gestured behind him and moved to the single third statue. Lykon lurched inside of him, and Galen pressed a hand against his heart as he touched Dexios's hair. "Soon, my friend, we're halfway there."

SUZANE stood before his desk, hands on her hips, and fire in her eyes. "What do you mean a harpist isn't sexy? This is an exhibit opening gala, not a toga party. You have enough sex going on in that room to set any kind of mood. What would you like instead, pounding drums?"

"Don't tempt me." With the mood Nick left him in this morning, pounding, tribal drums seemed to fit. Add in the anticipation from having to wait to talk to him and show him the new statue, and it was all Galen could do to sit still. "A harpist makes me think heavenly choirs or put-me-to-sleep elevator music. I don't want people associating that with the exhibit. Maybe a sax."

"Too loud and screechy."

"Growly and sexy," Galen countered and pointed to the paper with the layout of the room. "What if we set him up in this corner?"

"Can you pick any other instrument other than a sax? Please? What about a piano?" Despite Suzane's pacing and glowers, Galen could tell she was enjoying herself by the way her mouth twitched to hide a smile. It was good to see her like this, and Galen couldn't help adding more fuel to her fire.

"I think it would make the room seem crowded." Galen's thoughts went right back to the drums; as soon as Suzane said it, he knew it was just the right thing, but he wasn't sure how to set it up. "You know, I like your drum idea."

"Be serious." Suzane grabbed a chair and pulled it up to his desk. "We cannot have drums and cymbals crashing. It would be too much. Steel drums would be even worse in the room. No one would be able to talk."

"I am being serious," Galen said as he considered it further. "Drums are more versatile than you think. I'm thinking a single person and hand drums, very organic, wood and hide. Drums are old and primal. I think it would go over very well."

Suzane's expression turned thoughtful. "You might be right. I'll look into it tomorrow." She stuffed her notebook into her oversized purse. "On that note, I'm calling it an early day. Thank you for not hovering over me too zealously. I appreciate it."

"After two weeks of not having you here, I'm surprised this place is still standing. And boy, did I miss arguing with you." Galen grinned at her and waved his hand toward the door. "Go, relax, I won't be too far behind you."

"I'm glad to see you getting out more. I'll fuss at you later. Too tired tonight." Suzane patted her bun, blew him a kiss, then left.

As soon as his office door shut, Galen sagged back in his chair, exhausted by his efforts to keep Lykon from ripping control away. Sweat popped out on his brow, and he fumbled for his cell to send a text to Nick before he remembered that he'd broken his phone. He'd ended up having to send the picture of the second statue through Knox's phone earlier.

He started to reach for the desk phone when Lykon tugged again, and Galen slumped with a wave of dizziness. "Please don't, just stop." The last thing this place needed was for Galen to pass out and scare the hell out of poor Heather. She didn't need to walk in and see Galen like Suzane.

Lykon answered with another sharp tug that made Galen groan as his control slipped even more. He gripped the edge of the desk as his vision blurred, and when he could see again, Lykon stood by the desk watching him with exasperated concern. "Why do you do that? Hold on so hard? It's why you get so dizzy."

"I didn't realize it was me." Galen let go of his death grip on the desk and straightened. "What, no attempts to possess me this time?"

"Nick has convinced me that it would not be wise to try." Lykon studied him, his eyebrows drawn together in puzzlement. "I apologize if I offended you."

"I wasn't offended. I was pissed off. I don't know you well enough to trust what you're doing with my body." Galen gestured to the door and tried to quell the trembling. He felt as though he'd had too much sugar and caffeine mixed together. "Dexios is in the exhibit room. Did you want me to take you there?"

"No, I wouldn't be allowed to see him except for a too-brief encounter. That's all the goddess allows us. Little moments. It was you who I wanted to meet, the other half of me."

"Goddess? You're kidding me, right?" The seriousness on Lykon's face stopped Galen's skeptical laughter before it could form. Nick had mentioned a goddess once, and Galen had shrugged it off as another little piece of mythology. Though at this point, he supposed he shouldn't be surprised by anything when it came to the statues.

"Cythera, or Aphrodite, or Eve. She has many names, many aspects, but they all are the same being. Whatever name you choose to call her." Lykon leaned closer with a frown. "You appear ill. Are you sickly?"

Galen laughed shortly and scraped a hand through his hair. "No, I'm fine. I've been fighting with you all afternoon. It's very tiring." He wanted to lay his head down on the desk and sleep for a bit, but the thought of Lykon wandering through his museum kept him awake. He needed to get up anyway and lock the place down.

"You have a very strong will. The others let me take control gladly." Lykon watched him as Galen rose to his feet. "You do not need to escort me to Dexios. As I said, I wanted to meet you without the distraction of the curse and the statues. I think you are strong enough to handle what is to come."

"Don't say that," Galen snapped, fear grabbing a hold of him with a sick little lurch. "I don't want to be strong enough. I want to be left in peace. I want to be happy. Look, I'm sorry for what happened to you and your lover, but I don't want it screwing with what I have with Nick. I want to be happy again. He makes me happy."

"I do not want to interfere in your relationship. That is not what I meant. Some things should be left alone to work out on their own. We weren't given the option." Lykon followed Galen out of his office as he began to go through the museum checking on doors. "Life occurs whether we are braced for it or not. There are bad times as much as there are good ones. I think you know that already. What I meant is that you give me hope, for the first time in a long time, and that is painful."

Painful and frightening. Galen could read it in his eyes. Maybe because he understood how hope could be both of those. That's how he felt about Nick: hopeful, afraid, aching. All those emotions had welled up so hard and fast that he'd run. And by some miracle Nick had taken him back and was showing such patience too. Now that Galen knew he loved Nick, he wasn't going to budge an inch away from him. If there ever was a time when he would've cut his losses and run, it was yesterday morning.

"I don't know how I could give you hope," Galen said as he turned on the alarm after the last door had been locked. "I have no idea what I'm doing with the statues or the curse, though I'm starting to think that there's nothing really that we can do. The statues are reacting to the progress of our relationship. So, that's what we really need to concentrate on and let it take its course."

Galen glanced at Lykon to see his reaction regarding his theory, but the other man's expression remained unchanged. "I'd like to see the curse broken and to know that you are reunited with Dexios. I don't suppose you can let me know if I'm wildly off the mark."

"Cythera would consider that cheating. The decisions you make have to be your own and for your own reasons." Lykon hesitated and leaned closer. "There will be tests before she is satisfied."

"What kind of tests?" Galen didn't like the sound of that, but if his theory was right it made sense. All relationships had tests. It didn't matter how long a couple was together; it was a constant growing and changing process.

Lykon shook his head and turned away. "I cannot say any more. I've spoken too much already. Just know that I regret taking you over without your permission."

Galen shuddered as he remembered coming out of a half trance to find himself outside of Nick's apartment. "So, no more trying to take me over?"

"After all these centuries, what is a little more waiting going to do to us?" Lykon said the words with a light tone, but his eyes were haunted. Galen suspected that though he was referring to the forced separation, that wasn't the only bad memory he carried. He was also haunted by those other lives torn apart because the curse hadn't been broken. But if Galen dwelled on that he'd make himself crazy.

How strange it must be to be split, to look at another person and know that you are a part of them, to watch generations of them, Galen thought. He couldn't begin to imagine, and he had to take a mental step back from the realization. It was easier to concentrate on the fact that Lykon had been cursed and that somehow Galen had been picked to help. Trying to unravel the mysteries of reincarnation and looking any deeper into his connection to it was unsettling.

They both paused at the entrance to the exhibit room, their gazes going toward the statues, and Lykon sighed. "He will not appear tonight, I think. As I said, we only get moments."

"There's never enough time with the ones you love. You think you have forever, and then it's snatched away," Galen said. Lykon looked at him sharply and nodded. "So I'm going to hold onto the now. May I ask you a question?"

"If I can answer, I will."

"After you were cursed, did you get to see Dexios at all? Were you granted any of those moments in your own lifetime?"

Lykon looked back toward Dexios, his eyes far away. "Just once, when I was a dying old man. The goddess relented, and he held me until the end." He looked back at Galen, his eyes penetrating. "I wasn't alone. Do you understand?"

Galen nodded. Oh yeah, that he understood.

NICK stood outside the museum side entrance, trying to decide whether to bang on the door or give up and go home. Since he'd driven all the way to this part of town, he thought he might as well at least try. Perhaps it would be better to go home until the simmering annoyance died away.

He'd gotten the text with the picture of the statue from a phone number he didn't recognize. He'd tried Galen's cell all day only to have it go straight to voice mail. He'd even dug up Galen's office phone and hadn't gotten an answer there either. He wanted to know what was going on, and he wanted to know now.

Nick tested the door, found it locked, and banged on it hard enough for the sound to echo between the walls of the surrounding buildings. Minutes later, the door opened and Galen peered out. He looked wan, with dark circles under his eyes, though his face lit up when he saw Nick. "Oh good, you're here. I was getting ready to call you."

He grabbed Nick's hand, linking their fingers together, and the little surge of warmth that the gesture brought spiked Nick's annoyance even more. "Do you know that you're a pain in the ass to get a hold of? And who the hell sent me that text?"

"I did, from Knox's phone." Nick frowned, but he couldn't find fault with that answer. Knox was forever hanging around the museum, though that didn't explain why Galen had been so inaccessible after sending him that text. "I meant to call to ask you to stop by, but I kept getting interrupted. I'm so glad you're here."

Nick stopped, forcing Galen to stop too, as irritation bubbled over and sparked his temper. "You mean the entire day you couldn't take five damn minutes to give me a call? You knew how I'd react to a text like that. You knew I'd want to talk about it, ask questions. Five minutes, Galen. You couldn't have spared that?"

"I'm sorry." Galen touched his chest in that odd gesture he had whenever Lykon was being active. "It's been a long day. I didn't even get a chance to go get a new phone when I broke mine. I'll explain it all later. Come on, don't you want to see it?"

Nick let himself be pulled along again as he tried to fight the stirrings of jealousy and irrationality. Just because they were together now didn't give him the right to demand to know every little thing about Galen's day or who he was with and what he was doing. He'd end up shoving Galen away, and he'd have no one to blame it on but himself. Galen had a life outside of his relationship with Nick, and the museum was a big part of that life. Just because Galen was living his dream job and that it sometimes took his attention away from Nick didn't give him the right to act like a butthead over it.

Dexios's words also haunted him. Lykon hadn't been the only one to break faith. He knew what that implied, that Dexios had been at fault too, which meant that Nick needed to watch himself. But dammit, Lykon wasn't Galen. So shouldn't that work the other way too? Nick wasn't Dexios, so he didn't have to repeat his mistakes. Who was he really irked with, Galen or himself? At times with the statues and the curse, it just all got to be very confusing.

Nick's eyes lit on the second statue, and a surge of excitement leapt up. Galen released his hand as Nick walked toward it, as awed by the sight of them together in this statue as he had been by the first. This was worth it, worth all the worry and wondering, worth the broken heart that was coming if it would just see these two back together again permanently. How many men in his family going back how many generations had worked toward seeing this, and they were halfway there? Making this right was in his blood. It was his destiny, and that meant he had to face his fears about losing Galen.

He turned around to see Galen looking at him, his expression soft, his gaze caressing. Despite the tiredness on his face, he looked so happy, and Nick's heart flipped to see it. He wanted to see more of Galen with that exact same expression.

"What?" Nick asked. "You're looking at me like I did something."

Galen shook his head with a half laugh. "I love you." Nick froze, and then his heart began to thunder as Galen walked toward him. "I told myself I would give you time. I would wait until you were ready to hear it, but you disarm me. You did when we first met and you continued to do so every day since then."

Nick's hope rose up again, strong and brutal. "Don't say it if you don't mean it. Please don't."

"Hey." Galen wrapped his hand around the nape of Nick's neck and drew him close until they were eye to eye, their breath mingling as they looked at each other. "Have I ever lied to you about how I felt? I know me. I know my heart. I love you."

Nick wanted to believe him. Out of the corner of his eye something shimmered in the air, and they both turned to look at the same time. Moonlight had gathered around the third statue, even though there wasn't a moon to be seen through the skylights. Somehow though, it was there, gleaming pale and wavering, shining along limbs as Lykon slowly appeared underneath Dexios. The image wasn't solid yet, but the potential was there.

Nick's breath caught, and he reached for Galen as Galen reached for him. For a moment, Nick thought he could hear the two men caught up in the moment, the groans and pants. He almost smelled sex and sweat, and it caught him in the gut with a visceral punch.

"Oh wow." Galen went to kneel by them. Lykon's head was thrown back, his lips parted as if in a groan, his expression taut with pleasure and momentary discomfort as Dexios penetrated him. His legs were wrapped around Dexios's waist, and his hands dug into Dexios's muscled shoulders. "They're beautiful, even more so knowing them now, knowing what they meant to each other."

"Yeah." Nick tore his eyes away from Galen's jubilant expression and stared again at the statue. One more step closer to them being fulfilled. One more step closer until Galen left him and he had his heart shattered. Somehow he'd have to find the strength to work through that, keep faith and win Galen back. He wished he didn't know that everyone else who'd tried, failed. "We're so close. We have to fix it. Marry me."

Galen twisted around, his mouth falling open in shock. "What?"

Nick pulled him up, searching Galen's face. "Marry me. I love you. You love me. Why wait?" He glanced toward the fourth statue, hoping for a shimmer, a sign, and nothing happened.

Galen tugged his arm free and stepped back, running it through his hair in agitation. "Dammit, don't do this."

"Don't do what?" Nick snapped, feeling everything start to crumble, and what pissed him off was that he knew he was to blame and he didn't know how to take it back. He could only force his way forward. "Are you ready to commit or not?" Nick bit back the rest of his angry words, knowing he was going too far, pushing at Galen and giving him reason to push back.

Galen's expression went from shocked and bewildered to furious. "I'm saying no, not because I don't want to be with you, but because you are asking for all the wrong reasons."

"I—"

"Let me finish. I can't marry someone who doesn't trust me, who's only asking me because he thinks it'll give him another tie to me; make it harder for me to leave." Galen flung his hand back toward the statues. "Who's only asking because he wants to be the one to break the curse because he thinks it'll bring back his family."

Nick couldn't look at him anymore, look at those eyes so full of hurt beneath the anger. He glanced at the fourth statue, still incomplete, and felt it all falling away. How could Galen read him so well?

"No. Look at me, not the damn statues." Nick's gaze snapped back to Galen at the sound of those hard, furious words. "Which do you want, me or breaking the curse? Who are you really asking for? If you're going to be with me you have to accept me with all my shortcomings, just as I'll have to live with your insecurities until you get past them. This isn't about the legend, it's about us. And if your focus can't be on us, I'm not going to be a part of this. Remember when you said you wouldn't take anything less than me giving our relationship a real try, not a halfhearted one? Well, that's where I am now. Don't ask for a commitment that you aren't willing to give in return."

"No, don't. I'm sorry. I fucked it up." Nick turned his back on the Collection and reached to take Galen's hand. Galen drew back, shoving his hands in his pockets, and the rejection cut deeper than Nick wanted to admit. He followed Galen into the hallway, trying to find the words that would keep Galen from leaving. The look on Galen's face reminded him too much of the night that Galen had walked away. He couldn't let that happen again.

Galen was right. Nick had let panic and anger get in the way. He'd blasted Galen for being afraid when he'd left him the first time, reacting out of fear, and now Nick wasn't acting any different. He wanted Galen to have faith in him, but he wasn't showing any of that faith in return.

"You loving me, I believe it. I believe you."

Nick felt himself steady as soon as the words were out of his mouth. Galen wouldn't lie about something so important, so it had to be true. Maybe the first step in getting his heart to have the same faith would be to acknowledge it. Galen stopped, turned around to search Nick's face, and the smile that crossed Galen's face made Nick's heart skip a beat.

"Okay," Galen murmured. He took in a deep breath, and the tension uncoiled from his body. He reached out and took Nick's hand. "I think that's a good start. I'm not saying I'll never consider marriage, but if I do, I need it to be for the right reasons."

"Then I'll shelve that question for another day." Nick drew Galen closer, touched his forehead to Galen's. "I'm sorry about grilling you over what you were doing today and worrying over why you didn't call. I need to trust you, trust in us. That's my own problem, not yours."

"Let's go to my place. We can talk there."

A CONSEQUENCE REALIZED

LYKON studied the swirling dark clouds over his head with a wary eye as the wind picked up again. The boat shuddered, rocking in the rough sea, spray lashing over the side. The cold water smacked him hard, forcing the breath from his lungs as he held onto the wooden rail. He barely noticed the splinters driving into his palms and fingers as he searched for the shore with increasing desperation.

He'd been trying to find Dexios for months without any sign to give him hope. Too much time had passed with no word from him despite Lykon's messages to his home village, more than enough time for regret to sink in past his fears. He'd started to miss Dexios before the dust had settled on the road from his passing. As the time stretched longer, Lykon had gone from being hurt to being angry before his anger faded to sorrow. He'd injured Dexios far more than he'd let himself acknowledge, and the last expression in his lover's eyes haunted him still.

The waves rose higher, so the little boat seemed to be climbing each crest before plunging down the other side again. The fishermen screamed orders at each other over the wind, and Lykon tried to help, doing whatever task they demanded of him. He and Dexios had dreamed of owning such a boat and plying the waters around the island they were headed to. It was far away from either of their villages and the last place that Lykon could think of to search.

He'd find Dexios and figure out a way to close this rift that he'd caused. They'd build a home by the sea. Dexios loved to watch the play of water on the shore. Lykon would spend the rest of his life proving to Dexios that he wouldn't be ruled by his fears anymore. He only had to find his elusive lover first.

Lykon searched the horizon again, straining to see any sign of the rocky shoreline that Dexios had often described to him as they lay together at night, wrapped up in each other's arms. He had to be there.

Lykon could sense the place calling to him, a whisper on the wind, a murmur in Dexios's voice.

A terrified scream jerked his attention away from his thoughts, and Lykon twisted around to see a huge wave bearing down on the boat. He stood frozen, Dexios's name roaring in his mind, as he faced an enemy he could not fight. The boat lurched, timbers cracked, and Lykon shouted as they tumbled down toward the dark, seething waters. There seemed to be a face on the waves, angry and vengeful, its maw opening to swallow him whole.

Dexios. I am sorry. I tried to make it right.

As the waters sank over his head, Lykon felt a hand grab his hair before he blacked out.

LYKON *awoke to the sound of Dexios calling his name. For a moment, he thought he sensed his lover's strong arms about him, and he smiled, turning to reach for him, only to have his arms find nothing but air. He opened his eyes and found himself lying on a stretch of lonely coast. Sand clung to his wet, shivering body, and the remains of his garments clung to him in tatters.*

"Lykon."

He lurched to his feet as he heard his name again. "Dexios! Dexios, I am here."

He searched wildly for any sign of his lover and thought he saw a figure in the distance. He stumbled toward it, calling out Dexios's name with no response. Dread grew in his heart as he drew closer. The figure had Dexios's stance and breadth of his shoulders, but it was too still.

Lykon sank to his knees, his stomach churning as he gaped at the man. His back was to him as he faced the sea, and the sunlight glinted off his armor, surrounding him in a halo of light. Lykon stared, the light hurting his eyes as he silently willed Dexios to move.

He seemed frozen in midact, as if some Gorgon had gotten a hold of him. "No, no, Dexios."

"Lykon."

The whisper of his name had Lykon back on his feet, running toward Dexios. He stumbled to a halt in front of him, his eyes stinging as he stared at the statue of his lover. It was perfect in every detail, the strong line of his jaw, the tender fierceness of his brow, his empty arms circled as if to enfold Lykon in his embrace.

Lykon reached out a hesitant hand and wept as he wrapped his fingers around the cold, hard arm. "What happened?" There had to be some way he could free Dexios from this curse.

"You broke a pledge sworn in my name."

Lykon closed his eyes at the sound of the woman's voice behind him. He leaned closer and rested his head against Dexios's shoulder while the ache inside of him threatened to drown him as the waves had not. "Why punish him, Cythera? The sin was mine. Lay your curse on me instead."

"You both failed, and therefore you both carry the cost. You are punished as much as he, perhaps more. He merely waits for you with the utter faith that one day he will look upon you again and hold you in his arms. He will be waiting for a long time before you both redeem yourselves. He asked for the time to wait for you, so I granted it, and in return he promised he would be patient. Perhaps he will remember that vow."

Lykon looked at Dexios's face, the desire and love captured there as he waited with parted lips to kiss him. At least he was not afraid or in pain. Lykon touched Dexios's jaw, then turned to face the goddess, sinking to his knees. "Set him free. I beg of you."

"You have the power within you to set him free yourself." Hope stole the air from his lungs only to have it dashed away again when Cythera smiled. There was no mercy in her expression. "Though not in this lifetime."

She waved her hand, and three new objects shimmered on the sand, solidifying into more statues of Dexios. "Lykon, make me whole. Please." The whisper seemed to come from all of them at once, and Lykon stumbled from one to another, trying to rouse them.

"What must I do?" Lykon knelt beside the final statue, where Dexios lay in repose with such a familiar expression of sleepy, loving contentment that Lykon wanted to weep. Again Dexios's arms were empty as he held onto air, and the wrongness of it screamed out at him. Lykon should be within that circle. "If you will not free him, let me join him. Let us be statues together. Let them be made whole."

"One day perhaps. Not today. Dexios will no longer be alone, now that you are here to care for him while he waits." The goddess touched Dexios's bronzed hair with a fond look in her eyes. "His love sings. Can you not hear him calling to you? You have broken your vow, and I will not free him so you can hurt him again with your empty promises or to have him give up the fight so easily. You will be reborn, and when you are you will have the chance to free him. Fail and the statues will remain uncompleted in that lifetime, and you will have to wait again. Only when all four stand complete will the curse be lifted. You both must be steadfast. Look to the statues, they will be your omens."

"You came back." Dexios's voice shivered in the air and Lykon wept.

"I was such a fool." Lykon clung to him, hoping this was just a nightmare and that Dexios's limbs would unfreeze to take Lykon into his arms again. "Forgive me."

"There will be challenges of your commitment to each other."

Lykon's head jerked up at that silky tone and the threat implicit in it. "Challenges?"

"Of course, one has to betray another to see if the faith will be kept." A slender hand fisted in his hair, and Lykon's heart slammed against his ribs as her lips twisted. "Yes, I think you will be the instrument of betrayal."

"Wait!" Lykon reached out to the goddess as she faded. "Tell me more. What must I do in this lifetime?"

"Care for him, see that he comes to no harm while he waits for you. That is all you can do for Dexios now."

"Wait! Please wait!" Lykon shouted as the goddess disappeared, but she did not return. Desperate, he looked up and down the beach, searching for another living soul. Storms often lashed this area of the coast. He had to find shelter or make it. He had to keep Dexios safe until he could find a way to make it right.

"Lykon." The whisper hung in the air.

"I am here." Lykon kissed the cold brow. "I will not forsake you again. I am here."

CHAPTER NINETEEN

GALEN laid his head against Nick's chest and listened to the rapid beat of his heart while Galen's own breathing calmed. They tangled their limbs together, as Nick slid his hand down Galen's sweaty, slick back. "I have been dying to do that all day," Nick rumbled.

Galen smiled and turned his head to kiss Nick's chest. His body had that pleasant ache from the aftermath of intense sex instead of the not-so-pleasant ache of blue balls. "So was I, whenever I was given a moment to think." And every one of those quiet moments had been filled with Nick: naked Nick, Nick telling him he loved him, the sometimes wary look in his eyes, and the way he would always put on music for Amy and Rory so they could dance. All of those little things had filled up the emptiness inside of Galen.

"So what was it that kept you running around all day?"

Galen was relieved to hear curiosity in Nick's voice instead of suspicion and jealousy. He couldn't handle that all the time. Either Nick trusted him or he didn't, but they wouldn't get very far without trust.

"The opening gala is in a month. I can't believe how quickly it's looming closer. And Suzane's in a tizzy getting it all together since she missed so much time. Since she's naturally contrary, she keeps demanding my opinion just so she can argue with it. Today she was hell-bent on finalizing the catering, and she decided we needed a little music, so we had it out over that."

Nick chuckled and squeezed Galen's shoulders. "I like her. I'm glad she's doing better."

"Me too." Galen trailed his fingers down Nick's chest, exploring and thinking of teasing him into a second round. "We had the security lights installed in the exhibit room. That's when I noticed the second statue. I was getting ready to text you. When I saw Dexios and Lykon together, it startled me so much I dropped the cell and it broke. I think the installation guy thought I'd lost my mind."

Nick laughed again and captured Galen's fingers before giving the tips a gentle nip. "I can only imagine the scene you made."

"I wanted to send you a picture, and I couldn't ask him to borrow his phone, not when the picture was R-rated. So I waited until Knox got in. You've met him, remember? He hangs out at the workshop and helps us around the museum part time. Suzane wants to hire him in a more permanent capacity. Though, I suppose I probably shouldn't have used his either, not if he's a potential employee. You're the HR manager, what do you say?"

"Definitely not, some people would say using an employee's phone to send R-rated pictures could be considered grounds for harassment."

"Hmmm, well, I'll apologize to him tomorrow." Galen rolled onto his stomach, crossed his arms over Nick's chest and smiled at him. "There was nothing at all underhanded about me using his phone. It was a freaky turn of events."

Nick's expression turned regretful, and he smoothed Galen's hair back from his forehead. "I'm sorry about that. I was reacting to you suddenly being unavailable and uncommunicative more than anything else. Which goes back to when you left and stupid shit with my family, but it's not fair to hang it all on you. You get busy at work, so do I. It happens, and I just have to deal with my own issues."

"It's different now. It was different from the moment I got up the courage to call you. And now that I know I love you, it's even more different than before." Galen kissed Nick and repeated the sentiment. "I'm going to keep saying those words until you believe them. Before, we had sex, and I'd like to think, the start of a friendship. Just because you can't get a hold of me doesn't mean I'm going to up and disappear on you."

"Are you sure you won't reconsider marrying me? I know it all came out wrong earlier tonight, and maybe I'm rushing us—"

Galen pressed his fingers against Nick's lips and shook his head. "One thing at a time. You have your hang-ups about the past and so do I. And one of them is being proposed to for all the wrong reasons. It's a commitment, not a lark, not an excuse to have a hold on somebody or doing it for another person, like Dexios and Lykon. When you can say that you want to marry me because you want a future together, because you can see that future, and it's not an excuse, then you ask me."

Nick cocked his head, his gaze becoming curious. "You've been proposed to before?"

"Not tonight. I don't want to talk about past relationships when I'm naked in your bed." Galen straddled Nick's body. "The only person I want to think about is you. But I think if things keep going the way they are and you're not sick to death of me by the time the gala is over, then we can discuss taking things to another level."

Nick cocked his head, slid his hands up and down Galen's ribs before his hands settled on Galen's hips. "Another level? And I'm assuming you're not talking about eloping, so... maybe moving in?"

Galen leaned over him and gave Nick a small smile. "That's a possibility. Let's just take this one day at a time. We both have issues to work through. Okay? And it just so happens that my lease will be up around that time. Why don't we keep that thought as a possibility?" And if not Nick's, then Galen knew he needed to get out of the place he'd shared with Bryan anyway. He should've done that a year ago.

"I know I rushed things, and I know we're starting over, not really picking back up from where we left off." Nick lifted up to press a kiss to Galen's mouth. "When I see something I want, I go for it, but I should be giving you time. I didn't give it to you last time. I guess what I'm saying is it's okay, we can wait until after the gala to talk about it again."

Galen's heart started beating faster as Nick's hands wandered over Galen's body, and he pressed more of those kisses down from Galen's lips to his jaw, then his throat. For a moment Galen worried Nick would refuse, that he wouldn't be ready to take a step back. They had enough pressure on them with the statues and their past heartbreaks. They didn't need more.

"I have another seven months on my lease." Nick slid his arms around Galen and turned them both around so Galen was under him. "When that's up we can find a place together if that's what we decide."

Galen warmed inside. Together. He liked the sound of that. And maybe in seven months they'd both be ready to consider making their relationship permanent. He wanted it. He was a little frightened by how much he wanted it. That permanency. But only if Nick truly believed that it could work. Galen wasn't going to go into it already handicapped. "That sounds like the best thing you've said all night."

"Is that right?" Nick said with a mock growl.

Galen laughed and nodded. "Yep, and I think we should celebrate."

Nick's lips wandered down Galen's jaw to his throat, eliciting a thrilled shiver from him. "And how do you propose we do that?"

Galen slid his leg up along Nick's and hooked it around his waist as he arched his throat. "Oh, I'm sure I can count on you to be very inventive."

THE early-morning light filtered through the blinds as Galen lay curled up next to Nick, watching him sleep. This was a simple pleasure he didn't want to take for granted. If he had a say in it, he would choose to wake up like this every morning for a very long time. Galen kissed Nick's temple, then rose to shower and make a quick breakfast for both of them.

He could've handled their confrontation better last night. He'd been too tired and too excited to notice Nick's tension. Galen stepped under the hot spray and let it wash over his face. And admittedly, he'd been hurt to realize that Nick still didn't trust him. He'd just have to earn it, bit by bit if that's what it took. It had taken Galen almost two years to get to this place again, where he was willing to risk his heart. He owed Nick the time to heal as well.

It would take a while, especially with the way Galen had reacted when Nick proposed. It had grabbed him right by the gut. Galen leaned his hands against the wall, letting the water relax muscles knotted by memory. Bryan had asked because it was a lark, something fun to do, to add to his bucket list, not because he really wanted to settle down. He'd loved Bryan, and he knew Bryan had loved him in return, but trying to hold onto him was like trying to hold onto running water.

That's what they had been arguing about right before the accident. Galen shuddered. It was almost enough to make him go to

Nick and say yes. They could grab the license and go before the justice of the peace and get married. Nick wasn't Bryan; he wanted the same stability that Galen craved. They'd find a way to make it work. *We love each other, right?*

Sometimes love wasn't enough.

Galen laid his forehead against the tiles with a sigh and shut off the water before it cooled. Nick would want one too, this morning.

No, he couldn't jump into a marriage for the wrong reasons, no matter how much it stung Nick last night. In the meantime, Galen would keep doing what he was doing, keep being honest with Nick about how he felt. This was going to take work, like any other relationship. Hadn't that been Dexios's and Lykon's problem? They'd been too impatient to work through their troubles?

Galen toweled himself off and smiled as he heard Nick's light snore when he went back to the bedroom to change for the day. The snoring broke off, followed by a throaty, "Mmm."

Galen glanced over his shoulder as he pulled on his pants. Nick smiled at him, eyes half-lidded. "Morning, you hungry?"

"Waking up to see you bent over has me thinking of many wants, and food isn't one of them," Nick said in a teasing voice. "You sure have my complete attention. I'm not even remotely interested in going back to sleep."

Galen shrugged into a shirt and leaned down to drop a quick kiss on Nick's lips. "I left some hot water for you. I'll go make us food."

"I'd rather shower with you." Nick caught Galen before he could straighten and kissed him again.

"Tomorrow," Galen promised. "It'll give us something to look forward to."

"Tease," Nick grumbled as Galen moved back, but there was a smile in his eyes. "This is the second time you're going to send me off to work with blue balls."

"Ha, yesterday was your fault. I was fully prepared to finish what I started," Galen called back as he moved toward the living room. From under the draped cage he heard a twitter of greeting, and he made a detour to pull the cover off the cage. Amy cocked her head, fixed one eye on him, and let out a burst of sound.

"Good morning to you too." Galen said, opening the blinds. The twittering and cheeps followed him into the kitchen where he pulled out the ingredients for an omelet.

Breakfast was ready and being slid onto plates when Nick appeared, wearing a pair of sweats and a Chewbacca T-shirt. It made Galen's lips twitch. Nick would do just about anything to hold off putting on a suit for another five minutes. It was the last thing he put on in the morning and the first thing he took off at night.

"I'm probably going to be working late tonight," Galen said as he brought the plates to the table. "Until the gala is over, I'm afraid I'll be spending more and more time there."

Nick frowned and poured himself a cup of coffee. "I could help you out some if you want."

"Thank you. The more hands, the faster it'll go," Galen said as he buttered his toast. "I used to spend every waking moment there. It worried Suzane a bit; now I look forward to getting off at a reasonable hour."

"Do you want to go out tonight or stay in?" Nick asked before taking a long drink of his coffee, then topping it off.

"In, please. I want to relax. We could come back here. You have pets to care for. I don't."

Nick had sounded jealous last night over something. Galen made a mental note to get Nick more involved with the workshop at the museum since he was interested. Then Nick would see that he had nothing to worry about with any of the men that Galen saw over the day. Nick didn't accuse him of cheating. He didn't try hounding Galen about what he did during the day and who he did it with. Still, the thoughts had to be there. Galen had really been a selfish SOB in the past. Regret twisted inside of him.

Galen couldn't imagine being in love with someone, being with them, and not just knowing but seeing that person with someone else, engaging in empty sex, when you knew you had more to offer them. It would've driven Galen batshit too.

On impulse, Galen covered Nick's hand with his own. "I know I put you through hell last time we were together and more hell during the six months after I walked out." Nick's expression moved from surprised to wary. "I'll make it up to you."

"I don't think you have anything to apologize for, but thank you. And I'm sorry if I make you think that you need to keep apologizing for that. I guess I have my own baggage to work through." Nick turned his palm up and tangled their fingers together. "I knew what I was getting into. You weren't being malicious, and I appreciated your honesty. I'm a big boy; I can make my own decisions."

"Yes, you are a big boy." Galen gave him a mock leer to lighten the mood, and Nick laughed. He wanted to ask Nick what his emotional baggage was, but they didn't have time for an in-depth conversation before Nick had to be at work. He'd get Nick to open up about it tonight.

"You are something else." Nick touched his knuckles lightly to Galen's jaw, his gaze softening. The way he looked at Galen made him feel so alive. "I love you."

"I love you too." The wariness flickered back for an instant before it was gone, and Nick smiled. Well, at least he wasn't telling Galen to stop saying it, so that was progress. Eventually it would really sink in that this was real.

Galen refilled their coffees. "I've got a question for you, something that's been nagging at me from the beginning."

"What is it?"

"If it wasn't for the statues, would you have called me back?" Galen didn't know why he asked; the answer didn't matter. It was just one of those questions that poked at him. How close had he come to letting Nick slip through his fingers by waiting so long? Nick had been so intent on the statues when they spoke again, and Galen had let him, taking whatever connection he could.

Nick got quiet as he pushed the food around on his plate. Finally he looked up at Galen, his expression troubled. "I don't know. I'd like to think yes, I was definitely considering it, but I don't know."

"It's okay. That's fair enough." Galen smiled at him, and Nick's expression eased. "I knew I might have to work to get you back. I'd hoped that you'd want to try, and I was willing to jump through a lot more hoops than you gave me for the chance to get back with you."

"I may have fought the idea of getting back together when you first brought it up, but it didn't last long. Why say no to something I had wanted since I first saw you?" Nick glanced at the clock and slid the rest of his omelet onto his toast. "Damn, I've gotta change. I have a harassment accusation to look into today. I want to get the investigation started as soon as possible."

"That sounds depressing."

"It's going to be. No matter what happens or what we find out, there are going to be some very unhappy people." Nick leaned down and brushed a quick kiss on his lips. "Give me a call tonight if you need to be rescued."

"I'll let you know if I manage to escape the dragon lady unscathed." Galen tugged him down for another quick kiss. "Love you." Again and again, until Nick believed, and Galen thought he might be starting to come around. Somebody else had hurt Nick and hurt him badly. Tonight he'd find out who that was, and maybe then Nick could let go of some of the past himself.

"Love you too." Nick disappeared down the hallway, and Galen grabbed the dishes to bring them to the sink. He'd better get moving himself. He shoved his wallet in his back pocket and searched for his keys.

"Holy shit! Galen!"

Galen spun around at the sound of alarm in Nick's voice, half expecting to see Dexios or some other odd apparition, but it seemed quiet. "What's wrong?" he called as he went down the hallway toward the sound of Nick's voice in the bathroom.

"Bring me a shoe, a big-ass fucking shoe." There was a definite sound of panic in Nick's voice. Mystified, Galen peered into the bathroom. Nick was half-dressed, staring intently at a spot on the floor, his face pale. A large spider sat on the floor in the corner, a pretty ugly-looking one. "Where's my shoe?" Nick demanded, holding out his hand and keeping his gaze on the spider.

"You're wearing shoes." Galen nudged Nick's foot in case he'd forgotten that he already had squishing power.

"No way in hell am I getting near that thing. I need a shoe to throw! Better yet, grab me the fucking broom. Hurry, before it moves."

Galen couldn't help himself. He started laughing and Nick tore his gaze away long enough to shoot him an incredulous look. "It's not fucking funny."

"It's hilarious. Who would've thought you had a spider phobia," Galen said, still laughing as he pushed Nick out of the bathroom. "Go on and get dressed. I'll take care of it for you."

"It's not funny," Nick insisted as he retreated down the hallway. "Spiders are evil."

"I think from its viewpoint you're the evil one. How many of its brethren have you killed?" Galen asked as he upended the cup from the sink over it and went to fetch a piece of cardboard to slide under it.

"Not enough, because they keep breeding."

Galen carried the spider outside and let it go, still chuckling under his breath. "Okay, all taken care of. It's safe to come out."

Nick emerged from the bedroom fully dressed, with an aggravated expression. "You spared it didn't you?"

Galen shrugged with a smile. "I gave it a second chance and a warning. If it comes back, I promise to kill it for you."

"Spider lover," Nick accused. "I'm never going to live this down, am I?"

"Oh hell no."

NICK asked Sean to screen his calls and shut his office door during his lunch hour so he could pore over all the journals, photographs, and copies of the myth his family had collected over the centuries. His conversation with Dexios still plagued him. There was something they were missing about the statues, some key piece of evidence that might allow them to break the curse.

He wanted to believe. He needed to believe. Galen had him all mixed up inside. One minute he was telling Nick he loved him, and the next he was hung up on something from his past, something to do with a marriage proposal. Maybe he could get Galen to talk about it tonight, because Nick got the feeling that he'd shoved his foot into his mouth so damn deep that he almost choked on his knee when he asked Galen to marry him. It was better to think that there was another reason for

Galen's refusal other than the thought of being married to him made Galen shout "Hell no."

Nick gathered the notecards he'd made and spread them out on his desk, looking for a pattern. Then he pulled out the notes he'd made about Galen, Dexios, and Lykon and all the little incidents since the statues appeared. As he did, guilt twisted inside of him. He'd been keeping secrets too, such as how much he knew about the statues and the myth. Galen would not be happy when he found out Nick had been holding out. That had been rather asinine of him. He'd have to tell Galen the truth tonight. At this rate it was going to be like a tell-all confessional after dinner. He hoped that Galen wouldn't be too pissed. Nick winced. He'd have to find some way of making it up to him.

He'd tackle that once he had answers to give to him. Nick picked up the first notecard. The first statue had become whole before Nick and Galen had even laid eyes on each other. The only contact that they'd had was when Galen had called him. Nick stared at the card, his fingers drumming on the table.

The myth stated that Lykon would have to accept Dexios's offer four times. It had taken Nick a while to figure out how that one applied to the first statue. Then memory had tickled. When Galen had left all those months ago, Nick had given him an open invite to call him anytime.

Nick flicked the card and considered their conversation this morning. Would he have called Galen back if the lure of the statues hadn't been there? He'd been hurt when Galen left, not just his feelings but his pride too. The statues had fired him up, but that was just an excuse, wasn't it? A safe reason to call Galen back, something that wouldn't risk his heart, because if Galen was still looking for only a lay, he had a way out.

Yeah, he would've called Galen back. It might have taken a few days while he argued with himself, but the chance that Galen wanted something more would've had him taking the risk. He'd had it real bad. Nick smiled and picked up his phone, trying Galen's office, and to his surprise, he picked up on the second ring.

"Galen Kanellis."

"The dragon doesn't have you pinned down in a cave?" Nick asked, picturing Galen with that slightly abstracted look and the way it would sharpen when he heard Nick's voice. Whatever Galen felt for him now, it was certainly stronger than before.

"Are you trying to get me killed? If she knew I said that about her, I'd be dead. How's your day going?"

"Good, I just wanted to let you know I've been doing some thinking about what we talked about this morning." Nick sat back in his chair, tapping the notecard against his fingers. "I would've called you back, Galen. There's no doubt. My feelings for you hadn't changed. It just might've taken me a couple of days to get my head out of my ass."

Galen was quiet at first, and when he spoke again his voice was warm. Nick loved that sound, the way Galen spoke to him now without any of the distance he'd had before. "Thank you for telling me."

"You're welcome. I'll talk to you later." Nick hung up, smiling to himself as he turned to another notecard. It was hard to remember who had said or done what, but when the second statue had become whole, it had to have been because Galen had opened up about Bryan. Nick had asked him to tell him why he had been so reluctant to commit, and Galen couldn't tell him at first. Nick had offered to listen when he was ready.

That had to be it, Nick making a literal offer and Galen accepting it. There wasn't any twist to the legend. It was as straightforward as it got. So all Galen had to do was accept his marriage proposal, and it would be over with. If Galen loved him as he claimed, then what was the big deal? Say yes, and they could work out the details later.

Somehow he had to make Galen see that. Nick picked up the third notecard and frowned. This was the one that still perplexed him. Both he and Galen could see Lykon, could see how the statue would look when it was complete, and yet something was holding it back from fully materializing.

Nick hadn't been able to miss what had happened. They'd been looking at the second statue. Galen had given him a look that had pierced him right through and told Nick that he loved him. His heart still flipped every time he thought of it, hearing those words the first time with the oh-so-sincere expression in Galen's eyes. The third statue had come together right in front of their eyes… almost.

So what was missing?

Nick told Galen not to say the words unless he meant them, and Galen had said them anyway. If Galen didn't mean them, nothing should've happened with the statues at all. Nick's heart stopped and started again in a rapid drumbeat.

Galen loved him. He really did, even if the thought still scared Nick. He'd allowed himself to start to believe in the hallway after the disastrous proposal. And he remembered how right it felt when he told Galen that he believed him. He had to let go of his fears and embrace it, the way he had when he'd called Galen back, or when he agreed to go on the date. He'd been afraid, but the fear was worth the gain. Galen had to have been afraid too, when he'd talked about Bryan.

The missing element wasn't Galen, it was Nick. Nick had to acknowledge Galen too. Really acknowledge and accept the fact that Galen loved him without waiting for the emotion to be snatched back. Galen wasn't his mom. Galen wouldn't tell him that and then cut him off cold.

Nick shoved aside the journals and dragged the copies of the myth to him again. He scanned over the pages, searching to see if his theory was right. *"...until your fickle lover fulfills his promise four times over and you accept him."* Nick had to accept Galen's love. He had to believe it. And the offers couldn't be just anything. They had to be offers from the heart without any ulterior motive.

He'd bet that the first statue didn't become whole until after Nick had called Galen back or the second statue until after he'd listened to Galen pour his heart out without judgment or jealousy. That's why the third statue remained cursed. Galen had done what Nick requested, but Nick hadn't taken him at his word.

That meant if Nick was the missing element, he had to face the fact that the family journals were biased. They were all from the Dexios reincarnation's point of view. So the breakups and betrayals were one-sided. Cythera blamed Dexios as much as she blamed Lykon. Dexios gave up on Lykon; that's what he'd been referring to in his last visit. And he'd been right too, about the journals clouding the truth.

Nick had a part in this legend too. If he stayed strong and didn't give into doubt, all of them would be okay. Nick and Galen would break the curse together. His heart began racing.

Nick grabbed the phone and called Galen back. "Go check the third statue."

"What?" Galen asking, sounding puzzled. "Are you okay?"

"Set the phone down and go check the third statue now." Nick heard the sound of the phone hitting the desk and running feet. He waited, hardly daring to breathe. He didn't need confirmation. He knew, he knew it in his heart.

The pounding of feet signaled Galen's return, and Nick squeezed his eyes shut, his heart loud in his ears.

"What the hell? How did you know?" Galen said, breathless as he came back. "It's perfect, it's beautiful. What did you do? You have to come see this."

Nick laughed and sank back into his chair. "Tell me again you love me."

A startled silence followed, and then Galen's voice went warm again, the same warmth that Nick had not quite grasped last night. "I love you. You believe me now, don't you? I love you. I swore I'd pound it into your head and ears until you got it."

Nick closed his eyes and smiled. "I've got it, Galen. I believe you."

CHAPTER TWENTY

"I ALMOST feel like this is a second home," Nick said as he climbed into Galen's tower office. The hint of defensive wariness in Nick's eyes had disappeared, and Galen's heart skipped a beat. Nick did believe him. Even if Galen hadn't seen the third statue changed with his own eyes, he would've recognized that faith in Nick's gaze.

"Suzane has accused me of treating the museum like a home. She has booted me out of here on more than one night." Galen tipped his head back when Nick approached and sank his hand into Nick's hair at his kiss. That same surety was there in the possessive sweep of Nick's tongue, in the firm touch of his lips. It made Galen smile all over again.

"I hate to interrupt this interlude," Suzane said in a dry voice. Galen broke away and looked around Nick at his assistant, who had poked her head up through the stairwell. "But I thought you should know that I found the drums you wanted for the gala."

"Yes!" Galen pumped his fist with a grin.

A smile flickered over Suzane's lips before she continued, "The museum is locked down for the night, and if you decide to do something that I absolutely would've done in my younger days, keep it off the security cameras."

"Thank you, I'll try to keep my baser instincts under control."

"I hope not," Nick murmured as Suzane echoed the sentiment with a wicked glint in her eyes and told them good night. The sound of her footsteps echoed through the stairwell, and Galen found himself listening until he was sure she'd made it to the bottom.

"I called my mom today," Galen said as Nick took one of the chairs in front of his desk. "Told her all about you."

"Does this mean that there's a family dinner on the horizon that I'm going to have to attend?" Nick asked with his head cocked and a smile quirking his lips. "Because I've got to warn you, you can expect that from my family after I talk with them."

"Of course there will be a family dinner. Though, she is planning on a quiet meal first before she inflicts the sisters, the cousins, and all the rest of the brood on you." Galen's mother had been overjoyed to hear that he was dating someone seriously again, happy enough that she didn't even quibble over the likelihood that he'd move in with Nick after the gala. And that was a major block for her. He'd heard her views on shacking up on more than one occasion.

"Speaking of my family, they'll probably try to get you to San Francisco either for the holidays or for the christening, but I had another thought in mind," Nick said. "I'm taking a trip to Santorini at the end of summer, and I was thinking of swinging by home for a day or two as well. Why don't you go with me?"

"To San Francisco or Santorini?"

"Both." Galen frowned, and Nick cocked his head. "Let me guess, bad timing again?"

"I don't want to leave the entire place in Suzane's hands and go out of the country, not until she's better, and that's going to be right before Heather leaves us too. And if the new exhibit brings us the increased traffic that we want, I just don't see how I can get away from here anytime soon."

Nick picked up a stack of order forms and began organizing them. Galen hated to see the quick flicker of disappointment in his eyes, but he didn't see a way around it. "I understand. Really, I do. You know, I could help out around here in a more official capacity," Nick said with a neutral expression. "If I wouldn't be stepping on any toes. I know you have plans for this place, long-term ones. I'd love to lay the groundwork with you."

Galen hesitated. He should've thought of that before. Nick was already involved in so many ways; why not make it more official? Nick would be an asset. He had a background with business and HR that Galen didn't, but it would be a totally different dynamic than what he had with Suzane. The museum had been Galen's dream for a long time. Nick had had similar dreams. If Galen involved him it would become more of a sharing, and that was a little intimidating.

"You don't have to say anything now." Nick stuck the organized invoices into a file. "Just think on it."

"I will, I promise."

"Sooo… anything else happen today?" The air of suppressed excitement around Nick returned, betrayed by the tone of his voice and the way he couldn't seem to stay quite still. "Did you get your new cell phone?"

"Yes, but you didn't run over straight from the bank to talk about that." Galen shut his laptop and gestured toward the fire pole. "Let's go see them."

There was an extra bounce to Nick's step as they walked to the exhibit room. Galen was a little surprised that he hadn't stolen a peek before coming up. He didn't know if he would've had Nick's restraint. He'd been down here more times than he could count today to ogle. He wouldn't have blamed Nick one bit if he'd stopped by first to ogle as well.

As soon as they reached the exhibit, Nick headed straight for the third statue. Tonight Galen found himself lingering near the first one. The sight of Dexios and Lykon caught in that passionate embrace never failed to make him smile. That and he didn't want to experience those urges that hit him whenever he was close to one of those unfinished statues. Even knowing that it was Lykon responding and not really him didn't make it easier. It was too intimate. With the finished statues it was more like seeing old friends.

"Pictures don't even do them justice," Nick said, crouching down next to where Dexios and Lykon stretched out on the floor. "It's so real, as if you can sense them almost. Maybe it's because we're connected, but it's strong. I wouldn't be surprised if it translated to your patrons."

"I know what you mean." Galen touched Dexios's shoulder. "They seem happier. It's weird; I would've thought that they'd be more anxious since it seems like we're so close to actually breaking the curse. Instead it's like they're too busy reveling in each other, so engrossed in the moment that there is no worry about what might happen next."

"I think you're right." Nick looked across the bronzed limbs toward Galen. "Maybe we should take a lesson from them."

"I've had similar thoughts along those lines. I could be afraid of loving and losing again, but that would be a mistake." Galen sighed and dropped his hand from Dexios's shoulder. "I wish this could be over for the gala. I'd love for this nightmare to end for them and for people to see them as they should be seen, together."

Galen had given a lot of thought to Nick's proposal and his knee-jerk reaction to it. Maybe Nick wanted to get married for the wrong reasons, but he believed Galen loved him now. Maybe Galen needed some faith himself, faith that they could work through this somewhat shaky start of theirs, faith that what they felt would win out over their fears. He wanted to give Nick that sign of faith as much if not more than he wanted to break the curse.

"Nick, I've been thinking a lot today, actually. You know, maybe I—"

"Wait right there before you say what I think you're going to say," Nick interrupted as he rose to his feet. "I've been doing some thinking too, and I have both an apology and a confession to make."

Galen stared at Nick, caught off guard. "What could you possibly have to confess?" A twinge of foreboding hit him when Nick wouldn't quite meet Galen's eyes. Surely he was blowing this all out of proportion. Galen couldn't imagine Nick doing anything to betray his trust.

"Apology first." Nick took Galen's hand and led him out to the bench in the hallway. Thoroughly confused now, Galen didn't say anything as they sat down. How could Nick apologize if Galen didn't know what for?

"I shouldn't have asked you to marry me last night. It was wrong of me to try to use you like that. When I do ask you," Nick paused and gave him a nervous smile, "and I hope to one day get that chance, I want it to be because it's the right step forward, the right time. I don't want there to be any regrets later on. I don't want to ask you for somebody else's benefit. It should be just between us."

Nick's words eased a weight on Galen's heart and mind that he hadn't even realized he had been carrying. He didn't want to wonder later on if that was the only reason why Nick had asked, or if he'd asked as a preemptive strike to keep Galen from leaving and moving onto somebody else.

"Thank you. Bryan proposed, the night of the accident. That's what we had been arguing about. He didn't believe in forever, and I wasn't ready to tie myself to somebody who didn't. He thought I was being oversensitive and making too much of a situation that wasn't a really big deal."

"I guess I doubly fucked up when I asked." There was genuine remorse in Nick's expression and an unguarded sincerity that Galen had been waiting to see. "I don't think it's being oversensitive to want the real deal. That's what I want too, that forever kind of commitment."

Galen studied Nick, his concern growing as Nick seemed even more nervous now. "What's going on?"

"I haven't been entirely honest with you."

Galen went cold inside. He knew they still had issues to work through, but the one thing he'd counted on was them being honest with each other. Now that he looked back at it, he was the one who had made that promise, not Nick. He pulled his hand from Nick's and tried to ignore the quick slice of hurt that crossed his face.

"Okay, I'm listening." A thousand possibilities crossed his thoughts, and he shut them all down without considering them. He wanted to hear whatever it was from Nick's lips.

"Damn, you're pissed and shutting me out," Nick muttered, dragging a hand through his hair. "Please, don't shut me out, not now."

"Just talk to me. I'm not shutting you out; I'm trying not to jump to any conclusions. Tell me what's bugging you."

"You already know that you're the reincarnation of Lykon, and you know that my family owns the Collection, but it runs a little deeper than that. I know more about the statues than I let on." The words came out in a rush, and Nick grabbed Galen's hand again. "I can read those journals that I showed you, the ones in Greek."

Galen frowned as his thoughts whirled in a confusing dance. "I don't get it. Why try to hide that you knew?"

"It's complicated. First off, though my family technically owns the Collection now, they originally belonged to your family. Lykon was given the charge to watch over Dexios, and he passed that on to his brother's children. Sometime a couple hundred years ago my ancestor got pissed at your ancestor and took them away. We've been in control ever since. I don't think my people trusted your people to care for them."

"Wait a freaking minute…." Galen scrubbed a hand through his hair. He didn't know why he hadn't picked up on it before. He'd been so preoccupied with Lykon's journey that he hadn't even considered Dexios's. But it all came together in a flash of insight. "So what you're trying to tell me is that you're a reincarnation of Dexios. How the fuck does that work if he's stuck as a statue?"

Nick shrugged with a perplexed expression and lifted his hands in a helpless gesture. "I don't know. They both died. They both had families that carried their blood. And they both have spirits that linger; Lykon's in you and Dexios's with the statue. We've said it before, and they've said it too: though we're supposed to be their reincarnations, we're not them. Our experiences, our lives have made us different. I don't know if solving the curse ends the reincarnations or if it just reunites Dexios and Lykon. I don't know how it works, it just does."

Galen stared down at their linked hands and tried to make sense of it all. The romantic inside of him liked the thought of Nick being the one for him throughout all their different lives. Nick would probably argue that they'd managed to screw it up for a couple dozen generations, which raised the question: how much could that be blamed on the curse, on the weight of all those broken dreams? He hated how the curse seemed to dictate so much of his new relationship with Nick. He could imagine previous incarnations crumbling, as the pressure to fix it eroded what they were trying to build. It was a different situation. It needed to remain separate. He believed that wholeheartedly.

"Every generation or so Dexios is reborn as someone in my family," Nick continued. "The last time was during World War II, my great-uncle who I was named after. I used to love the stories my dad told me about him, and he gave me the journals when I was a teenager. Even though I used to study the journals, I never suspected that I could be one of those men until you called me about the statues."

Galen was silent as he recalled Nick's intensity that first morning after seeing him again. He'd been too nervous to read too much into it, too happy on seeing Nick again. He felt… used, and he tried telling himself that Nick would've called anyway. He'd said so. Galen didn't like this feeling of manipulation, and it wasn't just Nick. It was as though everything in their relationship had been instigated and influenced by those damn statues. He wanted a reboot, to go back to that phone call and start over again without Dexios and Lykon imprinting themselves on the situation.

"For God's sake, say something," Nick snapped, running an agitated hand through his hair.

"I'm just trying to figure out what's real and what's them." Galen touched a hand to his chest where Lykon waited and Nick paled.

"Don't say that." Nick cupped Galen's face. "I fell in love with you long before the statues were found. It's real. I fucked up, okay?"

Galen closed his eyes and nodded, fighting back his fears. That was true, and he'd started to feel for Nick back then too, when he knew nothing of Lykon and the curse. There had been no other man inside of him, tugging him toward Nick. Suzane had been right when they'd found the statues in the storeroom. They had brought so much trouble and so many questions. Yet Galen knew he couldn't bring himself to part with them. "You're right, you did. I did. Why didn't you tell me?"

"I knew too much. I was afraid. Take your pick. All those journals of men in my family who'd failed and had their heart broken. I just knew it would happen to me next. I was waiting for it." Nick gestured toward the exhibit room and the statues that waited inside. "I couldn't see my part in it, my responsibility. I just kept waiting for the ax to fall and wishing I could stop it."

Galen was supremely grateful now that they hadn't gotten engaged. Thank God Nick had stopped him, because Galen couldn't handle this without trust. He could work on his relationship with Nick, but he wasn't about to take that step into that level of commitment if Nick didn't trust him in return. Galen wasn't sure if he entirely trusted Nick anymore either, not unless he made honesty a policy as well.

"Is there anything else you haven't told me?" Galen asked, looking into Nick's eyes. "I don't want more swerves."

"No. No more surprises. I just thought you should know that agreeing to marry me wouldn't work, because breaking the curse is going to take both of us and it involves how we feel about each other, not what we're trying to do for Dexios's and Lykon's benefit."

"I came to that conclusion myself. I tried telling you, but I guess you weren't listening." A stricken expression crossed Nick's face, and Galen turned away. He didn't know what to think. He wanted some time to himself, a night alone to work through everything that was spinning in his mind. But he knew that if he suggested staying here and sleeping on the couch tonight it would go very badly. Nick would take it as confirmation that Galen wanted to run. Galen knew that was a knee-jerk reaction of his: shut down, tune out, put some space up until he got his thoughts and feelings back under control. And that wouldn't work with Nick.

"I don't know if this will make you feel better, but I decided to come clean before I had my epiphany about the statues and about how you felt about me. It came before, not after."

Galen shook his head, and Nick fell silent as Galen tried to work through what he felt about all of this. "I don't care right now. I just don't. I don't want to hear about them. I don't want to talk about them. Let's just go."

THE silence in the apartment dug under Nick's skin like a maddening itch that he couldn't quite get to. It didn't matter that he had the radio on for Amy and Rory, or that they let out their occasional flurry of chirps and twitters. No, it was Galen's silence that ate at him.

Galen sat at the other end of the couch, reading through some papers in a file folder with a thoughtful frown. He didn't completely ignore Nick and pretend he didn't exist, which was something, at least. Galen answered when Nick asked him a question, but then he buried himself back in his work with a single-mindedness that was driving Nick batshit. Now that he knew Galen with the walls down, he didn't want to go back to the protective distance that Galen had maintained the first time they were together.

If it wasn't for the fact that Nick knew he was irked over their conversation, and maybe a little bit hurt, he wouldn't think anything of it. But he did know, and dammit, he just wanted to find some way to make it right. Nick couldn't fix anything if Galen continued to refuse to talk about it.

Honesty was important to Galen. What if he decided that Nick wasn't worth the effort?

Nick picked up his cell phone before he gave into the urge to poke at Galen again and ask something stupid like "Are you okay." He'd been getting better about keeping in touch with his dad and Jason, and he'd even worked up the guts to give Damian and Stefan a call, though they hadn't returned it yet. It was crazy that he still got nervous when he picked up the phone. So far none of the fears he'd built up in his head had played out.

That's what he needed to do with Galen, stop letting his fears rule him. That's what he'd tried doing tonight when he came clean with him. He wanted to show him that he was trying to change too, to let go of the past and give this a real chance.

His dad answered on the third ring, and the sound of his gruff voice was very welcome. "Hey, Dad."

"Nick." Warmth suffused his dad's voice, and some of the conflicted jangle of emotions in him died down. "How're you doing?"

Nick flicked a glance at Galen, who was scribbling a note on one of the papers. "Good, it's been a whirlwind here lately. How are things going with you?"

Galen's pen paused and what might've been a smile touched his lips, though Nick wasn't sure. He was tempted to reach out to him, even if it was just nudging Galen's foot with his own, but he didn't. He didn't want the rebuff. He listened to his dad talk about the shop and the nursery he was working on with Jason for the baby.

"Are you still dating that young man you were talking about? Galen?"

A whisper of unease touched him as Nick looked at Galen again. He didn't want to lose him. He didn't want to go through what his Uncle Stavros had, or Dexios, or any of those other luckless men who'd lost their soul mate. "Yeah, we're still together, though I think there are times when I make him nuts."

Galen's head lifted, his gaze questioning, and Nick couldn't take his eyes off of him.

"It happens. Jason has been making Sophia crazy with his hovering. So when am I going to meet this guy? You bringing him home for the baby's christening?"

"I think I could talk him into a short trip to San Francisco. Hey, Dad, I know it's late notice, but I was wondering if you could make it up to Seattle at the end of June? Galen is having a big gala opening for the new exhibit. We'd like you to come."

"End of June, huh?" Nick's stomach knotted at the hesitance in his dad's voice.

"I know you don't like leaving the shop for just Jason to run. Galen feels the same way with his museum," Nick said, steeling himself for the refusal. "But it wouldn't be for long, just the weekend. I can reserve the plane tickets for you."

"No, no. I can pay for my own tickets. Don't you worry about my end. I think Jason can handle the shop just fine. He's been hounding me for more responsibility, him and Sophia both." His dad paused, and a little bit of hope crept in. Until now, his dad had refused to talk with him about the Dexios Collection. Every time Nick brought it up, he changed the subject. "So this is the exhibit with Uncle Stavros's statues?"

"Yeah, they're amazing, Dad. A little NC-17, but really amazing. There aren't any words to describe them."

"Sure there are, a whole bunch of words written on decaying paper." A concerned note entered his dad's voice. "I suppose they need to be insured. How much is that going to cost us?"

"Actually, Galen and I have that covered. We split the cost, so don't worry about that." Nick waited for his dad to ask him where he got the money from and if he'd thought it through, but he didn't.

"I know I give you a hard time about having your head off in la-la land and of dreaming too big without thinking things through. I don't want you losing that part of yourself; it's what makes you Nick. I was so hard on you because I didn't want it to control you. So that being said, don't get obsessed with the Dexios Collection. You can have many dreams. They don't have to all be around one thing."

Too late for that. Hell, it had been too late from the time when Nick had heard the first story. He'd dreamt of those statues, of finding them, long before he'd been estranged from his family and sought them anew as a peace offering. The last few months had only added to his fevered preoccupation. Galen was right to worry.

"I won't. Galen's got his head straight about them, and he's making sure I keep my perspective."

Galen's head lifted again, and there was no question about it this time—the smile lit up his brown eyes.

"Good to hear. I'll call you when I get the details settled for the flights."

Nick tossed his phone on the couch and folded his hands behind his head. He needed to say something, to close this gap of silence between him and Galen, but the words failed him.

Galen smiled at him from the other side of the couch and set the file on the coffee table. "I'm glad you're talking to him more often."

Nick's tongue unknotted with that first offering from Galen. "I...." He leaned forward and rested his elbows on his knees. "I'm sorry I didn't tell you everything from the beginning. It was stupid."

Galen shook his head and waved the apology away. "I've been thinking about it, and you don't have anything to apologize for. I come bursting into your life after all these months and expect you to tell me everything about something that obviously means a lot to you. That's not fair. You had every reason to not trust me at the beginning. I needed to remember that. I can't honestly have expected you to spill your guts on all your secrets right away. That would make me a real asshole."

Galen's gaze softened even more. "It also occurred to me that you opened up the very same day that you realized I wasn't bullshitting, that I do love you. I think we both need to stop being so damn prickly and touchy."

The unhappy knot of tension in Nick's chest unraveled. "Trust is not something that comes easily for me. But I think half the time it's my own fault."

"Again, understandable, and I think not just because of how you felt when I left."

Nick squirmed inside from Galen's insight. After all these years the memory of his mom leaving was still seared into his brain. He never wanted to be in a situation like that again, where he was begging somebody to stay. And he'd come so close to that with Galen. "I...."

"Talk to me," Galen said, his voice soft. "Who else broke your heart?"

"It's not what you think. I don't have some long-lost lover that hurt me." Though come to think of it, that was rather sad itself. He had protected himself so much that he hadn't allowed anyone else to get that close.

"But somebody hurt you and hurt you bad. I can see it." Galen turned his body toward him and leaned his head on his arm on the back of the couch. "Let me in a little."

"It's no big deal. It happened a long time ago." Nick played with a mechanical pencil, ejecting the lead and pushing it back in until it broke. "My mom left."

Nick stole a glance at Galen, who was continuing to watch him with a look in his eyes that made Nick's throat ache. "My dad was at work, he worked a lot then, from before opening till after close, Jason was helping him. I was at home with my brothers and mom, and we were just screwing around being stupid, and I broke a window. Stefan and Damien ran next door to a friend's house when it happened. Mom lost her ever-loving mind. She began yelling, then crying and the next thing I knew she was packing up all the suitcases in the house."

"Oh God, how old were you?" Galen moved closer on the couch, bridging the distance between them.

"Ten." Nick swore he could remember every word that was said that day, every accusation that was hurled when the rest of the family came home to find Nick alone. Not his dad, though. His dad had been quiet, and he'd tried reassuring Nick many times that it hadn't been his fault. "Nothing I said convinced her to stay. I cried, I begged, and it only upset her more."

"I'm so sorry." Galen took his hand, and even that slight contact made the memory hurt a little less.

Nick looked up, drawn by the gentleness in Galen's voice. "It was a long time ago."

"Did you ever see her again?"

"Yeah, for a little bit. About a year later she wanted to see me and my brothers, so she contacted Dad, and he agreed. I would've done anything to get her to stay, and she promised that she would, but my brothers they were still pretty angry, and they didn't make it easy for her. Not that I blame them, I just wanted to pretend that it never happened. We got a few months of visits with her before she disappeared again. I haven't seen her since."

"I…." Galen leaned in and kissed him. "She missed out on an amazing man."

"I'm glad you can still say that when I know I drive you crazy. I'm sorry."

Galen shook his head and tapped his finger to Nick's lips. "I can easily still say that. I'll drive you crazy at times too. But at the end of the day the two of us together are better than us apart. You let me be myself, which was something I think I was missing before."

"I wouldn't want you any other way." Nick slid his hand into Galen's hair, both relieved that the subject of his past was over and grateful that Galen knew the story. It had really torn him apart inside. Maybe now he could let that go, just as Galen had let some of the guilt and pain over Bryan's death go when they'd talked about it. And maybe now he understood his brothers and their reaction to his move a little more too. He wanted to help Galen in return, get him to take another step forward.

"How about we work on getting you to drive a bit this weekend?" Panic flashed across Galen's face, leaving behind a distinctly ill look. "Not far, I promise not to send you out onto any highways, just enough to break the ice a bit and get you behind the wheel again."

"Fine." Galen drew in a deep breath and rubbed his palm on his jeans. "Can we do it Sunday, before we go to Mom's for dinner?"

This time Nick felt the hot rush of prickling nerves. "Sunday dinner? This Sunday? You didn't say that it was going to be so soon earlier."

"I got distracted, sue me." Galen grinned, a wicked glint in his eyes. "Trust me; you don't want to try avoiding her. Mom has a way of tracking people down that's uncanny."

Okay, dinner. Nick could do this, no problem.

"Looks like you'll get a chance to meet my dad at the gala." Nick slipped his arm around Galen's shoulders, and a sense of contentment settled over him.

"That would be cool. Think your brothers might show?"

"Not likely, but you know, one step at a time, right? Jason and Sophia will have to run the shop, and it's going to take Stefan and Damian a little longer to come around. But I think I have a little more insight into them. I think if I keep doing what I'm doing, calling and visiting, that things will eventually be okay." Galen took Nick's hand and laced their fingers together. It felt good to be so relaxed around someone again, without the weight of the past or the worry for the future hanging over him.

"You'll get there. Rebuilding trust is a step-by-step process." Galen brushed a kiss on his jaw. "You taught me that."

CHAPTER TWENTY-ONE

GALEN hadn't mentioned Nick's crazy-assed notion to get him behind the wheel of a car again. He'd been hoping that Nick had forgotten all about it, and he didn't want to do anything to call attention to the suggestion. When Nick didn't bring it up the rest of the week, Galen thought that he'd managed to escape.

Then Nick shooed them out the door an hour earlier than they had to leave for his mom's, and Galen realized that Nick hadn't forgotten it at all. Nick was never ready early. Galen's stomach began to knot as they left the apartment, and by the time they were loaded in the car and Nick pulled off, Galen's palms were sweating.

"This is a bad idea," Galen muttered and bit at his thumbnail. "We should try this another time."

Nick shot a quick sympathetic glance at him. "There's never going to be a good first time, especially now that so much time has already passed. It's like getting on a bike again, but on a much bigger scale. What happened was far worse than a simple accident, but if you do nothing you still let it have power over you, and I know that's not what you want."

Galen rubbed his hands on his jeans and stared unseeing out the window. His stomach churned. He wanted to argue, but Nick was right. He couldn't live the rest of his life with this fear and self-imposed handicap. Still, did it have to be today? He had so much on his mind. After the gala would be a much better time.

"We won't be out long today, and you can relax after at your mom's," Nick said, interrupting Galen's thoughts. He reached over, caught Galen's hand and brought it to his lips for a quick kiss.

Nick got them on the highway heading out of Seattle, toward the suburb where Galen's mom lived. Galen closed his eyes, not wanting to see all the other vehicles on the road today of all days. "The sun's too bright. I didn't bring my sunglasses." He couldn't drive with the sun in his eyes.

"That's okay, you can use mine." Nick squeezed Galen's hand. "Besides, I thought it would be better today than on an overcast or rainy day."

Galen went cold inside at the thought. "Good point."

It was daylight, sunny, and they were headed toward quiet, back roads. This couldn't be any more different than the night of the accident. Galen kept telling himself that, concentrating on breathing slowly in and out, as he had so many nights after Bryan died when panic or grief would strike. Gradually, they had faded, though he still got the occasional panic attack. One seemed to be building up to strike now, and Galen refused to break down in front of Nick.

By the time Nick pulled over in the empty parking lot of a high school, Galen had managed to calm himself down somewhat. Okay, this he could do. A large space. Nobody else around. It would be similar to when he was fifteen and his big sister had taken him out to show him the basics without his mom knowing.

Nick pulled his car over and stuck it in park. "You ready?"

Fuck no, he wasn't ready. Galen's stomach jumped, but he nodded and got out of the passenger side before he could change his mind. He could do this. He slid behind the wheel and took his time adjusting the mirror and seat. His stomach was fluttering so badly he was surprised it didn't take flight right out of his throat.

"Nothing complicated at first. Why don't you go around the parking lot a few times?" Nick suggested and handed him his sunglasses. Galen set his hands on the wheel. He could feel the sweat on his palms. That wasn't good. He wouldn't be able to grip it if he kept this up. He had to get over this.

Galen found himself putting the car in drive, and it crept forward a few feet. His heart hammered, and he gripped the wheel tighter.

"Hey." Nick touched his wrist, and Galen heard the concern in his voice. "It'll be okay. Trust me. We can keep it to the parking lot today."

"It's not you I don't trust."

Nick hadn't killed his partner in a car accident, Galen had. And God, now Nick was sitting next to him…. He couldn't do this with Nick sitting next to him. The first turn came, and Galen's arms felt stiff as he maneuvered the wheel. He was going to be sick.

"You've got to relax." Once again Nick touched his arm, and Galen found his grip locking even tighter. "Don't hold on so tight. You won't be able to adjust."

Nick's voice sounded tinny and far away. It became a nonsense blend of words. The sense of Lykon bloomed to life in his awareness and panic lurched. *No!* Galen clung to the wheel, his gaze fixed ahead as he searched for the brake. Lykon couldn't come now. Galen couldn't allow himself to get dizzy, or even worse. Nick was there. He could get hurt. He could….

"Galen!"

What if Nick wanted him to take the car out on the road the next time? There would be other drivers, people Galen couldn't control. He could take care of his end, but he couldn't predict theirs. That night flashed through his mind again: the rain, the blurry lines on the road, and the other vehicle's swerve into his lane. That god-awful scream, only this time the scream was Nick's.

Galen slammed on the brakes, jerking the car to a stop. Moments later he was outside on his knees, dragging in great gulps of air that seemed to do nothing to ease the pressure on his chest. Lykon didn't fight to get free; instead, the sense of his presence remained steady and strong, bolstering him instead of trying to take over.

"It's coming, be ready, stay strong. There is a test. There is always a test, I'm sorry." The inner voice shivered over him with a looming sense of dread.

Right now Galen didn't want to be strong. He wanted someone to take care of him. He wanted to just let go in a way that he hadn't allowed himself in a long time. For a moment he almost longed to let Lykon take over, and the presence inside of him grew stronger. Galen let it happen and sensed Lykon bolstering him without the same dizzy spell. Something deep inside him clicked, like a deadbolt sliding open.

Galen shook his head and shoved the voice back. This was embarrassing enough without making it worse with self-induced hysteria. A car door slammed shut, and then Nick was there, kneeling in front of him.

"Galen? Galen, talk to me." The sense of Lykon drew back a bit, though it still hovered.

"I can't. I can't do it. Not today." Galen shook his head and closed his eyes, not wanting to see the pity on his face.

"Hey, hey. Hush." Nick's arms came around him, holding on even though Galen tried to push him away. The thought of Nick seeing him like this brought the panic screaming back. Nick's arms tightened around him. "It's okay."

"Dammit." Galen shoved him away and stumbled to his feet. He didn't look at Nick as he paced back and forth and tried to pull his jumbled thoughts together. He was an idiot for attempting this. Nick could've been hurt. Galen lived in the fucking city; he didn't need to drive anywhere.

"I'm sorry. I just wanted to help."

Galen spun on Nick. "It was a stupid, fucked-up idea."

Pain flashed in Nick's eyes, and his jaw tightened. "I can see that. You've made your point. I won't push you again."

Frustrated, Galen turned away and shoved his hands in his pockets. His shirt clung to his skin, damp from sweat, and his limbs still felt shaky. "Nick...." His voice cracked. "If something happened to you because of me...."

Then Nick was there again and this time Galen didn't resist when he pulled him into his arms. Everything he wanted was right there. Everything he feared to lose. "That accident wasn't your fault. But you're right, this wasn't the best idea. Maybe if we found someone else to go out with you, someone other than me until you get used to driving again."

Galen turned his face into Nick's neck and breathed in his scent. He drank in the sensation of the sun on his skin and Nick holding him tight. Gradually, the cold sensation inside of him warmed. "I'm an idiot."

"No. That's me." Nick kissed the top of his head. "I didn't realize how deep it had a hold of you. You were gripping the wheel so hard that I couldn't turn it half an inch. And when you went white…. We'll find another way of tackling this problem."

We. Galen had just about bitten his head off, shoved him away, acted like a complete jackass when Nick had only been trying to help him to move on, and still he'd said "we." Galen held on tighter and kissed the side of his neck.

"Thank you," he mumbled.

Nick sank his hand into Galen's hair and tipped his head back. Galen's eyes half-closed, and longing filled up the empty place inside of him that the panic had stripped bare. He wanted Nick's hands on him, rough and wild, leaving his ass stinging, the skin hot to the touch. He wanted Nick's mouth leaving marks on his neck. Just then, Galen wished they hadn't promised his mom dinner tonight.

"I know that look," Nick said with a soft chuckle. "That's a much better expression on you."

"What? Other than bald-faced terror?"

Nick's gaze became serious, and his knuckles grazed Galen's jaw. "Yeah. Are you feeling better?"

Galen nodded and took a step back before Nick could ask any more questions. "A little wrung out, but better. Look, we should get going. Mom's expecting us, and I'd like to stop somewhere and pick up a new shirt. I've sweated through this one."

"Okay." Galen sensed Nick's worried eyes on him as he walked back toward the passenger side. His legs still felt a bit shaky, and he'd really rather be anywhere, doing anything other than getting back in that little metal coffin.

"Hey, Galen."

Galen looked up and met Nick's eyes across the top of his car. "When we get home tonight, I'm going to answer that look you gave me a moment ago."

A little thrill went through Galen, and it gave him a boost of energy. The sense of Lykon seemed to subside, as if he knew that the time for fear was over. Galen found himself smiling as he leaned closer, folding his arms on the roof of the car. "Is that a promise?"

Nick's answering smile was wicked to the core. "No, sweetheart, that's a fact."

NICK had enjoyed the chance to meet Galen's mother. She hadn't been anything like what he had expected, which just went to show that his whole viewpoint of mothers was skewed. She had been zany and warm without any of the abstracted distance that Nick's mom had hidden behind more and more before she'd left. And it was obvious that she cared about Galen. It made him miss his dad. Nick had a lot to make up for with him, but that was a problem he was working on.

Nick touched the small of Galen's back as they climbed the stairs up to the apartment and sensed Galen's answering shiver. He'd been a little quieter than normal during dinner, though gradually the lines of strain around his eyes and mouth had eased. There had to be another way for him to get past this terror. As much as Nick hated to admit it—because he wanted to be the one to help Galen—it would probably be best if he weren't the passenger at first. Galen might be better off with a generic driving school.

Galen fumbled with the keys at the door, and Nick swept aside the hair at the nape of Galen's neck. He leaned in closer, breathing in his scent, and heard the catch of his breath. "I haven't forgotten that look you gave me earlier."

Galen shivered again, harder this time, and Nick felt the raised hairs on Galen's neck as he brushed a kiss over the spot. "I was hoping you hadn't," Galen replied in a husky voice.

"Once you walk through that door, you're all mine."

"I'm all yours anyway." Galen turned his head and looked back at him in the dim light coming from their neighbor's apartment.

"One rule before we start—"

Galen's eyebrows knitted together in a frown. "Rule?"

"Yeah, and it's not one I'm going to compromise on either." Nick wasn't sure how far Galen wanted to take a submissive role, and Nick didn't want to step over that line and do something Galen wasn't ready for. That could damage this fragile trust they'd worked so hard to build. "If it reaches a point where you want to stop, you tell me. If I find out later that you didn't and we went to place where you weren't comfortable, it's going to piss me off. Trust goes both ways with this. Do you understand?"

They were both pretty new to this submission/domination game, and Nick didn't want there to be regrets later on. He knew that Galen wasn't into the idea of punishment, even if he liked spankings, and that was an important distinction to know. And that was just tapping the surface of what they could do.

"Yeah, I trust you to be in control, and in return you trust me to let you know if I get freaked." Galen's eyes were solemn as he held Nick's gaze. "I swear, I'll tell you."

Nick smiled and took the keys from Galen's hand. He reached around him to unlock the door and gestured into the darkened apartment. "After you."

"How do you make two words sound so sexy?" Galen didn't hesitate as he stepped over the threshold, and a hot thrill went through Nick in anticipation. His hands trembled, and he almost dropped the keys. He'd never been in this position before, where someone wanted to hand over that much power, and he wanted a few minutes alone to make sure he was in complete control of himself.

"I'm going to let the kids out for a bit. Go take a shower and be waiting for me." Nick flipped on the light and gave Galen a gentle shove toward the hallway.

"Don't be long, okay?"

"Trust me." Nick winked, and Galen headed off with a light laugh. Thoughts of Galen naked, Galen begging, Galen writhing occupied Nick's mind as he let Amy and Rory out while he filled their water and feed dish. He let them roam about until he heard the sound of the water shutting off in the bathroom. "Okay, you two, sorry for the short break, but in you go."

Amy protested loudly as Nick bundled them back in the cage, though she settled down when he covered it with the blanket. He didn't feel too bad for them since they had been out all day until he and Galen had left. Nick washed his hands, listening to the sound of Galen moving about in the bedroom. He couldn't help but wonder how far Galen wanted to take this.

Nick went back to join him and paused in the doorway to the bedroom. Galen had stretched out on his stomach on the bed, his skin damp and flushed from the heat of the water. Nick's cock grew heavy at the sight. His gaze traveled down the length of Galen's spine, over the tempting curve of his ass and down Galen's legs to his toes. Galen watched him with mock innocence, crossed his arms and rested his chin on them. "You're too far away."

Nick crossed his arms as well and leaned against the doorjamb before he gave into the temptation lying in front of him. He'd thought about this more often than he should have over dinner, and he wanted to play, not rush things. "You haven't told me what you wanted."

Galen wiggled his ass and raised one eyebrow. "I want your hands on my ass."

Nick's cock jumped, and he rubbed a hand over his chin as he contemplated that ass. "That's a given, but I want you to say the words."

Galen's eyes went hot and his squirming stilled. "I want you to spank me, hard enough that you leave handprints. And I want you to keep spanking me until I'm hot and sore and it stings even when you touch me gently."

The image that Galen's words gave him filled Nick with a rush of adrenaline. "That's a good start. What else?"

Galen's brow furrowed. "Isn't that enough?"

"You tell me." Nick shrugged out of his shirt and tossed it in the direction of the dresser. "Given the way you were looking at me earlier, I think that's not all you were longing for. What were you thinking when you looked at me like that?"

Twin spots of color appeared on Galen's cheeks, and he wet his lips. He looked so damn beautiful like that, with a touch of shyness and a lot of desire. "I was thinking that I wanted to be helpless with you," Galen said in a quieter voice, lowering his gaze.

"Look at me." Galen snapped his eyes back up, and the color on his cheeks deepened. "How helpless?"

Nick wasn't sure if Galen would answer as he shifted restlessly on the bed. He looked away, then jerked his gaze back to Nick. "Completely."

The possibilities that rose in Nick's mind…. They really needed to go shopping together for toys sometime soon. Nick retrieved a few silk ties from the closet. At least they'd be good for something other than choking him on a weekday. Galen stared at the ties as Nick emerged and groaned under his breath. "The next time you wear those to work I hope you can't function the whole day."

Nick laughed and tossed the ties on the bed before kicking off his shoes. "I think I'll retire them, maybe make a shrine on my wall." He drew Galen's hands behind his back and bound them. The gray silk looked better there than it did around Nick's throat. "Is it too tight?"

"Nope."

"Good." Nick picked up another tie and scooted down the bed to bind Galen's ankles together. "If you want me to stop, flip me a double bird."

"What's wrong with just saying stop?" Galen craned his neck to look over his shoulder, and Nick gave him a wicked grin.

"It might be a little hard to understand you when you have a gag in your mouth."

Galen's eyes widened, and Nick waited to see if he'd change his mind about wanting to be completely helpless. Then he shivered, and his muscles relaxed as he nodded. "Gagged it is."

Nick brought his mouth to Galen's ear as he picked up another tie. "I bet you're harder than you've ever been at the thought."

"You would be right."

Nick grasped Galen's chin and kissed him. Galen groaned, his mouth going soft in surrender. Nick kissed him more deeply, stroking Galen's hip, and when he pulled back, Galen's eyes were hazy. Nick smiled and tied the gag on. The sight of the red-striped gray silk between Galen's lips made Nick's cock ache even more. He dropped a kiss on the corner of Galen's parted lips. "You okay?"

Galen nodded with no trace of the panic that Nick had seen earlier in his expression. If anything, he looked even more eager to get on with it. Nick stood and savored the heat in Galen's eyes while he watched Nick undress. Galen groaned and stared at Nick's cock with that look he got when he wanted to go down on him. Nick's heart quickened.

That was definitely a thought to explore later, after he had driven Galen out of his mind.

He scooped up the final tie, bound it over Galen's eyes, and looked down to admire his handiwork. Galen laid his cheek down on the bed, his breathing deep and even, his body relaxed. A surge of tenderness made Nick breathless. They had something special together despite the rocky start and the lingering issues they were struggling to overcome. He wasn't going to let it end.

Nick straddled Galen's body on his hands and knees and hovered over him. "Helpless suits you, Galen. You should see yourself right now."

Galen made a sound behind the gag and tilted his head to give Nick better access to his neck. "It's not going to be that easy, sweetheart," Nick murmured as he lowered his mouth to Galen's neck. He nuzzled, brushed kisses, and breathed against the sensitive skin. Galen squirmed, making pleading sounds as Nick remained gentle.

Nick felt the goose bumps on Galen's neck when he scraped his teeth, but he didn't do anything harder than that. The sound of Galen's wordless begging was too intoxicating to give in so soon. Nick moved lower and pressed open kisses along Galen's spine. He paused on occasion and sucked, leaving little red marks behind.

"I know what you want. Well, this is what I want, having you out of your mind, anticipating that spanking until it's an acute ache and not knowing when I'm going to give it to you."

Galen's squirming rocked the bed, but whenever Nick glanced at his hands, Galen gave no indication that he wanted this to stop. And the last thing Nick wanted to do was stop tormenting Galen. When he slid his hand beneath Galen to fondle his cock, he found it rock hard. Galen's hips rotated as he pressed against Nick's palm, and when Nick didn't squeeze, the sound of pleas changed to curses.

"Do you feel helpless yet, sweetheart?"

Galen whimpered with a frantic nod.

"You don't know how much you're turning me on right now," Nick said in a rough voice and palmed Galen's ass. His heart pounded while he squeezed Galen's cheeks, and he traced his fingers down the cleft. Galen moaned and tried to lift his ass higher in supplication, though he didn't have the leverage to do it. Nick smacked him lightly, just hard enough to tease, and the curses started up again.

"Fuck, Galen," Nick rasped. He stretched out beside Galen, one hand rhythmically squeezing his ass as he sought out Galen's neck again. He could smell how turned on Galen was, and Nick nipped his throat. Galen whimpered and turned his head so that Nick could get at his nape. Nick fisted his hand in Galen's hair and used that handful to hold Galen in place as he bit the side of his throat again.

Galen struggled for a moment before relaxing with another groan when he realized that Nick wasn't going to release his grip. Nick glanced at Galen's hands again, then went back to tormenting his neck. He nipped Galen's jaw, dragged his tongue back and tasted the clean skin from Galen's shower. He kissed Galen's favorite spot and smiled against his skin at the frustrated groan. "This is where you want it, isn't it?"

Galen made a frantic sound and nodded as much as he could with the leeway Nick gave him. He smiled again and kissed the spot as his hand came down and smacked Galen hard on his ass. Galen cried out and stiffened before trying to lift his ass up for another. Nick draped his knee over Galen's thighs to pin them down. It only seemed to spur Galen on to writhe even more. He panted around the gag, and the edges of the silk started to dampen.

Fuck, Galen was beautiful, his desire evident in the flush of his skin and those oh-so-sexy sounds coming from the back of his throat.

Nick's cock pressed against Galen's hip, and every move that he made had Nick's cock aching a little more. He slapped Galen's ass again and watched the flex of his muscles as he squirmed. His hips circled, grinding into the bed. "I think one of those toys we're going to buy is a cock ring. Then you can grind all you want and keep working yourself up with no relief."

The long, drawn-out moan was the only answer Nick needed. He traced his tongue over Galen's favorite spot, smelled his scent sharpen, then bit him, just hard enough to make Galen cry out. He shuddered, and his hips jerked against the bed. Nick sucked on the spot and kissed the mark he made. It was hard to choose which he wanted to play with more, Galen's neck or his ass. It was wonderful to know they'd have many more nights just like this so he didn't have to choose.

He began spanking Galen—hard, measured slaps that quickly began to redden the sweet globes of his ass. The small bedroom was filled with the sound of bare flesh smacking against bare flesh and Galen's muffled pain-tinged, pleasured-laced cries. Galen's body moved in an erotic dance. With each blow he jolted and tensed, then his hips would grind as he moaned before he'd lift his ass again in anticipation of the next one.

Nick's handprint stood out stark white against Galen's skin before the blood rushed to fill the space. And when he would rub Galen's ass between the strikes he could feel the heat burning hotter. Watching Galen rub himself into the bed, searching for the right amount of friction to get himself off as he was spanked, made Nick's mouth go dry. He stared at Galen's ass and thought about how it would feel to fuck him with that scorching heat pressed against his hips, to hear Galen's hoarse pleas as his tender skin was given even more stimulation.

Nick groaned and squeezed Galen's ass as he circled his cock against his hip. Fuck, if he kept this up he'd be coming himself, and this was not where he wanted to do it. Nick pulled his hips back and brought his mouth close to Galen's ear again. "You going to come for me? You think you can get off from being bound and spanked?"

Galen moaned, sweat dampening his body as his cries became more and more frantic, and his body tensed. "That's it, sweetheart," Nick breathed, his gaze fixated on Galen. "You're almost there. Fuck, you're beautiful to watch." His heart pounded, and he leaned down to nip Galen's shoulder blade.

Galen's hips jerked hard and his muscles stiffened even more. The gag did little to mask his shout of completion, and the scent of his orgasm rose hot and heady. Galen's hips stilled, and he trembled, limp and sated next to Nick.

"Damn, that was hot." Nick eased him onto his side and stroked his fingers over the ankh tattoo on Galen's hip. Galen's ass pressed against Nick's hips, and Nick's cock jumped, pressing forward eagerly. Galen whimpered and squirmed, and Nick's jaw clenched under the onslaught of raw need. As much as the thought of fucking Galen now tempted him, while he was still on edge from that intense orgasm, Nick wanted his mouth even more. "I'm not done with you," he said hotly, and Galen shuddered.

Nick eased him off the bed and onto his knees, supporting Galen until he was steady. The sight of him, still bound hand and foot, gagged and blindfolded made Nick wild inside. He didn't think he was going to last long once Galen's mouth was on him. As he stood up, his cock brushed against Galen's cheek, leaving a smear of wetness behind. Galen moaned and leaned toward him.

When Nick stripped the tie from Galen's mouth, he wet his lips and searched blindly for Nick's cock. Nick's heart jumped, and he threaded his hands in Galen's hair, cradling his head and guiding him. Hot, sucking heat swallowed his shaft, and Nick groaned. Arcs of tingling need jolted through him, and he allowed Galen to take the lead. He bobbed his head on Nick's cock with hungry sounds, and already Nick's balls began to tingle and tighten.

He had to remind himself that this wasn't what Galen wanted for tonight. He wanted to be helpless. Nick tightened his hands in Galen's hair, holding his head still. Galen moaned, the sound vibrated around Nick's shaft. He pulled out, the head of his cock brushing against Galen's slick lips, and Galen retaliated with teasing flicks of his tongue.

"Please." The husky, urgent note in Galen's voice was enough to make any man's knees weak. Nick stripped the blindfold off him, and Galen blinked before his gaze focused on Nick. The expression there, a mix of desire and trust, made Nick groan. He nudged his hips forward, sinking his cock into the welcoming heat of Galen's mouth.

Galen's head became heavy as he relaxed even more. He sucked harder, his tongue rubbing, his stare spurring Nick on. Nick's heart pounded. "Fuck, Galen. Oh fuck."

He didn't last nearly as long as he wanted to. It was fucking impossible with the way Galen kept looking at him and the sight of Nick's cock disappearing into his mouth. He came hard, the sensations rolling over him in hot waves. Galen pulled back and Nick let him. Come splashed against his cheek. Galen sat back on his heels, panting. "Oh God, that was intense."

Nick dropped to his knees in front of Galen and gathered him into his arms, feeling shaky as his emotions tumbled about, love and intense protectiveness. Galen kissed him, leaning into him as Nick reached behind him to untie his wrists. He wrapped his arms around Nick and deepened the kiss, and Nick tasted himself on him.

He pulled back and nuzzled against Galen's mouth. He wanted to keep on kissing and holding him until they were ready to go again. "Is that what you were looking for?"

Galen groaned and yanked off the tie around his ankles. "All that and more."

CHAPTER TWENTY-TWO

GALEN sat back so the waiter could refill his coffee and signaled that he wanted the check. Ella laughed at something Nicole said and poked her in the ribs before wrapping an arm around her shoulder and kissing her temple. Galen smiled to see her so carefree after the intensity of weeks spent on the mural. Her nerves would be up again on gala night, but for now she was relaxed.

The sun shone on his face, and Galen glanced over the crowded plaza. It was a perfect day to eat outside, yet he couldn't stop the little niggle of dissatisfaction. He looked around the table and wished once again that he'd been able to get a hold of Nick. Suzane was there with Clint, Knox and Heather. Everybody who'd helped put the exhibit together was having a celebratory luncheon, everybody but Nick, who remained missing.

Galen frowned and took a sip of his coffee. Nick deserved a little of this impromptu celebration too; after all, he'd helped Galen keep it together when Suzane was gone, and the Dexios Collection belonged to him. Nick's assistant had promised to pass along the messages as soon as Nick got out of his meeting, but it looked like he would miss the whole thing. This was what Galen got for setting it up at the last minute.

"I would like to propose a toast," Galen said, picking up his water glass after he handed the waiter his credit card.

"Mr. K, shouldn't we have wine for that?" Knox asked with a little smirk.

"Some of you are underage, and the rest of you have to get back to work," Galen replied, waggling his finger first at Knox, then leveling it toward Suzane.

Suzane rolled her eyes. "A little wine never hurt anybody; a lot of wine is another matter."

"Hush, you." Galen cleared his throat at the outbreak of laughter, smiling himself, and waited until everyone else lifted their glasses. "As I was saying, all of you have been instrumental in bringing this exhibit together, whether by keeping me in line, doing grunt work, adding to the beauty of it, or keeping the rest of us sane while we worked. And I wanted to thank each and every one of you. And no matter what the critics say the day after it opens, we all can be proud of what we accomplished."

"Hear, hear." Ella echoed and clinked her glass to Nicole's before touching Galen's. "Hot damn, the madness is over. My parents even said they'd come." Her dusky cheeks flushed with emotion, and Galen grinned at her. He knew how much her parents' conservatism bothered her, but he had to give them credit for continuing to try. It was a far better deal than what Knox got with his mom, who hadn't said one word to him since he came out.

"That's great news, Ella."

They talked for a few minutes more, and then the party started to break up as Suzane's son left for class, and Knox and Heather went back to work, until finally it was just Suzane and Galen. "I like what you've built with those kids," Suzane said, touching his hand.

"I like your help in doing it." Galen sat back in his chair and pulled out the newspaper he'd saved from the morning. "I'm going to finish my coffee and the paper before heading back if that's okay with you."

"Since when do you ask my permission?" Suzane slid her purse strap over her shoulder. "What happened to Nick? I didn't get a chance to ask."

"I tried inviting him, but he's been in a meeting. You can grill him next time. I know you've been dying to."

"Please, I wouldn't do anything of the sort," Suzane sniffed. "That would be stepping over the line."

"Like that's ever stopped you before." Galen laughed.

"I'm trying to mend my ways." Suzane assumed a pious look, pressing her palms together with a glance skyward that had Galen laughing again. He took his coffee and paper and moved a few chairs over so the sun slanted even more against his face and he had an unobstructed view of the plaza. There were a few tourists about, the crush of the busy season was just getting started, and the fountain splashed merrily, providing a musical backdrop. He sent Nick another quick text as he sipped his coffee, then pulled out his paper.

He needed a few minutes of quiet time. Life had gotten more and more chaotic in the last several weeks. Not only were they wrapped up in the work at the museum, but as Galen moved more and more of his things over to Nick's apartment, and they were spending every night there, they'd decided, why wait until after the gala, and he'd moved in. Even with Knox's help, it ended up being a logistical mess with boxes everywhere. The first thing he was going to do once the gala was over would be to get all that organized before he lost his mind.

A shadow fell across the page, and Galen glanced up in irritation, blinking to see who stood between him and the sun. "Galen? I thought that was you. Where the hell have you been? I haven't heard from you in ages."

Galen grinned and rose to clasp Vincent's hand, pulling him into a quick, one-armed hug. "Good to see you too. Come on, join me. I have a bit of time before I have to head back to the museum."

Vincent stepped over the barrier and took a seat opposite from Galen. "How's that going for you?"

"Keeping me busy. That's one of the reasons why I've been so out of touch. We're opening up a new exhibit soon. How's your store doing?"

"Slow but steady. In this economy, I'll take it." Vincent ran a local art supply business, and he kept Galen's workshop well stocked. He found him to be a lot more reliable for actual art supplies than the bigger chain stores. Come to think of it, he should have Suzane look into the state of their supplies. Or maybe Nick, since Suzane really enjoyed the promotional side of the business and hated the day-to-day grind of operations. Nick had taken over a lot of those little details while she was out, and he had suggested more than once that he'd be happy to continue to help.

"We're having a gala for the opening in eight days. I'd love to see you there."

"Are you asking me as a date?" Vincent said with his quirky smile. "We haven't hooked up in a long time. You're not still playing that abstinent card, are you?"

"Sorry, Vincent. I'm playing the happily-in-a-committed-relationship card." Galen finished off the rest of his coffee and set it aside. "I finally gave in and called Nick."

Understanding crossed Vincent's face, followed by a grin. "You know, I'm not surprised. There was this vibe between you guys. I always thought it was just a matter of time. And to be honest, the couple times the three of us hooked up, I kind of felt like an intruder."

"Was it really that bad?" Galen asked with a laugh as he tucked his paper away. "I knew Nick got a little possessive there at the end when we hit the clubs, but I didn't think he was that obvious."

"You were just as bad. Trust me, all those sidelong looks and little touches. There were times when you both were wrapped up in your own world." Vincent stood up and pulled Galen into another hug. "I'm happy for you guys. Send me the information about the gala, and I'll see you there."

"Good to see you too." Galen watched him go, and then his eyes caught Nick standing by the fountain. He started to smile and lift his hand in a wave, but Nick's fierce glower froze it in place and his heart sank. Oh boy.

THE shock that crossed Galen's face was another blow to Nick's heart. For some reason, he had believed that Galen's clubbing, partying days had ended when he left Nick, that he'd cut himself off from that old life. Only it was clear that he'd remained friends with what's-his-name. Nick tried to recall it, but the names of all of Galen's conquests blurred under his anger.

Nick couldn't figure out what it was about himself that made it so easy for people to cut themselves out of his life so completely. First his mom, then Damien and Stefan when he'd moved out of state, and then they wondered why he was leery of letting them back in, why he didn't jump to make the first step.

But Galen…. As much as Nick had tried to keep that wall up, somehow Galen had crept under it to make him believe again.

Just as his mom had when she'd returned, Nick had believed every promise, every lie. Maybe she had come back with the best intentions of staying. He'd never know for sure, but what he knew deep down was nothing lasted, no matter how much he wanted it to.

Galen shot him a glance and moved toward the exit. Fuming, Nick turned away and stalked across the plaza. He didn't trust himself to talk to Galen now. He didn't want to see him, didn't want to hear his damned excuses.

Things had been so intense between them lately as they explored more with sex. They'd talked about scenes both before and afterward, and he'd thought that Galen was being up front with him. But if it was intense for Nick, it had to be that much more intense for Galen. And what did Galen do when he got afraid? He put up a damned wall, kept his distance.

Nick knew that all too well, and he really couldn't handle seeing it right now. Galen had run once, and Nick was trying so hard to believe that he wouldn't do it again. Deep down he knew he was overreacting, so he needed to put some distance between them and get some perspective.

Vincent. That was his fucking name. Galen had fucked that bastard more than once. Vincent had kept coming back, sniffing for more in those last few weeks before Galen had walked out on him. Were there other times that Nick hadn't known about? Because clearly, Vincent and Galen were awfully fucking chummy.

"Nick, wait!"

The sound of Galen's voice cut through him, and Nick tried to move faster, but it seemed as though everybody got in his way, slowing him down as Galen drew nearer, still calling to him. A hand grabbed his elbow, and Nick jerked away, spinning around to face his tormentor.

"I don't want to talk to you. I don't want to even see you right now," he snarled.

Galen took a step back, paling then flushing. "It's not what you're thinking. Just let me explain."

"There is nothing to explain. I have eyes for myself." Nick didn't want to believe that Galen had remained friends with Vincent after he'd split with Nick, that he'd kept in contact with another fuck buddy and left Nick in the cold and dark, wondering if he could've done something else to keep Galen close. It had been in the past and should stay there; only that little seed of doubt had crept into the dark cracks of his heart.

"I shouldn't have to explain, but obviously, I need to," Galen retorted, his voice tense. He looked around at the plaza and the curious gazes. "Can we go somewhere else?"

"No, I'm not going anywhere with you. I don't want to see you. I just need some damned time to think." Galen's face drained of all color, and for some reason the hurt there just pissed Nick off even more. It all felt like it was crumbling wildly out of control and he lashed out. "Did you fuck him again after you left me?"

Nick wanted to take the accusation back as soon as he said it, but it was too late. And he'd almost rather Galen confirm that it had been meaningless sex than something deeper.

"Name me one damn time that I haven't been honest with you, one time that I ran around behind your back. Yes, I had a history of screwing everybody that came my way, but you knew it, and I didn't try to hide it." Galen stepped in close, his voice lowering and becoming harder. "And you know what? You weren't a celibate fucking monk either. What were you doing the night we met? Looking for a hookup. How many times did you join me with someone else? Stop throwing my past in my face."

"Why were you all buddy-buddy with him?" Nick said through clenched teeth.

"It's not what you think," Galen said in a gentle voice, laying his hand on Nick's arm.

"You don't know what I'm thinking." Nick pulled away, stepping back toward the fountain. He just needed space to think, some quiet, but Galen wouldn't quit poking at him.

"We're friends, that's it. We've done nothing more than have coffee together or hang out for some conversation. I haven't screwed him since the last time the three of us were in bed together. Yeah, he might flirt on occasion. He might ask me out even though he knows the answer is no. I don't want him, I—"

Nick cut him off with a quick, jerking motion of his hand. There lay the crux of it, the real hurt that underscored his anger. "You remained friends with him, but shut me out for six fucking months?"

Galen's eyes widened and his mouth formed an "o" of surprise. "Nick…."

"You couldn't call to check up on me? Maybe we could've gone out as just friends with no strings attached, no sex, just seeing each other without the pressure." Nick flung his hand out in the direction Vincent had disappeared. Galen had left him in the complete dark, had given him nothing but a vague someday promise, and goddamn it… now he was pissed at himself for holding onto it so long, for letting it get to him like this. Galen hadn't given a damn about him and his feelings. He'd been more concerned with himself.

"You know what? Never mind," Nick snarled, turning away. "I don't want to talk about it. I don't want to think about it. Just leave me the fuck alone, please. I just need to get my head together."

"Wait." Once again Galen grabbed him, Nick shoved, and Galen shoved him back with a curse as they grappled. Nick stumbled back; his heel struck stone, followed by the backs of his knees, and he lost his balance, toppling back into the fountain. A stream of cold water struck him in the face, dousing his fury under pure shock.

He looked up at Galen, who stared back at him, his eyes widening further as water soaked every inch of Nick. Concern quickly replaced the shock, and that only infuriated Nick more. He'd rather Galen laugh at him than show concern. Seething, Nick held out his hand, and without hesitation Galen grabbed it.

One quick jerk and a startled squawk, then Galen was there next to him, sitting up and pushing his sopping hair out of his face. "Are you satisfied now?" Galen asked acidly.

"Not by a long fucking shot." Nick clambered out, ignoring the squelching of his shoes, the dripping of his clothes. "Just leave me alone. That's what you're best at."

There was an ancient pain in Galen's eyes, and for a moment he looked tired, as though he'd been through one too many battles. "You seem to be pretty good at walking away yourself. Do you think I'll wait, like you waited?"

Nick turned to face him, shock rendering him incapable of speaking or thinking. Galen's expression was so cold, so alien that he suddenly felt like he didn't know him anymore. "Galen...."

"Go ahead and leave, get the fuck out of here. I don't want to see you either."

Nick clenched his fists and turned away. He didn't trust himself to speak, didn't trust himself to touch Galen. This time Galen didn't call after him as he pushed his way through the crowd. His heart was buried up in his throat, cutting off his breathing. Fury kept warring with the feeling that he'd just lost everything that made the day-to-day bullshit matter.

GALEN watched Nick storm off, water splashing around him, people goggling at him, and it stoked his anger. Where the hell did Nick get off accusing him of...? Well, he hadn't really accused Galen of doing anything he hadn't done. Galen had assumed that Nick thought he was cheating, but Nick hadn't thought that at all.

He should've known better than to confront Nick right off. It was best to give him a little time to cool down and start thinking rationally, but the thought of him leaving, furious like that, thinking the worst, it was just something that Galen couldn't do. And now the situation was even more fucked-up.

He sighed and pulled himself out of the water with as much dignity as he could muster given the circumstances. He ignored the whispers and titters as he stripped off his tie and began heading off in the opposite direction, even though he really longed to chase Nick down again so he could knock some sense into him. That would be a very bad idea, considering the mood they were both in. He didn't want to say anything else that couldn't be taken back or hear similar things from Nick's lips.

Oddly enough, Lykon was silent as well. Galen thought that after an argument like that the man would've been eager to make his presence and thoughts known. He touched a hand to his chest and headed out of the plaza, his clothes clinging to him.

By the time Galen got to their apartment to change into dry clothes his anger had started to turn to regret. Nick wasn't anywhere to be seen, and there was no evidence that he'd been by as well. He didn't know who he was more upset at—himself or Nick. Nick was blowing the whole incident out of proportion. So what if Galen had remained friends with Vincent? It hadn't been anything more than that. And the silence between them during the time when they were apart went both ways. Nick could've tried calling him too, once or twice, but he hadn't.

Galen shoved a few overnight things and a change of clothes into a duffel bag. Nick wanted some space; well, he could damn well have it tonight. Galen needed it too, because it seemed like no matter what he did, Nick shoved him away. And Nick was so caught up in fixing the statues he wasn't looking at fixing his own issues.

They both needed some distance for the night. Tomorrow they could sit down like rational adults and discuss things, because the thought of hashing it out right now made Galen ache too much. He had enough on his mind with the gala coming up. Couldn't Nick have waited just a little bit longer before being hit with this sudden spate of insecurities? He couldn't handle this right now.

Galen pulled out a piece of paper, frowning in thought before he scrawled a note. Nick wanted a little free time to think? Well, then, Galen would oblige. He hoped that Nick just meant a little time and wasn't seeking a breakup. Galen closed his eyes against the pang that the thought brought him and replayed the whole argument over in his mind.

The only thing that stood out was the horror and heartbreak in Nick's eyes when Galen had gone off on him after their dunking in the fountain. Galen shouldn't have said what he'd said about not waiting. It was cruel, especially considering how Nick had just opened up to him about his mom abandoning him. Remembering it had him squirming inside. God, sometimes he really hated his temper. It took a lot to get him going, but when he did blow, he always regretted what he said and did.

Nick,

*Look, I'm sorry, we both need to chill out a
bit. You're right. I did shut you out completely.
And I know it seems cruel that I did it only with
you and not Vincent, but he was safe. He was safe
because I didn't have the same feelings for him
that I had for you so there was no risk in being
friends with him. And if you thought that I meant I
stopped hanging with everybody we used to screw
around with when I stopped partying, I'm sorry
for the confusion because I didn't mean that.*
 *And I never should've implied in any way that
I'd screw someone else. That was me being an
asshole. I think we just need to cool down. You want
some space from me and I have a lot of work to do
at the museum so I'm going to bull through it and
crash on the couch. And I promise, I'll be alone.*
 *Let's meet for breakfast tomorrow, at the
café around the corner from our apartment. We
have got to hash this out before we tear each
other apart. Tomorrow at 10, I'll save us a booth
in the corner. I don't want this to end, but damn,
when are you going to start believing in us?*

I love you.
Galen

Galen stuck the note on Amy and Rory's cage where Nick would
be sure to see it, threw the duffel bag over his shoulder, and headed out
the door. As he locked it, a wave of dizziness struck him hard and fast.
He leaned against the door with a groan as Lykon overwhelmed him.

Instinctively, he began fighting back, and then he stopped
himself. What did it matter? Galen was too heartsick to care right now
if Lykon went looking for Nick or Dexios. He just wanted an escape for
a little bit. And maybe somehow, Lykon would find the solution
because Galen didn't know what to do anymore. At least Nick would
know that it wasn't him, and that was a small comfort.

"Fine, I'm not going to fight you this time," Galen whispered as the other spirit washed over him and his sense of self vanished.

NICK shifted the grocery bags to one hand as he pulled out his keys. It was still early enough that he was pretty sure he could get dinner started and the table set before Galen shut down the museum for the night. He'd really fucked up this time. Galen's silence proved that. He hadn't called or texted once the entire day.

And despite the fact that Galen's parting words had cut deep, Nick knew that he'd pushed Galen to it. He had to get over his fear of abandonment and stop punishing Galen for leaving him before. If he could take that step and believe Galen loved him, if he could open up about his mother and the rest of his family, he could let this go too.

A happy twittering answered him as he opened the door, and the sound never failed to make Nick smile. He set the grocery bags down and went into the living room. Amy and Rory were still in their cage, so Galen wasn't home yet. Nick let them out, flipped on the radio, and started dinner. He might not be the cook that Galen was, but he did know how to marinate and grill a steak at least.

Amy flew into the kitchen and landed on the back of the chair to watch Nick's progress. He wished her presence helped ease the empty feeling that the apartment gave off. Maybe he should call Galen so he would know not to work late. Things had been hectic for him lately, and he'd been working longer hours.

Nick stripped off his tie and jacket and tossed them on the counter. He wasn't sure if dry cleaning would salvage them or not. Wouldn't Galen laugh on a normal night to see him rushing to get dinner started before changing out of the clothes he hated? Nick stuck the potatoes in the oven and set the table, bringing out the candles and the wine that he'd bought.

The nagging sense that something wasn't quite right came back to him as he returned to the living room. Nick frowned as he looked around. Something seemed to be missing. The photograph of him and Galen at the convention still hung on the wall with Nick's other photos, but the pictures of Galen's family were missing.

A deep sense of foreboding grabbed a hold of him and froze him in place. Nick looked down the darkened hallway toward their bedroom. He remembered all too clearly how empty it felt when his mom left with all of her things. And he remembered the look on his dad's and brothers' faces when they came home and noticed as well.

He could not do this again. He couldn't. He didn't want to go into their bedroom and see the empty drawers and hangers. Galen may not have had a chance to move in all his stuff yet, but there was enough to make his presence felt and now that was gone. Nick fisted his hand in his hair and turned away. The apartment suddenly felt claustrophobic, and he headed outside to the landing to get some fresh air.

This could not be happening. Galen had promised. It was one thing to say that he'd had enough, but to leave like this? Nick pulled out his phone and called Galen before he could change his mind. He had made a promise to himself a long time ago that he would not do this again, he would not beg, but this was Galen.

The call went straight to voice mail. Nick closed his eyes, and his throat tightened. "Galen, I… I'm sorry, please come home."

Telling himself that he couldn't put it off any longer, Nick went back inside to check only to confirm that everything Galen had moved in was gone. He sat down on the edge of the bed, set his phone on the nightstand and willed it to ring. *Please, Galen, please, not like this.*

Dexios appeared in front of him with a whisper of sound, and the sight of him looking as lost as Nick felt turned his heartbreak into rage. Nick had known the betrayal was coming, and it still hadn't prepared him for how much it would hurt. He had an overpowering urge to hurt something in return.

Dexios opened his mouth, no doubt to chastise him, and Nick didn't give him a chance. The punch landed on Dexios's jaw and he staggered back against the dresser. "Fuck you," Nick snarled.

"Butt the hell out of our lives, because you and Lykon make things more complicated than they already are. Don't Galen and I have enough to deal with without having to worry about your curse? How many damn tries have you had, and you still can't get it right? That is not going to happen to us, dammit, so fuck off."

CHAPTER TWENTY-THREE

GALEN had been so sure that Nick would show up at the café, and he couldn't have been more wrong. It was one o'clock, and no matter how much Nick liked to sleep in on a Saturday, he wouldn't have been this late. Galen tried to ignore the sinking in his heart as he checked his messages one more time without any luck. Nick hadn't called or texted either.

He was tempted to call Nick, but decided that it would be better to have this out face to face. Maybe Nick's cell got damaged in the dunk in the fountain. Maybe Galen's had as well. That could account for the silence if not for Nick's no-show.

His heart beating double-time, Galen rose, his muscles sore and aching. They didn't used to ache like this when he'd slept on the couch before, but the dunk in the fountain probably hadn't helped. He must be getting older, to feel this sore the next day. He paid the bill and headed over to the apartment, but Nick's car wasn't out front. Galen growled under his breath. Nick was making it impossible to apologize, and Galen couldn't stop the awful feeling that he'd fucked up big time by crashing on the couch last night. If there was anything he could've done to bring Nick's fears front and center, this was it.

There had been so much to do after Lykon had let go of him that Galen had pushed aside his exhaustion and buried himself in all the tasks vying for his attention. By the time night came he'd crashed and crashed hard on the couch, only to wake up sore and aching all over. Galen returned to the museum, and Heather pounced on him as soon as he came through the door.

"There you are! I've been trying to call for the last two hours. Suzane left the write-up for Monday's newspaper ad on your desk, then went to her son's soccer game. Knox can't come help close today because a project came up, and he has to go out of town. Some guy called and wants to know if he can get a preview for the exhibit to write up on his blog."

Galen pulled out his phone with a frown. "You called?"

"Yeah." Heather rolled her eyes. "Like half a dozen times, Mr. K."

Damn, that was the second time in the last few months that he needed to get a new phone. At this rate he was going to beat last year's count. "Sorry, my phone got soaked. Let me take a look at the messages and the notes on the desk, and if you want, I can cover while you go to lunch. Anything else happen?"

"Nick stopped by."

Galen spun back around to face her and his heart skipped a beat. "He did?"

"Yeah, I think he was here for a bit and left maybe thirty minutes ago?"

"Okay, thanks." Galen tried to not let his conflicted emotions show, but he wasn't sure if he was successful or not when Heather gave him a puzzled look. He turned away before she could ask questions. He'd just missed seeing Nick. As he climbed the tower steps, he argued with himself over Nick's actions. Maybe he'd tried to call because he overslept and came here to look for Galen. That didn't explain why he didn't at least try to see if he was still at the café. It was just around the corner, it would've taken five minutes. Maybe the note Galen left had fallen and he hadn't seen it.

He tried calling his cell from his desk phone, and sure enough it didn't go through. A headache began to form at his temples. *What a fucking mess.* He called Nick and Suzane, though neither answered, and left a message letting them know about his cell phone. Nick had to have been trying to get a hold of him and must be going nuts.

Galen stared unseeingly out the window as unhappy, worried thoughts crowded his brain. For once he didn't want to be at the museum. He wanted to hunt down Nick, but he had no idea where to start. After Heather had her lunch, maybe he could sneak away for an hour. He grabbed the paperwork on his desk and headed back downstairs.

Heather was busy with a customer, so he laid his work down on the counter and went to check on the Dexios Collection. Trepidation slowed his steps. If he went in there and found them starting to revert back to their former state, he didn't know what he would do. No. That was asking for trouble, and he'd be damned if he let things get that bad between him and Nick over a stupid argument.

Galen rubbed his chest as he walked into the exhibit room. There was an air of hushed expectation around the statues, as if they were someone steeling themselves for another blow.

Galen walked over to the final one, where Dexios lay on his side, his arms empty, and this time the longing that swept over him was so strong that his eyes stung. He wanted to lie in that embrace and just sleep, knowing that he was finally where he belonged. Galen closed his eyes and rubbed his chest again. "Hey, you there, Lykon? Dexios? It'll be okay."

Silence answered him, and Galen went back to work with a sigh. He kept trying Nick's phone without any luck, and no matter how many times he tried telling himself it was just because Nick's cell was probably trashed, it didn't ease his nagging sense that something was terribly wrong.

"Okay, Galen, you look like a kicked puppy. What's going on?"

Galen grimaced at the sound of Suzane's voice. He did not want to get sucked into a soul-baring conversation right now. He couldn't handle it. "I thought you were at Clint's game."

"It's over; they won. Clint's off celebrating with his friends." Suzane pulled her wild mop of blonde curls back from her face with a colorful scarf and came behind the counter with him.

"Well, now that you're here." Galen handed her the folder with the ad write-up and Heather's notes on the calls. "I think the ad works. Good job, we should get some last-minute buzz from that."

"Screw work. What's wrong?" Suzane laid her hand on Galen's arm, and his chest squeezed around his heart. "Does it have anything to do with the stack of boxes in the storage room?"

Galen's head jerked up as an icy-cold jolt hit him hard. "What boxes?"

Suzane's expression turned from concern to sympathy, and her hand tightened on his arm. "I'm sorry. I thought you were the one who put them there. It looks like your stuff. I stole a peek, and I didn't mean to pry, but after the last time boxes showed up without warning, I had to know if it was something similar."

"Do you mind covering the desk for a minute?" Galen didn't wait for Suzane's answer. He had to see for himself. It could be the rest of his belongings from his old apartment. Maybe Knox moved them before going out of town and didn't have a chance to tell him. Telling himself that kept his feet moving forward.

The boxes were stacked against the wall. Galen steeled himself and took the lid off the first one. His heart plummeted with a sickening lurch, and his eyes stung as he recognized the contents, the things he'd brought over to their place.

Galen replaced the lid. He didn't want to see anymore. Now he knew why Nick had stopped by, and the realization that he'd ended their relationship without even a word.... His chest tightened to the point that he couldn't breathe, and then fury erupted through his heartbreak. *Oh fuck no.* He wasn't going down like this.

THE apartment was quiet, too quiet, and it was making Nick crazy. Nothing seemed to break the stillness, not even Amy and Rory's presence. Nick had tried to exhaust himself swimming, but it hadn't helped, though for at least a bit he was out of the apartment and doing something. Nick shoved a hand through his wet hair and tried to bury himself in his comics, but it was useless.

So this was the night that Galen had decided not to try calling him. When Nick had gotten that first voice mail about Galen's phone he'd been ready to rush back over to the museum to apologize. Then he'd made the mistake of listening to the second. Galen had been so pissed off that he'd made little sense during his rant other than to tell Nick to fuck off. Nick got the message though. He'd screwed up and screwed up big time.

He'd tried; he'd really tried to understand where Galen was coming from. Nick had let his issues sabotage them from the first meeting in Galen's tower. Still, Nick had to admit that trying to understand Galen's viewpoint didn't work too well when he was still reeling from how Galen had ended their relationship.

It didn't stop him from listening to the message again, or the ones that followed a few days later. The messages where Galen apologized for being so angry in the last voice mail or for what he'd said when they'd fought outside the restaurant. He never apologized for leaving, though. He never mentioned wanting to come back home. And Nick didn't know if he could handle letting him back in a little bit only to find out that it was over past any hope of fixing.

It didn't stop him from wondering when Galen would decide it wasn't worth calling to try to get through to Nick. It had eaten him up inside. He hadn't been able to decide what was worse: waiting and wondering if this was going to be the night that Galen gave up; or enduring the chime of a text coming in, the ringing of his phone, the sound of Galen's persistent voice, sometimes angry, sometimes sad; or the dead silence after Nick had listened to the new message.

Now he knew the answer.

Fuck, it hurt. He never should've allowed Galen back in as much as he had. He'd been a fool from the moment he'd called Galen back, lured in by the perfect bait. Nick glared at the journals on the coffee table and swept them off with a jerk of his arm. The fucking Dexios Collection had been the bane of his family forever. He should've listened to his dad's warnings. They weren't the golden ticket home he'd been searching for; they'd been a trap that led him into a nightmare.

Rory's screech broke the silence, and when Nick glanced his way he found the cockatiel's crest lying flat and his feathers slicked down. Great, now even his bird was depressed. "I'm sorry, buddy. I didn't mean to scare you." Nick got up and flipped on the radio to fill the silence, the first time he'd done so in days, and Rory's crest lifted a little.

Nick threw himself back on the couch and pinched the bridge of his nose. The gala was a couple days away. Surely Galen had better things to do than to continue to torment him. That's why he hadn't called. It was better to think he was tied up doing last minute things for the opening of the exhibit than wondering where Galen was sleeping tonight.

Nick sat up again as realization struck. *Fuck.* His dad was planning on coming. *Fuck, fuck, fuck.*

His stomach twisted at the thought of calling his dad and cancelling, but he couldn't let him waste his money and come up here for nothing. When his dad's voice mail picked up, some of the tension knotting Nick's insides let up.

"Hey, Dad, ummm, about this weekend, cancel your tickets. Galen and I broke up, so there's not really going to be much of a celebration. I'll be heading out to Greece in September for vacation. Why don't I stop by in San Francisco on my way home? We can catch up and discuss what we want to do with the Dexios Collection, though really I'm all for leaving it with Galen. He'll take good care of the statues. I'll call you again sometime next week. Don't worry about me. I'm cool."

Nick tossed the phone down, feeling sick to his stomach. He should cancel his trip to Greece. He didn't really feel like heading there of all places, and he sure as hell didn't feel like wreck diving for statues. And to think, he'd been plotting on how to get Galen away from the museum to go with him.

He heard a rush of wings, and Amy alit on the arm of the couch next to him. She cocked her head to the side and half lifted one wing, sticking her leg out to the side in invitation. "Hey there, beautiful." Nick gently scratched her feathers. Somehow the motion and loving contact was profoundly depressing. He missed Galen with a fierce and unending ache.

He thought he hurt the last time they'd parted, but that hadn't even come close to what it felt like this time. It was as though something vital had been scooped out of him, leaving him scarred and empty. He closed his eyes and was confronted by the picture Galen made sitting in the fountain and the look on his face as he said those words. His heart constricted. It had cut so deep when Galen had stared at him with such cold eyes and implied with his words that he would be looking for someone else's bed. But that pain had been nothing compared to the realization that Galen had moved out without a word.

Nick couldn't wrap his head around it. There had been times when Galen could be distant when he was upset, but he'd never been deliberately cruel, not like he had on that last day. It didn't make any sense. He couldn't fathom Galen leaving him in that way, not after he'd told him what had happened with his mom. It would be far easier to just say fuck it all if Galen would've left him alone after that. But no, he had to keep fucking calling and twisting the knife a little deeper. Until tonight, that is.

Despite how much Nick wanted to keep blaming Galen for hurting him, a voice inside of him questioned his part in this whole mess. At the end he'd believed Galen wouldn't leave again. That's why it had been such a shock when he had. So Nick must've done something to convince Galen that leaving was the only thing he could do. And if Galen really wanted their relationship to be over, why keep calling?

Nick leaned back with a frown as the aching band across his forehead tightened even more. He had to stop obsessing over it. It didn't even matter. Everything was destroyed now anyway. He hadn't heard from Dexios since he'd shown up to berate him and they'd gotten into that altercation. He was probably locked inside the statue again, waiting to be reborn.

Nick's thoughts flashed back to Galen as he continued to pick at the problem despite his best efforts not to. It was like worrying at a scab. He knew he shouldn't, yet he couldn't stop himself. Galen had said more than once that Nick was too focused on the statues, and he had been right. If he'd put the same amount of drive into their relationship from the beginning they wouldn't be in this mess.

He'd held himself back, worried over Galen eventually betraying him and leaving, when in reality he'd been the one with his foot half out the door, ready to bolt at the slightest provocation. He'd kept pushing Galen further and further away so Galen couldn't hurt him in the same way that his mother had, and by the time he'd started to set those fears aside Galen was already at an erupting point. It was no wonder he'd said what he said and left.

It had been a self-fulfilling prophecy from the start. Just like any good Greek tragedy. Nick had spent so much time and energy trying to avoid his fate that he'd set up his own downfall.

He was such a fucking idiot.

Those words…. The expression on Galen's face were etched into his brain with acid regrets. He'd hurt Galen too, and it hadn't stopped Galen from continuing to try with him. He didn't want this to be over. He wanted to be with Galen, really give this thing between them a try. The first time Galen hadn't been ready. This time Nick hadn't. Maybe they could get their shit straight with a third try.

Only Nick couldn't imagine that Galen would want to hear from him after Nick had spent the last week ignoring him. Nick stared at the phone, gnawing his lip. He wanted to rip the scab wide open, in the hopes that it would heal cleanly.

The phone rang, and Nick straightened so fast that Amy let out a startled cry and took flight to the top of the window. She began berating him as Rory joined in with a hiss. His heart pounding, Nick picked up the phone, and a flash of disappoint went through him at the sight of his dad's name. He almost let it go to voice mail and stopped himself. Isn't this what had partially led to his estrangement from his family? Hiding and nursing his wounds?

He had to take a step forward.

"Hey, Dad."

"Talk to me, and don't tell me you're okay." The quiet strength in his dad's voice made Nick ache even more. If there was anybody who would understand what it felt like to come home to an empty place, it was his dad. "What happened?"

Nick leaned back against the couch cushions and closed his eyes. "I think I've forgotten how to dream, Dad."

"HEY, you."

Galen looked up at the sound of Suzane's gentle voice. She stood at the top of the stairwell in his office, her face soft with concern. He must seem pretty pathetic for her to use her gentle voice. "We're all set for tomorrow?" he asked, setting aside the invoices he was going over. "I can't believe you managed to stay within the budget we scraped together."

"What can I say? I have skills. We're good to go for tomorrow. Knox and his friends will be here at five to set up the tables. I've recruited a few others to help finish the decorating. The caterers will be here at six, and we'll be all set to open the doors on time. I think we can get some good donors out of this."

"Good." Galen wanted to muster more enthusiasm. He'd put months into this opening and gala. And even more than time, he'd poured his heart into this project. But Nick hadn't called back. He hadn't stopped by again. Galen didn't know what to do anymore. He didn't know how to reach him. He'd even tried stepping back a bit to let Nick come to him in his own time, and even that hadn't gotten him a reaction.

The thought of going to the gala without Nick didn't seem like any kind of a celebration at all.

Suzane came over and sat down on the arm of his chair. "I hate seeing you hurting like this. And if you say you're fine one more time, I'm going to thwap you."

Galen stifled the automatic response, and it showed him how bad off he was when he really had the urge to lay his head against Suzane's shoulder and let her hear the whole sordid, sorry mess. "Do you think kidnapping would be excusable under these circumstances?" he found himself asking instead. "It's the only way I can think of to make him listen."

"Honey, if I thought it would help, I'd buy the duct tape for you and be your alibi." She slipped an arm around his shoulders and gave it a pat. "But if a person's determined not to listen, all the shouting in the world won't make a difference. Now, I'm not sure what happened between you two, but spending another night on your couch in your office isn't the answer either. Why don't you come out to dinner with me and my boy?"

"Actually, I do have plans tonight. No really," Galen insisted at Suzane's skeptical look. "There's someone I need to talk to before I lose my chance and he disappears completely."

"You're not planning on trying to go see Nick, are you? Because sending your belongings to the museum was a dick move on his part. And until you get some indication from him that he wants to make amends or at least talk, I think going over is a bad idea."

Those damned boxes. That kick in the face still made Galen clench his teeth. When Nick said good-bye, he didn't do it halfway. Then he thought of his own part in the fiasco and sighed.

"He wasn't the only one to pull a dick move."

Suzane raised an eyebrow, and Galen wanted to squirm under that expression. Women did that so well. Suzane was too much like his mom sometimes. Oh God, his whole family was going to be there tomorrow, and they would know something was wrong. Fuck. He could probably avoid them during the gala, but they would hound him the next day. He just knew it.

"Out with it. I know you're dying to blurt it out to someone, so lay it on me."

Galen's sense of outrage over Nick's actions fled under the weight of her stare. He didn't need to go into every detail, like how he'd taunted Nick with the idea that he'd go back to his former partying if Nick left. He should've just given him time to calm down instead of getting pissed and defensive himself. Besides, that wasn't what made Nick respond by kicking him out. Galen really knew what was to blame.

"Let's just say that I'd finally gotten Nick to open up about why he had such trust issues over people leaving. It had taken him months to open up like that, and the very first argument we have afterward I decided it would be a fine idea to not come home that night."

"Oh, Galen."

Galen shrank inwardly and winced at her tone. She didn't need to say anything else. "I left a note," he said, coming to his own defense even though he knew that it was a lame excuse.

"Well, that's something I suppose." Suzane squeezed his shoulder again. "I hope you two figure it out. Maybe after the gala, you can try that kidnapping idea. Some time alone without the stress of pulling all of this together might be just what you both need. You've been working nonstop for a long time. You need a vacation. And if you really want Nick, go off with him to somewhere private, and don't come back until it's resolved."

Galen nodded and dragged a hand through his hair. He liked the thought of dragging Nick off somewhere, but he wished Nick would give him some fucking indication that he gave a damn about them at all. "Until then, I'm leaving Nick alone. No calls, no e-mails, and no stopping by. Harassing him didn't work, so I'm hoping that maybe giving him some time to think will."

"I've heard worse plans." Suzane rose and patted her blonde curls back into place under her scarf. "Are you sure you won't join us?"

"Another night, I promise, before you go back for your next treatment. We'll do something fun. Maybe have a night on the town."

Suzane wrinkled her nose, and then her eyes lit up. "We can celebrate early. This will be the last one. Lordy, I'm looking forward to never having to go back."

Galen squeezed her hand and smiled at her. "That calls for a huge celebration."

Suzane paused at the top of the stairs and fixed him with a look. "Promise me you won't stay in this room all night by yourself."

"I promise."

Once Suzane left it seemed like she took all of the zest with her. Galen didn't know how she did it, how she filled each moment with such life. He almost called out to her to ask, but decided against it. She was worried enough as it was.

Lykon stirred inside of him as if sensing that Galen intended on seeking Dexios out. He'd been strangely silent since that afternoon outside of Nick's apartment, and Galen ached for him too. "Not just yet," Galen murmured. "Soon, my friend."

Even if things didn't work out with Nick, he'd find a way for Dexios and Lykon to be together, at least for a little while. He hated to think that way, but relationships took two people, and if Nick chose to shut him out forever, Galen couldn't think of anything to change his mind. He didn't want to cross the line into stalking Nick if he just needed some time to think. Now he knew how Nick felt when he left—completely shut out. And he knew that if Nick had tried to call or text back it would've only made him retreat more. So this was him giving Nick space.

Galen dug through the few boxes he'd hauled up to his office, searching for something more comfortable to wear before he headed to the exhibit room. He really needed to find a new place after the gala was over. Suzane was right; he couldn't continue living in the tower and sleeping on the couch.

The last rays of the sun shone down through the windows, wreathing the statues in a warm golden glow. He loved how they captured the light like that when it was just him and Nick visiting. As if the statues had their own aura.

He slowly walked over to the last one, where Dexios lay alone on his side, and the pose, his empty arms, struck up a yearning so intense that Galen's entire body ached with it. That's how he felt right now. Unfinished. Incomplete. His own puzzle piece was missing, and Galen didn't know how to win him back. He missed Nick's smile. The way that he made Galen feel complete in his own skin, as if his wants and desires were perfectly fine. The way he tried to support Galen even when he got all touchy over it. Those were the vital elements that had been missing in his relationship with Bryan. With Nick, Galen could see a future if they could just let go of the past and move forward, and he wanted Nick to be able to see it too.

Galen sank down next to the statue, his eyes pricking as a new urge hit—to sink himself into the statue's embrace and let Lykon take him over. At least Dexios and Lykon could be together for a short while, and Galen could lose himself in their emotions, just as he'd lost himself for so long until Nick had woken him up again. He'd awakened him, made him want a connection again, made him want to love, and then he'd taken it away.

"Why are you here, Galen?"

Galen pressed a hand to his chest as Lykon leapt inside of him at the sound of Dexios's voice. He could let go, and at least tonight he wouldn't be alone. Wasn't that why he'd sought out the lovers night after night? So he wouldn't be alone, only to be afraid that they'd leave him, too, so he'd left after only a few minutes. He watched him, hurting for them, hurting for himself, and the only thing that gave him any hope was that the first three statues were somehow still whole.

"I didn't want to be alone tonight." Galen closed his eyes with a humorless laugh. "I guess I should've taken Suzane up on her offer."

A strong hand closed on his shoulder, and Galen wanted to sink back and let someone hold him, someone who gave a damn. It would be so easy to let go, just for tonight. He gritted his teeth and hung on a little longer. He'd made that mistake after the fight with Nick. Maybe if he hadn't been such a coward then and hid, he could've found Nick and fixed things before they'd gotten so out of control.

"It would be a lie, wouldn't it? If I let Lykon out so you could be with him. You two might have a night together, but unless Nick and I work things out you'll have to wait until another reincarnation is born, and in the morning I'd be right back where I was before."

"I will not lie, it is a temptation. I miss him. I do not know when I will see him again." Dexios's quiet words tugged at Galen's heart. "To be able to hold him tonight…. It would seem like a blessing."

"But it would be the wrong decision, wouldn't it?" Galen twisted around and looked up at Dexios. "It would be taking the easy way out. This is a part of that test that Lykon mentioned."

Dexios's eyes were far away and thoughtful, then after several long moments he nodded and crouched next to Galen. "It is strange how fate twists us about. At the beginning, I was the one forced to wait for Lykon, and I didn't. Instead I sought an easier way and a way to punish him for hurting me, for throwing my love away. And if I had waited, been more patient, we would have been together."

Galen shifted into a sitting position and wrapped his arms around his knees. "Now I am the one who has to be patient, who has to wait for Nick to realize…." *Realize what?* Not that he loved him… but that what they had was worth the fear and the uncertainty… to be willing to work through the rough times instead of hiding from them. Galen needed to know that Nick would fight for them. That was why he was waiting, because if Nick wasn't willing to let go of his fears and fight, this wouldn't last long at all.

"I think you understand." Dexios squeezed Galen's shoulder, and this time Lykon didn't struggle to free himself. It was almost as if he just accepted that touch and reveled in it. "Nick has his own test as well. He has to fight for you, fight through his own sense of betrayal, be willing to see beyond the surface and to look for the truth and then to face up to that truth."

Galen rubbed his palm against his chest as Dexios's words echoed his own thoughts. He could sense Lykon's regret, and it mixed with his own. He still felt as though he only knew half of what was going on.

There was something else there. He just knew it. This whole thing had blown up beyond any sense of reason.

"Would you sit with me tonight?" Galen met Dexios's eyes and gestured toward one of the benches. "I don't really feel like going back to my couch upstairs and a pizza box." The thought of being alone again made him so cold inside. He didn't want to be cold anymore, not after Nick had shown him how things could be different.

"That is an offer I can gladly agree to." Dexios settled down next to Galen. "I recall you promising me a story about someone called Sleeping Beauty'?"

CHAPTER TWENTY-FOUR

NICK sat in his car across the street and stared at the old-fashioned lamps that were aglow outside the museum. Galen had really gone out of his way to dress the place up. Potted trees were covered in twinkling white lights, colorful baskets of flowers hung from the old iron hooks. The rainbow paneling on the bay doors had a fresh coat of paint on them. Through the glass he could see people milling about in the shop, looking at the items that had been donated for the silent auction.

Now, sitting here only yards away, his courage failed him, just as it had failed so many other times when he'd picked up the phone to call Galen back or almost stopped by the museum to see him. There was nothing he could say or do to make it up to him, to apologize for shutting himself away just as he'd so often accused Galen of doing. He hadn't wanted to be another painful distraction before Galen's big day. Or at least, that was the lie he'd told himself yesterday.

History had proven time and time again that they were better at breaking up than staying together. Nick really wanted to prove history wrong. He wanted to go in there and tell Galen he loved him and that he was willing to do whatever it took to prove that to him, even if it meant starting back at the beginning with a date.

Nick adjusted his cuff links and straightened his tie in the rearview mirror. This was a mistake. What right did he have to just show up on this night of all nights? Galen had been looking forward to this opening since before they reconnected. The press was there, along with some of the more prominent players in the town. Galen was counting on donations to expand his place, to find new ways to help the growing community he'd started. The last thing he needed was Nick coming in and making a scene. He should wait until tomorrow when it would be calmer.

That argument was the fear talking, though. He'd let Galen go without a whimper of protest, the way Dexios had let Lykon walk away. Despite Galen's angry message the day after their fight, Nick had known that Galen probably hadn't gotten his first plea to come home. He should've followed it with another and another instead of remaining silent and pulling back to sulk over his wounds.

The crazy fucking thing was, now that he'd gotten the guts to come this far, now that he was sitting here, he was frozen, so damn afraid of taking that next step, just like he had been with his family. And the terrible twist in this situation was it had been Galen who had shoved him in the right direction with them. It was Galen who had given him the support he needed to make that call to his dad.

Nick could handle Galen's texts, the e-mails, and the voice mails that he would play over and over. Maybe it was a form of self-torture, he didn't know. But those he could handle. They were an affirmation that no matter how stupid he was being Galen, for some crazy-assed reason, still gave a damn about him.

What Nick couldn't handle was Galen being heartbroken. The expression on Galen's face when Nick had gone off on him outside the restaurant gnawed at him in the middle of the night. And the look of entreaty in his eyes as he sat in the fountain, wet shirt plastered to his chest before Nick prepared to walk away, before Galen had gone so cold, haunted his thoughts during the day.

He'd completely booted Galen out of his life, and Galen would have every reason to tell Nick to go fuck himself.

Nick picked up his cell phone and replayed the last message again. "I really miss you." There was a pause, as if Galen wanted to say more, then the click of the phone.

He swallowed the lump in his throat and stared at the museum doors. Galen had tried to cover it, but he hadn't been able to hide the wounded tone to his voice. And every time Nick heard it, his mind flashed back to the fight and Galen's hurt expression. He had to find a way to make Galen stop hurting, to stop it for them both.

All Nick had to do was go in and scope out the gala. If Galen looked at him like he'd grown three heads and he was the last man that he wanted to see, then Nick would slip quietly back out. There was no need to embarrass them both. In the morning, he could look for Galen in private so they could hash this out.

He loosened his tie as he got out of the car. Damn thing was too tight, choking him. The sound of the car door shutting and the beep of it being locked seemed unnaturally loud in the still night. Light spilled from the doorway out onto the street, and Nick's heart hammered as he approached. A young woman sat behind the counter in the gallery, and beyond the doorway Nick could hear the hum of conversation, the low, throbbing beat of some drums, and laughter.

"Your invitation?" the woman asked, holding out a slim hand.

"Uhhh." Nick flushed and cursed himself. He'd forgotten that little detail. Maybe he had one in the car that Galen left behind. He hoped this wasn't a sign that it was a mistake to come tonight. "There isn't a list of invitees?" He asked, as he checked his wallet for a spare one and the woman shook her head. "Hold on, let me check my glove box."

"And just where do you think you're going, Nicholas Charisteas?"

Nick winced at the absolute steel in Suzane's voice and turned around to face her. Her dark hair was short and spiky, and she wore a snazzy purple dress that glinted back all of the light like a scintillating disco ball. "I was going to tear apart the car to look for an invite."

"Wouldn't it have been easier to ask for me or Galen?" She gestured impatiently at him. "It's okay, he's one of the organizers, though if he'd been any later he'd have been here early for our grand closing. Come on, no sense dragging your feet now that you're here."

There was no way that Nick could escape Suzane without a ruckus, and now that he was here he had to at least see Galen. "How is he?" he couldn't stop himself from asking.

She led him down the hallway, snagged two glasses of champagne off a tray, and handed him one. "Here, you look like you could use one."

Nick took it with fingers he didn't trust. The glass was so fragile, and his grip was uncertain. Everything was uncertain. He took a sip as they neared the entrance, and still Suzane hadn't answered his question. "You were the only one he ever talked about," she said as they stopped in the archway. "Even back when he was running around town every night, you kept coming up."

With that little nugget dropped, Suzane abandoned him and disappeared among the throng of people inside the exhibit room. Nick hung back, scanning the room and taking another sip of champagne before he gave into the urge to tug at his tie again. At first his eyes were drawn to Dexios and Lykon, somehow miraculously still together except for the final statue. Nick thought he heard the voice Galen had described. *Make me whole*, it whispered. Only Nick wasn't sure if it really was Dexios or the urgings of his own heart.

He took a step farther in, faces blurring, conversation nonsensical as he searched. His heart flipped, then twisted as he saw Galen intent on the man before him as they conversed. He stood there, drink in hand, the other hand in his pocket, missing the animation he usually had. Nick knew that look, that stance. Galen was in pain and hiding it by putting on his social mask. It made Nick ache to see it, because he knew he was the one who had robbed him of his joy tonight.

Nick was a fool for considering not coming, because next to Galen was where he belonged, and walking out now would be a regret he'd never forgive himself for. He began slipping through the crowd, making his way toward Galen, nerves fluttering along his skin. *Please don't let him freak out. Please let this be a good thing for him.*

Their eyes met, and the both of them froze. Nick's heart pounded louder, drowning out the sound of the drums, the conversation around him, as his entire focus centered on Galen. This was the moment when he'd know if they had a chance or if he'd fucked up past any hope of redemption.

Galen's expression softened, and his eyes lit up as he gestured to Nick. Relief poured through him, and Nick smiled as the room around him came alive again. He stepped up next to Galen and took his hand, lacing their fingers together. They were going to be okay. They had a lot of work ahead of them, but they were going to be okay. "I'm sorry I'm late."

"I'm glad you came." Galen turned to the other man. "Commissioner Pople, I'd like you to meet my partner, Nick Charisteas."

For a second Nick couldn't speak. God, nobody could undo him like Galen Kanellis. For someone who liked being helpless, Galen definitely had Nick bound in the palm of his hand. Nick shook the

Commissioner's hand, and they made small talk for a few minutes while he silently willed the man to disappear.

After several long, agonizing moments, the Commissioner excused himself, and Nick set his champagne glass on a proffered tray before he dropped it and drew more attention to them. He was so shaky on the inside that he was surprised he was still standing. "I...." A thousand things flashed through his mind, but only one stumbled out onto his tongue. "I love you."

Galen's eyes flashed a warm brown, and he stepped closer, a smile tugging at his lips. "I love you too."

"Look, I'm—"

Galen shook his head, cutting Nick off. "Hold that thought for later. We can apologize when we're alone. Right now I think there's someone you need to see."

He turned away before Nick could argue and pulled him through the crowd toward the buffet table. There wasn't anybody here that Nick wanted to see except for Galen, and it occurred to him that it was going to be a very long night of socializing before he'd get the chance to drag him off for a little alone time and a lot of groveling.

Galen was excited about whoever it was, probably a big potential donor, so Nick plastered on his pleasant business smile and went along with the flow. An older man with silvering, brown hair stood at the tables overlooking the selections, and it took a moment for recognition to sink in.

"He's here!" Galen crowed.

Nick's dad turned around, and for the second time that night the world seemed to stop spinning. There was a suspicious wetness to his eyes, then he grinned and pulled Nick into a rough hug. "What are you doing here?" Nick asked, hugging him back. He pulled away to stare at his dad in stunned delight. "I thought you were staying home."

"I realized after our conversation the other night that maybe I pushed being realistic and cautious a little too much with you." His dad patted Nick's cheek, then squeezed his shoulder with a broad grin. "So I decided that maybe you could teach me a little about being spontaneous and living for the moment. I want to see you get a little of that back."

Nick had a long way to go with both Galen and his dad, but for the first time he truly believed that he could show them the same faith that they had given him. He cleared his throat to ease the tightness in it and gestured to the room around them. "Have you had a chance to look around and see what Galen built?"

Galen nudged Nick with his hip. "I had help."

"No." His dad's gaze slid to the first statue in the Dexios Collection. "I wanted to wait for you."

"Well, come on. We'll show you around." Nick took Galen's hand. "Unless you have to get back to your guests."

Galen's brown eyes sparkled. "Your dad is one of our guests; besides, I think I've earned a little break."

THE moonlight shone down into the now-deserted exhibit room, and the museum was quiet once more. Galen loved the museum at night. It was almost as if he could hear the pulse of the place, the energy it collected during the day shining back at him. And tonight that energy had been very good.

Nick came up behind him and slid his arms around his waist. "You and Suzane did an amazing job, pulling this exhibit and gala together. What are you going to do with all the donations?"

"Oh, I have plenty of things in mind, activities I'd like to sponsor with the workshop, maybe putting in some computers for digital art and a photo lab for the purists. As much as I love the museum part and do want to open a third, final room someday for the public, I want to work more with the kids first."

"I think that will make you very happy."

They stood in silence, and Galen let Nick's presence be a balm to the ache of the last week. He was here. He'd come. Galen didn't know what spurred Nick's change of heart, but he was determined that he wasn't going to let past resentments steal their tomorrow. That was, if Nick still wanted a tomorrow. Galen hoped for it, and he'd find a way to fight for it.

Nick let go of Galen and turned him around. "Apologies aren't enough, but here they are. I'm sorry I blew things way out of proportion with you and Vincent. I know that I have to let go of my past and my fears. I swear to you, Galen, I really will focus on getting past that. I had no right to go off on you like I did."

Galen smiled as one of the worries that had been nagging him about their relationship left him. He could see a conviction in Nick's eyes that had been missing before. "I have my faults, God knows, too many of them, but I won't take you for granted. And I have to apologize too. I didn't realize how much I hurt you when I walked away like that. This last week has given me a taste of what you went through, so I think I understand where you're coming from a little more. I'm sorry, and I wish I could say that I would have done it differently, maybe had lunch on occasion, hooked up on the net, I don't know. I was coming out of a bad place and trying to work through it day by day."

"I know you've tried telling me that so many times, and I didn't listen like I should have. There are so many things I regret. I kept telling you that I wanted you to stay, and I didn't realize how much I was pushing you away at the same time. I was so afraid that the past would repeat itself."

"Like what happened with the other couples and the curse?" Galen asked, and even as Nick nodded he knew that wasn't the real driving force behind the fear that had been his excuse. "And with your mom?"

"Yeah."

The quiet way Nick said that tugged at Galen's heart. "I was a jackass too. I shouldn't have walked out like I did, especially after you told me about your mom. I'm so sorry for pulling a stunt like that. There was no excuse for it."

Nick tilted his head up to look at the skylights and drew in a breath, as if to fortify himself. "I… after you left I did call you and asked you to come back. I'd always told myself that I wouldn't ask somebody to stay when they wanted to leave, but I couldn't not call you. When I got your message the next day I realized that you hadn't gotten mine, and I punked out. I should've called you again. I should've at least tried to beg you to come back home. You are worth me laying aside my damned pride." The raw pain in Nick's expression and voice made Galen ache inside too, and it took a moment for his words to register. "It just... I... I was so afraid that the answer would be no and that you were gone for good."

"Wait a minute. I left a note saying I was just going to be gone for the night. I asked you to meet me at the café for breakfast." Galen broke off as Nick stared at him in confusion, and a horrible sinking realization struck him. "You didn't see the note?"

"I... I didn't see a note." Nick searched Galen's face, his brow lined, his jaw set. "I don't understand. If you only wanted to be gone a night why did you move out?"

"I didn't move out. I packed a duffel bag. You brought all my stuff here. You kicked me out." Though as he thought about it he realized that he hadn't actually seen Nick move the boxes, he just assumed, and the expression of confused heartbreak on Nick's face told him all he needed to know. "Lykon."

"You're not making any sense. I swear I didn't kick you out. The last thing I wanted was for you to leave."

Galen touched a hand to Nick's chest. "Oh God, I'm so sorry." The weight of the realization struck him even harder, and his eyes stung. He couldn't imagine what Nick had felt when he came home to an empty apartment, with no note, no word, just Galen gone. "It's my fault. I was so upset after the fight that I let Lykon take over for a while. I assumed he'd go back to the museum to be with Dexios. I never thought that he would do something like this. He must've been the one to pack everything."

"That doesn't make any sense," Nick said, sounding bewildered as he turned his head to look at the statues. "Why would Lykon do something like that? He had so much at stake. Why would he try to sabotage us? Didn't we have enough shit to work through?"

"I don't know." This time Galen touched a hand to his own chest, but all he got from Lykon was a sense of stillness. "He mentioned tests, but I didn't really pay that much attention to him. Every relationship is tested, so I thought he was just talking in metaphors."

"I... I feel like such an idiot." Nick turned back to Galen, still looking a little lost. "Why he did it doesn't really matter, though I think there's something in the old myths about it. What matters is that I should've done more, sooner. After everything that has happened, you taking that time away and what has been going on with the statues and the family legends, I just played it all up in my head. I just kept waiting for you to leave, like you already had, like how Lykon had left, and I was forgetting that you came back like he had come back. I focused on the wrong thing. I've been such an asshole. I don't know how you can forgive me."

Galen stared at Nick, his thoughts tumbling over themselves in a chaotic rush. Nick had believed Galen had walked out on him the way that his mom had walked out. And despite that belief, despite his fears, he'd shown up tonight. His heart started beating faster, and his throat ached.

"Shut up, Nick."

Nick's apologetic litany stopped, and Galen smiled at him as an aching joy filled him up. "Forgiving you is easy. For one, you didn't make me wait six months. And you came back too. Just when I needed you the most, you didn't let me down. Thank you for coming tonight. I needed you."

"I was worried that I'd ruin it for you by coming."

"No, you made the night for me. It wouldn't have been right without you," Galen said, sliding his hand through Nick's hair. "You had every reason in the world to give up on us, to be so damned afraid that it would be easy to choose to let it all fall apart, and you still came. That tells me everything I need to know."

A look of profound relief crossed Nick's face, and then he was kissing Galen, holding him tightly. Galen had missed this so much. Just the chance to hold Nick again lifted the weight that had been holding him down.

"I love you," Galen said softly when they broke apart.

"I love you too." Nick cupped Galen's face and kissed him again. "I've got to give it to you. You're one persistent bastard. Thank you for that."

Galen laughed at Nick's lighter tone, feeling so damn free after the misery of the last week. "A note of warning, I can be a serious nuisance when I want something, and I want you. Whether you knew it or not, when I was hurting you gave me something good to strive for, you helped me to find the strength to heal the broken bits inside of me.

Even after we got together and I was still afraid of taking new steps to put the accident behind me, you were there for me. Thank you."

"I'm choosing you, no matter the risk," Nick swore, his expression becoming serious. "You helped me too, even when I didn't know I was broken. You helped me to reach beyond my fear so I could connect with my family again. It's kind of funny, we've been concentrating so much on the statues, but really we were the ones who needed to be whole first."

"We did it. Together," Galen said, looking up at him.

"No more running, for both of us."

"That's a promise I can live with."

Nick's thumb brushed across Galen's cheek, and he leaned closer, touching his forehead to Galen's. "Come home, Galen. I've missed you so much. Please come home with me."

"You don't know how much I've been waiting to hear those words. I can't believe I thought you'd moved me out. I should've known better."

"No more regrets. No more looking at the past. We're just going to look forward from now on."

Galen smiled and felt Lykon tug free. Lykon appeared next to them and crossed his arm over his chest in a private salute before turning toward the final statue. Nick tensed, and Galen held his breath as they watched Lykon go to Dexios, who reached up and pulled him down into his embrace. The statue shimmered, and Galen could see Lykon lying down and facing him, both of them so lost in each other. The outline was there, but they weren't whole yet.

"So close," Galen groaned, aching for them. "Have they ever been this close to being together again?"

"I don't think so." Nick turned Galen away, his gaze unshadowed. "But I know it'll happen now. It's just a matter of time."

Galen smiled back at that certainty and nodded. He felt it too, in Lykon's joy as he left him, in the contentment and love in the statue's embrace. He felt it in the way Nick held him, in this confidence in their own love. "Yeah, very soon, I think."

"I wish we had a chance to say good-bye," Nick said softly as he looked at Dexios and Lykon.

"They're happy, they're together, and they intend on just holding each other until the last threads of the curse are broken." Galen laid his head against Nick's shoulder, content in a way that he couldn't explain, in a way that he had not been in a long time. "I could sense it when he left me."

He sighed and kissed Nick's temple. "Take me home."

Nick squeezed him hard and held him just a moment longer, conveying how much he wanted that in his embrace, and his voice was rough when he finally answered. "Gladly."

EPILOGUE

"WE ARE gathered here today in a place that celebrates love of all kinds, to witness the joining of Nicholas Charisteas and Galen Kanellis."

Dexios woke up with a shudder at the sound of those words as the last tie tethering him to bronze and copper snapped. He rose from the confines of his prison and looked back at the final statue, where Lykon lay permanently locked in his embrace. They had lain together just like that for the last year, ever since Galen had gone home with Nick. They had waited, content to hold each other, for the final chain in the curse to be broken when Galen and Nick made their vows to each other.

"I thought they would disappear with us," Lykon said as he took his place by Dexios's side.

Dexios drew a breath and picked Lykon up, swinging him around in a tight embrace as a feeling of completion, of coming alive again struck him. Trembling, he set Lykon down and stared into his flushed, beaming face.

"Perhaps they'll serve as a reminder," Dexios said softly, touching his hand to Lykon's cheek. "They are almost there, and she is allowing us to witness it."

They looked at Nick and Galen, who stood in the center of the exhibit room and faced each other with smiles on their faces and tenderness in their eyes. Their hands were linked and their voices confident as they repeated their vows to each other. An older woman with a cap of silvery-blonde fine curls smacked Galen on the arm when he pretended to look in his pocket. She handed him a ring with a shake of her head.

"With this ring, I thee wed," Galen said as he slipped the ring on Nick's finger before lifting his hand to give it a kiss.

"They look happy," Lykon said in a low voice as he leaned against Dexios, moving under the curve of his arm.

"They are happy." Dexios's arm tightened around him. "They are a part of us, and we are a part of them. Their joy is our own."

"I would make my own vow to you, one that I should never have broken. For an eternity, I am simply yours. Where you go, I will follow, until we are no more."

Dexios turned and faced him as Nick slid a ring on Galen's finger. "I have my own promise to make as well. I acted in haste. I did not give you the understanding that you needed. I will not do so again. If you need my ear, you have it. If you desire my patience, it is yours for howsoever long it is needed."

Lykon tugged Dexios to him and kissed him hard. "These promises will not be forsaken. We should go, the Elysian Fields await us."

"Why?" Dexios grinned as Lykon looked at him in confusion. "We have an entire world to explore, an island to make ours. That is Cythera's gift to us." As Lykon's eyes widened, another voice brought their attention back to the couple who had broken their curse.

"Nick and Galen, I pronounce you husband and husband. You may seal your vows with a kiss."

Dexios sensed the leap of Nick's heart, and his own joined it as he and Lykon turned to face the couple again. Nick grinned and caught Galen up in an embrace, bestowing on him a heated kiss that left Galen flushed and breathless. They turned with linked hands to face their friends and families, and Galen gasped, his mouth falling open as his gaze landed on the fourth statue.

He nudged Nick, thrusting his chin toward it, and Nick's eyes widened. They both turned, searching the room, and went still as they saw Dexios and Lykon. Nick lifted their linked hands in a salute. Dexios and Lykon did the same.

"Cythera," Dexios called out in a silent prayer. *"We are ready. Please, take us home."*

MARGUERITE LABBE has been accused of being eccentric and a shade neurotic, both of which she freely admits to, but her muse has OCD tendencies, so who can blame her? Her husband and son do an excellent job keeping her toeing the line, though. Together with Fae Sutherland, Marguerite has found a shared passion for stubborn men with smart mouths. With her solo work she often likes to explore darker themes as well.

When she's not working hard on writing new material and editing completed work, she spends her time reading novels of all genres, enjoying role-playing games with her equally nutty friends, and trying to plot practical jokes against her son and husband.

Visit Marguerite's web site at http://www.margueritelabbe.com.

Romance from M<small>ARGUERITE</small> L<small>ABBE</small>

A<small>LL</small>
B<small>ETS</small>
A<small>RE</small>
O<small>FF</small>

M<small>ARGUERITE</small> L<small>ABBE</small>

http://www.dreamspinnerpress.com

Romance from LABBE & SUTHERLAND

http://www.dreamspinnerpress.com

The Triquetra Trilogy by MARGUERITE LABBE

http://www.dreamspinnerpress.com

Romance from MARGUERITE LABBE

Marguerite Labbe

GHOSTS
IN THE
WIND

www.ingramcontent.com/pod-product-compliance
Lightning Source LLC
Chambersburg PA
CBHW051529260626
47170CB00003B/845